THE WOLVES OF ESSEX

Robert D Hastings

Copyright © 2024 by Robert D Hastings

All rights reserved. No part of this publication may be reproduced, distributed, or transmitted in any form or by any means, including photocopying, recording, or other electronic or mechanical methods, without the prior written permission of the publisher, except in the case of brief quotations embodied in critical reviews and certain other noncommercial uses permitted by copyright law

TABLE OF CONTENTS

CHAPTER 1 7

CHAPTER 2 12

CHAPTER 3 19

CHAPTER 4 23

CHAPTER 5 35

CHAPTER 6 43

CHAPTER 7 48

CHAPTER 8 52

CHAPTER 9 56

CHAPTER 10 59

CHAPTER 11 68

CHAPTER 12 74

CHAPTER 13 76

CHAPTER 14 79

CHAPTER 15 85

CHAPTER 16 91

CHAPTER 17 97

CHAPTER 18 103

CHAPTER 19 111

CHAPTER 20 115

Chapter	Page
CHAPTER 21	121
CHAPTER 22	126
CHAPTER 23	129
CHAPTER 24	136
CHAPTER 25	142
CHAPTER 26	148
CHAPTER 27	156
CHAPTER 28	158
CHAPTER 29	166
CHAPTER 30	174
CHAPTER 31	179
CHAPTER 32	184
CHAPTER 33	186
CHAPTER 34	189
CHAPTER 35	192
CHAPTER 36	195
CHAPTER 37	200
CHAPTER 38	204
CHAPTER 39	206
CHAPTER 40	209
CHAPTER 41	214
CHAPTER 42	216

CHAPTER 43 228

CHAPTER 44 236

CHAPTER 45 241

CHAPTER 46 245

CHAPTER 47 250

CHAPTER 48 261

CHAPTER 49 269

CHAPTER 50 274

CHAPTER 51 279

CHAPTER 52 281

CHAPTER 53 286

CHAPTER 54 291

CHAPTER 55 294

CHAPTER 56 298

CHAPTER 57 302

CHAPTER 58 312

CHAPTER 59 321

CHAPTER 60 324

EPILOGUE 330

CHAPTER 1

Essex – August 1948

Sheriff Venter picked up a form from the top of the tray that resided permanently on his desk. "Complaint—Domestic." He shook his head slowly as he read the name on the top line, aggravated by what he read. He glanced at the date held in place by a small, plastic device that displayed the month and date. The twenty-fifth of August, 1948, stared back at him.

Domestic issues were not an area that Venter enjoyed in upholding the law. When he took the role, the mayor had been clear regarding his responsibilities. To foster community relations, resolved disputes before they escalated to charges, subdue civil disputes, ensure speeders and defective vehicles were fined on the highway, and provide a sense of security to the residents of the county of Essex.

Country folks kept their lives private. Reports of domestic issues occurred, but rarely. Men stayed silent, and women retreated from the problems. To receive a report like the one on the desk in front of him was rare. This time, he needed to protect Lena Peterson from her violent husband.

He had lost count of the times he had been to the old ranch house on the outskirts to the North of the town. The report described the discussion with Chances" wife, Lena, at Doc Lowe's surgery. He sent her to hospital in Winslow and called Venter the next morning. "He will kill her one day." He said slowly and unequivocally. The tone of his voice laden with concern and the experience of a doctor who had seen the proof of abuse too many times before. He had treated Lena before. Yet, each time she refused to lodge an official complaint.

Yet again, Chance was drunk and had beaten his wife, and this time, her injuries were significant. The report noted a broken jaw and contusions bad enough for her to be in hospital in Winslow. The report was the first written complaint Venter has seen. A report on which he could take further action.

"Goddamit, Chance." He hissed under his breath as he reread it. He had confronted the man several times before with the same result. Peterson denied what had happened and ordered him off the property. Tom complied, but this time, he had an official complaint from his wife, which meant he could charge him. With nothing better to do except investigate a stolen bicycle and a lost bull, he decided to take the matter up with the man.

Picking up his hat, he walked outside to the nine-year-old police cruiser, started it, and motored down the main road, past the aging water tower still standing higher than anything else in Essex.

He drove at a leisurely pace down the old town road towards the new highway. North Eighty-five comprised a recently built, two-year-old, four-lane blacktop that bypassed the town of Essex. The town no longer offered a thoroughfare to Winslow. The days of frequent visitors and passing traffic were slowing as a result.

The brown gravel road edges of the town road gave way to reddish-colored road shoulders with barbwire fences stretching as far into the distance as he could see. Farmland, bleached by the sun and nourished by rain, surrounded the highway on both sides.

Aged oaks, wide trunked and heavy with deep green foliage, lined the fields, interspersed with areas of cleared timber in various stages of regrowth in the reaches of the hills that led up to the granite cliffs, which changed color: light grey in the sunshine, turning to a dark, foreboding somber grey after the rain.

Several flashes, thin arcs of brilliant white light, appeared in the sky far beyond his vision through the windscreen as he traveled down the far reaches of the old town road towards the eighty-five turnoff. With a look of resignation that more rain might head his way, he put the cruiser into fourth gear and increased his speed. The flashes became indistinct and irregular, finally moving over the top of the high escarpment to the west.

In the distance, parallel to the cloud formation, he noticed a deep red flash in the underbelly of one large, menacing cloud. He had never seen a color like that in the sky before, and as he glanced across at the hilltop, it happened again.

He swerved suddenly, and almost skidded onto the shoulder of the road as a group of jackrabbits flew across the blacktop before him. Their faces showed panic, with eyes flashing left and right as they skittered across the front of the cruiser. They looked to be evading capture. Within seconds, they moved well beyond the road as they dodged and twisted, pursued by an unseen enemy. Finally, the group disappeared into the distance towards the trunks of a thicket of gigantic oaks on the lower part of the hillside.

It was the damnedest thing, he thought to himself. He had never seen so many rabbits at one time and never on the road because they seemed to avoid traffic and stayed away from any thoroughfare.

As he headed for the turnoff, he saw a large buck deer bounding down the bottom of the hill. Within a moment, it stopped still, looked up towards the top of the rise, and galloped off into the brush with a swiveling head, looking for its invisible pursuer.

Venter pulled the cruiser over, retrieved an old pair of army issue binoculars, and surveyed the hillside up to granite cliffs above the forest. There was little to see except the buck disappearing up the side of the hill. He thought he missed something as he brought the binoculars down and raised them again. He could hardly recognize what looked like a face, grey and menacing, at the bottom of a tree near the middle of the rise. It was hard to discern against the timber of the trees. He lowered the binoculars and used his naked eyes. Nothing.

He got back in the cruiser and headed down the road. As he neared the corner, he heard the radio crackle and picked up the microphone. "That you, Beth."

"Might be." She joked. "Where are you, sheriff?"

"Trying to avoid Jackrabbits."

"What?" she asked with surprise in her voice.

"Heading out to Peterson's place, you know, off the eighty-five. By the way, I read the report. When did you put that in my box?"

"Yesterday. You just read it?"

"Yep." There was no point in lying. She knew him better than he knew himself. "How's his wife?"

"Lena? From what I hear, she will survive. Thank God. Beaten up pretty badly, I guess. He's no better than an animal, Tom. Something needs to be done."

"I will make him understand."

"Okay." Replied Beth in her slow drawl. "That's a start, at least. He is a tough sonofabitch. You need to be careful."

"Did they send a copy to Winslow?"

"Yessir."

"Has Lean been discharged?"

"Nope, still at the hospital. The doctor says she will be okay. Hopefully, she will get better and give that bastard husband up for good."

"Seems he can't keep his hands off her. This must be the second time in two months, right?"

"Last time, it was a broken arm," Came the curt reply.

"Then how did she get to Doc Lowes this time?"

"Dunno, Tom. Maybe she drove herself."

"That would not be easy with those injuries. See if you can find out if anyone drove her to the hospital. Maybe we have a witness if she had a companion."

"Will do," Beth's voice came loudly over the two-way.

Venter clicked the microphone. "I don't know if anything will change with Chance. He's a stray cat, that one. He seems to care less about his wife than the dogs on his farm. I'll check it out. Over and out," He placed the handheld microphone in its cradle.

CHAPTER 2

Thirty minutes later, Venter steered the cruiser onto the road to the old farmhouse. It came into view two hundred yards up a dusty dirt road from the junction of the North eighty-five.

The old farm was similar to others in the Essex district. The property held low-lying pastures of rich soil, abundant wheat fields usually harvested in July and August, and a flock of sheep. Peterson kept te sheep in the upper pasture above the homestead.

As he drove up, Venter considered the timber cedar board dwelling. The house sat in a state of disrepair. Bowed, bent and faded cedar boards held together by nails and not a lick of paint in years.

When he started as sheriff in Essex he realized that most homes in the county stood cowed and scarred by the elements. Buildings that held a long to-do list for farmers and ranchers who had more important chores to do with their time. The Peterson house displayed signs of age and neglect: weathered paint, cracked door and window frames, and evidence of settling unevenly on old stumps. This resulted in challenging door closures and window openings. Venter had visited enough homes in the district with hard-to-close doors to realize it verged on normal.

Placing his hat lightly on his head, Tom walked up to the front door. There was no answer, so he knocked again and finally walked to the back of the old farmhouse. As he strolled down the side of the house, he glimpsed a shape out of the corner of his eye moving fast towards him.

Instinctively, he stepped quickly back and away as a large, black dog came bounding towards him, grinding savagely to a halt as the tether chain strained against its anchor, set firmly in the ground some twenty feet away. The dog snarled as saliva dripped from its bared, yellowed teeth. Straining against the chain rope, the dog jumped up, growling menacingly as it strained on the leash.

In the distance, the weathered barn walls reflected a faded, rust hue like the sunset skies of late fall. The front doors of the barn remained permanently open, fixed by rusted hinges and propped by long sticks, which barely held the doors as they swayed in the light breeze.

"Chance." He called out. "Chance, you there?" Venter walked into the gloomy barn with the familiar smell of manure, stored hay, and age. He made his way to the rear, listening to the creaking from a light easterly wind blowing soft against the side of the barn. He finally ended his short walk near an old tool bench, which looked barely used. Old tools and implements lay strewn on the table under years of dust and barely used.

At the back of the barn, he heard what sounded like a fox scurry under a bale of straw as he walked cautiously towards the back wall. He looked around at the various piles of junk, including a variety of old hessian bags lying haphazardly inside the barn. Watching his step, he moved towards the rear wall and returned, thinking whoever tended to the barn cared little about neatness and order.

He called out again and retraced his steps just as the sounds of footsteps made him look towards the light that spilled in through the barn doors.

"Well, well, if it ain't the local sheriff. Now, what can I do for you, boy?" The voice was raspy, low, and guttural. Chance stood at the doors with his arms at his side.

"Came to see you, Chance."

"Really. Now, you ain't been asked here, sheriff. To my reckoning, you'd be trespassin', now wouldn't yer? I don't remember asking you around here, so no matter your business, you jes move along."

Tom reached the doors, pushing his hat off his brow as he approached. Chance stood before him with his feet apart and hands on his hips. He was a big man with a protruding stomach. His shoulders appeared heavily muscled from farm work. He was dressed in an old shirt and dungarees covered with dirt. Venter guessed that one knee had almost worn out with the fabric, leaving a small patch of visible skin, dirty from keeling.

"Could do with some cleaning up, Chance. The barn, I mean."

"That's none of your business, sheriff. Whatcha doing here, anyway?"

"Come to see you, Chance."

"You said that. Why would you come out here?"

"Received a report, Chance." Tom replied, holding the white paper that he had grabbed from the cruiser in his hand. "Now Chance, this report says you were beating on your wife again, and this time your wife is in hospital," Chance glared at him. "And this time, she's laid down a complaint."

"Maybe, Sheriff. I'll need to have a quiet talk with her about that piece of paper you're holding."

"Well, I wouldn't advise that, Chance. Before you start off, this report is all about you and your hitting on your wife, and that's against the law, boy."

Chance stiffened his body to his full height, looking slightly down at Tom, who stood before him." That so? Says you and who else?"

"The law, Chance, the law. It would be best to lay off her son; here is some advice. Charges are pending, and that means you are in trouble. Do you understand what I'm saying, Chance?"

Chance scoffed and half turned away. "So, you say sheriff. The way I see it, Lena's my wife, and I will goddamn do what I want. Now you need to leave. This is between her and me, and that don't include you!"

"You won't be beating on her again, Chance." Tom said authoritatively. "If you do, you can consider an imposed fine and a stay in a jail cell."

Chance turned again and put his nose next to Venter's face with a snarl. "That'll be my business. You need to leave the property, sheriff, and don't be slow about it. Now move off!" Chance snarled at him angrily. He walked over to the inside of one of the barn doors and hefted an axe handle. "I hope I am makin' myself clear about your goddam piece of paper. It's between her and me, and just so you know, she is gonna get a beating about this mess as well, clear?"

"Nope, don't get it, Chance," Venter replied, locking their eyes together. "You can't beat her up, and it cannot continue. One day, you will kill her, boy, and no one wants that. Now, we have a written complaint, and that changes everything. Next time, you will be in jail."

Chance lifted the axe handle and pushed it towards Venters face. "Time for you to go, Sheriff. That dog over there will make a dinner of ya, if I let it off."

Venter lowered his voice and stepped towards Chance. "You're not listening, boy? You will have to defend this complaint as well. Now, are you clear about that, Chance?"

Chance looked at him and started to snort. "I ain't the one complaining, Sheriff."

"She is, Chance."

"Well, I guess I'll make sure that bitch don't complain again," Chance smiled grimly at Tom as he turned and walked towards the back of the old farmhouse.

"Don't walk away, Chance. This is me talking to you, not some defenseless woman," Venters voice deepened as he called out.

"Well, I'll have to talk to her about that as well. It's my understanding that she ain't made no complaint," Chance kept walking towards the house.

"Chance, you are going to face a charge. You can be sure of that."

Like what, sheriff?" Chance sneered at him as he moved back to where Tom stood.

"I have the medical report, Chance. That is all I need. If this continues, you will face jail. Understood?"

"Really. Says who? You?"

"You can't beat on her. It's a crime."

"I can do what I goddam like, sheriff. Not you, nor no one else, will tell me different."

"The law is the law, Chance. You need to do the sensible thing. Understood?"

Chance moved towards Venter and grabbed him by the throat. Venter pushed his arm away and laid a fist into Chance's jaw. The big man clutched at his face as he fell back. "Don't go touching me, Chance. I am not your wife."

Chance glowered at him and spat at his feet. "You stay away, boy. I see you here again. I'll make you wish you didn't come."

Venter looked at Chance as the man stood up to face him again. "If you have any sense, which I doubt, you'll listen."

"See that dog? You stay here, and I'll let him off that rope, and if he doesn't rip your hide, I will." The big man spat onto the ground and turned to walk away. Venter looked over at the massive hound slavering at the end of the rope tie. It had an enormous head and jaw. "This is not the end, Chance. You will be charged with assault."

"Fucker." came the reply.

Tom strolled towards the driveway after making a detour around the large dog that had stood to attention when the commotion started. He inspected his knuckles, noting a thin trickle of blood forming. He used an old handkerchief he kept in his pocket and wrapped it around his hand. "Mind what I told ya, Chance. I will see you real soon," He shouted as he slowly returned to the cruiser on the dirt patch next to the front fence.

As he got to the Ford, he turned to see Chance release the dog off its tether. The dog bounded, snarling and barking towards him. Venter got into the cruiser just as the dog pawed at the car door.

He watched the dog jump up against the door as he started the cruiser and headed back down the dirt road to the highway. The dog continued to claw the cruiser side, so he opened the door quickly, slamming it into the dog with as much force as he could muster. He watched it fall to the roadside with a yelp. It instantly got up to its feet, left behind in the dust from the wheels of his car.

Once he hit the highway, he raised the microphone and clicked the side button.

"Sheriff?" came the reply.

"Hey, Beth. I went to the ranch house and had it out with Peterson.

"Who won?" Beth asked dryly.

"Well, we can put attacking a police officer onto the list of charges, but I doubt he will do it again. We heard anything back from the Peterson woman?"

"I checked. They will release her tomorrow. What are you going to do about the written complaint?"

"I need to speak to her."

"Rodger," she replied. "It will take more than a talk, Tom. I don't think she will cooperate. From what I hear, she wants to return to the farm."

"So, she wants to withdraw the complaint?"

"She is a frightened woman. May not give you the information you need."

"But, she submitted the complaint, didn't she?"

"Nope." came the curt reply. "It was the Doc."

"Hang on," Tom pulled the cruiser over on the shoulder of the eighty-five. He opened the file and read the bottom of the document. He had failed to note the name and signature. Beth was correct. "Is the Doc in town today?"

"He's in Winslow this week."

"I'll call him, but I can't see it will do much good," Beth replied as she signed off.

CHAPTER 3

The following morning, Venter stood in front of an aged, slightly faded mirror. It was affixed to the bathroom wall above a leaking basin tap that left a trail of brown stain to the sinkhole.

Out of tune, he hummed along to a song playing on his unreliable radio with a barely functioning dial, so he usually left it alone. He switched stations only when the static became irritating. There were three stations the old radio could pick up, and the choice was limited. Invariably country music came out of its speaker. Eddie Arnold sang Bouquet of Roses, and the tune drifted softly through the house.

As his hair fell across his forehead, he combed it back after applying a little hair oil and dropped the brush onto the vanity after briefly looking in the mirror. He held the sort of tan that came from wearing a hat most of the time. The top of his brow looked almost white towards his hairline, with the rest of his wide face covered in a deep tan.

Venter looked briefly at his reflection. Like his father he had a broad face with wide-set brown eyes. Deep-set lines around his mouth and eyes offered proof of his life experience, most of it through difficult times. The fields of France remained etched in his memory.

The war taught him many lessons. How to survive, how to contain grief without showing it and how to fight for his life. The days where he wondered why he had survived when so many had lost their lives seemed to wane each passing year. However, the guilt of survival followed him, and many others, like a black dog.

He straightened the dark brown, military-style tie he hated wearing and gave his reflection a cursory glance in the mirror. What the hell was the point of a goddam tie, he thought briefly. Out of habit, he tied it on and straightened it around the collar line. After all, he was still the sheriff. As always, he led by example.

Entering the kitchen, he put an old, green kettle on the wood stove after stoking the coals beneath and walked out to the verandah that adorned the sides of his cottage.

He looked in the distance at the stark gray sides of granite hilltops, where solid, tall oaks and taller cypresses reached up from the steep inclines, pushing out branches above thick brush on the hillsides below the cliffs. Trees competed for space with periwinkles, long-frond ferns, and wood anemones on the forest floor.

Across the distant ridges, broad branches sprouted to reach the uppermost layers, where they basked in the diminishing sun of the fall season. Bright gold, orange, and red-brown leaves highlighted the lingering patches of green on the hillsides.

Winter was on the march.

A lilting song from the radio took him back to his honeymoon and a time on a beach in Los Angeles. They were the best of times, he thought without any real emotion. He recalled standing on the shore of Long Beach, looking across the expanse of golden sand, marveling at the ocean. He had never seen the sea before and regarded it as miraculous. It stretched to the horizon like a broad, blue canvas, calm and resolute on that perfect day.

As he stood with his toes in the sand, the ocean raised small, perfectly formed waves that reflected the sun. Each time a wave rose, it crashed onto the shore, spent its force against the sand, laid flat, and surged forward until the next wave pulled the water back. It was a sight to behold.

The memories of their time in love, with dreams so distant from where he stood that day, pushed his mind back into regret. Now, he lived alone, with the occasional visit from his daughter. For the first time in his life he was by himself, and he freely admitted there was an upside and a downside, to that reality.

When he returned from the war, his wife, Frankie, remained distant over the ensuing weeks. She finally confessed to an affair with the man who lived in an ordinary house in Winslow and worked as a dentist—a man who never went to war. Frankie chided him when he raised the subject, saying professionals were needed at home.

He argued and finally shook his head in disbelief. After his return from Europe, he lost his wife and his job within two months. The joy of his return was laced with the depressing prospect of an entirely new life. A life that differed from the one he envisaged while he sat in foxholes awaiting the onset of battle. Reality bit him hard.

Venter exited the front door and threw the gun belt he never used on the cruiser seat. Stuck in thoughts of Frankie, he lay his head back on the seat with a sigh as he rubbed his sore shoulder. The constant ache of his shoulder joint made him remember where the injury occurred. The past presented itself at the strangest times.

He tried in vain to forget the battle of Mortain, when his 30th infantry division fought to a standstill, losing over four hundred men. He lay near a clutch of trees holding his shoulder and wondering if the bullet had passed straight through? He was lucky, he knew that much. Over the three years he served he gained the ability to shut out the grief. It lay in the past, like his marriage and his old job.

He shook his head to dislodge his thoughts and checked his watch. At least the sun shone combined with the comforting thought that Essex offered an undemanding job as sheriff, well away from the war.

Over the past two years he had learned a lot about the town as he managed the county. Essex had evolved into a large, bustling town for over a hundred years. However, a closed copper mine, lost jobs, and the army airfield closing during the war without explanation within the same year did not help. Then, they built the eighty-five highway, routing traffic around Essex and into Winslow.

The bustling days of constant traffic waned over several years as motorists chose the eighty-five on their way to the west. The old town road was filled with local trucks and pickups from the district farmers and ranchers, and an occasional lorry bringing deliveries. The days of frequent visitors who drove to Essex to stop overnight on their interstate trip had changed irrevocably.

The old ways of peaceful life, unchanged for many years, were almost over as the process of change, of being left behind, became more apparent. Inevitably, Essex became a victim of progress. The Eighty-five assured that outcome, thought Venter as he drove slowly along.

To his mind, Essex had become a town stuck in a time when it had no impetus to grow or the disposition to push against decline. It steadfastly held onto its identity through farming, ranching, and a populace proud to be on the land. The war had ended and Essex would need to change if it was to survive.

CHAPTER 4

Deputy Marvin Rusk parked his cruiser in front of the office with infinite care. He reversed it slowly and straightened it to align perfectly in his allocated area.

He looked at his reflection in the cruiser window as he closed the door. He stood taller than Venter, a point of pride against the heavy set, muscular physique of his boss. Rusk's long, thin face sometimes looked gaunt beneath his wavy blond hair. He had a slightly aquiline nose and his grandmother's blue eyes.

Rusk ate sparingly to keep himself slim. He liked the way the gun belt hung low on his hips, sitting on top of his immaculately pressed uniform of a khaki shirt and dark, long pants. His mother had told him numerous times, "Clothes make the man." Deputy Rusk took this lesson into his life. For good measure, he shined his gun belt with wax each week and took pleasure from ironing his uniform each Sunday night. Marvin Rusk took his deputy role with the relentless intensity of a Sunday preacher.

That morning, he assiduously spent the previous four hours scrutinizing a particular section of the eighty-five highway for speeding vehicles. He sat just off the road, where he could sight cars and trucks traveling around a long corner before passing him on the roadside. If they were over the speed limit, he switched on the lights and the siren to pull them over to write a citation, relying on his calibrated speedometer and his unerring ability to move at high speed in pursuit. They never got away.

Marvin prided himself on an uncanny sense of someone else's speed. By watching the angle and movement of oncoming vehicles, he could tell with unerring accuracy whether they were over the county limit. He rarely made a mistake.

There were no warnings, just a deserved fine. He never could understand speeding. Why be in such a hurry to get a ticket for your efforts? Made no sense to him. The sheriff always wagged his finger at him when giving him a lesson in the law. "You are the deputy and paid to uphold the law." At the young age of twenty-six, he could not think of a better job.

That morning, Marvin sat at his desk, sipping contemplatively on over-brewed coffee and waiting a little impatiently for the sheriff to return. The sheriff received most of the paperwork and immediately processed what little trickled through to his tray. Waiting for the sheriff to pass the paperwork to him sometimes took a while.

"There's a call for you". Beth shouted out between chewing a pastry she had bought from the diner. Rusk liked her. She didn't take crap from anyone. She was very efficient in her work and neat as a pin. Qualities in a person that Marvin respected. "Who is it?"

Beth just shrugged her ample shoulders. "He asked for you."

Marvin picked up the receiver as the call came through from a man whom Rusk, the deputy of Essex, could best describe as a vagrant. A call from one of the town drunks surprised him. Bing and his pal came and went, and no one cared where or how as long as they did not help themselves to items that did not belong to them.

On his rounds, Marvin had pulled Bing in countless nights for reckless behavior and being seriously inebriated. He charged him with an added misdemeanor of disorderly conduct, which seemed to be the occupation where Bing most enjoyed himself. Bing spent most of his time looking for handouts, and the generosity of the townsfolk never waned.

A night in jail and a meal brought Bing in with some regularity, more for the comfort of a warm cell than any other reason. Despite a stern caution about reoffending from Rusk in his most officious manner, Bing ignored the instruction and went on his merry way the following day.

All towns seemed to have them. In Rusk's experience as deputy, he thought they had either failed at life, could not give up the sauce, or, for some inexplicable reason, they liked the vagrant's life.

Most citizens avoided Bing and his friends. However, they learned where the soft touches lay and handouts lived. Somehow, they survived. They were few and far between in Essex town. Winslow, directly fed from the eight-five gained vagrants each year as service members returning from Europe and the Pacific returned to limited jobs and hardened hearts. Alcohol offered a cheap escape.

Rusk was too young to enlist, and by the time he could attend a medical, induction had stopped. He tried repeatedly, but the war no longer needed the bravery of young men, and GIs were returning stateside looking to resume their lives.

Old Bing was a casualty, but not from war, or so Marvin ruminated as he thought about it. Bing was a casualty of his life, just another alcoholic and a man who walked away from any responsibility thrust on him and appeared more than happy about it.

Leaning back in his chair, he listened briefly, trying to feign some interest regarding the call from a faulty phone box in the middle of the town. Bing mumbled, which made it harder to understand, but finally, he came to the point of the call.

"On the field behind the old warehouse on a town road, near the end, deput*ee*." Bing had a way of singing at the end of each sentence.

"The end of what, Bing? Try hard to be more specific, okay?"

"The road, deputee. The old store, the one with the rotten gates."

"The old Sturger grain store road, that one?"

"Yessiree." Came the reply. "There's a bull there."

"Great news?" Rusk said sarcastically, which he realized was lost on his caller. "So, what?"

"You need to have a look," Came the slow reply.

"Are you sure, boy? This had better not be a hoax by y'all. If it is, trust me you're gonna pay."

"Not a hoax, Marvin," A limited response came with his rasping breath, the result of too much alcohol, but it might have been the onset of older age or maybe a little of both.

"Deputy Rusk to you, boy."

"Yessir."

"Where you calling from?" Rusk queried.

"Right here in town, deputee." Bing coughed into the mouthpiece. The phone box on the main street was famous for not taking coins. If you hit the side of the box, the call started. Every kid in the district knew if they needed to call someone, even if they used it for prank calls.

It occurred to Marvin that Bing had decided on a call rather than turning up in person. The only question in his mind was whether the call was a practical joke by Bing and his crony, who always seemed to hang with him.

"Let me tell ya, Bing. If this is not true, I will tan your hide, boy. I'll go there, but you better be there as well. So, let me guess, you'd be heading there now?"

"Yessiree."

"Y'all, better be there!" Marvin replied with a tinge of aggravation in his voice.

"I'll be there, deputee. That's the reason I called. You wanna pick me up?"

"Nope," The curt reply hung in the air. "We don't like being mucked around in the law. We are busy! so get there now!" Marvin replied brusquely as he waited for Bing to hang up the receiver.

He spent the next half an hour filing some of the paperwork he had been processing and finally took a breath and stopped. Hey, Beth. You feel like doing a little filing?"

"Nope," She looked at him over her spectacles and returned to her work.

Marvin shrugged. It was worth a try. "Beth, I'm heading out to the old warehouse on the South side. The old Sturger place."

"Why?"

"Well, that call came from old Bing. Says Carter's missing bull is over there."

The word stopped Beth from cleaning the coffee pot and made her turn to face him with a questioning look. "Carter's bull? Marv? What the hell would that big bull be doing down there? That's way away from its ranch. That don't make sense."

"I agree." Rusk replied sourly.

"And the information came from Bing? You trust him?"

Marvin nodded knowingly. "I have my doubts."

"So, have I!"

Marvin nodded in the officious way he offered when something he felt was important enough came up. "Any lead on that bull has to be checked out. God knows we don't want Bob back here complaining. I am sick of everyone talking about it. I'll report when I find out if it's nonsense," Rusk sighed as he picked up his hat. "Which it could be."

Beth nodded. "OK, I'll let the sheriff know when he comes in."

With urgency and the need to be involved in something new, Marvin got in his cruiser, turned the light on but not the siren, and drove off.

Heading down Town Road, he took a right turn at a street opposite the empty diner. He checked his watch, thinking it might be due to the time of day. He continued driving until he got to the end of the street, where old cypress trees lined the grassy roadside, and took another right down 2nd Street, towards the end of the town.

Essex had changed he thought to himself as he drove slowly down the road. For many years, well before his time as deputy, this old part of town held thriving businesses that manufactured farm machinery parts and a large granary and farm supplies business. How long had it been? He thought briefly as he continued driving. Years.

The old warehouses and buildings fell into disrepair and mournful neglect with the war and the recession in the late thirties. It bordered on ghostly. A part of town that no one visited. Finally, it became the subject of discussion in the area. Nothing was proposed in the absence of any binding decision by the town council as to the future of the buildings. The Winslow town council, like everyone else in Essex, gave up over the years, and the area ended up firmly in the too-hard file at the council office.

There was little point in trying to beat Bing to the site, so fifteen minutes later, he finally came to a stop outside a single-level, old warehouse with weather-greyed window frames and old stucco walls with a stale brown color on the wide, disused doors of the building.

Above the old entrance door, a sign held fast to the wall, slightly crooked from age, with the name "Sturger Feed & grain in faded white. Almost as if someone erased the left side.

He got out of the cruiser, donned his hat, checked his sidearm, and walked past the rusting wire fence at the front of the property. He noticed the timber side fences were falling apart, with many palings lying broken and scattered.

As he approached, he saw Bing leaning casually against the front gate. He looked furtively at Rusk with a smile that showed his lack of teeth.

"I'm here, deputee, jes, as I said I would."

Marvin nodded at him. "Lucky for you, boy. Now, where is this bull you been talking about? Or have you been drinking too much?"

Bing ran a dirty hand across his balding head and pointed to the back of the warehouse twenty feet away. "Right out the back, deputy, and after you, sir," Bing said grandiosely as he stood up.

"Where?"

"It's in the back area behind the shed, but you ain't gonna be happy with what you will see. Let me tell you that before yer' get there." Bing pointed in the general direction. 'You'll need something for your nose.'

"What? Why are you being so tender about this, Bing? You sure it's there?"

"Oh, deputee take my word for it. It's there alright." Bing stared at him sheepishly. He seemed reluctant to follow when Rusk started. "We ain't got nothing to do with this deputy."

"With what? Keep up with me!" Marvin's voice sharpened as he waited for Bing to catch up.

"Me and the boys. We drink. Maybe too much, but that's all we do."

Marvin felt suspicious of the man standing beside him. Contemplating whether to wait for the sheriff, he stopped, turned and retreated to the cruiser to contact Beth. "Won't be long, boy. You jes stay here. "

Rusk grabbed the two-way radio microphone. Beth's reply about the sheriff's whereabouts was negative, so he walked through the old gate toward the back of the warehouse, making sure Bing walked with him again.

He reached the double door at the front, moving several broken branches from a long, dead tree, and peered in before heading up towards the fence that lined the back of the warehouse lot. Once painted and upright, many fence joints hung forlornly and crookedly, threatening to fall to the ground.

"How'd you find the bull, Bing?" Marvin asked. He walked slowly towards the rear of the warehouse, nimbly sidestepping several pieces of what looked like bull dung.

Bing pointed to the back of the fence. "Sometimes we go through here as a shortcut, and sometimes we sleep in the back. There's an old shed behind the warehouse with a couple of old bunks in it. We stay there."

"That's a lot of 'sometimes' Bing. Why do you stay here of all places?"

Bing shrugged as he pulled his old pants up above his waist. "No one to bother us none."

"With booze?" Bing nodded as if the question did not need to be asked. "Last night you were here?"

"Nope, the night before."

"How did you find the bull?"

"Came here this morning to pick something up, and you could smell it a mile off."

"Smell?"

Bing backed away. "Might be the wind, but you'll see it, deputee, you'll see. Old Bing is right."

As they turned the corner of the building, Marvin stopped abruptly and let out a long breath. "Goddamn, boy, is this what you were talking about?"

The scene was hard to acknowledge because it seemed unreal. Rusk stood transfixed on the spot and did not make another step. It was as close to brutal violence as he had seen in his life. "When did you say you first saw this?"

"This morning. Yessir, this morning."

The mutilated remains of a massive, black bull covered the back area of the warehouse. It was ripped to pieces. Dismembered body parts lay on the ground in all directions. The head was pulled entirely from the body of the bull.

"Goddamn!"

"Yessir," Bing replied promptly. "One hell of a mess."

As the deputy walked around the area, he tried turning his head to avoid the nauseating stench, but it hung like a foul-smelling cloud above the remains. He took his hat off and scratched his head, trying to take in the scene. "What the hell?"

"Told ya," Bing said defensively.

"Don't get smart with me, boy! How does a bull of this size get ripped limb from limb?" Marvin said to himself as he looked around the area.

"Beats me." Bing scratched his beard as he looked.

Marvin felt physically ill as he stepped gingerly around the gigantic carcass and proceeded to inspect each of the dismembered limbs. Each part looked to have been violently pulled from the rest of the body with deep rips into the flesh. He winced as he looked at the bull. "This is one hell of a mess."

The bull's eyes, glassy and whitened by the sun, remained open and locked in a what looked like a bewildered stare. The disturbing thought entered Rusk's mind that the brutality may have occurred while the big bull was still alive. Was that scenario possible?

"Pretty messy, huh?" Bing said quickly.

"You got that right" He offered the curt reply as he retreated to the cruiser. "You stay here until I return."

He sprinted to the cruiser, picked up the microphone. "Beth, come on," he said urgently.

"Here, Marvin, what's up?"

"Hey, Beth, has the sheriff called in?"

"Nope."

"I am over at the old Sturger warehouse. I need him here as quickly as possible."

Beth replied quickly. "OK, I'll find him. Did you find the bull?"

"This you would need to see to believe."

"Meaning?"

"It's that missing bull of Bob Carters? That big bull is here alright, but it's long past dead. Something ripped that goddamn bull to pieces."

"No kidding? Ripped?"

"No joke, Beth."

OK, I'll find him. Over and out."

"Pretty mean, huh? What the hell would have done that damage?" Bing said with a sly look, leaning on the front of the cruiser as Marvin walked past him walking to the back of the warehouse. He was holding his handkerchief tightly against his nose and mouth.

"I thought I told you to stay out back?"

"Well, I was investigating, deputy. I mean, no person could've done this damage, no sir? It looks to me like one of those coyotes or something."

"A coyote down here in the town?" Marvin looked at Bing with surprise. "It would have been a lot of coyotes or maybe one the size of that bull. I ain't seen nothing like that," Rusk laughed at Bing, who stood looking at him with a stupid grin. "Coyotes? It must have been a giant."

"Then what was it, deputee?" Bing kept his grin as he thoughtfully stroked his chin with his hand.

"Take another look at the state of that big bull, boy. It's in pieces. What's that over there? What the hell is that?" Rusk peered at the other side of the yard, which took up the width of the warehouse.

Bing looked quizzically in the direction and finally shook his head. "It looks like the gizzards."

Rusk moved cautiously to the other side of the bloodied grass. "It's the goddam heart of that big bull, you idiot. Look at the size of it," He bent over to inspect it. "It's been chewed in half."

"Well, I can smell that old thing from here," Bing replied with a shrug. "Don't need to go any further."

Rusk finally made his way around the rear of the building to assess the situation. He examined the head again, noticing broad, reddish stains pooled on the grass for the first time. The attack caused the beast to bleed heavily, and he wondered momentarily how much blood a beast of that size might hold. A hell of a lot, he thought.

What the hell was the bull doing here in the first place? He asked, more to himself than to Bing, who stood on the other side of the grassy area.

"What did you say, deputee?"

"Boy, think about it! Why this, and why here?" Suddenly, the stench overtook him, and he vomited into the remains of an old tire near the side fence. After several long breaths and the contents of his stomach removed, he took stock of the scene before him.

"You okay?" Bing asked as Marvin walked back. "Gotta tell ya, I lost my stomach when I first saw it."

"I'm okay, Bing." He replied gruffly, feeling a little embarrassed. "That smell is god awful, ain't it?"

"Wasn't exaggerating, now was I?"

Marvin looked over the site again and motioned to Bing. They walked back to the cruiser deep in thought. After sitting heavily on the wide seat of the old Ford Tudor cruiser for several minutes, he clicked the microphone, but there was no response. The sheriff was probably on his way.

CHAPTER 5

Rusk spent time away from the nauseating stench of the bull remains as he waited for Venter to arrive. He sat comfortably in the cruiser, with the windows closed against the stench, which came and went depending on the direction of the breeze.

As he sat in the warm interior of the cruiser, he thought about the bull's remains. What the hell would rip a bull of that size apart? Why would, whatever it was, kill a bull, anyway? How did it end up at the back of an old disused warehouse? To kill a bull of that size without a bullet was a big task. It seemed to be a senseless kill.

Bing sidled up to the window. Rusk waved him away, watching as he walked off unsteadily towards the front of the warehouse and sat near the gates.

. "Hey Marv, what's up?" Rusk startled at the knock on the window of his cruiser. He nodded at the sheriff, noticing, not for the first time, that the sheriff was not wearing his revolver. He never understood why the sheriff hardly, if ever, wore his belt. "No need." Venter offered as his explanation when Rusk queried him. "What am I going to do? Shoot a horse?"

The sheriff never carried his weapon, which was the last thing Rusk put on when he dressed. He treasured his Smith and Wesson Model 10 above all else. He wore it pridefully and cleaned it weekly by removing the cartridge and oiling the breech.

"You're not looking too good, Marv. You okay?"

"Use a handkerchief, sheriff; the stink is godawful."

"What stink?"

"You can't smell that, sheriff? I can smell it from here."

Venter looked at him, puzzled by the remark, until the stench hit his nostrils. It made him feel nauseous. "Sweet Jesus, I can smell it now, Marv. What the hell is that?" With a look of disgust, he inhaled the stench of the decaying carcass coming from the old building.

He grabbed an old handkerchief from his shirt pocket, wiped his brow, and finally put it over his nose and mouth. "Okay, Marv, let's go." Together, they strolled to the back of the warehouse. When they got to the scene, Venter stopped in mid-stride.

"A goddam mess, if ever there was one." Rusk said as he looked at Venter.

Tom Venter pulled his hat back off his forehead. He stood still, transfixed by what he saw before him. It took him a while before he spoke. "What the hell happened?"

Marvin pointed to several areas. "How's that for something different?"

"Different, Marv? Goddamn it, Marv! This is horrific."

Marvin shrugged and pointed to where Bing was standing. "Bing and his friends use the back shed to sleep over some nights. They found the bull this morning."

"Did they sleep here last night?" Venter asked.

"Nope, said he didn't. They slept in town. "I can't see they had anything to do with this mess."

Tom just looked at him and then back at the dismembered bull in front of him. "Hardly possible, I guess."

"Besides the bull, there is very little to see," Marvin replied seriously. "There are bits everywhere. Even the bull's heart was ripped out. It's over there," He pointed to the mass of flesh in the middle of the yard with flies swarming.

As Venter moved around the area, he stopped, looked carefully, and moved on. Something had torn the left front leg of the beast in two. Deep rips in the flesh of the torso were a yard long. The wounds showed deep teeth marks, showing something tore off the flesh. The brutality of the attack became more apparent the longer he inspected the carnage.

He shook his head as he walked around. "How could something like this happen to a young bull of such size? "Coyotes or dogs, perhaps?" He said abruptly to Rusk, who stood beside him.

"That was my thought, sheriff. We don't have wild dogs around here. Could a pet dog do this? Has anyone seen a coyote near the town? Ever?"

Rusk shook his head. "Nope, not to my knowledge."

Venter sighed as he looked down at the torso of the bull. "Can't see how dogs could take down something of this size. More than one? Maybe something else?" Venter had seen traffic accidents with broken bodies and dead children, but he had never seen anything like what lay at his feet.

"Like what?" Rusk asked.

"Dunno, Marv." He checked the length of the building and walked carefully around the bull parts to inspect the old shed that Bing had noted he sometimes slept in. The crumbling shed stood immediately behind the warehouse.

He peered inside, and as old Bing had mentioned, it held two old bunks with what looked to be old horsehair mattresses, partly covered by old army-issue blankets greatly in need of a wash.

He poked around and found nothing of interest, so he stepped to the back of the warehouse, where he discovered a small opening to the rear of the building.

It was not large enough for a man to get through and might have been the opening to a fan vent in days gone past when the old warehouse was a bustling enterprise. Days when the building held workers and a busy entrance next to a bustling street, as trucks came and went, picking up and delivering as instructed.

He peered down at what looked like an indistinct, partially formed footprint. Curious about where the bull had come from, he moved to the back fence, keeping the handkerchief hard to his face. He stopped and looked over at the long grassy fields to the rear. The fields at the rear of the warehouse lot led up to the forested area below the hills and grey granite cliffs around Essex. There seemed to be nothing out of the ordinary that he could pinpoint except the carnage behind him on the grass at the back.

Finally, he stepped through the broken paling fence and looked around but found nothing interesting except other smaller, indistinct prints that he could not make out. It had rained the night before, and the damp earth softened any prints that might have been visible. He turned back to look at the rear from a different perspective.

The backyard of the old warehouse was no more in size than a house lot, but the bull's carcass and dismembered limbs seemed to be everywhere. It was almost as if something had thrown each part of the head, legs, tail, and torso in different directions. He stopped now and then to inspect the parts and the reddened earth beneath them.

"You see a problem here." Tom said as he stepped back to survey the area. "That's one hell of a mess, but no prints, nothing. How can that happen, Marv?"

The deputy looked back over the area and finally nodded his head. "Maybe from the rain late last night. You know, maybe washed them away. The ground is wet, and maybe the larger pools of blood have disappeared."

"How much blood does a bull have? It must be a lot," Venter said as he pointed at the reddened grass.

Marvin pointed around the area of the carcass. "There are a few indistinct footprints around the building, which I can show you, but, you know, they don't lead to anything?"

Tom nodded his head as if the suggestion made sense. "There should be some sign around to show a fight, but I can see nothing except a bit of churned earth around here. Why here of all places? Why would that damn bull be here?"

"I've been asking myself the same question," Rusk replied briskly.

Tom whistled softly as he looked back at the bull's remains in front of him. "See, to bring down an animal of this size, it would take something of the same size or a lot of them. Maybe it was dogs? Wild dogs, back of the old Sturger warehouse. Seems ridiculous to me."

"Maybe it was a lot of them."

"Maybe."

Marv shrugged as he looked around again at the spread carcass. "I ain't ever heard of a dog attacking a bull."

"Pack of dogs?" Venter said as he looked around. "I've never heard of that either, but then, as you say, the area has many of them. It might have been dogs, though. You have been in Essex longer than me. Has this happened before?"

Rusk shook his head slowly." Nope, not to my knowledge. Why would a group of dogs target such a bull of this size? There would be easier prey around."

"I agree." Venter said with a perplexed look.

"Do we take photographs or something?"

Venter looked at him strangely. "Not our problem, Marv. We'll get McNab out to have a look?"

"Yeah," Rusk fiddled with his gun belt as he motioned to Bing.

Tom looked towards the front gates as Bing sauntered up the side of the old warehouse. "Why is he still here?"

"Can't get rid of him." Rusk laughed as he watched Bing.

Tom pulled out a door-eared, thin book from his top pocket and wrote several notes. "Hey, Marv, how long you think this bull has been here in this state?"

Marvin adjusted his gun belt and shrugged. "This carnage has to be fairly recent. There are no maggots on the flesh, but they will come."

"Plenty of flies though. Yeah, something to look forward to, I guess," Venter replied sourly.

"Maybe a couple of days. Can't think it might be much longer than that."

"Marv, grab some rope and tie the area off at the front. Let's move away from here and close the gate," Marvin nodded and walked back to the front with Tom towards his cruiser parked on the dirt shoulder beside the road.

Marvin pulled the rope from his trunk and strung it across the gates. "Hey Bing, come over here and help me with his rope. Don't return to that shed until I tell you to. Okay?"

Tom continued making notes on his black pocketbook as he stepped out of the back area and walked casually towards the front gate.

"What now?"

Tom shrugged. "It ain't possible to believe dogs could have done this. I mean, why would they? There is easier prey around this town, and most of it is unprotected." He said firmly, lifting his hat off his sweating forehead and wiping his brow with the blue handkerchief he held over his nose. "In all my years, I have never seen something like this."

Rusk nodded. "You want me to get McNab?"

"Maybe call him when you get to the two-way. I'll wait here for him."

Rusk nodded and called to Bing. "Follow me!"

Venter called out to Rusk as he walked off. "When you have done that, Marv, drive to Bob's ranch and give him the bad news because that is one expensive animal to lose. He ain't gonna be happy,

I can tell you that much, so go gentle on him. There is little point in visiting this site until McNab has a look-see."

Marvin nodded and headed back to the cruiser to call Beth. He returned some minutes later as Tom, who was still inspecting the front of the warehouse. "Beth is trying to get a hold of him, sheriff."

Venter nodded as he checked his notes. "See you later."

Rusk smiled, looking over at Bing, who stood by the cruiser with a blank look. "Bing! You keep in touch, and there is no going back here until it's all cleaned. Got it?"

Bing smiled quietly. "Sure thing, deputee."

"I'll see you back at the office, Marv." Tom replied briskly as he inspected the tied rope. Within a minute, he had retied the rope so that it spanned the entrance and the gates. "Keep quiet on this, Marv, until we review it. No one comes anywhere near Sturgers warehouse until then."

"You hear that, Bing?" Marv shouted out, making his way back to his cruiser.

Bing nodded with a wry smile. "You driving, deputee Rusk?"

Marvin nodded with a frown. "I'll drop old Bing back to town and head out to Carter's farm."

Tom nodded absently, watching as the cruiser moved back down the potholed blacktop. He leaned against the old gate with a perplexed look on his face. The dead bull was a huge Angus, a giant breed of bull favored by the cattle ranchers of the area.

He knew enough of the breed to know the bull carcass at the back of the warehouse probably weighed more than a ton or even a ton and a half. He thought the size of the giant bull might have given it protection against any attack outside of a bullet. It was a long way from Bob Carter's farm. So, why the back of the old warehouse?

The more he thought about it, the less sense it made. He had witnessed death and the broken bodies of dismembered men and animals from shells during the war, but a mutilated beast in the back streets of Essex town? He might have witnessed stranger things, but the brutality unnerved him.

He leaned against the cruiser and wiped his sweating forehead again with his old handkerchief. On a hunch, he walked to the front of the warehouse, looking carefully around at the concreted area at the front of the disused building. He looked for prints or any signs of the horror at the back. Nothing.

The bull could not have come from the roadside. The driveway up the side of the building was narrow, and he wondered if any bull could make it up the side of the building. It must have come from the field beyond the back fence of the warehouse. But why was it attacked?

Beth came on the two-way as he returned and opened the cruiser door. "You there, sheriff?"

He clicked his button twice. "Did you get a hold of Harold?"

"Nope. Not around."

Venter sighed, thought momentarily, and clicked the side button. "Okay. I'll head in."

CHAPTER 6

The twenty-minute drive to the farm was uneventful, except for when Rusk questioned himself why he should inform Charlie about his bull. It seemed a menial job for a deputy sheriff.

He pulled up to the farmhouse and made his way to the door, where Bob Carter greeted him as he headed out with a bucket in his hands toward the chook pen at the side of the house.

"Deputy?" Carter looked surprised as he stopped mid-stride and adjusted his glasses that had slipped down his nose. "What brings you out here?"

"Good to see you, Bob. Need to speak to you about something."

Carter nodded. "Well, now, rarely do we get a visit from the law. How about a coffee, deputy? You look like you have had a bad day. Let me take the slops out to the chickens, and I will get Mable to put a pot on."

Rusk nodded. Carter pointed to chairs on the veranda. "Won't be long. Black coffee, okay?" Rusk nodded and promptly sat on one of the wicker chairs that had seen better days. It creaked as he sat down.

The house provided a wide view of the main paddock, built high enough to overlook the fields and hills extending towards the faraway ridgeline. He lit a cigarette and waited for Carter, who finally arrived with two cups in his right hand. He set one on the table beside Rusk, who smiled at him. "Just what I needed, Bob. A cup of joe."

"Sounds serious, Marvin. What the hell would take you out here? We don't get much in the way of visitors these days, especially the law.

Rusk took a long breath as he picked up his coffee and sipped. "We found your bull."

Bob sat upright as he heard the news. "Well, now, that is great news, Marv. Where?"

"Before I get into that, let me ask you. How long has it been missing?"

Carter thought about it for a moment. He rubbed his eyes and looked up. "Close on a week. Let me see. Friday before last. Why do you ask Marv?"

The news ain't that good, Bob."

"Meaning?" Came the suspicious response.

Bob, we have just been to the site. The news could be better. When we found it, it was dead."

Carter looked at him strangely as he lowered the coffee cup from his lips. "Dead, you say?"

"Old Bing found it and called me. I went out to investigate, and it's dead alright."

"What, hit by a truck or something?"

"Well, I wish it was that simple, Bob. We found your big bull at the back of the old Sturger grain store. You know it?"

"That area off the town road?" Carter asked quietly. "Yeah, I know the area."

"Yep, down the back of the old town road. You know that old disused area?"

Carter nodded at him. "Ain't been there since old Sturger died and his relatives closed his shop."

Rusk shifted on his seat with a concerned look and lit another cigarette. "Might have been attacked."

Carter winced as he looked at Rusk. "That don't make sense. What did you say happened to it?"

"Well, that's the thing of it, Bob. Something got at that big bull at the back of the warehouse. Unfortunately, that's how we found it. Bing found it this morning. We are all wondering how that bull got there."

"That might be the least of the problems, Marv. What the hell do you mean, attacked?" Carter asked quickly. His face had whitened, and his eyes bored into Rusks. "What are you saying, Marv?" Carter asked quickly.

Rusk watched Carter's growing aggravation. "I wish we knew, Bob. We looked around thoroughly. There was nothing to give us an idea of what happened. It rained heavily last night, which washed away any tracks. Bob, I don't know what to say, but something ripped that poor bull apart.

"Goddam it." Carter got to his feet angrily. "You're not making any sense, Marv. What the hell are you saying?" Carter stared at him blankly and finally called his wife to come out.

"What is it, Bob?" She looked at Rusk with a light smile. "Morning, deputy. Something up?"

"Deputy here found our bull, but it's dead, Mable. It seems something killed it, but they don't have the foggiest what or who did it."

Mable rubbed her wet hands with the tea towel she was carrying. "That's our prize bull, Marv? Are you serious?" Mable looked at him suspiciously and then stared at her husband. "Now, that don't seem possible, now does it? Are you saying something pulled down that fifteen hundred-pound bull? That makes about as much sense as a snow day in summer."

Carter peered over his spectacles, finally removing them and cleaning them with the bottom of his shirt. "It makes little sense to me, Marvin. We better go look-see," he said.

Rusk held up his hand, attempting to stop them talking. "Not yet, Bob. The sheriff says the area is off limits until McNab inspects the area."

"Hey, that's our goddam bull, Marv!"

"We want to see it, deputy. Right now," Mable said in unison.

"If someone done this, I want them caught, Marv. And thrown in that jail you never use. You need to get on and do your job, Marv."

"Not that easy, Bob."

Carter moved on his seat, clearly agitated. "Don't you go telling me about easy, Marv. You need to find who done it and charge them for Christsakes! Let me tell you that this is a prize bull and worth a lot of money. Money we don't have."

Rusk exhaled slowly. "I'll talk to the sheriff."

"You can talk to God, Marv, but either way, you need to find out who done this?"

Marvin's face suddenly reddened. "I'll do what I can. This ain't exactly police business."

Lena put her hands on her hips and looked him squarely in his eyes. "If this ain't police business, what is?"

Carter chipped in. "Our bull goes missing, and you find it dead at the back of the old warehouse? You don't think this is police business, but something killed it? We want answers, nothing short of that, Marv, and you tell the sheriff I said so."

"The sheriff is asking McNab to have a look."

"McNab, huh? That useless bastard."

"Yessir," Rusk replied affirmatively.

"I need to go have a look," Carter stated quickly with his eyes on his wife.

"Not yet, Bob. Sheriff has asked everyone to stay away until McNab looks at the site."

"Why?"

"Needs an expert to have a look, I guess."

"You tell the sheriff to call me afterward. We got a phone, so you tell him to call. You got that, Marv?"

Rusk rose, put on his hat, and adjusted his gun belt. "I'll let him know. Thanks for the coffee," he said.

"When is McNab heading out there?"

"Not sure. I'll let you know."

"You do that!". Carter replied. "Tell the sheriff we want to know what done it and why?"

Marvin walked towards his cruiser, feeling that Bob Carter was rightfully angry. A dead bull, miles away from his farm, lay dead, and no one had an answer. Least of all, the sheriff and himself.

CHAPTER 7

Venter had met his predecessor briefly before the man left Essex to retire. They had two catch-ups over coffee, during which they discussed law and order requirements in a rural town. Venter learned all he thought he might need to know, and after an hour of conversation, he was convinced that the man on the other side of the table knew his business and had managed the town with great care. He intended to do the same.

The previous sheriffs name was Joe Lenthen, and, like Venter, he had experience upholding the law in a larger town. Venter guessed his age in the middle sixties, but he might have been younger. He appeared unfit, with a pronounced limp from his left leg, but eager enough to explain his role and to make a change in his life, so Venter felt no reason to ask him his actual age.

"Life is easy here, son," He drawled when they first met. Lenthen was a large, imposing man with a ruddy face and hair resembling the color of rust. "The idea is to keep it that way. There is no point in stressing or creating big change! You have experience as a big city sheriff, but you now manage in a county where most of the population lives outside the town. So, most issues are different, and getting used to the pace takes a little time. But, Tom, I am sure you will manage."

Venter smiled at the genial man across from him. "When you say *different*, what do you mean, Joe?"

Lenthen sipped his coffee as he gave it a thought. "Well, Tom, the place is real quiet overall, and in the policing business, that's about as good as it gets. I never attended a murder, for example. There is petty theft and the constant pressure for income from the eighty-five fines. Mind you, there are the day-to-day issues of keeping a large rural population represented. However, you won't be attending much in the way of murder scenes hereabouts."

"Why are you leaving?"

Lenthen nodded. "There are several reasons."

Venter nodded as he listened. Most of the problems he discussed could only be associated with farming and the ranch community. Lenthen had made it clear that his primary reason for leaving was his distaste at the prospect of living in Winslow if and when they closed the Essex sheriff office. 'Too big' and 'too many people over there.'

"When did you decide to retire?" Venter asked as he leaned his large frame into the back of the chair.

"The town has changed over the past five years with the war and the losses of all the farmers and rancher's sons. They lost a lot of young men in these parts," Lenthen said with his slow drawl. "The town is finding it hard to push on with the eighty-five heading to Winslow and not here. The old town road used to be busy, but now it is local traffic or supply trucks from somewhere delivering goods. There is nothing and no one to push growth. If you understand my meaning, things might change, but I doubt it."

"Too quiet? Boring, you mean?" Venter asked Lenthen.

"It's never too quiet," Lenthen guffawed. "The truth is there is a minor crime issue. Now and then, we get domestic issues. There are always land disputes on fence boundaries and the like, but all in all? Well, it's quiet enough to manage with yourself and a deputy."

"What about your deputy? I have met him once. He seems okay."

"Marvin Rusk? Well, he is a straight arrow when it comes to the law. He takes it real seriously if you get my drift. He will make a fine sheriff one day, but I have reminded him that the day to take on that responsibility has not arrived," Lenthen smiled quietly and patted Venter's arm. "Give him time. I am sure he will get on with it. He wants to learn, so give him something to do, and he'll do it."

Venter looked out of the diner window, wondering if there was anything else he could ask of the aging sheriff before him. "So, there is little in the way of hard crime?"

No murders in the past years. At least none I know of!" Lenthen laughed, which turned into a light smile. "A few houses done over, mainly by young and bored sons of local farmers. We get our share of grifters, but I move them on quick enough before they do too much damage. There are spinsters out there who will believe what a grifter says and mark my words, it's important to keep that gullibility in mind. I think the secret to managing this town is to listen."

Venter nodded knowingly.

"Like any community, there are domestic disputes and usually drunks beating on their wives. You get to know the people and how they behave." He said solemnly.

"Anyone in particular?"

"Some. You will get to know them soon enough. The closest hospital is now in Winslow, as they closed the small one they had here last year. We have a good doctor, but he spends his time between Essex and Winslow, and these days, he spends more time in Winslow."

"I guess that is not going to change." Venter responded.

Lenthen stared at Venter momentarily as if making up his mind to keep talking. "In confidence, there is one other thing, Tom. Winslow is controlled by a little bastard named Perkins, and you would have met him, right?"

Venter nodded. "Twice."

"That man does not care about this Essex office or what goes on. He cares about revenue from the eighty-five and keeping the place clean of any problems that might be escalated to Winslow, and make him look bad. You understand what I mean?"

Venter nodded his head as he listened.

"Now, thankfully, Marvin does a first-class job regarding the fine revenue. Do you want support from Winslow? Forget it, Tom; it won't happen unless Perkins becomes personally involved, and that is rare. I don't know how long it will take, but as sure as hens lay eggs, Perkins will close this Essex office. Might be some years or less, but that little shit will do it if he thinks it will help him."

"Duly noted." Venter added.

"So, to keep your job, you need to keep the fines up each year and try not to let any matter escalate to Winslow if you can handle it."

"Yep, understood. What did Perkins say when you resigned?"

"Could not give a damn. Goddam councils. They are all the same. So, keep the place clean and attend to the matters. Life will be, hopefully, peaceful."

"When do you leave?"

Next week, I'm heading to San Clemente, an hour down from the big city. I will live near the sea and my daughter, so I look forward to a change. I wish you the best of luck, Tom Venter, and I have left the town in good order for you."

CHAPTER 8

Venter walked briskly through the office door. In a practiced motion, he dropped his hat on his desk, eying the top of the desk suspiciously. He leafed through several top pages that lay comfortably within the sides of the worn, three-sided tray.

Around him, the office walls were constructed of bare, old common bricks marked by age and wear. The doorways and windows held ornate framing once painted white. The passage of time and neglect had pitted and discolored their surface.

Two disused jail cells lay at the back of the office as reminders of past crimes and the once-larger town of Essex. They were complete with sturdy metal bars that were slightly rusted, each holding a door that remained unlocked and slightly ajar due to the lack of use. The brick construction of the walls at the back of the cells showed the graffiti of bored inhabitants. A middle wall of bars separated the two cells. Each cell held a small window with a view of the distant granite cliffs soaring above the forest lining the hills around the town.

One cell was half full of old furniture, stashed in the back because the office held little space. The other had a basin and two beds that folded down from the wall via two sturdy chains. Placed haphazardly on each bunk lay old, army-issue blankets and pillows stuffed with straw at one end.

Venter sauntered over to the radio desk where Beth usually sat. The desk looked neat and orderly because that was how she liked it. As he neared her, she turned and smiled. "Busy day, Tom. Just the way you like it."

"Some days," He replied without enthusiasm.

The front of the office held two sizeable windows. One faced the street, and the other lay in front of Beth's desk, situated to the side of the office. It offered a view up the main street to the main intersection, close to a hundred yards away.

Muttering to himself, he sat on the old desk chair he had made comfortable in the first week of his tenure. He located an old cushion under one of the iron beds and re-employed it on the hardwood surface of the chair. The cushion color did not suit the timber, but comfort overrode any other consideration.

Tom sat back in his chair to look at his mail. After scrutinizing the stamp on one envelope, he opened it and withdrew the letter. As he read, he recognized the signature at the bottom. It was from the medical office over at Winslow, with the top sentence reading "Case update."

Venter read the first sentence and promptly put it on the 'in' tray for a later date when he was bored. He pulled out a pad and wrote a report on his visit to the Peterson farm and his altercation with Chance.

His desk held a three-sided wooden container, scratched and worn, with the title 'in tray' stacked with paper. The tray title sat on the front, neatly written with ink on a small piece of blotting paper about twice the size of a postage stamp. A piece of paper remained stuck to the front of the tray with sticky tape, yellowed by the years it had kept the writing in place.

The tray held a repository of notices received in the mail or brought back from Winslow, showing printed pages with indistinct photos and information of wanted felons and persons of interest. The only perp who showed up was seen on the main road in a pickup. By the time Venter was alerted, the man had moved.

He guessed some POI may have even stayed at the old Travelers motel out towards Winslow, but as far as he knew, they have yet to make their presence known in the town.

He rose to pour himself a coffee from the old pot, hissing like a disturbed snake onto the hot plate of the stove. He wondered what to do if someone on the felon list turned up. It would cause a stir, that was for sure. Maybe an arrest? He shook his head to dislodge the thought from his mind. That meant putting them in jail and taking them across to Winslow. The goddam paperwork would send him insane.

The job was a far cry from Decorah, where serious crime increased. The short-lived role due to the war gave him a respected identity in the community in the three years he held tenure. Essex was different. The job was not as intense, and the duties were not as wide-ranging as in Decorah, but at least he held a job and received a paycheck.

At times, he felt he had fallen to his knees at the loss of his marriage and job at Decorah. He had never been good at talking things out. It was his nature to hold the disturbing thoughts of the war and the brutality he witnessed almost every day within his mind. Frankie had often complained bitterly about his attitude but found it impossible to change. His father had instilled in him. "Keep your problems to yourself, son," Venter could hear his voice as he remembered it.

He tried to balance the most negative thoughts with the knowledge that he had survived France, and many did not. Whether he liked it or not, reality in Essex was consumed by lost bulls and petty issues. As the previous sheriff, Joe Lenthen had confided in him on the day they met to discuss the role, "Life is reasonably quiet, Tom. Let me be more specific. Quiet has many upsides."

For the rest of that day, he fielded calls from two shopkeepers about a man they had not seen before. The man moved in and out of the shops after buying something insignificant and then left the shops. They were concerned the man was a grifter, but Tom doubted it. He thought it was time to visit the street.

He strolled up the road to the grain store and asked Forrester if he had seen the man, but the man shook his head in his laconic, somewhat disinterested way. Venter patted his dog's head, a border collie named Jay, who padded with him for a while and then ran back to the grain store.

Venter waved at Forrester, crossed the road to the gas station and checked the five-dollar note the man had used, but it seemed legit. "You'll keep a lookout?" Eddie said suspiciously. "I don't like the look of him. He looks like a grifter."

"What does a grifter look like, Eddie?" Tom questioned.

"Like a grifter." Crooks gave a gravelly reply. "But that's your job, not mine. Too many around here for my liking."

"Can you give a better description?" Venter smiled as he asked him.

"Like I said. He looked like a grifter. Tall and shifty."

CHAPTER 9

Early the following day, Venter opened the door and edged his body onto the front seat of the cruiser. He put the key into the ignition, gave it a spurt by pushing down on the accelerator to warm it up, put it in gear, and headed down the gravel drive to the road, some two hundred yards from his house.

As the cruiser moved along, he picked up the hand microphone, clicked the button twice, and listened for several seconds. Then, he placed it back in its cradle and looked at his watch. It was still too early for Beth to come on air. The engine coughed as Venter kicked the gas pedal several times, coaxing it along.

By 1948, the cars allocated to the Essex office were over eight years old, ex-Winslow, and pushed off for use by Venter and Deputy Rusk. They worked—not well and not fast, but they did the job. Two sirens sat on opposite wings. Only one was functional, but he never used it.

Despite being washed several days before, it remained as dirty as it looked before the hose down, which is the only cleaning it received. It was ubiquitously adorned with two colors and offered a presence anywhere, with the broad emblem on the doors and two red lights in the middle at the front of the roof. The tires needed changing, but the car kept going, and that was all he cared about.

All panels of the cruiser were painted black except for the rear wings, dusted in white. On the driver and passenger doors, a large gold star sat in the middle below the window with "police" underneath the star in bold capital letters.

After driving for a while down the dirt road, he reached the junction of the old town road. In earlier days, it was a thoroughfare for traffic heading through Essex and beyond on the old road parallel to the eighty-five highway.

In earlier times, people used it around harvesting time. However, as fewer farmers tended to it and some switched to ranching instead of the rigors of farming, the old town road started showing signs of dereliction with potholes and ragged edges.

Venter took a right on an old blacktop road rather than his usual left turn to the main street and headed out towards the South end of the town. He was thinking about the issue with Chance Peterson and his unfortunate wife. The abuse happened, and more often than not, it remained unreported and covered by absence from the town.

Suddenly, a large dog ran out onto the road in front of the cruiser. Venter swore as he stood on the brakes. The frightened dog bounded off towards a house at the end of the street. Venter decided to follow it out of interest. The dog walked off towards one of the houses on the side street. Tired, it sat beside a picket fence outside the home and fell asleep. Venter sighed as he moved off. It was not a bull killer.

It sparked a long-forgotten memory that pushed itself into Venter's mind: the memory of a large, black, and brown-colored Alsatian dog that attacked its owner, a woman, in a park in Decorah as she pulled on its leash. He had been driving past the park perimeter when it happened.

The raw physical strength and the savagery of the attack shocked him as much it did the woman who it attacked. It took the strength of several men that day, including himself, to subdue the dog. The animal's size and physical strength made it challenging to keep it under control.

One of the men received a ripped left hand as the dog savagely bit anything it could attack. Trying to suppress the dog, he finally knocked it out with his cudgel as it repeatedly tried to rise. The woman finally got to her feet in shock at the dog's behavior. She had never experienced it before.

The next day, they shot the dog because of the injuries it inflicted on its owner and the man who helped him subdue it. The sheer physical force of the attack stayed so vividly in his mind.

What defense did a human have against the muscles of a one-hundred-pound dog with jaws that could snap a bone in two? Even after they pulled the dog off the woman, it continued to snarl and drool at her as she lay on the ground.

That memory brought a question to his mind. Was it possible that a dog, or dogs, pulled down a strong bull of that size? But if it was a pack of wild dogs, where the hell were they? As he thought about it, he realized it would be difficult to track a pack of dogs, or even a large dog on the prowl.

Over the past two years, he had never seen marauding dogs, let alone a hunting pack that might take down a bull. It seemed impossible to believe that a single dog, no matter how large, could kill and dismember a bull the size of a small tractor. That meant more than one dog, but where the hell would they be?

CHAPTER 10

It drizzled the night before, and a heavy ground fog had moved in that morning. By the time his cruiser coasted down the road, the fog was beginning to disappear from the low hills of the forest. The trees offered a fragrance in the heavy air. The view stretching up the broad hills and the warming feel of the sun made the day immeasurably enjoyable.

He spent the trip looking through his side window for evidence of dogs, stopping momentarily at several old and disused buildings. In the west of Essex town, three derelict warehouses with old, weed-infested storage and loading docks offering defunct grain and trucking facilities. He inspected each of them, and outside the last, he left the cruiser and strolled around the lot. There was nothing to see.

As he looked up at the towering trees and dense scrub reaching well up into the hills on the outskirts of Essex, Venter realized the search for any animal would be difficult. He could not find any evidence of dogs amongst the tall spruce and cypress that dotted the higher reaches of the hills or the lower fields.

At one point, he pulled his binoculars out and spent five minutes surveying the vast hills. Nothing of interest, he thought, and he realized he was wasting his time. He saw a hungry-looking, stray black cat, but that was all.

He returned to the Ford, checked his army-issue watch, and heard a familiar double click on the two-way. As he picked it up, the voice came over. "Sheriff? Are you there?"

"I'm on Beth. What's up?

"Nothing, really," She replied in a strange accent she had developed over the years from listening to her husband. "I'm going early today. I'm not feeling too well."

"What's up?"

"Might have caught a cold.."

"Okay." Venter replied solemnly. "I'll be in soon enough."

His watch read nine-thirty as he pulled into his park at the front of the sheriff office. The radio desk lay empty, and her familiar cheery hello was missing, so he walked over to his desk, looked at the in-tray, and sighed.

After quickly inspecting the paperwork, he put his hat back on and headed out toward the diner. It was situated up the main street and a short five-minute walk away.

The thought of a cup of coffee and perhaps a couple of eggs remained a luxury to him after he had eaten powdered eggs and salted meat out of cans for the three years he had trudged the fields of France.

As he walked he cheerfully waved to Madge, who stood just outside the front of the fashion shop. She nodded but didn't wave, but then she never did. She returned to her labors of changing the window displays with a grimace as if the result was not what she desired.

Across the street, he heard a shout, and Bobby Ray smiled. The local grocer waved his hand at him from the front of his small but well-frequented grocery store. He wore the white apron he always wore—his balding head adorned by a Dodgers baseball cap that he wore pushed up from his brow.

"How's it hanging, Sheriff?"

Venter smiled as he kept walking and replied as he always did to the same question Billy Ray asked every time. "Could not be better!" He omitted the, *and you*, because the discussion could take half an hour or more.

He finally made his way to the diner. The broad window front had gilt edging around the glass window, door, and the lower portion of the wall. Red tiles, faded from age, lined the bottom of the walls.

The diner facade had windows framed in age-worn brass that had long lost a sheen.

He walked in and sat at the bar, returning a courteous nod and light smile as a cup of coffee landed with a light thud in front of him.

"Sheriff."

"Jane." Tom replied.

"What'll it be?"

"Eggs over easy."

Jane pushed her blond hair back from her face and smiled. "What about something different for a change, Tom? You always ask for eggs. Don't you eat at home?" She asked as she moved away from him to deposit a coffee at the other end of the long counter.

"As little as possible." He replied. "And I'm happy with that."

Jane pushed several biscuits on a plate towards him, which he declined. "I'm Trying to lose weight, " he said as he rubbed his stomach.

"You only live once!" She replied with a broad smile that lit up her eyes. She nodded and moved on to the next customer.

Venter picked up a copy of the Winslow newspaper sitting on the counter beside him. He glanced through page after page, using his moistened thumb to turn. Farm machinery, feed, and stump removal using a tractor rather than a horse were prominent ads. Women's clothing comprised most of the pages, with very little else.

"No news?" she said as she returned to fill his cup. Tom looked at her, noticing not for the first time the clarity of her light brown eyes, which contrasted with her blond hair. "I haven't seen you around the last couple of days. How come?"

Tom shook his head. " Busy trying to find lost bulls and handle complaints. A bicycle was stolen near Grays, and I think I know who did it."

"Who?"

"Probably Chuck. You know, Bing's pal. They hang out together. However, old Bing is the man of the moment. He is not right in the head but a veritable source of information."

"Like?"

"A lost bull."

"He found Charlie's Bull? Everyone has been looking for it. You don't sound happy about it."

Tom nodded as he sipped his coffee. "Bing found the bull behind the old Sturger warehouse. Dead as a doornail."

Jane looked at him blankly. "What do you mean? Someone shot it?"

"Nope, weirder than that. The bull was in pieces on the ground, at the back. Inside the fence."

"How did Bing know?"

Venter shrugged. "They sleep out the back in an old shed some nights. That is, after downing as many hooch as they can afford or steal. He is the one who found it. He contacted Marv yesterday."

"That's weird. Any idea how it happened?"

Venter suddenly became wary of what gossip it might cause. "No one knows, but McNab will have a look. He will let me know. It is a bit of a mystery, so keep it to yourself until we find out. Okay?"

Jane nodded as she pulled several strands of hair from her eyes. "Gotcha. By the way, did you hear about Chance's wife?"

"Yep, went out to see Peterson after I received the report."

"How did that go?"

Venter winced as he thought about it. "Not real well, to be honest. That man is as thick as a post. The report said Lena was beaten up pretty badly."

"She's still in the hospital, from what I hear. He's a pig, you know, that goddam husband of hers. He ain't got any sense, " she said with anger. "On top of that, he is just plain rude. If he comes in again, I won't be serving him. He stares at me. Creepy, really. A strange man, if you ask me."

Tom nodded as he thought briefly about Chance. He had made trouble for ages, but his wife never complained, even though he had once almost beaten her to death.

"Something has to be done about him?"

Venter nodded. "There is a limit to what we can do." He tasted his coffee, finally putting in a little more sugar.

"Sure." Came her curt reply.

Over his cup, Venter looked at her as she fussed around filling coffee cups and delivering meals. She possessed a clear beauty, a clear complexion, and a bright personality. Despite marriage, she maintained the figure of a younger woman. However, he thought briefly, the uniform did little to compliment her.

From his talk over the past year, he knew Jane was a mother of one child—a boy she adored in a marriage hanging by a thread. The relationship ended the year before, or so the gossip mongers noted. Her ex-husband had also taken off to Winslow. "Good riddance," That was the term he heard of her regard for him.

"Here's your eggs, Tom. Not much happening, is there?" She moved her hair out of her eyes with a light shake of her head and looked at him as she pointed to the open page in the newspaper. "It's real slow in the town at the moment. Even Madge is complaining, and she never complains," She frowned slightly as she said it. "Essex seems to have run out of news."

She collected bread from the server counter inside the kitchen, placing the plate carefully in front of him. She looked at Venter, her face slightly flushed. "Hey, now here's a question out of the blue, Sheriff. You don't have anyone from what I hears, and neither do I. Am I right?"

"You mean a partner, right?" Venter nodded cautiously.

She nodded in the same manner. "You know, we should go somewhere. Maybe we can go out one night? What do you think about that idea, Tom?" She stared at him intently, gauging his response with her eyes.

Venter looked at her momentarily and shifted uncomfortably. "What would the town say, Jane? Is that the best she can do? That old Sheriff."

"How old are you?"

"Now that's a personal question, Jane." Venter replied defensively

"So?" she replied with a wide smile.

"Thirty-six," He said as he sipped his coffee.

"Well, I'm pretty close."

"I bet I am older than you."

She smiled at him. "You ain't that old, Tom Venter. I don't think they would say anything. If they do, well then, let them. This is a sleepy old town with nothing going on unless you raise cattle or plant crops. None of the young people want to be here. We all know that. If the rest gossip about us heading out to dinner, they can go to hell."

Venter nodded as if he had heard the remark before. "True enough," He replied flatly.

She nodded as she refilled his cup. "I don't care what the town might say. They can mind their own damn business for a change. To be honest, I am sick of not having fun. I'm not even suggesting a date. Even going out for a friendly meal would be nice. What do you think?"

"I can't remember ever being asked out on a date, Jane."

"Well, there's always a first time." She chuckled as she said it. "What else do you have to do this coming weekend? Chasing criminals? Splitting the atom, maybe? Finding dead bulls?"

"No criminals, no, not at the moment, as far as I know. If you finally see one or two of em' call me," He smiled in response.

"Now, maybe we could catch that movie? The Eternity one, over at Winslow."

Tom looked at her with a questioning look and shrugged his shoulders.

"Yes or no?"

"Okay. Dinner, right?"

"Of course, and you get to pay." She winked as she wiped the counter in front of him. Her eyes smiled for the first time. She looked younger than what he guessed her age to be in her middle thirties somewhere, but he had no desire to push the subject.

"Okay?" she questioned.

"Okay, " he said again, glancing surreptitiously at her figure as she hurried to the other end of the counter. She served a customer who sat patiently on one of the red stools, his arms resting on the metal counter. She glanced back at him, which he returned before she averted her eyes.

The man looked over at Venter and nodded, which Tom returned. Rusk told him that the man sitting stiffly at the counter, Frank Ficco, had lost his three sons in the war and never recovered. Tom nodded back, thinking that if he lost his daughter, it would be the end of him. "Howya" doing, Frank?" Venter said to him.

The man responded with a nod. "A little more rain would help, sheriff, but it seems unlikely. Those clouds ain't got enough rain in their bellies."

Tom shrugged with a smile. "Never enough or too much!"

"That's for sure." He returned as he diverted his attention to his coffee. "Hey, I heard about that big bull of Charlies. Did you find it at the back of some warehouse?"

Venter sipped his coffee and nodded his head.

" Go figure. How the hell did it get there."

Venter nodded grimly. "How did you hear about that, Frank."

"Forrester told me."

"How the hell did he know?"

Ficco looked at him briefly before returning to his coffee. "Sheriff, it's a small town."

Venter glanced at Jane with a knowing look and rose from his seat. She immediately came over to him and whispered. "What does a girl have to do to arrange a dinner out? Saturday, seven? Don't be late, OK? You are picking me up?"

"OK, don't tell everyone!" He replied with a wide grin. He dropped several notes on the counter, donned his hat, and nodded curtly to two older men sitting in one of the red leather booths at the side of the diner wall. He made his way out into the sunshine that splashed along the sidewalk with the thought of where he might go Saturday night.

He walked outside to find Billy Ray in front of him with a parcel in his hand. "Make way, delivery!" He shouted with his permanent smile. "Now, how are you going, sheriff?" He questioned trying to stop Venter so he could talk further.

Venter put his hand on Billy Ray's shoulder. "Now Billy, I'd love to talk, but I have sheriff business at the office." Without waiting for an answer, he strode towards the only town road intersection.

"See you when I see you," Billy Ray shouted behind him. Venter quickly crossed the road, tipping his hat to a woman on the opposite sidewalk. "Mrs. Constant," Venter said politely.

"Susan," She replied stiffly.

"Susan," Venter corrected himself.

"Sheriff, did you see that weird light last night in the sky? It lasted a couple of minutes. It was the strangest thing I've ever seen."

Venter shook his head and smiled. "Nope. What did it look like?"

"Green waves in the sky!"

"Waves?" Venter asked with a wry glance. Are you sure it wasn't a reflection or something? I can't say I have ever heard of light that looked like waves in the sky."

"Have a look tonight. It's the weirdest thing," She said with a smile as she walked off.

CHAPTER 11

After stopping at a post box at the other end of town road, Venter eased the cruiser into his designated parking spot around a rubbish bin left haphazardly by Beth. He left the Ford window open. The interior smelled of heated rubber, and maybe that meant something bad, but he didn't know enough about cars to make an assessment.

Looking in the office window, he could see Beth waving at him to enter. Unhurried, he entered the door and looked at his radio operator, coffee maker, secretary, and voracious town gossip, who stood impatiently as she waited for him to move closer. "Mornin" Beth, everything okay?"

"Sheriff, " she nodded, shifting her considerable bulk on her chair. She had long dark hair, with a touch of gray around her temples, which she fashioned most days into a bun so that strands fell to her shoulders. Her face held a mask of mild anxiety. "I got some news," she said breathlessly as he approached her.

"What's up?"

"Someone saw a group of wild dogs early this morning up towards the lake on the Winslow side."

Tom shrugged and waited. "Really?"

"Well, Marv says it must have been dogs badly mauled that bull. Might have been those dogs."

Venter looked at her. "Have you ever seen a pack of dogs attacking anything? Anytime?" he added quickly.

"Nope, but what else could it be?" she said quickly. "It beats me why dogs or anything would take down a bull. You know the size of that thing?"

"Makes no sense to me, but Marv is on the case. You know what he's like. A determined bull ant. We will find out soon enough." He added a wry smile. "The case of the dead bull."

She laughed. "I'd be careful about any thoughts Marv might have on the subject, sheriff," Beth added with a sideways glance. "Far as I'm concerned, it has to be dogs. That'd be my best guess." They took that big old bull down and disappeared into the forest.

"It was probably coyotes. That explains the forest." He replied with a sigh.

"Maybe?" Beth shook her head as she thought about it.

"Well, think about it for a moment. If it was dogs, and I ain't saying it was dogs, why would they do it? Dogs are domestic animals, and they get fed. So why take down a bull? It might be wild dogs, but no one around this town has ever seen them, let alone a pack. My best guess is coyotes."

"Coyotes, huh?" Beth laughed as she sat back at the radio desk. "Same question, Tom. Why would a coyote take down a bull if they could attack a sheep or a cow? Don't make sense."

Tom nodded quietly. "I can't believe we are wasting our time on this nonsense and searching for something that took a goddam bull down. I couldn't care less. But, the clean-up is gonna take time. You should have seen that beast. Pieces everywhere."

Beth shook her head as she returned to the radio desk. "Marv, you on?"

A crackle came back. She clicked the button twice as the deputy's voice filled the room. "All done, Beth. I finished the eighty-five. There is very little traffic."

"Any pickups?" Beth put the two-way on the loudspeaker as she listened.

"Yeah, three. Old Jones was in a hell of a hurry for the market. I pulled him over. I was going to let him off, but this is the second time this week. He'll complain, so no doubt he'll put a call into Perkins."

"For sure." Beth replied authoritatively. "But, I bet they don't let him off the citation." Who else, over?"

"The second was an out-of-towner in a real hurry to get to Winslow, doing well over sixty, so he got the big ticket. The third was a strange one. He was towing a trailer with huge dogs in it. No rear lights and real early this morning."

"What time?"

"Maybe eight thirty or thereabouts. I gave him a ticket and a defect, but he's an out-of-towner. Nice guy, though. Wasn't happy, but what can y'all do?" Rusk said in his mild Texan drawl. "Hey, did ya know a dog show is set up tomorrow at the old showgrounds? I never heard of it. Seems he…"

The two-way died. The green light on the console changed to a steady red. She hit it with her hand as it sometimes worked to give it some life. She swore under her breath, studied the unit for a moment, flicked two switches, and hit the control button on the microphone stand. Finally, in frustration, she hit it with her hand again, but the unit refused to respond.

"Don't kill it." Venter shouted with a laugh.

"Damn thing!" She roared as she flicked the plug switch point, waited a moment, and watched as two lights returned to the front of the console. She clicked the talk button. "You there, Marvin? Come on." Several seconds later, she heard a reply.

"Still here, Beth. What happened?"

"I'm not sure. There must be something in the air. It's been doing it all morning. It's the hills around here. They're full of iron. Maybe it's the Martians. Everyone is saying they are coming."

Venter shouted out from his desk. "Could be, but then it could be the two-way. When the Martians come, you can tell them from me. It needs to be replaced." He winked at her as he sipped his coffee.

"More likely." Beth added as she moved to get a coffee.

"Probably." Marvin added. "Definitely the Martians. They are flying here soon. I read it last week."

"Where?" Beth asked, with a questioning tone. "In the newspaper?"

"No, space monthly. They know everything about the planets. Y'all should get the two-way unit replaced if it's breaking down, just in case those Martians arrive." His voice resounded through the two-way static. "We will have to let people know."

"No chance on a replacement." Venter added as he pulled paperwork from his tray. "Perhaps they could help with the paperwork from Winslow?"

"Perhaps we need a mechanic." Beth replied.

"Mechanics don't fix two-way systems," he said as he moved towards the radio desk. "We need a… What do you call em?" a technician. That two-way issue only happens occasionally, right? "

"Worse lately."

Beth sighed. "Worse over the last few days. What would happen if we had an actual emergency?"

"Like what?"

"Dunno. Maybe one of the cruisers broke down."

There was a crackle as Beth clicked the microphone button several times. "Hang on, Marvin. Hey Sheriff, you know about a dog show?"

"Dog show? News to me, Beth." Venter sat on the side of the desk as he thought about it. "Probably put it through council.

Sometimes, they forget to tell us. Come to think of it, I was told there was a show some years back,. Before me, anyway, Why here?"

"Didn't ask," came the crackle and answer from the deputy. "I pulled him over on the eighty-five hill. He had a trailer of those dogs heading towards Essex from the Winslow end. Get this! Those dogs are American staghounds. So, he said, but I never heard of the breed. Y'all heard of em, Beth."

"Nope. What did you call them? Staghounds?"

"The guy holding the show told me. Apparently, the ranchers love them. I had a look at them, and I can tell ya, they are large, ugly-looking things. They are an original dog breed in the old US of A. Go figure."

Tom shuffled the papers on his desk without any intent. "Well, that'll bring the ranchers in. How many dogs were in the trailer?"

There was silence for a moment. "More than a few, but really couldn't say for sure..Maybe six or eight."

"These staghounds, What the hell do they do?"

"You hear the question, Marvin?" Beth replied quickly.

"Say again?"

"What do the dogs do? What's their purpose?"

"Don't know. Maybe they hunt jackrabbits?"

Beth looked at Tom, slightly shaking her head, and rolled her eyes for good measure. "Doubtful."

"Ranchers buy em". The reply came through the static crackle.

"Well, there you go." Beth shrugged her shoulders as if to get rid of the thought. "You said the showgrounds?"

"Sure. You know, where the circus comes around now and then, over on the twelve-mile road."

"Okay. You gave him a citation?"

"Yes, Ma'am."

"Well, that's the right thing to do, Marvin. No lights, so he should have known better."

"I'm heading in."

"Rodger that."

Beth put the receiver down on the desk and wrote the citation in a book used for that purpose. They recorded the date, the amount and the address of the person fined.

Marvin would fill out the details when he returned. Most paid, their fines, some didn't, but Essex never had the resources to chase the non-payers up so the pressure was to get them to pay at the time of the fine.

Mayor Perkins grew fond of stating that revenue was used for the greater good. "This is about safety." Perkins would offer as a reason to increase the tariff. "However, the revenue helps us in other areas."

Venter nodded his head in the meetings. On returning to Essex, he would meet with Rusk, and the number of fines would increase. He disliked the direction of fining folks who were in a hurry to do their business. However, there was little he could do about it.

"Marv, this is about us keeping our jobs. Keep that in mind." Venter said after each of the fine increase meetings.

"Yessir." The reply was always prompt and laced with disdain. "We gotta keep the council running."

CHAPTER 12

Outside of his ambition towards a more prestigious sheriff role, there were reasons to stay in Essex. Sheriff Lenthen had been right about the job and how it might suit Venter. He worked to keep the peace with the upside that the job kept him near his daughter in Winslow, just thirty-five minutes away. He could get there slightly quicker if he put the siren on and pushed the old cruiser up to a higher speed towards Winslow, but common sense dictated he kept within the speed limit.

There was also the matter of respect. The Sheriff role offered prestige as part of the job. Many people looked up to him and sought his advice on the issues where he had reasonable experience. Everyone was polite to him. Country people respected the law.

His daughter's well-being lay like a heavy ominous cloud, on his mind. It was challenging to meet with her because of Frankie's interfering insecurity. She jealously guarded access and his emotional relationship with his daughter. He had her tacit agreement on visiting times, but the last time, his daughter was not there, with Frankie explaining afterward that she had forgotten the visit. He no longer believed her and tried to quell his rising frustration.

Perhaps Allie would understand, and Frankie's influence would wane. Either way, he realized he needed to do more to spend time with his daughter. The house provided by the authorities was remote and not in the best condition, especially for a young daughter. He needed something closer.

"No matter what I do, this desk never gets clean, " Venter said as he stood beside it.

"Not by itself." Beth smiled as she arranged her hair based on the reflection of the small mirror she had attached to the wall in front of the two-way. "I'm getting more grey hairs!" She shouted. "My God, sheriff, I am too young."

Tom ran his hand through his hair. "Have a look at me, Beth. I am going gray all over."

"At least you have kept your hair, sheriff. Many men have little or none around your age." She looked at the clock on the wall and picked up her bag. "I'm going, Tom. See you tomorrow."

Tom barely nodded as he reread the report on Chance Peterson, wondering how his wife was recovering. He checked his round-faced watch, the same army issue he had kept through the European fields. Marvin had headed off, so he decided to call it a day. After locking the door, he picked up his hat and walked to the cruiser.

CHAPTER 13

The trip home remained uneventful. Twenty minutes later, he pulled up in front of his house, grabbed his hat from the seat, and walked to the front door. He turned in complete surprise when he heard a voice. His daughter stood up from the swing chair on the wide porch. She took him by surprise. "Allie, what the hell?"

"Hi, Daddy," She said and hugged him.

"Come in, come in," He said, gesturing to the front door, which he opened in front of her.

"I don't like that old dog, Daddy, " she said with a wary look, pointing to the dog and ensuring she kept up with her father.

"Allie, he's old but harmless. Like your old man."

Tom glanced at Butch, who sat on his hind legs near the door. He realized there was a low growl coming from its throat. "C'mon, Butchy. Good boy." Venter moved to pat his head. As he moved his hand the dog immediately moved back and away. Venter dismissed it with a wave of his hand. "He's old and a little grumpy like you when I have to wake you up!"

Tom ushered her inside and poured her a glass of milk. After vainly searching for cookies, of which he had precisely none, he poured himself a stiff gin and tonic and sat across from her at the old kitchen table.

"What are you doing here, Allie? And where is your mom?"

"Back in Winslow for all I care."

Tom looked at her. At sixteen, she was already growing up too fast, with a mind of her own. She wore what he might have expected for a fashionable girl. A pale pink shirt and a black skirt, too short, but he felt the argument was not worth starting. She wore sneakers and short socks that somehow complimented her age, except that she was developing faster than he might have liked.

For the first time, he realized she was becoming a beautiful young woman, which worried him. "Allie, let's just get a few things out of the way, OK? How did you get here?"

"I got a ride from Jarrad."

"Who?"

"A friend, Daddy, nothing more."

"How old is he?"

Allie looked him directly in the eye. "Why?"

"Just answer the question."

"I dunno. Maybe eighteen or nineteen."

"A friend?"

She shrugged, unaware of her beauty that seemed to have arrived out of nowhere. Tom nodded sagely as he listened. "Sure. What else?"

"Does your mom know you are here?"

"I left a note."

"Get serious, Allie. Does she know you are here with me?"

"No."

Tom shook his head and walked over to the old telephone on the wall. "I don't want to go back, Daddy. I hate that man. He treats mom and me badly, as well."

"Physically, you mean?"

Allie shook her head and looked at him. "A bit."

"Has he hit you? Be honest with me, Allie. Has he touched you or mom?"

"He pushed Mom because he just gets drunk and shouts a lot."

Tom nodded and finally lifted the receiver to dial the number. "You can stay the night, Allie. I will take you back tomorrow."

"No!" she screamed as she jumped to her feet. "I'm not going back. You can't force me to go," She walked towards the room he had set up for her and slammed the door. Tom just sighed and dialed the number. It was looking like a long night.

He rang Frankie and calmly received her abuse for not taking her back to Winslow immediately. As he neared Allie's room, he heard her crying softly, and as he started to open her door, he heard her shout. "Stay away. I'm not going back."

"You are," He said softly, feeling a distinct lack of control.

CHAPTER 14

Venter closed the door softly so as not to wake his daughter. He left his house early and headed to the warehouse. The drive took maybe twenty minutes, with a view of the powder blue, cloudless sky that stretched into the distance. The journey was uneventful. Just as he pulled up on the roadside, he saw McNab waiting beside the rope they had strung across the site the day before.

"Harold." Venter spoke loudly as he got out of the cruiser.

"sheriff." Came the curt reply. "What's up?"

When Venter first met McNab, he admired the man's seriousness and obvious expertise, and his impression had not changed. McNab had a studious look, half-height glasses, and a slight paunch. Venter always thought he fit the caricature of a town veterinarian perfectly. The man never told a joke and regarded farmers as mostly morons because they never listened. However, he was mindful that they were necessary to his business.

Tom saw him as a fixture of sorts. He had been around Essex for over thirty years, and it seemed everyone had a positive word to say about him and his practice. He attended to his old veterinarian office on the main street near the hardware store and treated everything from birds to cows.

Harold built an enviable reputation and renown in the district for his ability to resuscitate and heal almost any animal. Over the years, he had saved many a calf, many lambs stuck in their mother's birth canal, sick cattle, and more than a few horses. Added to that came a range of dogs and cats if the owners cared enough about them.

"Hey, Harry, thanks for coming. Did Beth fill you in?"

McNab looked over at the warehouse and then back at Venter, who was, by this time, in front of him and walking to the main gate.

"Yep, she gave me the gory details. That girl can talk the hind legs off a cow!"

"She has that ability," Venter said with a half-cocked smile. "But, I tell ya, Harry, she is the best in the office. Everything is neat and tidy, just the opposite of Marv and me. Well, maybe. Marv is better than me!

"The bull?" Came the reply as McNab adjusted his spectacles.

"Well, you need to see this." Venter nodded as he walked briskly to the back of the property after ducking under the rope that lined the entrance gate. As they neared the back area, he stopped and pulled out his handkerchief, motioning to McNab to do the same. He declined and rounded the corner together as McNab pulled up abruptly and looked at the scene before him.

"Whoa, sheriff, am I seeing things?" McNab instantly produced a pair of black rubber gloves from his bag and put them on as he kept his attention on the bloodied grass.

Venter pulled his hat off to run his hand through his hair while deftly holding his handkerchief to his face. He stepped back towards the old fence as the smell became worse. "Seen nothing like this in my life. It's like a damn abattoir."

Flies and insects buzzed around the carcass, attracted by the same smell that revolted Venter. He took a deep breath through his cotton handkerchief, trying to remove the smell of rotting meat from his nose. It permeated everywhere he moved. He watched the town veterinarian pace carefully about the backyard of the old warehouse, ensuring he inspected each area before moving on to the next area. He looked to be cataloging the area in his mind.

"Anything?"

McNab glanced briefly at Venter, sighing as he surveyed the pieces of carcass meat lying on the back grass. Finally, he walked amongst the ripped, rotting pieces of the bull, stopped, tutted, and moved on to the next area.

THE WOLVES OF ESSEX

He stopped, squatted down to view the bulls, sightless head and then rose to move to the torso. "Well, well." He muttered almost to himself as he rolled the torso over and finally stood. "You are close, sheriff. The last time I saw pieces like this was in an abattoir, but cut cleanly, unlike this mess. And it wasn't a bull of this size. However, there is something unexpected here."

Tom looked at him with a perplexed look on his face. "Which is?"

"Have a good look around at the flesh," He replied. He adjusted his gloves, pulling them above his wrists. "This bull has been torn apart, not eaten. What does that mean?"

Tom looked at him, perplexed. "I was hoping you would know, Harold."

"It might be coyotes, but it would take a large, maybe a very large pack, to take this bull down. Have you or Marv checked around the area?" McNab bent to inspect the side of the bull's neck. "Ripped." He said to himself.

Venter shook his head as McNab continued. "If a coyote or more than one attacked this bull, then it stands to reason they would have consumed some of the carcass. But, in my opinion, that has not happened here. So that is a mystery."

Venter shook his head as he pointed to several of the ripped limbs. "Coyotes or dogs?" he asked.

"What else!" came the curt reply. "It makes little sense; all of this carnage for what? Not for food, that's for sure. Coyotes would have consumed at least part of it, but that is not evident. It may be a dog pack."

"Then where are they, Harry?" Venter asked as they walked back to the entrance and ducked under the rope.

McNab stopped briefly before they reached the police cruiser. "To be honest, Tom, I have no idea. Do you have any idea of the force required to bring down a bull of that size? We are inspecting a bull weighing around a thousand pounds plus, maybe a ton and a half. How long has the bull been missing?

"Not sure. Maybe a week or more."

McNab nodded as he thought about it. "This is a long way away from the hills. However, dogs are not as territorial as wild animals. The question on my mind is why dogs would pull down a ton and a half of Hereford bull and rip the animal apart, and then not eat it."

"What about wolves? You must have some idea."

"Can't be wolves, Tom. There hasn't been a sighting in years. More likely to be coyotes, because they will move from their territory if they are hungry. However, there should be evidence."

"Like what?"

"Prints, maybe."

"We checked the area at the back and the front. Nothing."

McNab shrugged. "Let's assume the bull was wandering. So, it might have wandered through those hills behind that adjacent field and made its way down here to the flat terrain and grass," McNab pointed to the field at the back of the warehouse lot. "That makes sense, don't you think?"

"Why here?" Venter questioned.

McNab shrugged his shoulders. "There is more than enough space in that broken fence for it to mosey into this area. The question is, why was it attacked here and not in the forest?"

"Have you heard of something like this happening before? You've been around a long time."

McNab shook his head. He pulled his glasses off, inspected them in the light, and replaced them perfectly. "Nope, not to my knowledge."

"Are we finished here?"

"I think so." Came the curt reply as he walked around the area. "These paw prints are so indistinct that it is impossible to say what sort of predator made them. I can't see anything else. I contact Winslow and let them know. We need to have this mess cleared quickly. It's already rotting."

Venter nodded. "Call me if you need me. Thanks again, Harry. Hey, before you go, how long has this bull been dead? Do you have any idea?"

McNab shrugged. "I reckon in the last two days from the decomposition and the congealed blood. However, there was rain last night, which would have wet the area, so maybe, just maybe, a little longer. Some days, perhaps."

Venter nodded his head thoughtfully. "Can you write the report?"

"Sure. This place is unsanitary. It needs to be cleaned up as soon as possible." McNab pointed around the area.

"If we assume it is a group of dogs, do we let the county know? Your decision, not mine, Harold." Venter looked at him intently as he waited for an answer.

McNab shrugged as he walked back with Venter to the cruiser. "By the way, that old dog show is back. I know that fellow pretty well. His name is Nesbitt, Charlie Nesbitt, and he knows a lot about dogs and their behavior. It might be worth calling him in to take a look here, because I am out of ideas. He's over at the showgrounds setting up."

"You think he might have a clue?"

"He might. More than us, anyway."

"That is more your area than mine, Harold. Why don't you talk to him?"

"We are coming into lamb season, Tom, and I don't have time. You discovered the bull, so finish the investigation, and I will furnish the report. Okay?" McNab looked over his glasses as he said it. He held Venter's gaze until he consented.

Tom shrugged and got into the cruiser to click the two-way. "Okay, but this Nesbitt guy won't be too happy to help."

"Why?" McNab asked.

Tom smiled thinly. "Marv gave him a citation for a backlight issue. By the way, have you heard of this American breed, a staghound?"

McNab laughed. "It's a specialized breed, Tom. That's the breed that Charlie offers. You never heard of them?"

"Nope." Tom replied.

"Well, they are big and ugly. They can easily take down other predators. A coyote couldn't stand a chance."

"Okay." Venter replied, slowly moving off.

He got into his pickup, did a U-turn, waved and disappeared in the opposite direction towards his home.

CHAPTER 15

Venter put the coffee pot on the burner after stoking the fire beneath the hot plate of the wood stove. He watched his daughter, bleary-eyed, walk into the kitchen. "Good afternoon." He chirped.

She grumbled as she sat down at the table. "What time did you leave, Dad?"

"Can't remember, Allie. Anyway, you were asleep when I left. Did you have breakfast?"

"No, I wasn't hungry."

Tom looked into her blue eyes, knowing he was looking at his ex-wife's eyes. Her stare, the same as Frankie's, was unnerving. "I spoke to mom."

Allie sat down on the end of the bed and stared blankly at the open entrance door. "And?"

"You gotta go back, Allie. You have several weeks before vacation and can't miss school."

"I hate school."

"Everyone hates school, Allie. That's a given."

"Yeah, but I really hate it."

"You need to go back."

"Why? She said defiantly, with one hand clasped inside the other.

Venter sighed. "However, the good news for you is that mom agreed for you to stay a couple of days over the vacation. Okay?"

"No." She pouted, sitting forlornly at the table. "I want to spend my time here."

"Well, you can't. There is an excellent reason," He whispered. "I work! Since your mom doesn't have to work, you can stay with her."

"I could help out at your office? I want to stay here."

"Not going to happen."

"You just don't understand."

"What?" Tom said as he placed a glass of milk before her. He put his hand softly on her young shoulder. "What?"

"It's him."

"Who."

"Jack, who else?"

Immediately, Venter felt uneasy and worried. "What is the problem?"

"He's always at me about something."

"That's it?"

"Now and then, he seems to make an excuse to come into my room or even the bathroom without knocking or calling out."

"Have you asked him to stay out?"

"I tell Mom, and she nods and reckons she will speak to him, but nothing changes."

"Has he ever touched you?" Tom asked, feeling exasperated. He wondered if his daughter was telling the truth or if she did not like the change to a new home and a stepfather.

"No, " she replied blankly. "I don't like him, Dad, and I don't want to live there anymore."

Venter sat down beside her, trying to calm her down. "Yeah, honey, I know it's been tough, and if I could have changed it, I would have. Try to understand that it has not been easy with the war and coming back home to find a new job."

"What's that got to do with it?" She looked up at him with a distressed look on her youthful face.

"Well, your mom ain't happy with me. Perhaps she was right about many things, but I can't see you coming to live here at this stage. I'm an old bachelor who cooks badly and is only home when he's not working. Allie, I work long hours most days."

"You don't want me here!"

"Exactly the opposite, Allie. What you are saying could not be further from the truth. Your mom has a mind of her own and wants you in Winslow. There is not much I can do about it."

Allie nodded softly as she turned her eyes back to her father with a pained look. "Well, it wasn't the right decision. I want to be back with you and Mom together," she said.

"Ain't gonna happen, Allie, not this side of anything I know."

"What happened? Why couldn't it stay the way it was back then?"

Tom shrugged, unable to think of anything to say to soothe her and make her see reason. Perhaps it was just the way of the war and another marriage casualty. Things that happened with little or no reason except the turmoil and death and its effect on everyone he ever knew. There was little chance that Frankie would admit she was in an unhappy marriage.

Venter placed his hand tenderly on her arm. "It's a long story, Allie, and probably my fault. It was tough over there. I felt bad about surviving, and I don't expect your young mind to understand why, but it is true. When I came back, I felt unable to share what happened. Your mom and I grew apart."

"And she found someone she liked better, right?" Allie said with maturity that shocked Venter as he listened. "But I am glad you stayed around." She said in the most pleasant tone she could muster.

"Yeah, well, me too. You are the most important thing in my life, Allie, and I know I could have been a better dad, but I will try my best. Okay?"

Allie softened mildly and finally moved to lay her head on his shoulder. "Ok, can I visit more often?"

"Sure can, kiddo, and I will make you a promise. If things get tough, I will speak to mom, okay?"

She nodded as she got up from the bed. "So, do I get a coffee?"

Tom pointed his finger towards the glass on the table. "You are too young for coffee."

She turned her nose up at the milk. "Pancakes would be better."

Tom shrugged. "Okay, but eggs are better for you. How is school going?"

"Like I care!" came the response as Allie sat at the kitchen table and disregarded the question. She seemed content to sit back and listen to his monologue on the need to be successful at school and do her homework. She rolled her sixteen-year-old eyes and finally sauntered out to the outside deck. She walked back in briefly. "Has anyone fed Butch?"

Venter nodded his head as he beat the batter for the pancakes. He was about to pour it onto an old griddle pan that sizzled softly on the wood stove. "There's a bone in the fridge. Give that to him."

Allie grabbed the bone by the part that held the least meat and took it outside, calling for the dog. "Butch, Butchie!" She sang out in a loud voice. Usually, he would respond to her calls, so she walked around the deck to where he would generally lie on an old wheat sack on the sunny side of the house.

She rounded the corner and found him sitting on the deck. "There you are, sitting in the sun." As she approached and held out her hand, the old dog bared his teeth, yellowed and blunted by age. Cautiously, she pulled back, finally threw the bone at him, and headed back to the kitchen. "He was growling at me, Dad. What's wrong with him.."

Tom looked up from his cooking. "He's old, Allie, that's all. Let him be. By the way, I am taking you back in the morning. I have to go back to Winslow for a meeting with the council."

"I don't want to go?" She said defiantly slumping down on the chair as she pulled her long hair back.

"I have to go to the meeting and I am taking you back with me!"

Allie looked at his serious face and thought about it for a moment. "Why don't you leave your job? We could leave Winslow and live near the beach."

Tom sighed as he placed the pancakes and maple syrup before her. "I have bills to pay," he said.

"Well, you always said you wanted to live by the beach."

"And how do I pay for you?"

"I come and live with you. I'll get a job."

"And, mom?"

"She can live with the idiot."

Tom glanced at her and shook his finger. "Don't be disrespectful, Allie. He also works to take care of you and your mom. And you need to finish your schooling before there is any talk of you moving elsewhere."

"You need to have some fun, Dad. You are always working."

"I am having fun. I have a date tonight."

Allie looked at him with a mixture of curiousness and surprise. "A date!" Her voice carried her immediate interest. "Now we have something to talk about. Who is it?"

CHAPTER 16

Tom received a not-very-good haircut from his daughter, shined his boots, put on his best shirt, applied a little aftershave, and headed out the door.

As he walked out onto the veranda, he looked over to the edge of the house where Butch sat with a tiny wag of his tail. The dog was staring intently at the forested hill behind the house. "Bad day, eh?" Tom said as he watched the old dog get up and stroll away. It growled softly as it rounded the corner of the house out of sight.

The trip from his house to the edge of town took fifteen minutes. He spent the time thinking about the previous day. The remains of the bull had him perplexed. How did the bull get from Bob Carter's farm to the back of the old warehouse? McNab's observation seemed to waste time because his conclusion added more questions than answers.

He cruised down the main street towards his office and into the main street, his eyes surveying the area. Like most police officers, it came as an occupational habit, looking for something unusual, but it seemed quiet. In his experience, it was the habit of towns that folks ate early; even if they went out to dinner, they went home early to bed.

He stopped at the only red light in the town at the intersection of the war memorial; he nodded his head to several people as they courteously touched their hats or half-waved as they walked past.

Marvin had called to tell him that Bob Carter, the bull's owner, was livid when he heard the news. However, the bull's death meant it needed to be cleaned up. Who would complete that work? The council? He needed to raise this issue when he met with the Mayor.

They could find no animal prints. There were no discernable prints anywhere around the bull. Marv had shown two indistinct footprints near the warehouse wall the day before, but they could easily have been from Bing or his other cronies.

The grass around the bull carcass was heavily churned, indicating the bull had endured a great deal of suffering before it died. He immediately felt remorse for the creature, possibly in the wrong place at the wrong moment, and did not expect the attack that killed it. There was little doubt in his mind that dogs were the likely culprits, but it would help if he could find evidence that his assumption was correct.

Tom sighed as he pulled up outside Jane's house and let the thoughts flow out of his mind. If there was no answer to the killing, time would take its course, and the incident would be forgotten. What did his father say about waiting? 'All things happen in the fullness of time, son.'

He checked himself in the side mirror, feeling nervous for the first time as he left the cruiser and went to her front door. He barely knocked before she opened it with a wide smile. "You made it." She chirped.

Did you believe I would not make a grand entrance on my first date in years?"

"You never know, Tom Venter, you never know," she said, ushering him in and picking up her purse. He glanced at her as he stood by the door. She wore a white and yellow flower dress, highlighting her blond hair. "You look beautiful," he said honestly.

"Well, that's the first time I've heard that in a long time. Having a man's attention rather than ordering coffee and pie makes me feel better. You know, Tom? There are days I get real sick of serving idiots."

"I know how you feel," He said with a smile. "Is your son here?"

She smiled lightly. "He is at his father's this weekend. He is always reluctant to take him, but I insisted. A middle-aged woman is rarely taken out, especially by a sheriff!"

"The town will talk."

"I'm betting on it." She laughed out loud and offered him a drink, which he accepted. They moved out to the front of the house to an old porch swing where they sat and spoke about the town. He watched one of her neighbors, an elderly man, walk past. He waved politely, and Venter returned the gesture. "The town will know about this in five minutes," He added as he watched the man walk past the front picket fence.

Finally, she looked at him with the bluest eyes he had ever seen. "So, where are we going?"

"Out." He replied softly as he opened the door.

"We could eat in." She offered in a soft voice.

"I thought you wanted to be taken to dinner? What about we go out for a meal and return for a nightcap? It's been a long time since I took a beautiful woman to dinner. Since you have dressed up for the occasion, what about it?"

"Beautiful? Keep it up, I like it." Jane nodded and smiled as she took his glass inside and returned with her bag and a light shawl against the mild, but cool air. They walked out to the cruiser, and with a flourish, he opened the door and waited for her to sit comfortably.

"Can we go with the lights and siren?"

He smiled as he opened his door. "Only for official police business."

"This is not official?"

"Nope." He replied flatly. "Not even close."

"Can I wear your hat?"

"Nope, I haven't got it with me," he replied as he moved the cruiser onto the blacktop and towards the town center. There were few options for food after five o'clock in the afternoon. The diner had closed, but there was Megs, a restaurant as old as the town.

They ate and talked until Meg informed them that the other patrons had left and it was also time for them to depart. Tom paid the bill, and they walked out into the mild night air together. "Nice to see you without your uniform on, Tom." Meg chided him as he left.

As they reached the cruiser, Jane pointed to the far hills. "Wow, did you see that?" She said suddenly. Their view was directly down the main street towards the granite cliffs that towered above the dark, forested hills. "I just saw a flash of light. Like a pulse."

Venter moved over to where she was standing. "Lightening, maybe."

"No, the light was green across the horizon. Look. there it is again." Low on the horizon, between the hills and sky, a brief flash of light happened and abruptly stopped.

Venter watched for several more minutes. "Lightening, I think. It radiates light a long way off.

"It doesn't look like lightning to me. When has lightning been a shade of green?"

Venter shrugged. "What else could it be?"

Ten minutes later, he pulled up outside her front gate. He stared at the old stucco house in desperate need of a paint job. He noted the garden and path were meticulously kept.

"I can read your mind, Tom. It's not my job to paint. You want to come in?" She said with a smile.

"It's a big day tomorrow, Jane. We found the bull, and I need to go to Winslow. I have to see the mayor and drop off my daughter.'

"How does that stop you from coming in for a drink? I won't bite if that is your issue. Not yet, anyway!" She laughed aloud as she said it, and Venter joined in with a chuckle. "Worse than that, I have a daughter who does not want to go home."

"Oh Boy. Now that's serious!" she scoffed. "What happened to that bull seems to be the topic of conversation in the town. It's a real mystery, don't you think?"

Venter nodded. "We think maybe coyotes killed it. Now we have an unhappy rancher and there are no clues as to how it happened."

"Are you serious? coyotes? I have never seen a coyote near the town. But, in saying that, they must be up in the hills. Still, can't see why a coyote would take down a bull. There must be easier prey, right?"

"Agreed. We seem to be spending a lot of sheriff time on the bull, and honestly, I am sick of it already. I am not usually the one that handles it. McNab can take it over."

"It's Harold' responsibility?"

Venter shrugged as he thought about it. "It's a good question. He is the town vet, so who else would take it over? There is one thing I am sure of: It's not my responsibility or my deputy. We have other responsibilities."

She then sat in silence for a moment as the conversation lapsed. Finally, she leaned across the seat and kissed him softly before nestling into his arm. "Okay, rain check. Don't be a stranger."

Venter drove slowly up the dirt road towards the house. He realized Allie would be safe, so he turned the car around and returned to the town. Fifteen minutes later, he stopped, slammed the cruiser door behind him, and went to the front door.

Jane opened it and smiled at him as he was about to knock on the door. She ran her fingers through her hair. "Good choice." She scolded. "What about your daughter?"

"Is that the welcome I get?"

"I'm serious. What about Allie?"

"She'll be okay. She is sixteen going on forty. She has your telephone number. She'll call if something happens."

CHAPTER 17

Outside the house, Venter gazed at the morning sky. The day offered a clear sky with a light wind from the northeast. The pine scent from the forest surrounding the house hung heavily in the air. He made his way to his cruiser after finally getting his daughter prepared and in the passenger seat next to him.

"You need a new car, dad." She said caustically.

"Really? Never guessed.".

"Are you going to tell me how the date went?"

"None of your business, Allie. All in good time."

"You got in late. Very late!" She scolded.

"We talked."

She snorted as she turned her face to the window. "Oh yeah, it's okay for you and mom to ask me about boys, but I can't ask about what you did."

"That's why I'm the dad and you are the daughter. By the way, what boys in particular?"

"You and mom are such squares." She made the sign of a square with her fingers and stuck her tongue out.

He smiled at her comment as he motored down the old forest road towards town, finally turning onto the eighty-five towards Winslow. As the cruiser sped along the highway, they watched the changing colors of the vast fields stretching to the hills beyond. Some cropped, others left fallow in the off-season to replenish the soil.

Several times, he slowed the car as they encountered a wandering cow from a broken fence, but he sped up as the ten-mile-to-Winslow sign appeared on his left. He looked across one of the vast fields to glimpse the old Winslow road, used only by farmers and ranchers, while everyone else used the 85.

Venter slowed his speed five miles from the city outskirts, and several minutes later, he entered the main street of Winslow after motoring down the long hill from the Essex end of the road. The entrance finally plateaued to a long street with stores and shops and people milling about as they did their business. He turned to Allie, who had been mostly silent and deep in thought on the trip. "Nice to see customers everywhere," he said.

"Home, sweet home." She replied sullenly.

"Make the best of it, Allie. You live in a pleasant town and a nice house. It could be worse. Are you, at least, enjoying school?"

"You know the answer to that, Dad. It's okay."

"Just okay?"

"Barely okay."

Venter pulled up outside Frankie's house. He watched her as she walked towards the house, waiting until she reached the front door. He then made an about-turn and headed for the main street and the council buildings at the center of town. Several minutes later, he found a park outside the building.

Like much of Winslow's main street, the building held its original façade, but the interior had undergone extensive renovation. The *executive* floor was accessible via a grand wooden staircase that rose two levels.

Gray tiled floors paved the entrance with extensive wood paneling on the walls which highlighted the internal gloominess. Venter disliked the place. Impatient to get the meeting over, he took the wide steps two at a time until he reached the landing and went to the mayor's office.

"He will not be long." Perkins secretary said politely as she sat serenely at her vestibule desk. She paid him little attention and focused on another pile of khaki folders, each with neat notes on the top indicating the contents. "And how are you, Sheriff Venter?"

"Well, thanks, Ma'am." Venter replied quickly, trying to remember her name and whether she had been at that desk the last time he had been called in for a meeting. "And you?" Without saying a word, she smiled at him and returned to her neatly arranged paperwork on the desk.

To her left, a telephone with a black receiver and four buttons was positioned within reach. Less than a minute later, a light appeared on the top. "Mayor Perkins will see you know, " she motioned to him to go in with a hand wave practiced over time. Venter nodded and opened the heavy oak door to enter the largest office in the building.

The mayor walked his sizeable girth around from the other side of his desk to greet Venter as he entered. "Well, Sheriff, good to see you. I am busy so let's start. I hear you have some issues over there in Essex. Domestic matters, am I right?"

Venter smiled thinly, shook his hand, and took the seat offered to him. Perkins then returned to the large chair that swiveled with a creak as they faced each other.

"A particular gentleman who has a history of beating his wife."

The mayor nodded knowingly. "It seems to be on the increase these days. It's hard to know why, but you need to keep a lid on it. Will this man, eh, Peterson, be charged?" He questioned after perusing a thin folder on his desk.

Venter shrugged. "It wasn't his wife that brought the complaint. It came from Doc Lowes. He made the report, so I am unsure if we can charge him. I did meet with Peterson and warn him."

"How did he respond?"

"Not very well." Venter replied without offering details.

"Good news. Keep on top of it. By the way, my secretary got a call about a dead bull?"

Tom was surprised that Perkins knew of the issue, which must have originated from Beth gossiping with Winslow. "Strange one, really, mayor. It was a young bull that got lost and ended up near the back of an old warehouse outside the town. It appears it got taken down by something. Coyotes, probably.."

"Killed?"

"It was ripped apart."

"Coyotes, you say?" Perkins asked, surprised. "There are wild coyotes around Essex?"

Venter shrugged. "Well, it's a mystery. No one I spoke to can say they ever saw a pack of coyotes or dogs in or around the town for quite some while. Years, apparently."

"Well, we got a work order from your office to send men to clean up the mess." Perkins said as he pointed to the file on the desk.

Venter nodded, "We don't have the men to do it in Essex, mayor."

"What about the rancher?"

"Farmer! Bob Carter is his name."

Perkins drummed his fingers on the desktop for a moment. "Well, sheriff, as far as the council is concerned, it's Carter's property. It surely is not yours or mine, and I can't see how this is the council's mess. It is his job to clean it up as soon as possible. We can't have health hazards near the town."

"I doubt he will comply, mayor."

"He will." Perkins replied curtly.

Venter nodded, frustrated at the mayor's response and reluctant to pass the news to Carter, a complex man at the best of times. "Can the council assist?"

"No." The word stopped in the air. Venter nodded.

"As you know, we are in the process of making a decision on the sheriff office at Essex. I can't see you having time to chase coyote packs, or whatever it is. The bull is this farmer's problem, and we'll leave it at that, eh?"

"It is not a small site, Mayor. Where would he dispose of the bull remains."

"Dig a trench! How would I know, sheriff? That is his problem."

Venter stared at Perkins for a moment. "Anything else?"

The mayor nodded. "Fine revenues are down, again."

Venter exhaled slowly to calm himself. "There seems to be less traffic these days. Mayor. Also, we can't pull drivers over for nothing and give them a fine."

"Yes, of course." Perkins nodded at Venter. "However, safety can only be imposed through infringements to wrongdoers. Perhaps talk to Rusk and check that he spends the right amount of time on the eighty-five. He does the patrols, correct?"

"Correct." Venter nodded again as the mayor approached from the other side of his desk.

"Then I will leave the issue of the patrols in your hands, Tom, and we will speak again next month. Anything else?"

Venter shrugged as the mayor rose from his desk. I'll leave the clean-up to you and the farmer, Tom, but get to it quickly. It must be a godawful mess, right?"

"Right." Venter replied, shook his hand as the mayor walked him out of his office. Venter, slightly worried about his tenure and the upcoming elections and aggravated about the cleaning of the bull carnage, walked out of the outer office without speaking to the mayor's secretary. In response, she gave him a dour look. Goddam bureaucracy! More infringements? Hardly possible. He wondered if the mayor had ever been on an official police call in his entire life.

He reached the cruiser and drove slowly out of Winslow. Once he had traveled for ten minutes, he clicked the two-way and waited until Beth came through with a large amount of crackling on the line. He was close to the maximum distance for the two-way to work.

"Where are you, sheriff?"

"I'm driving out of Winslow, Beth. Can you call Marvin and tell him I'll go back to Bob Carter's farm to let him know the council order is for him to clean up the bull carcass! The mayor reckons he owns it, so he has to clean it."

"That don't seem fair, sheriff?" Beth said with surprise.

The mayor refuses to do it. He reckons its Bob's responsibility because it's his bull. Do you have any idea how they found out about it?"

"Guilty as charged, Tom. I mentioned it because we need a clean-up order for someone to do it," Beth coughed quietly. "How long is that going to take?"

"Well, we will need to help him. Perkins says it has to be done as soon as possible. Do you know where Marvin is?"

"Picking up Nesbitt, the dog breeder. He's meeting you at the site."

Venter groaned lightly. "Yeah, I forgot. I'll head there."

CHAPTER 18

Deputy Rusk began his journey out of town heading towards the old showgrounds south of Essex. Before the war, the grounds had been the epicenter of community activity for as long as most townsfolk could remember.

As a young boy, Marvin vividly recalled playing minor league baseball on the short-cropped grass field. That memory, like the showground itself, remained isolated after the war. Many of the local young men who played baseball died on the battlefield.

For many parents, the absence of young men remained an insurmountable grief. The happy days of Little League and Circuses remained a memory, waiting for a younger generation to take over when the war stopped most of the activity.

The old ground lay in disrepair. Days of annual cattle shows, Sunday community picnics, and little league baseball had disappeared during the war and had yet to return to when life was more accessible and the threat of world war non-existent.

As he neared the turnoff, he could still see the old picket fence, which had long since surrendered its white paint to the sun and buffeting, heavy northerly winds that brought cold temperatures and driving rain.

Marvin inched along, looking for the dog breeder and his trailer, which he saw moments later parked near the old, rickety seating that once held fifty participants with a view towards the showground field. The tiers of seating stood above a barely legible sign that read, 'refreshments' next to where green canvas tents were erected.

Marvin left his cruiser and walked slowly towards a group of large, green canvas tents. The flaps of the tents moved slowly in the breeze from the north. He stopped to read a sign held by a rope. "*Dog *show -. Come and see the original American Staghound - puppies available for purchase - Charlie Nesbitt, expert dog breeder."*

Marvin searched the area near the trailer, finally calling out several times. He then walked towards the tents at the back. A man appeared with his wife at this side, and the look on his face was not welcoming. He glared at Marvin, who immediately pulled his hat off and proffered his hand as he walked over.

Reluctantly, Nesbitt put his hand out and removed his hat, an old Stetson, at the same time. "Another citation, deputy?" Anger showed on his face.

Marvin smiled thinly as he stood next to him. Nesbitt was a full head shorter than Rusk, and the deputy was not tall. "Call me Marvin or Marv if you like. Can I call you Charlie?"

Nesbitt looked at his wife and pointed to the deputy. "You remember him, don't you, Jesse? He's the man who gave us the citation. No warning. Just the fine."

Marvin looked sheepishly over at Nesbitt's wife before putting his hand out. "Deputy Rusk, ma'am."

"What do you want, Deputy? We are busy and have a lot to do before opening the show."

"I have come to ask you a favor on behalf of the sheriff."

"Really? Well, deputy, you've got a hide coming out here with a request! Maybe you should have thought about it before you gave away that ticket."

"Doing my job, sir, just like you are doing yours. Nothing more, nothing less. It wasn't against you folks; it's a council ordinance. Those trailer backlights? Well, they should be working."

"Okay?" came the curt reply as Nesbitt finally stopped pacing. He leaned against the extended trailer with closed arms. He looked at the deputy with a shrug and a continuing scowl. "I can't say I feel friendly towards you, deputy. So perhaps you move along, and we'll talk another day."

Nesbitt wore a peaked cap above the weathered skin of someone who spent much of their time under the sun. "I understand, Mister Nesbitt, but we have an issue. I believe you know our town veterinarian, Harold McNab."

"McNab? Yeah, I know him. So?"

"Well," Marvin started sheepishly. "He suggested to Sheriff Venter that we come and say hello as we have a problem. We sure could use your help."

"Who?"

"The sheriff."

"As you can see we are setting up a dog show for Thursday. Do you have a reason why I should help?"

Marvin pulled the citation from his top pocket, tore it up, and returned the remains. "Well, that's a start, Charlie. I understand I was doing my job. I understand you are busy, but it would not take an hour or so. I am willing to take you there and back to the showgrounds."

"No, I don't need help, deputy." Nesbitt unfolded his arms. "Go on."

According to Harold, you've got a strong understanding of dog breeds and how they work, right?"

"You mean dog behavior, deputy?"

Rusk nodded, wondering if Nesbitt would help. The man had not moved from his position against the trailer wall.

Nesbitt removed his cap and ran his hand through his grey hair. "Okay, so what's up?"

"Well, bluntly, we have a problem with a bull. Maybe I should preface it by saying it's a dead bull."

"What the hell are you talking about, deputy?" Nesbitt asked. "Why do you need me to see a dead bull? I've got better things to do with my time."

"We found this bull at the back of an old warehouse near the south end of town."

"So?"

Something has torn it apart."

"So."

"Hell, of a mess. We think it may be dogs or coyotes, but we're not sure."

Nesbitt looked at his wife and then at Rusk. "Have you seen any wild dogs around the county? Maybe it was coyotes?"

"Well, Mister Nesbi…."

"Call me Charlie, son." Nesbitt said with his hand raised.

"The issue is how the bull was killed, Charlie. We don't know. McNab had little clue either and said you might be able to understand what happened and help us find out what or who did it."

"If it was dogs or coyotes, what difference does that make? You got a dead bull. So?"

Rusk gave him a perplexed look. "Charlie, we really need to see this!"

"That bad?"

"Dead bulls at the back of Essex town, especially ones that have been pulled to pieces, are not something we normally see. Ever"

"McNab doesn't know? He's got more experience than me."

"Not about dog behavior, apparently."

"When?"

"Well, now. I know you're busy, but if you have the time, we will meet the sheriff there."

"It sounds like a waste of time to me," Nesbitt replied as he considered it. He looked at his wife, who shrugged.

"Can't hurt, Charlie. Just have a look."

"What about the back-stop light?" Nesbitt nodded at the end of the trailer as he looked at the deputy's face.

Marvin smiled. "Should be okay, Charlie, and if it is still an issue, I'll help you fix it."

Nesbitt nodded and directed his attention to his wife. "You be okay, hon?"

She smiled lightly and waved her hand around. "Don't be too long. We have a host of work around here for Thursday, and no going for a beer. You come right back, you hear? Deputy? You take care of him."

Nesbitt nodded his head and pointed briefly to the cruiser. "You offering to drive me, deputy?"

Rusk nodded his head vigorously and waited for Nesbitt to respond. "I'll need to chain the boys and girls up, so follow me," Marvin followed him towards the tents. They entered one tent and found four dogs lying patiently on the ground, away from the outside heat.

Marvin took a step backward as he approached. "These are the males, deputy. Quite big, aren't they? Once you get near them, I mean. Have you seen them before?"

"Can't say I have, Charlie," Rusk replied, waiting patiently for Nesbitt to finish his work.

Nesbitt nodded as he patted the closest dog under its chin. "One hundred percent American breed, deputy, and one of the few native dogs. An interesting history as well," Charlie commented as he walked around the tent. He took the time to inspect several dogs as they sat obediently and quietly. With practiced ease and a soft voice, he chained them to a central point on a long individual lead, carefully ensuring it was long enough for the dogs to move around.

He picked up a bucket from the front of the tent and filled several old metal bowls until the water overflowed. "Okay, one more thing to do before we go." He moved to a second tent where two younger dogs sat restlessly, their broad tails wagging furiously when he entered through the tent flap. "I thought there were more dogs," Marvin said as he stood waiting.

"Nope, that's it. The big ones are for the show, as I put them through their lessons on the day to demonstrate how trainable they are. I usually travel with six full-grown and several young ones in case a rancher or a farmer wants to buy one. You never know. Hey, Jesse, can you unload the feed bag?" he shouted as he rechecked the lead lines.

"Don't be long." She scolded with a wave and a look.

"You heard the boss." He said with a cocked eyebrow as they made their way to the cruiser.

"These dogs, they eat much?"

"Well, dogs are always hungry. They are a full breed, no crossbreeding if you know what I mean, and they have to be cared for, and that means eating good food, not scraps."

Marvin nodded his head. "Staghound, you say? I can't say I have ever heard of em," Marvin said as he pulled the cruiser onto the dusty side road and drove towards the run-down industrial area and the old Sturger grain store.

"A pure American breed and the best for ranchers. They have quite a history, but they didn't start off as the breed you just saw. The early pioneers from Europe and other places moved out West for new land and opportunities. Their only real assets were their wagons, goods, and, of course, their livestock."

Rusk nodded as he listened. "That much history, huh?"

"Well, the livestock were an easy feed for roaming coyotes and wolves. In that time, they had these Sighthounds, or so they were called back then. As far as we know they originated from Europe, but god knows how they got them to this country. Maybe the early settlers could bring what they wanted."

"Makes sense." Rusk added as he listened to the story.

Nesbitt paused briefly as he wound the cruiser window down for fresh air. "Let me tell ya, deputy, I have watched these dogs pull down a huge stag, one big animal if you are ever close to one. To give you an idea, a big stag can weigh as much as five hundred pounds. My boys can pull down and kill something that size. They have the muscle and weight to pull down big prey. Perfect for ranchers."

"Never seen them before, Charlie, and honestly, I ain't seen you around either?"

"Have you heard of the American Lurcher?"

"Nope." Marvin replied flatly.

Nesbitt nodded with the look of a man who knew his business. "Well, as a breed, it comes in different names. Longdog of the Prairie is one, but it's best known for the name we breeders use, which is what you have seen today."

Marvin added as he lowered his green pilot sunglasses against the harsh light and slowly motored along. "How much are they selling for?"

"Why, you after one?"

Rusk laughed. "Nope, not much use to me, Charlie."

"Well, now, the answer depends on the dog. They are not cheap, but an excellent investment for anyone who hunts and keeps other preying animals away. They are very territorial but easily trained. Real smart as well."

"So, only used for hunting, I guess. I say that because the hills around here don't have much in the way of prey of that size. Mainly jackrabbits, raccoons and the rest."

Nesbitt nodded his head. "The early settlers used them mainly for hunting, deputy, as they hunted deer and bucks. These boys are good for keeping coyotes away. Maybe you have a few around here, right?"

CHAPTER 19

They arrived twenty minutes later and parked near the roped-off warehouse area. Venter stood next to the fence nearest the roadside as he waited.

Marvin introduced them, and Tom took over the conversation. "I want to thank you for coming with deputy Rusk, Mister Nesbitt, because we are at a bit of a loss on this one. Our local vet, Harry McNab, reckoned you know a great deal about dog behavior."

Nesbitt smiled at Venter and shrugged his shoulders. "That's high praise from Harold." He stopped to survey the building and the surrounding areas. "Deputy tells me this warehouse has been closed a long time."

"Correct, maybe twenty years, I believe. Well, before my time."

Nesbitt wiped his brow with his hand. "How long have you been sheriff in Essex?"

"Some say too long!" Tom looked at him with a smile. "A couple of years."

"You served?"

"France."

"You?"

"I tried. Too old." Nesbitt said with an irritated look on his face.

"So, Mister Nesbitt, would you be happy to come and see what we've got going on in the back?"

"Call me Charlie, sheriff. Lead on. Is it far?"

"Nope, not far at all." Venter stepped from the front of the cruiser. Just as he had walked with McNab, he escorted Nesbitt to the back of the warehouse. He noticed Nesbitt favored his right leg, and while they were walking, Nesbitt turned towards him. "I'm a bit slow these days. This right leg got bit by a snake some while ago. Took me a long while to recover."

"Well go slow." Venter mumbled. They walked along the broken timber fence at the side of the warehouse. Venter focused on the ground, wondering if the bull had come this far down from the back area. There were no prints he could see.

"Boy, that is some stench." Nesbitt whistled softly and stepped around the bloodied area where the bull remains lay inert on the ground. He took several minutes to take in the scene. "Did Harry know how long ago this might have happened?"

"His guess was several days ago."

"Okay," came the curt reply as he circled the carcass. He squatted to inspect the neck and head of the great bull lying sightless and lifeless. With its swell of flies and foraging insects, the main carcass had started to disintegrate in the sun.

Nesbitt stopped now and then and with a frown around the mounds of flesh, prodding occasionally with an old paling he picked up. "I think we need to take a closer look. Okay, if I move some of these pieces, sheriff?"

"You do what you need to do."

"Yo'all" need some help there?" Marvin asked as he moved closer.

With some effort, Charlie placed the paling under the bull's torso. With Marvin assisting, he lifted it until it rolled over with a heavy squishing sound. The stench wafted up after he moved it.

Marvin moved back quickly, followed by Venter as they held their handkerchiefs up. "My God, that is nauseating." Nesbitt said as he stood back in disgust at the rotting carcass.

He pulled an old rag from his pocket and placed it over his nose. Then, with his right hand, he pointed to the ground beneath the bull's torso. "There you go! " he said.

"What?" Venter moved closer and peered down without recognizing what Nesbitt was pointing at.

"Prints."

Venter squatted to examine the indented earth beneath the torso. The marks were defined and, to him, resembled dog paws.

"Wolf prints. Probably timber wolves. *Guipago*." Nesbitt said softly. He checked further around the rolled torso.

"What did you say?"

Nesbitt smiled lightly. "The native Indian word for a wolf is *Guipago*. There are others, but in this area, that is what they called them."

"These are wolves prints?"

"Exactly." Nesbitt replied, looking again at the ground under the carcass.

"What did McNab say?"

"He thought it might have been coyotes, but he wasn't sure."

"Did he see these prints?"

Venter looked directly at him. "Nope, don't think so. He didn't move the carcass."

Nesbitt held up his left hand and motioned to the prints he found. "Wolf paws, I believe."

Venter looked at him incredulously. "Are you sure?

Nesbitt rechecked the prints. "Yep, they are unmistakable."

"Wolf prints? There are no wolves around here!"

"They could be timber wolves," Nesbitt offered. "Certainly not coyote, that's for sure."

"Well, that is a first." Venter said as he looked carefully. He counted twelve prints in the area where Nesbitt was pointing.

Nesbitt nodded. "Based on the depth and difference in those prints, it's the work of a pack. Wolves are the best of hunters. They move together and work in unison. Family evolution at its best. That is what we are looking at, right here."

"What about dogs? Any evidence here to determine if they were involved."

"Maybe. Several prints over there look like a dog's paw, but I can't be sure because of the rain. They might have come after the attack. Have there been any reports of wild or domestic dogs attacking in the area?"

"Nope, not that we know," Venter said as he slowly shook his head. No one has seen wolves in this area, so are you sure they are wolf prints?

Nesbitt nodded. "I think so. They are not coyote prints because the paw print is too big. The paw print has a wide, distinct outline and four claws. I might be wrong, but I doubt it. You had better let McNab know as soon as possible."

"Could dogs have joined the wolves in bringing the bull down?"

Nesbitt stood up with his hand on his hip above his sore leg. "Highly unlikely. Wolves and dogs can look similar depending on the dog breed. However, that is where it ends. Dogs and wolves have evolved differently. A dog would be no match for a wolf."

Venter nodded his head as he listened. "What now?"

"Speak to McNab." Nesbitt offered as he turned to walk back to the cruiser.

CHAPTER 20

Utilizing his police training, Venter motored down the old town road, observing anything that might explain the attack on the bull at the Sturger warehouse. Finding nothing interesting, he picked up the microphone and clicked several times. "Beth, you there?"

"How did you go with the dog breeder, sheriff?"

"Not sure, Beth. He thinks it may be wolves, not dogs."

There was silence on the other end for a moment. Beth laughed. "Wolves? Nonsense! There hasn't been a wolf sighting for as long as I can remember. Is he sure?"

"Did you speak to Winslow?"

Beth smiled briefly. "Sure did. The council won't budge. It's up to Bob to clean it up. According to Winslow, it's his bull and his responsibility. I guess we will have to help somehow."

"I agree."

"Amen." Beth replied. She clicked twice. "You going to see him?"

"Yep. Over."

Venter slowed as he drove slowly past the gates, mostly off their old hinges, and drove up the potholed road. He could see the house in the distance. The house appeared as if it had recently received a fresh coat of whitewash. A white picket fence surrounded the house, highlighting the garden that Carters wife, Mable, lovingly maintained with the pride of someone who enjoyed such a task.

Bob Carter followed in the footsteps of his father and grandfather. They cultivated corn fields, raised livestock, and made ends meet in some years while accumulating debts in others. The farm was not large by local standards, being one hundred and twenty acres, but it was layered with workable crop fields on undulating ground, flat enough to be farmed efficiently. The quality of the soil, volcanic by origin, offered excellent yields.

When Venter met Carter in town, their conversations often revolved around the high crop and stock prices during the war and the unexpectedly low prices for corn after the war ended as prices slumped. Carter would nod his head and decry any authority. His ability to complain seemed in line with his officious, pedantic nature.

With the dead bull uppermost on his mind, Venter braked the cruiser to a halt, picked up his hat, and got out of the cruiser. He looked around briefly as he made his way to the front door.

Bob came out to greet him. "Beth called, sheriff. It is quite a surprise you are coming out here to see us. Mable is making my late-morning coffee, so come out the back and say hello. Two law visits in two days. You coming with more bad news?"

Cursing Beth under his breath, Venter removed his hat and walked around the long veranda, finally sitting on an old chair that gave a wide view of the cornfields surrounding the house and stretching up a low hill to the west of the house.

As he dropped his hat on the table, Bob's wife poured coffee, retreated to the kitchen, and ambled back with a fresh pot.

Venter leaned back in his chair, crossing one leg over the other. He looked at both of them before he answered. "I tell you plain, it has stumped all of us, but we got two experts, including McNab, to look, and they are telling us, it's not coyotes. The attack was from a wolf family."

"Wolves, you say?" Carter stared at Venter for a moment.

"You know that dog breeder, Charlie Nesbitt?"

"Nope." Bob replied laconically.

"Well, he's setting up at the old showgrounds for a dog show. He breeds Staghounds and sells them to farmers and ranchers. We called him to the site, and he inspected the area. He even showed us the prints. Must have been a pack of wolves, he said. The prints were unmistakable."

"Wolves? Nonsense, sheriff. There are no goddam wolves around these parts. There have never been any that we have seen in recent years. Right, Mable?" he said, looking at his wife. She nodded.

Venter shrugged. "Nesbitt's an expert dog breeder. So, he should know."

Carter winced as he peered over his half-rim glasses. "He's an expert, you say?"

"He's an expert dog breeder?"

"Is he some expert on wolves?"

"Not exactly, but he understands canines, I guess." Venter offered as he sat back on the old chair.

Carter dithered momentarily, looked askance at the ground, and finally lifted his head to look Venter eye-to-eye. "I'll tell you what's strange, sheriff. Why would a pack of wolves pull down a large, angry, obstinate bull when they can pull down a cow or a calf more easily? And, have a better meal! It just don't make any sense."

Venter nodded as he listened. "Yep, that is a mystery, Bob."

"There are still plenty of calves out there for the picking. Pulling down a bull of that size would take a big effort, even for a pack of dogs or wolves. To my mind, nothing could take that big bull down outside of a large bullet from a rifle."

"Bob understands this sort of thing." Mable chirped in support as she offered to refill Venter's cup. He declined with a wave of his hand and a light smile. "Still, I've seen stranger things in my time, that's for sure."

It did seem weird, Venter thought to himself as he sat on the old veranda of the clapboard house. Why would a pack of wolves attack a big, ornery bull when a small calf or even a defenseless cow was on offer if they were hungry and had run out of game to hunt?

He stood up to stretch his legs, sipped the remains of the second cup of weak coffee that Mable had deftly poured, and pondered the reason why the bull was attacked in the first place. Perhaps Bob was right. Why kill a bull when a cow is easier? Much easier.

Bob briefly lowered his head and looked at Venter over his glasses. "No more than three years old. He was a bigun". He would not have gone down easy, sheriff, I can tell ya that."

"Even on the ground, that bull looked huge. How long did you have him?" Venter asked.

Carter pursed his lips. "Maybe around twenty months, I guess. I can check if you need me to be more accurate, but I think I am right. He weighed more than a ton, I guess. Maybe a ton and a half. That is a lot of meat to pull down! Also, he was a young, angry bull. He would not have submitted easily and still had his horns, mind you."

"You ever seen wolves around here?"

Carter looked at his wife with a shrug of his shoulders. "We saw a timber wolf up on the hills beneath the forest. That might have been more than, how many years?" Carter asked his wife.

"More than five years ago." She answered confidently as he nodded at the memory.

Venter patiently waited for him to finish and cleared his throat. "Well, besides the loss of that bull, the news is the council has ordered you to clean up the mess. They say it's your beast, so you gotta clean it up."

"Pigs ass!" Bob said, suddenly annoyed at the order. "I'll be damned if I gotta clean up that mess!" Bob shouted at Venter as he stood up and paced, his face a little redder than before. He finally lowered his voice. "Now, I got to do the bidding of those assholes? Is that what you're saying to me? They got a hide, that group of people. Morons without a proper job. Try to find one when you need em!"

Venter nodded as he listened to the tirade. "Listen, Bob! Marvin and I will help somehow, but I can't get around the order. I was told by the mayor face-to-face only this morning."

"Lucky he ain't talking to me face-to-face, sheriff; otherwise, he might change his mind."

Venter finally stood and stretched with a loud grunt, ignoring the pain in his shoulder. The thought of wolves made him look out across the fields and up to the hills that always looked more imposing from this end of the town. Perhaps it was an illusion, but it always appeared that way—the colors were more vibrant, and the hills taller and more imposing—almost threatening.

In the distance, what appeared to be a light ground mist had formed. He studied it momentarily until he turned to place his cup on the green pattern saucer on the aging table between the two chairs. "Better sooner than later. I can tell you, Bob, it is one hell of a smell in that yard."

"No way out of this?"

Venter shook his head and gave a sympathetic look. "Nope."

"Anyone got any idea how the hell it got down there?" Mable walked over to her husband and put her hand on his arm. "I still can't see how this is our job, sheriff. Why should we clean up the mess?"

Venter nodded, wondering how to leave the house before it became a full-scale argument.

"Bastards! Let's just get it done, Mable." He whispered. "You can't fight city hall. You know that. Let's just get it done."

"No, damn it, why should we do it?"

"It's our bull." He sat down on the chair and thought for a moment. "Okay, okay. When do we do this thing, Mable?" Bob deferred to his wife for an answer, but she immediately shrugged, showing little interest.

Carter stood up to lean on the old railing. His brow furrowed as he considered it. "Maybe the day after tomorrow. Does that suit you? I'll bring my pickup, get the old tractor, and dig a big trench. It will cost me a bundle to get a new bull. We are doing their goddam work. It makes me angry, sheriff."

"Believe me, I understand, Bob, but I have no choice." Venter replied with a smile. "Let me know what time. Now, I got to push off."

"Will do.," Bob replied as he walked Venter back to his cruiser. As they neared the car, Bob pointed to the hill road that weaved up towards the top fields. "You got time to look at something that might tie in with what happened to my bull?"

Venter stopped as he leaned against the car and checked his watch. "What do you mean?"

"Maybe a coincidence. Maybe not. Want to take a look?"

"Get in. How far?"

CHAPTER 21

Bob Carter joined Venter in the cruiser. As they pulled out of the farm gates, he pointed to the hill at the top of the farm, offering directions. The cruiser took a hard right up the rutted hill road, winding up to the top area of the farm. Pale brown grass stalks stretched into the distance.

Two hundred yards away, a fence separated the area from the forest undergrowth at the back of the large field. Far above, granite cliffs glinted in the sunlight.

Carter stopped for a moment before he opened the gate. He looked directly at Venter with a severe look on his face. "Let me say something, Tom. I ain't been telling Mable, but I tell ya, strange things have been happening around here."

"Like what?"

"I saw this light up in the hills late last night, around ten or so, and it looked weird. A bit like waves. Yep, a wavy light in the sky. Strangest thing, if you ask me."

Venter glanced at him. "Where did you see it?" He looked up to where Carter was pointing. The cliff face soared above the forest of dense tree growth, reaching up the hills towards the granite tops.

. "Up there. The light was above the top of the cliffs, really, really bright green."

"How long did it last?"

"Hmm, maybe several minutes. Then it disappeared. Strange, really. That's the only word for it. I'm surprised no one has seen it. I called Mable to look, but the light disappeared before she joined me. Has anyone else seen it?"

Venter stared at the area above the cliffs. "I'm not sure." He replied uncertainly thinking of his discussion in town.

"What the hell would it be, sheriff?"

He patted him on the shoulder with a reassuring look. "Sometimes people see things that are not actually there, Bob. It's more like an illusion. You know, like the reflection of moonlight on tree leaves and that sort of thing. That light might have been as simple as a campfire someone had lit. What else could it be?"

"The light was a deep green, like the grass on the lawn. Your guess is as good as mine, sheriff, I suppose. I saw it, but Mable said I was seeing things. "Age, you know? They blame everything on age these days." Bob added as they reached the top of the rise. He stood for a moment, breathing heavily.

Venter shrugged. "Well, if you see it again, let me know."

"There's more." Carter scratched his head with this forefinger and looked out towards the hills. "Our dogs, the Collies? They have plumb vanished, and that's unusual. They are usually back by mealtime."

"How long?"

"Several days. Don't suppose if there are wolves around that they got them."

"I don't have an answer for that one, Bob."

Bob shook his head as he opened the wide farm gate at the front of the long, grassed field. Venter looked around but could not see any stock. "Over there!' He pointed. "Follow me."

Together they walked fifty yards into the field. Large boulders, common to the county, stood high out of the grass. "When did you find it?"

"Yesterday afternoon." Venter followed Carter until he stopped and pointed to an area of churned grass. "I haven't seen anything like it."

Venter walked around the dead calf. It appeared to be in the same state as the bull. Something had torn the head from the body and eaten out the tongue from its jaw. One leg was torn off and lay several yards from the body. "Ugly, huh?' Bob said as he looked at the remains.

Venter stooped to inspect a mash of paw prints deep into the rented soil around the carcass. He saw a pattern of prints similar to those he inspected around the bull carcass. "Similar to the prints at old Sturgers warehouse," he said almost to himself as he moved around the severed head and then towards the carcass.

Bob looked at him askance. "Do you reckon it's wolves?"

"Hard to know, but I guess so. Maybe dogs?" Venter moved around the area where the calf remains were scattered. The deep rips in the body and complete separation of the limbs resembled the mutilated bull.

What intrigued him was the pattern of paw prints that looked almost singular in some areas, mashed and imprinted. He motioned to the area he was inspecting. "Those paw prints look identical to me, but I'm no expert."

Carter pulled his hat and glasses off and ran a hand across his scalp. "But they haven't eaten it, have they?" He said with a perplexed tone in his voice as he waved his hand around the area of the dead calf.

Venter shrugged. "Weird. None of this makes sense to me. Have a look at that!" He said as he walked slowly to the side of the calf. Its head was severed, and its limbs torn and pulled away from its body.

"Well, if this is those goddam wolves, we must find where they are hiding out and take em' out," Carter said with determination in his voice. "I don't want to lose more stock. I looked around the fence line this morning, and unless they vaulted the fence and the barbed wire, the area is undisturbed."

"It may only be one for a calf of this size. The truth is, we don't know."

"To do this damage?"

"Well, Bob, after listening to Nesbitt, I have a newfound respect for wolves. It's possible a large wolf could jump this fence or easily get under the low strand of wire."

Carter looked at him in amazement. "Maybe I'll bring the rest of the stock into the pen at the back of the barn."

Venter nodded in agreement as he looked up towards the hills and then back at Carter, who looked at the calf sadly. "Anyone else lost stock?"

"I don't know. I want to get McNab to come have a look at this kill. We need to identify what took this poor calf down. He will know what we are looking at."

"You said it was wolf prints?"

"Could be, Bob, but I am no expert. That's why I want Harold," Venter looked down at the severed head of the calf with its eyes closed and mouth ripped open. A thin trail of blood had congealed on the ground next to its eyes.

"Why don't we just track and kill these wolves? It can't be that hard."

"To be safe, let's just find out what he thinks. Let's assume it's wolves until we are told a different answer. Okay?"

Carter shrugged as he looked at Venter, who was returning to the gate. "Listen up, Tom. I've lost a bull and a calf. I don't want to lose anymore. Bring whoever you like. I will leave it to you, but we need to kill those wolves before they do more damage."

Venter nodded his head. "I'll speak to McNab."

"Damn, McNab. I'm not losing any more stock."

"Leave it to me, Bob."

Carter looked at him fiercely. "If you won't help, sheriff I will start looking for them after I bury what is left of my goddam bull!"

Venter decided to push off as quickly as he could. "The bull is a significant loss, Bob. We all understand that."

"Sonsofbitches!" Bob replied sternly as he walked with Venter towards the cruiser. "If you see my dogs, let me know, huh?"

Venter drove quickly down the hill. As the cruiser came to a halt, he looked at Carter and shook his hand. "I will get McNab out here to have a look at the calf," he said.

Carter nodded as he waved goodbye.

CHAPTER 22

Venter pulled up outside the double-story building that Harold McNab called home on the main street of Essex, directly opposite the diner. McNab lived upstairs and left downstairs to his business.

The town veterinarian was famously frugal in his expenditures and advice. His surgery fronted the sidewalk almost directly opposite the diner, and he provided several parking spaces in the back of the building for clients. The surgery was a converted shop with a glass door and a wide window with the word *veterinarian* in wide, white letters on the front. The letters had paled over the years.

The room was sparsely furnished with five old, worn chairs and a small reception desk that had not seen a receptionist for many years. Harold was fond of saying, *cost issues,* to customers who suggested someone might be of assistance.

A moment later, McNab came through the surgery door, leaving it partially open with a brief view of cages that contained a bird and several cats. The smell of medicinal alcohol wafted into the room with him.

"Tom? What's up?"

Venter looked at him briefly. "Well, the truth is, I am doing work I should not be doing, Harold. It ain't my job to hunt dogs or wolves."

McNab stood slightly back at the tone of the sheriff's voice. "Wolves?"

"I've been back to Sturgers with Nesbitt, and he reckons it's wolf prints."

"Hardly likely around here, Tom." McNab replied calmly. "We haven't seen a wolf around here for years."

Venter shook his head. "I have also been out to Charlie's farm, and he showed me a calf that had been attacked and partially eaten. That is a bull and a calf. And guess what, Harold? There were real similar prints around there as well."

Harold adjusted his spectacles. He sat down beside Tom. "This is not my area, Harold. This is yours. Why am I involved in all this?"

"Well, if it is a wolf attack in the district, everyone is involved, Tom. I am a local veterinarian, not the council. If Nesbitt is correct, this is a matter for the county."

Venter stared at him momentarily. "Well, if Nesbitt is right. What the hell are wolves doing down here in Essex?"

McNab shrugged. "Wolf prints are very distinctive. You and I didn't notice any when we looked."

"Because it had rained recently. Nesbitt says the rain washed the rest of the prints to an indistinct point. With some effort, he moved that disgusting carcass of the bull, and the prints were underneath."

McNab nodded his head as he listened. "He identified them as wolf prints? That seems odd to me. We haven't seen wolves in these parts for quite some time. If a pack took down that bull of that size, they haven't been seen since. Where are they?"

"Good question." Venter replied. "However, assuming Nesbitt is right, we need to prevent further stock losses. Farmers and ranchers have a right to look after their stock. The only action needed is to cull, if and when we see them."

McNab looked at him with a glare. "I am against that course of action, Tom. If it is wolves, I assure you they will return soon enough to the hills. I'd like to have another look at the site and Charlie's calf. Come with me, okay?"

Venter thought about it momentarily and finally nodded to him. "Okay. When?"

McNab checked his watch. He disappeared out the back of the surgery and then returned. "Can we make it later this afternoon?"

"Sure." Venter replied. "I'll see you at four?"

McNab nodded and disappeared into the back, through the door to the surgery, tutting under his breath. "Wolves, no less."

CHAPTER 23

Clouds that offered rain earlier that morning cleared from the sky, leaving it an azure blue. Sunshine reflected off the cruiser roof as Venter drove to the old warehouse to meet McNab. It took less than fifteen minutes.

With handkerchiefs over their noses, they walked down the side of the warehouse. As they approached, swarms of flies flew off the remains and returned to feast as McNab walked around.

Unknown predators had mauled the head and legs. The torso lay slightly hollowed out by animals attracted by the rotting meat and stench of the rotting carcass. "Something has been busy," Venter said as he pointed around.

"Probably feral cats and foxes. They will eat anything." McNab approached the carcass and inspected the uncovered prints. He stooped down to take a look and nodded his head. "Hmm, now let's see." Harold put four of his fingers just above one of the indentations. He murmured to himself. "Yes, I think he is correct. These are wolf prints."

"Can you tell how many wolves might have been here?" Venter asked as he waited patiently near him.

McNab stood up with a grunt and his hand on his left hip. "Goddam rheumatism! No, that is not possible. If you look at the body, there were more than a few of them, but there is no way to tell how many. Look here," he commanded.

Tom approached cautiously. McNab looked up at him and then pointed to the paw prints. "Right there! They are quite unmistakable if you look closely. Wolves paws are around five inches long and four inches wide, and each paw holds four symmetrical toes. They are very different from a dog's paw. These are deep prints, even accounting for moisture in the ground. If the prints are anything to go by, they are big wolves. They are probably large timber wolves on the hunt."

"Big, you say?"

McNab nodded. "Wolves can grow to large dimensions. A big timber wolf can be six feet from nose to tail and well over a hundred pounds of lean muscle. They are highly evolved predators. Adult wolves can run above thirty miles an hour in short bursts."

"Really? Well, I didn't know that fact." Venter said as he looked carefully. He counted twelve prints in the area where McNab pointed beneath where the carcass had rested.

"Do you think any of the prints might be dogs?"

"Not in this spot. It might have been dogs disturbing the feed. If you look around, there are indistinct paw prints, which could be dog paws. I think it unlikely they initiated the attack."

"Why?"

McNab rose to look at one of the bull flanks laying nearer the back of the warehouse fence line alongside an old, upended tire. "Well, wolves hunt in packs. Sometimes as small as two and as many as eight or nine. It would take a big wolf pack, maybe as much as six to eight wolves, to bring down a bull of this size. I mean, have a *look* at the size of that torso!"

"So, why attack a large bull, a ton and a half in weight when they could go for a sheep or a cow? Charlie asked exactly that question," Tom asked as he approached the spot where McNab inspected the torn flank.

"Good question, Tom. It could be position. You know, the bull was in the wrong place at the wrong time."

Venter stared at him, perplexed. "Then, do we have a pack roaming around here?"

McNab nodded. "There is no other possible explanation."

"Why is the bull not eaten?"

"Hmm." Nesbitt looked briefly around. "Good question and not an easy answer."

"It has been ripped apart and left."

"Yes. I can see that." McNab replied curtly. "That is the question I have been pondering. A full pack of wolves would normally consume most of a carcass. This pack has eaten what appears to be the most palatable parts of the beast and left the rest. Maybe they were disturbed."

"Would they be moved on by dogs?" Tom asked.

"Could be. But, there is another option." Nesbitt nodded as he thought about it.

"Which is?"

"Dogs attacked the bull, and a pack of wolves drove them off. Sensing the dog's markings on the bull, they ate some and moved away."

Venter stopped and looked back towards the rear of the warehouse. "It's a goddam mystery. Why here?"

"Impossible to know, Tom."

"Would a wolf pack normally attack a bull of this size?"

"The short answer is yes. Wolves work in packs, sheriff. They corner, then go for the neck and bring the prey down. Now, I'm not saying it would have been a simple task to attack a bull of this size; however, let's assume the bull had somehow walked itself to the back of this warehouse near that broken timber fence. Then you have the perfect position for attack. Keep in mind wolves don't think about the odds of success; they just go for the kill."

"Still doesn't make a lot of sense."

"Might be the alpha was somehow misdirected and took on the

first kill it found."

"The what?"

"Wolves have a very rigid social structure. A family."

"So?"

Nesbitt stopped walking and put his hand on Venters arm. "Give me a minute to explain wolf behavior," he said.

"What is there to explain? They attack and eat."

McNab smiled thinly at him. "It's much more than that, Tom. In a wolf pack, a family unit, there is an alpha, the lead wolf. There is a Luna, who is an alpha female, plus there are betas and omegas in the pack, which is the lower hierarchy of the family. All levels are strictly adhered to. If one contests the Alpha, they will usually come off second best. The betas and omegas can be male or female. The alpha male is the one that coordinates the attack, and, in this case, he probably picked on that poor bull."

"Are there more than one alpha in a pack?"

"Nope."

"The alpha is male?"

"Absolutely."

"What's next? Will this happen again?"

"If these wolves are on a territorial hunt, there is not a lot you can do about it except leave them alone until they return to the hills."

"That's it?"

McNab inspected another indistinct print near some broken palings. He shrugged as he looked back at Venter. "Wolves are very much creatures of habit. They may have returned to their lair."

McNab stopped to look around the back of the warehouse. Ten yards away, a broken fence barely stood upright. The cross joints and palings were smashed and lying broken on the ground. "Say, did Nesbitt have a look in the field behind the warehouse?"

Tom shook his head. "Nope. Why?"

"Might be worth checking," He said as he went to the fence and looked into the field beyond. He pointed to a copse of trees some twenty yards away. "I'll look over there. Can you check along the fence to the other side over there? Call out if you find anything!" Nesbitt pointed to the fence that skirted the back of the warehouse.

"What are we looking for?" Tom asked

"Anything out of place, I guess. Look for prints and disturbed ground," McNab wiped his brow with an old handkerchief as he walked in the opposite direction.

Some five minutes later, Tom heard a shout. He moved back to where McNab stood in tall rye grass. As he neared, McNab pointed towards the ground. "That is what I was looking for. Right there."

Tom moved into the grass until he saw the gray and black fur of a wolf lying prone on the flattened ground. Its glassy, opaque eyes had long since lost sight, and its long, pink tongue lay outside its snout, covered by tiny ants.

"Timber wolf," McNab stated matter-of-factly.

"How do you know?"

As McNab bent closer, he pointed to the ripped body. "The fur color and size. On its left side, a gaping rent in its flesh lay open. "Boy, that is some mess! Have a look at that wound."

Tom shook his head as he looked at the remains and at the broken fence some thirty yards away. "What the hell is a wolf doing way out here?"

Nesbitt pointed to the ground near the entry to the grass. "Tom, if you look closely at those prints, they are the bulls. The ground is churned up here and over there. The rain has almost washed them away. "It sort of makes sense if you look at it logically."

"What do you mean?"

McNab inspected the fence and returned to where the wolf lay lifeless in the long grass. He checked the area quickly, stooping now and then to examine the grass. "I can see what has happened."

Venter pulled his hat off as he followed McNab to the fence. "The bull was attacked on the field and tried to escape the wolf pack. Under attack and probably in a blind panic, it careered off right over there and broke through the fence."

"How do you know that?"

McNab pointed to the fence line. "Have a look at the fence, at the area in the middle there. The bull has smashed it as it tried to get away from the attack. This where they cornered it and brought it down. It would not have been a pretty sight, I can tell you that much."

"Makes sense. So, what happened to the wolf back there?"

"Best guess? The bull attacked it as it tried to defend itself. The wolf is gored across its belly, becoming a casualty."

"So, it died here?" Venter asked as he inspected the remains.

"It's a fact that wolves will risk their own lives to save the pack if the group is in danger. I believe that this wolf did just that in assisting the family."

"Why here, in this grass? Wouldn't it be dead back there in the yard?"

"Maybe not. It may have crawled here to die after the wound it received. The pack would have left it here after they sensed it was dying.

"Wolves would do that?"

McNab nodded as he looked up towards the hills and foreboding cliffs in the distance. The afternoon light gave them a dark gray appearance, somber and stark. "They are a remarkable species. Wolves are highly intelligent and resourceful. However, they will leave a badly wounded member if it means survival for the family," He stepped closer to the wolf. Using a small branch, he prodded the torso, finally turning it over. "Those wounds are gore marks from the bull."

"Well, that brings up a question. Where is this mysterious wolf pack?"

McNab continued to look further around the grassy area. "My best guess is that they have headed back. Wolves are highly territorial, meaning they will return to protect their territory."

"So, there is no way of knowing?"

"They could be anywhere, but just stick with the facts."

"So, do we alert everyone in the district?" Venter asked.

"Well, Tom, I am just an old veterinarian. I don't have a crystal ball. However, I am sure they will return to the hills. It is just a matter of time. There is no need to start issues in the area; let's see what happens."

CHAPTER 24

The house, paneled with aged clapboards, was built in the early 30s and lay on the lower side of a barely used, potholed blacktop road accessed from the highway junction. After the war, the road was built to bypass the empty airport and runway, and traffic rarely came past the homestead.

Jack Milbrook pushed a large gate shut at the top field as he surveyed the cattle moving slowly across the pasture before him. The ranch comprised two hundred and eighty-three acres situated north of Essex towards Winslow; the area held long grass plains of rich, black soil, resulting in strong grass growth, ideal for cattle fattening and agistment.

The cattle were fattening up nicely, and that pleased him. After thirty-five years on the ranch, he had decided earlier that year to call it a day and sell the farm once he took the cattle to market towards the end of the season. Someone, and some other place, could provide meat for the market.

His wife had died the previous year, and there was little anyone could say that might lessen the loss. His son had died in England in an accident before he got to the war in Europe.

All he had left were his cattle, which grazed on the upper fields, and a house that lay empty of life, except for sheltering one man who had, for the first time, given up the need to pursue his daily life.

As he sat on his front veranda on hot summer evenings, Milbrook daydreamed where he might end up in his life. Near water of some form seemed the most attractive. The idea of living beside a lake seemed the most enjoyable. That was the sort of solace he felt he required to live out his life.

As habit dictated, he walked inside the back door to make breakfast after inspecting his cattle. Before doing so, he put a cross on the calendar on the wall. The 26th of August stared back at him.

The night before, he saw the sparking trail of a meteor in the clear night sky and felt it was an omen. It was his son's birthday. He never missed the date or spent time in anger at those who allowed it to happen. It took the effort to push the memories from his mind.

He broke the contents of three eggs, carefully dropping the yolks into an old, well-used frypan with a spoon of lard to keep the eggs company. He looked in the cupboard to see if any bread was left over from the previous day. He knew his memory was failing in his old age, which irritated him. He could not remember whether he had remembered to buy bread at the store two days before.

He cursed his old age. After a quick search, he found several pieces, and with his fingers, he dropped them into the frypan to fry with the eggs. He then sat down at the old pine kitchen table to pour himself a second cup of brewed coffee.

As he took his first sip, he heard a strange knock at the side of his house. It sounded like a light thump from a hammer onto timber but missing the high note of a nail head beneath the strike. He thought it may have come from the room closest to the kitchen.

Sometimes, birds mistook their bearings and hit the house. He shrugged and returned to his meal. Several minutes later, he heard a second thump on the clapboards and then four more thumps, increasing in frequency until it sounded like constant hammerheads striking the back wall of the house. Loud and concerning.

Several seconds later, the sound increased on the west side of the house. Quickly, he pulled the pans off the stove and headed out to the corridor and the back door. He stopped momentarily, thinking about grabbing his rifle and deciding against it.

He opened the door to the small landing at the back of the house. Suddenly, he heard a sound like a rushing wind. Above him, a large fleet of birds cast a long shadow on the ground beside him.

"What *the* hell." He said slowly as he watched them move together, transfixed by the sight.

In the sky, they arced and turned perfectly in unison. The flock resembled starlings cavorting in the evening sky that he had once seen on a trip to the seaside at Carmel. Was there a word for it? He tried to remember the term. What the hell was it?

He remembered it as a flock of finches arced low to the ground and moved skywards to what he estimated to be eighty feet under the morning sun. Murmuration! That was the term.

Red-beaked finches reached the peak of their climb, then followed each other in crowded unison and suddenly changed direction. He watched in horror, as the mass of birds flew towards the ground, and directly toward him. He didn't know what to do: stand there or hurl himself to the ground.

He stood still, more in shocked awe, than anything else. His feet were frozen in place as he watched the lounge room windows burst inward from the force of birds flying headlong into the wall. Some hit the window glass, while others crashed in full flight into the boards that lined the house. Shrieks filled the air as the boards turned crimson from the impact of the large flock of birds following each other in mass suicide.

He stood there, untouched, as the last finches passed him to smash into the wall and broken windows. Piercing cries echoed off the wall. He tried to block it out by placing his hands over his ears, which did little to muffle the sound.

Incredulous at the sight, he moved slowly to look inside the window nearest him. On the timber floor inside his loungeroom lay birds dying in agony with broken necks and ripped wings flapping helplessly on the floor. All in the throes of a horrible death.

He shook his head in an attempt to understand why hundreds of beautiful, red-beaked finches had cast themselves in full flight into the homestead wall. As he surveyed the bloodied boards and the ground beneath his feet, he realized, astonished, that not one bird had hit him.

He stepped back towards the door at the back of the small landing. He could only think of one reason why the mass suicide had occurred. The finches were pursued by something. He walked around cautiously, keeping his eyes on the sky and horizon. Nothing.

Finally, he shielded his eyes from the sun's intense light by holding his hand up and gazed for several minutes into the sky. He noticed the sky held strange haloes of light—three rings that circled each other around the glowing sun. Strange concentric circles shining brightly in the sky above where he stood.

The sound of dying birds filled the air. Masses of finches lay dead in twitching piles on the grass. Some injured birds flopped around helplessly while others lay still with broken wings and torn heads. Confused, his gaze shifted up and around towards the far horizon.

The day looked clear and undisturbed, so what in tarnation had caused what he saw before him? He walked quickly around the house, returning to the back and the carpet of dead birds on the grass. Would the rings around the sun have caused the commotion? He seriously doubted it. What were they anyway?

Birds lay clumped several yards from the wall; without counting, he guessed there might be more than a hundred birds on the ground with more inside. Why did it happen to his house? Where did so many finches come from?

Disbelieving and shaking his head slowly, he walked inside, peering at the birds on the floor, some entangled in broken window panes. They were the same breed of finches. Brilliant red beaks and dark plumage appeared even more prominent against the dark timber of the floor before him.

He waited for some minutes, wondering if there were more coming. He checked the perimeter of the house to satisfy himself that the other walls were intact and not targeted, and they lay clear of any birds. He sat for a moment trying to gather his thoughts, trying to make sense of what just happened. Why here? Had it happened in other places? What the hell?

Finally, Milbrook rose and reached the back door, walked inside the house, pulled on his work gloves, and went to the lounge where the birds lay. Blood from the suicidal birds dripped slowly down to the sills from jagged pieces of glass that remained in the window. The floor was a mess of feathers and broken, disheveled birds.

He felt a pang of sorrow as he gingerly stooped to pick up one of the finches. He inspected it closely. It was a beautiful bird, bedecked in tiny bright orange feathers across its neck and speckled feathers on its wing. In his hand, its bright red beak oozed a thin line of blood no wider than a needle.

He wondered if the wind was to blame for the deadly collision with his house, but even that idea made little sense. It must have been something. But what?

Another loud crash into the side of the house startled him. He ran outside with his rifle to find an eagle lying broken with shredded feathers, twitching on the ground. He stared at the bird momentarily, turned, and hurried around the house, looking to see if other areas were hit. Mystified, he returned to the rear and the sickening sight of the birds.

What the hell was going on? In forty years on a ranch, he had never seen anything like it.

He moved to where the eagle lay amongst the dead finches. It had hit the boards of the house with such force it lay slumped with a broken neck. Finches and now an eagle? Why would an eagle, a majestic bird in full flight, follow Finches into the side of a house??

Feeling exhausted, he sat on the back porch with his rifle resting on his knees as he waited nervously for another attack. He sat for an hour, swallowed a tot of rum to calm his nerves and finally, he felt more relaxed. He laid his rifle down, wondering how to clean the mess.

The shrill cries had stopped, and there were no more collisions. Maybe they lost their way? Would hundreds of birds possibly lose direction and fly, like Lemmings into a house? This was unheard of in his life. It simply made no sense.

"What the hell is going on?" He said out loud in frustration. He looked at the clumps of dead finches on the ground, motionless against a light breeze that ruffled the stalks of the mown grass and the speckled wing feathers of the dead birds.

Tears started to form in his eyes as he brusquely wiped them away with his shirtsleeve. It was such a waste. Above him, the concentric circles in the sky shone brilliantly and promptly disappeared.

CHAPTER 25

Angry at spending time on matters that hardly concerned him, Venter drove out towards the Carter farm. He picked up the microphone and clicked twice. " Are you there, Beth? Marvin, are you on?"

The two-way crackled, and finally, Beth's voice came on. "I've been waiting for you to come on air, sheriff. Marvin has headed to the old Romano farm. You know the place? It's on the East road at the back of the hills. There were stock kills there last night, the…they called him from the neighbors far..."

Venter nodded and waited, finally hitting the talk button on the microphone. "Beth, come in, Beth?"

Silence. Venter clicked the microphone again and waited.

A minute later, the radio crackled. "Sorry, sheriff, this thing has been acting up today, cutting out. It's worse than ever, and that's saying something. It seems to work and then stops; even the office radio cracks all the time, giving this sort of pulsing sound. Weird, really."

"You spoke to Marvin?"

Maybe fifteen minutes ago, I spoke to Marv and lost him. Maybe out of range. I could not raise him."

"Maybe someone needs to assist with a better two-way radio."

"Fat chance." She replied as the volume rose and fell.

"Did Marv say anything?"

"Well, I don't know the full details, but apparently, they have a few dead sheep on the property. Happened last night!"

"Did he say how?"

"Mutilated and left for dead. He didn't explain any further."

Venter took several seconds to answer and finally clicked the button. "I am driving to Carters farm with Harold next to me."

"Oh, okay. Hey, Harold. Having a good day?"

McNab smiled thinly at Venter. "Afternoon Beth. I could be doing other things."

"Yeah, you got me there. Me too."

"Is everyone okay?" Venter asked quickly.

"Not sure. That's why he took off."

"How did he find out?"

"One of the sisters rang in from a neighboring farm. They don't have a phone."

"Did he say how the sheep were killed?"

There was a momentary silence on the other end of the two-way, and Venter thought he had lost contact again when a crackle came through the speaker. "Lord knows, Tom, this sounds weird, don't you think?"

Venter grunted. "Yeah, to be honest, it is all strange, but one step at a time, Beth, just one step at a time. When Marvin comes in, get him to contact me on the two-way as soon as possible. Dead cattle and sheep are hardly in the business of upholding the law, Beth. Let me know if Marv discovers anything."

"Then it's up to Charlie. You know what the council says about it."

"Yes," came the curt reply from McNab. "Picking up the torso alone will need a tractor, and we will have to bury the remains in the field at the back. Do you know who owns that property?"

"I think it's public land from when the eighty-five was built."

McNab nodded to Tom. "Good news."

"Okay. When you hear from Marv, get him to contact me! How quick can a wolf pack move, Harold?"

"They can cover a lot of territory and very quickly. Like dogs, they can move over vast distances. Why do you ask?"

"If I do a quick mental calculation, the distance between the bull carcass and the Carter farm is at least twenty miles. If wolves are as territorial as you say, how did they get there so quickly?

McNab pursed his kips as he listened. "Let's have a look at the calf first. It may not be wolves. It might be a coincidence," McNab offered as an explanation.

"If wolves have been to the Carter farm and are the same pack as the killers of the bull, why travel out to the farm? Surely there are animals on farms between the two sites?"

Before McNab could answer, there was a crackle, and the two-way came to life as his deputy's high voice came bounding out. "Heading back in, sheriff."

Venter responded quickly. "Beth says you inspected the Romano farm?"

"Sure did. Three sheep ripped apart, really similar to that bull. Those two sisters, Meg and Jamie, heard the pack in the early morning. They saw them attacking the sheep, so they got their rifles and ran towards the holding pen. Three sheep were dead by the time they got there. Two were alive."

"Are the sisters okay?" Venter asked, his voice on edge.

"They are okay but a bit shaken up, as you can imagine. Meg said she may have wounded one of them as they started running at them and firing shots to scare them off. Then the wolves changed."

"Changed? What do you mean?" Venter questioned as he released the microphone button.

"Well, those goddam wolves stopped off a distance while Meg was firing off rounds at them. The wolves did not retreat they moved towards them, snarling and growling, and as the sisters watched, they separated and attacked from different sides."

"What did they do? Did they shoot them?"

"Nope, the women retreated inside as fast as they could."

"You mean the wolves attacked them even as they shot at them?"

"That's what they told me." Marvin replied quickly.

"How many were there?"

"Well, that's the strange thing, sheriff. They reckon the pack had wolves *and* dogs."

McNab looked directly at Venter. "Marv, it's Harold here. I am heading out to Charlie's with Tom. Did I hear you right? Did you say wolves and dogs?"

There was a pause on the other end of the line. "That's what they said. I went to the pen and had a good look around. I saw plenty of prints, but I couldn't tell one from the other. They were sorta mashed around."

"Did they say how many were there?"

"Quite a few, they said. It was a full moon last night. All they said was that the pen seemed full of em. They did say they were gray wolves and way bigger than any dogs."

"How far is the field from the house?"

"They were in a holding pen, maybe no more than fifty yards from the house itself."

"So, the wolves or dogs attacked. What did the sisters do?"

Marvin's voice came over the increasing static. "The sisters returned to the barn, closed the doors, and kept watch. Finally, the wolves and dogs took off. They jumped the fence, running off towards the hills at the back. Howling from the hills for some time in the distance."

Suddenly, the line went dead. Venter clicked his microphone more than once and placed it back on the seat. "We got a few issues here, Harold. I hope you are right about them returning to the goddam hills!"

The two-way clicked to life. "Sheriff, you there, over?"

"You disappeared, Marv. What were you saying? Howling?" Venter repeated but got no answer. "Marv, if you can hear me, I'm heading off to check Bob's farm. We have to find out if it is the same wolves that attacked the bull. Keep me posted if anything happens, and at least we will know about the sheep at the Romano place."

The crackle stopped. Marvin's voice came back from the ether. "Okay, sheriff, will do."

"Also, you need to calm them down. It might just be an isolated attack, and the wolves just happened to enter their farm. Maybe you revisit them tomorrow, just to check."

"Yessir." came the loud reply

"Also, when I get back, I think we need to alert the district."

"And the town?" Marvin questioned as he waited.

"I'll explain when I get in."

"Okay. Say, there was another thing."

"What?" Venter asked impatiently.

"The sisters. They talked about a strange light in the sky late last night. Above the cliffs."

"What sort of light?"

"Dunno. Green, on the edge of the sky, moving like a wave above the horizon, whatever that means. Those were the words they used."

"Moving like a wave? What the hell does that mean?"

"That's what they said. Been there for the last two nights."

"Just above their farm?"

"No, on the horizon."

"I thought I saw something the other night, but it's probably a reflection of campfires, Marv. People are up there this time of year. They camp out before the winter cold sets in. Maybe they were hunting before it got too cold," He replied without much interest.

"Reflection?" Marvin replied. "Maybe more than a reflection, sheriff. They said waves."

"I heard that, Marv. Over and out."

CHAPTER 26

McNab poked around for several minutes. He moved the calf head and carcass and stooped down to place his hand near a print in the mud. "See here and there," he pointed to the prints and finally stood. These are not just wolf prints," there was a cautious tone in his voice. He stood, removed his glasses, cleaned them, and stooped down again.

As Harold stooped down, Venter studied the top of his grey, thinning hair, feeling that the town's respected veterinarian had no sensible answer to the bull or the calf before them. Wolves? No one had seen a wolf in years. His senses were telling him to be cautious.

"Dogs?" Venter asked softly.

"Correct. Do you see the difference, sheriff Venter?" He pointed to the ground around the calf's ripped flesh. "Dog prints are in the middle of the group of wolf prints. If you look closely, you can see how different they appear." McNab picked up an old branch from the ground and pointed to each of the distinctive wolf paw prints embedded in the black, roiled earth around the calf remains.

"You see here?" The paw indents appear much more defined, longer, and heavier than the dog prints with the telltale four-pointed paw front, which he also pointed out as he spoke. "Here, sheriff; See? Wolf print, dog print, and those over there. All wolf prints."

Venter nodded his head as he listened. "I get it, Harold. There are different prints."

"Exactly." Came the studious reply.

Venter stood back from where the carcass lay. "I'm confused about this. I thought you said that wolves and dogs do not exist together? The wolf is from the wild, and the dog is domesticated."

Harold grunted and straightened his body. "Well, I don't remember saying it like that, but logically speaking, they can't easily coexist."

"Then what in hell is going on?" Venter demanded.

McNab shrugged as he looked further around. "There can only be one of two explanations. The first is the harder one to believe. They banded together to bring down this calf, ripped it, and took off without completely devouring it, I might add. But, that make little sense.'

"Or?"

"The second is more plausible. The dogs, or wolves, arrived after each other. The prints around the calf do not tell us. Either way, it is a guess."

"Your best guess, Harold? You're the expert. Which is it?" Venter asked with his frustration rising.

Nesbitt slowly raised his eyes at the hills that stretched up from the back of the field. After a time in silent deliberation, he strolled back to where Venter stood near the fence. "Best guess is the wolves arrived, and the dogs came later. The dogs may have been foraging for food. They waited until the wolves left."

"But they left it alone! It is not devoured!" Venter pointed to the carcass. "Same as the bull!"

"No, that's not quite correct. Some of it has been eaten," Nesbitt replied calmly as he pointed to several areas of the carcass, which had since bled out. There may be another explanation, but to be honest, Tom, I am running out of ideas."

Venter nodded because it left little for discussion. "Either way, a dead calf, bull, and now Marvin is saying sheep were attacked at the Romano farm."

McNab pointed with his hand across the expanse of heavily wooded hillsides, rising sharply from the back of the fence line to the light gray granite cliffs, imposing and foreboding above the tree line.

Sentinel ridges protected the farm from the northern weather and the full force of winds that cascaded above and over the escarpment. "Perhaps the hills hold less prey?" He said, almost to himself.

"That would be unlikely, Harold. Hunters still go on weekend excursions and return with a few deer and jackrabbits."

"Yes, that does not make sense, does it?" Harold said vaguely.

"So, it is wolves and dogs, but not together?" Venter added.

"It makes sense that wolves are present. Dogs may arrive afterward to inspect and eat the kill. Dogs can scent up to five miles away, so a kill would attract them if the wind blew in the right direction."

"Yet, I have never seen a wild dog or a goddam wolf, for that matter."

McNab stared blankly at him. "Yes, you are right. It is rare to hear of a sighting."

"Dogs are fed." Venter replied quickly.

McNab nodded his head. "Their owners feed them. But, anything is possible if there are wild dogs."

Venter waited for him to finish. "Why would a pack of dogs or wolves follow each other? You said the attack indicated the bull was at the wrong place and time. So, with this calf, why here? Why now?"

"How far are we away from the bull carcass in Essex?"

Venter pursed his lips as he considered it. "It's more like twenty-five miles away. It depends on which route from there to here. Why do you ask?"

McNab checked his watch. "The bull carcass is at the south end of town, and this farm is much further West. From experience, we know that established wolf packs usually live and stay within a specific territory, and they guard their territory carefully. If another wolf outside the family strays into the area, they confront and dominate it."

"So, this area is a territory?"

"Maybe it is, " he replied with a frown. "Wolf territories range in size based on what prey is available and, of course, the seasonal change in prey. A wolf territory can be large, maybe up to fifty square miles."

Venter checked the area just beyond the fence. It lay heavily wooded with a thick green and brown brush, which seemed impenetrable. "So, you're saying it's the same pack on the move? Is that possible?"

Harold thought about it momentarily. "It's certainly possible."

"Have you come across this before? Ever?" Venter asked him as his mind searched for a reasonable answer.

Nesbitt shrugged as he looked around for the last time. Finally, he moved across to where Venter was standing and patted his shoulder as they moved back to the cruiser, which sat beyond the gate. "I can't see what else would cause this killing," he said.

"Wolves kill to eat?" Venter replied calmly. "So, if hunger is not the reason, why would they kill for the hell of it? And there are no wild dogs around here or wolves last time I looked."

"There is now." McNab said flatly.

"Then where the hell are they?" Venter asked flatly.

Harold shook his head. "I don't know."

The wind picked up. In the distance, Venter could hear the unmistakable sound of leaves and bush bending as the gust rushed through the bushland on the hills above the field. Suddenly, his eyes picked up movement in the bushes; just a flicker of change appeared in the corner of his eye.

He stopped momentarily to look back again and finally saw a further movement at the back fence. "Over there, Harold, over there!" He shouted as he moved back to the gate.

As McNab joined him, Tom pointed towards the low brush near the fence uprights close to a large oak that spread its shade across almost twenty yards of the perimeter.

"Can you see it?" His finger pointed towards a moving mass of gray fur, almost inconspicuous, creeping through the long grass. Finally, they could make out the form of a large, gray wolf, moving slowly and cautiously. It bent its legs to keep low as it half-crawled through the fence wire and made its way across the field.

As the two of them watched the wolf stopped, stooped low in the grass, and raised its snout above the grass heads before moving slowly through the field.

"Look at the size of that thing, Harold?" He tugged on the vet's sleeve. "My God, that is one enormous wolf. I didn't know they could be that big."

McNab nodded in response, keeping his eyes on the wolf as it slipped through the high grass at the back of the field. "That wolf is the size of two large dogs put together," McNab said softly. "At least the wind is on our backs. It can't sense us."

Venter heard the wolfs low growl as it crouched toward the calf carcass. "You see it?"

McNab nodded in agreement. "The question is, where are the others?"

"Stay here, Harold. I won't be long." Venter moved quickly back to the cruiser, pulled his old rifle from its mount at the back of the cruiser, and returned. He loaded two cartridges and aimed.

Harold put his hand up and pushed the rifle away. "There is no need to kill it. It is marking the area. It is simply foraging."

Venter stared at McNab as he slowly pulled the rifle off the top of the gate. He watched as the wolf roamed around the calf carcass, sniffing and growling. It stopped quickly, raising its head again to snuffle the air. It stooped to rip a piece of flesh from the neck of the prone calf, gulping it down as it let out a deep growl.

Venter turned slightly and dropped his cartridge belt to the ground with a thud. "Damn." He whispered as he cursed his carelessness.

McNab stood back several steps as he watched the wolf. "The wind is changing."

Venter guessed its length to be at least six feet. It had long legs, a broad skull tapering to a narrow muzzle. Long canine teeth showed when it raised its snout to sniff the air. The fur was dark gray, with some white interspersed on its tapered back. He watched as it moved stealthily through the grass.

"What now?" He asked McNab.

"Nothing. It will take off soon enough."

Venter nodded unconvincingly as he replaced the rifle on top of the gate. He waited.

The wolf moved forward until it was twenty feet from where they stood at the other side of the farm gate. The closer it moved, the more agitated it became, finally stopping some fifteen feet away.

Venter could feel a distinct disturbance in the air. Deep growls from the wolf resonated around them as it changed direction. They watched it cautiously as the wolf moved into a crouched position, the hair on the back of its neck rising.

"It's going to attack!" Venter whispered, not daring to speak out loud.

"Wait, wait." McNab replied. "Look over there!" Venter followed his hand gesture to another wolf that entered the back of the field through the wire fence and towards the calf.

Momentarily, it stopped and let out a wild howl. The wolf nearest Venter turned with a snarl and sprinted towards the back of the paddock with the other wolf in tow. Within seconds they disappeared into the brush on the lower part of the hill.

"Timber wolves." McNab said quietly.

"I've never seen one in the county until now," Venter let out a sigh of relief as he and McNab turned to walk back to the cruiser. "That was the alpha of the pack," Harold said, seemingly unperturbed by the confrontation.

"How do you know that?"

"Well, studies have shown that, contrary to popular belief, the alpha is not the most aggressive or violent partner. The alpha moves around with an air of confidence and authority and displays leadership. The one at the back? That's the alpha. That is why the other one took off after it barked and howled. It was simply following orders."

"Would that first wolf attack us if the alpha did not turn up?" Venter asked as he turned towards the cruiser. He was happy to be moving back to the safety of the car.

McNab followed him, keeping an eye on the sides of the old dirt road and pasture. "Unlikely. It was simply protecting its territory. That is why it stalked us."

Venter nodded, unconvinced but relieved to be in the cruiser and on his way. "So, you are saying the wolf we just encountered would have ignored us and left us alone."

"Probably."

"Probably?" Venter questioned.

"Well, we were in its territory."

"I can't tell you how much that comforts me," Venter replied sarcastically. "At least we have proven there are wolves in the district, and Nesbitt was right about the wolf prints under the bull. "We need to alert the district."

McNab shrugged as he wound down the window. "We won't see them again."

"I can tell you Harold, hunger can't be the reason."

Well, Tom, I can't think of another explanation."

"I can?"

McNab diverted his attention from the calf carcass and looked directly at Venter. "Which is?"

"These packs are not killing for food. They are killing for the hell of it."

"That does not make sense, sheriff. Animals are highly evolved. They don't kill for the heck of it."

Venter nodded and immediately decided to direct Rusk to alert those he knew on the farms and ranches of the possibility of a wolf pack in the district. He felt no need to let McNab know.

CHAPTER 27

Rusk spent over an hour calming the Romano sisters of their hysteria over the killing of their stock and reassuring them the wolves and dogs would likely not return. They did not possess a telephone, so he promised to report the issue to McNab when he saw him.

The sisters pleaded with him to stay for the night to guard against the wolves return. He patiently checked the perimeter of the field and the pen after assisting Meg and Jamie in pulling the dead carcasses out of the enclosure towards a ditch they had dug using the tractor late that morning. He checked his revolver and the rounds in his belt, and walked around the general area. There was little to see, so he returned to the house.

The sisters had said they saw wolves and dogs in the attack. He inspected the area. Maybe they were dog prints, he thought to himself. Maybe coyotes. What else could they be? Maybe small wolves, but he noticed the larger indents held the distinctive paw pattern.

After promising to return, he finally pulled himself away from the two women, who tried to convince him to stay when he told them he was leaving under orders. He walked quickly to the cruiser in case they tried to stop him, and made his way out to the main road. He clicked on the two-way, and finally, he heard a crackle. "Beth, you there?"

"Damn thing." That is all he heard. "Why in hell is this thing not working? Marvin, Marv?"

"I'm here, Beth."

"This thing keeps going on the blink. It's worse today than yesterday. It seems there is crackling all the time. "Say again, you coming in, over?"

"Soon. That pack of wolves hit the Romano farm pretty hard. I have no idea if they are the same ones that took down Carter's bull. They savaged some sheep. The sisters heard the carnage and fought them off by firing at them. They reckon they hit one. I looked for blood, but nothing to be found. If you speak to the sheriff, let him know. Might have been dogs there as well."

"Still can't hardly hear you, Marv. You a long way out?"

"Far enough." He called back.

"I'm getting worried about going home tonight." She said through the crackling line.

"No, you'll be fin……"

Beth heard the first words and tried to reconnect without success. She was sick and tired of the two-way cutting out all the time. Over the last several days, its connection was worse, if that was possible. "Goddam council, " she muttered to herself.

CHAPTER 28

Under hushed orders from the sheriff, Rusk visited several properties closest to the town area and the bull kill. He stopped briefly at each farm or ranch and explained the presence of wolves, with the warning to be careful.

The cruiser rose to the top of a long hill as Rusk stared at a lone farmhouse in the distance. His final visit before returning to the office. Like bursts of sunlight, long-forgotten memories of hot summer days on the field, playing minor league baseball with the son of the man he was about to visit, entered his mind.

Fred Milbrook was the older brother he had never had as Marvin grew up. He looked up to Fred and wanted desperately to be like him. As he reached the age of fourteen, Marvin's parents relocated to Texas, where he grew from a young boy to a young man.

The memories remained. He and Fred sprinting to the kitchen to find cookies and homemade lemonade on the table and a motherly hug. Some hours later, usually around dusk, Marvin's father would pick him up, mouth a few pleasantries, and take him home. Once home, he would usually sit on the stoop, exhausted by the day, sated by the late afternoon treats, and just a little sore in his legs.

By the time circumstances returned him to Essex, Fred had disappeared from the face of the earth. He took off to war in the first intake of 1941, destined to fight on the fields of Europe with the zealousness that his father said could only accompany inexperienced youth. The news came back quickly.

Fred was not on army maneuvers or a glorious battle, but in an accident where two jeeps collided after an American soldier drank too much at the local pub and drove down the wrong side of the road. The drunk driver caused a head-on collision with the other jeep, driven by

Fred, resulting in the deaths of all involved, including a British sergeant-major who was in the car.

When Jack Milbrook was informed by telegram of Fred's death, he shook his head and walked away, unable to discuss the issue again. His mother, Mildred, went into a deep state of grief that verged on obsession with photos and old letters on display around the house and a constant melancholy that held a morbid stench in the air to anyone who spent time in the home. She wore black until the day of her death.

Marvin overshot the old road leading to the house by several yards before he stopped, reversed, and made his way down the four-hundred-yard drive to the homestead on a pebble-strewn road.

It had been months since he had seen the house. As he looked closely, the pristine condition of the property he remembered in his youth had irrevocably changed, and not for the better. Flaking paint, withered clapboards, and a front window, broken and unrepaired showed the state of the farmhouse before him.

As he neared the front door, the looming presence of Jack Milbrook came behind him and clapped one large hand on his shoulder. Marvin was short, and the man beside him made him appear even smaller. "Hello Marv, you're a long way out. What brings you out here?"

Marvin looked at him with a smile that was not returned. Jack had gained a heavy beard since he last saw him and an emptiness in his eyes he remembered. Marvin turned to face him. "Well, we've got issues with stock being taken down by what appears to be wolves, and the sheriff has asked me to alert the district. You don't have a phone, so a visit is the next best way of saying howdy and a warning to be on the lookout."

"You talking about out here, the ranch?"

Marvin shook his head as he pointed towards town. "Not these parts, but you never know. They took down a bull around the back of those old warehouses South of town, and got into sheep at the Romano farm."

"The sisters? Did they see them?"

"Yep, and fired on them, but I don't know if they hit one. There was no blood outside of the pen."

"Well, I got my problems."

"What?" Marvin asked, instantly wondering if it was wolves.

Milbrook turned on his heels. "Follow me." As they walked, Marvin noticed how gray Jack's hair had become. Marvin followed him to the back of the home, and as they were about to turn the corner, Marvin stopped at the sight on the ground. "What the hell is this?" he asked as he stepped over several birds lying disheveled on the short grass.

"That's nothing, Marv. Come around here."

In front of him, dozens of birds lay lifeless on the ground. Some lay on top of each other, while others were spread out on the grass up to what he guessed was ten feet or more apart. "Goddam, Jack, what the hell happened?"

"Beats me." Milbrook surveyed the scene with a strange look on his face. "I ain't seen anything like it in my life, Marv. You ever seen this?"

Marvin shrugged his shoulders in answer as he looked around at the carpet of mashed and broken birds lying on the ground, and the blood on the wall of the house. "They flew into the wall?" he asked.

Milbrook gestured with his hands in the air and towards the wall. "They flew close together up there, and then straight into that wall. All of em"

"Why in tarnation would birds fly into a goddam wall? Did they come out of nowhere?"

Milbrook nodded. "Exactly, Marv. Out of the air, and hit the wall. For no reason! That's what gets me."

Marvin looked towards the fields at the back of the house. "You haven't seen any wolves?"

"What the hell have wolves got to do with all this?" he asked, gesturing to the house.

"Don't know, Jack. Strange things are happening. That's all."

Milbrook shook his head. "Nope. I ain't seen a wolf around these parts for maybe fifteen years or longer. I thought they had moved or died off."

"When did this happen?"

"I saw a flock of these finches flying late yesterday afternoon. They settled on the fence and took off again, following each other in a strange pattern. They had disappeared by the time I went in for dinner last night. Well, I made breakfast this morning and started hearing strange noises, and all these birds just massed up and flew around in the sky, up there. Then! Bang, into the side of the house. Damn, did they make a sound! I thought it was someone hammering the wall until the windows broke. Have a gander at those windows!"

Marvin walked gingerly, trying not to step on any of the dead birds as he checked the back of the house. Five of the six windows barely held fractured shards of glass in their weather-beaten frames, and in several, the whole lower pane and some of the top pane were missing. "They flew straight through the glass as well?"

"Some," came the reply. "I threw those that were left flapping on the pile. They had no chance. I am going to put a lot of them in bags and bury them. Strangest thing, huh? I grabbed my rifle as I thought it was an attack by something, but then this happened."

Marvin just shook his head, unable to understand what he was seeing. "What time was it, Jack?"

Milbrook stretched his arms as he considered it. "Maybe around seven, but I don't use a watch, and I don't get up real early anymore. Maybe eight. I'm not sure."

"They look like scrub finches?" Marvin asked as he walked around the birds. One lay on its front, almost as if it might fly off.

"Yep. The trees are full of them around here, quails and house finches mainly. These finches are a small bird and fast flyers, so why they piled into this house, or any house, is beyond me. They broke their necks from the force of the collision; that's what killed them, except those who hit the windows and got torn to shreds."

"No warning? Just flew into the wall? Rusk kept his eyes on the birds as he spoke.

Milbrook looked at Rusk and shrugged his shoulders. "Goddam waste. There's an eagle over there as well," Millbrook motioned to the other end of the house directly below one of the broken windows. An eagle lay on the ground, looking like it was asleep.

Marvin nudged it with his boot as it lay motionless. 'You want help to clean this up?"

Milbrook gave him a thin smile. 'Nope, should be okay.'

"How many cattle you got out there, Jack?

"Only bout' three hundred. There is too much to take care of with Mildy not here and, well, you know the rest. I'm giving it up after these cattle go to market. Had enough, Marv. Only me left."

Marvin nodded lightly. "How you going, Jack, out here by yourself? You don't get lonely?"

Milbrook shrugged his large shoulders as Marvin followed him towards the house. "Nah, I got the radio. The cattle keep me busy."

They entered the back door and walked to the lounge where the silent embers of the previous night's fire lay faintly glowing in the fireplace. Window glass lay smashed on the floorboards. Rusk could see minute traces of blood on the internal sills. The floor had been wiped down. "That's some serious damage." Marvin said softly as he looked around.

Milbrook silently nodded and began walking out of the house. "Only glass, Marv, and glass is replaceable. Not sure about that many birds. Damn thing, these birds." He raised his voice a little to ensure Marvin heard him. "Such a waste."

"That's for sure." Came the stilted reply because Marvin could not think of a time he had heard of such a thing. He walked out the back to inspect the dead birds lying like a carpet of red and speckled feathers. "You sure you don't want help to clean this up?" Rusk asked, wondering if Milbrook had the energy to do it.

"I'll get to it. I've had other things to do. If I leave em long enough, they'll make good fertilizer, don't you think? " Milbrook half smiled as he stood with his arms crossed. "What are you going to do about the wolf sighting?"

"Good question, Jack. We've seen the prints so we know they are here." Rusk said with authority in his voice. "The Romano sisters had at least five sheep killed, and Bob Carter suffered the loss of both his bull and calf. We got an old dog breeder to look, and he says they are wolf prints. You need to keep an eye on the cattle."

"What did Harold say?"

"He agrees. He also reckons they'll move off to the hills soon enough."

Milbrook pointed skywards as he spoke. "Yep, sounds like McNab. He always takes the path of least resistance."

Rusk followed to where he pointed. "Can't see anything but blue sky, Jack."

Milbrook looked up and around the sky for several seconds before dropping his arm. "Well, I'll be damned, Marv. There were strange circles around the sun this morning, and now they have disappeared. They were up there, circles that looked like clouds, but noticeable in the sky. Where the hell have they gone, I wonder?"

Rusk looked up and back at Milbrook with a questioning look. "Strange circles? Tell you what, I'll will keep a lookout. I need to get back to the office. Now, you take care."

"Always welcome, Marv, you know that."

Marvin shook his hand as he got into the cruiser. "Holler if you need something, okay?"

"Will do, Marv, and good luck with the hunting."

"Might see you in church?"

"Doubt it. God hasn't been too good to me," Milbrook replied as he moved back from the cruiser and looked up at the increasing cloud. "Might be rain, " he said absently. "You know, I once read about whales that lose direction and beach themselves. You know, they die on the sand."

"So?" Rusk looked at him perplexed.

Well, the truth is, I have never read about birds losing their sense of direction and losing their lives by smashing full flight into the side of a house. Before they hit the wall, they were in full flight murmuration."

"What in hell does that mean?" Marvin asked quickly.

"They band together like a cloud and follow each other. This time, I guess, they followed each other into the side of the house. Why? Who in hell knows?"

Marvin looked at Milbrook, a man he had known for years, not knowing how to reply. Wolves, dogs, now birds? What the hell? "Jack, I've never heard of it, but I will tell the sheriff and McNab."

"You do that," Milbrook said abruptly, almost like it would be a waste of time.

Marvin waved his hand out the window as he drove away from the house. In the rear-view mirror, he saw a man who looked lonely and broken after losing his son and wife.

Jack waved as the disappearing cruiser. He rubbed his sore back and ambled to the barn to search for a sack so he could pick up the birds. He wondered if he was imagining the circles around the sun that morning.

CHAPTER 29

Venter pulled his hat off with a sigh as he sat at the diner counter. Thoughts paraded through his mind, not the least of which was McNab's attitude to culling the wolves. He saw Jane walking up towards him. "Just a coffee?" she asked. He appeared deep in thought. "Yep," Came the reply.

"Nice to see you too." She said with a soft voice. "After the other night, I thought I might get flowers, at the very *least*." She whispered, with emphasis on the last word of the sentence.

Venter nodded slowly. "I plead guilty." He smiled as she poured a full cup in front of him. "Perhaps another dinner this coming Saturday?"

"You paying?" She leaned over the counter, surveying him with intent, brown eyes.

"Of course. What sort of man do you think I am?"

"A preoccupied sheriff with too many issues on his mind. It's time to take a load off Tom and smell the roses. Coffee? That's all you want?" she said with a wide smile. "You look like you have the weight of the world on your shoulders. How about a piece of pie? It's fresh this morning, and if you ask nicely, you can have it for free."

Venter smiled back at her and nodded. "It's been a hell of a day."

The door opened abruptly. Venter looked up as he pushed it open and returned to placing more sugar in his coffee. Crooks looked unkept, with a long, bushy beard that reached to his chest, and a large stomach hanging precariously over his pants. With deliberate ease, he moved up to the bench, sat with a grunt leaving several seats between him and Venter, who was sipping his coffee contemplatively.

He looked at Eddie Crooks and nodded as he received one in return. "Hey, Eddie, how's business going?"

"Like everything else in this goddam town, sheriff, it's slow. It seems everyone is heading to Winslow on the eighty-five to get their gas."

Venter nodded. "Must be enough local business? The sheriff's department gives you at least two tanks worth per week, right?"

Crooks gave him a hard look. "You can't run a business on two tanks per week, sheriff. If it weren't for the farmers, I would be broke. Say, have you heard anything about the lighting in the sky above the hills late last night? Weird, if you ask me. Waving to and fro, and then disappearing."

"When was that?" Venter asked with a feigned interest.

"I saw it last night. It was around ten. It lasted quite a while and then disappeared. It was the strangest thing, if you ask me. Like waves, green waves in the sky."

Venter shook his head as he took a sip of coffee. It felt good as it slid down his throat. "I have looked up and seen nothing except the stars. It's probably the reflection of camp fires."

"I don't think campfires move around like waves on a pond, sheriff."

Jane poured coffee for Eddie, then replaced the coffeepot to make a fresh batch and returned. She poured a new cup for Venter and stopped next to him. "Are you listening, Tom?"

"I am." He replied defensively.

"Campers? I am told the light also pulses, sorta like turning around every little while and then disappearing, only to return. What campfire does that?"

Venter thought about it for a moment. "Well, a large campfire and the wind moving the trees make the light look like it is moving on and off. That would be my guess."

"Then the light disappears! That is when the campers douse their fire, right? "Jane replied flatly as she joined the conversation.

Eddie downed his coffee after pouring cream into the cup. "I gotta get back to the pumps."

"This light in the evening sky? It could just be a natural occurrence, like starlight or something," Venter added as he rose from the stool.

"Really, sheriff?"

Eddie smiled as he dropped several coins on the counter and took off towards the door. "See you all later." He called out as he left.

Jane moved slowly over to where Venter was sitting, leaning casually over the counter towards him. She put her hand softly on his forearm.

"What?" He asked sourly.

"Don't be like that, Tom. People around here have concerns, and word spreads fast. You got a bull taken down by wolves, at least that is what everyone is saying. Wolves and dogs have been sighted at the Romano sisters farm, killing their sheep. Bob Carter lost his prize bull and calf as well. You were there at the time to see the calf. So, you saw one of the wolves up close?"

"I did." Venter sat back and stared at her in amazement. "Can't see how you might have found any of that out, Jane. You must have sources I don't know about."

"The whole damn town knows, Tom. How do you keep that sort of thing secret? Why would you want to keep any of it secret, anyway?"

"McNab told us to keep it quiet in case it spooked the town."

"Don't listen to McNab, Tom, the town is already on edge because of what everyone is hearing, and people get worried. It's their livestock and their livelihood. Remember, you are in a town where nothing, and I mean nothing, really ever happens. Wolves is always gonna be big news." She placed a small plate with a piece of blueberry pie in front of him with a clean fork that she wiped with a dish towel before she laid it down.

"Thanks, " he replied with a nod. "Yep, I guess you are right. Bad news travels faster."

Jane smiled at him. "I thought you were coming in to ask me on another date?"

Venter smiled as he sipped his coffee. "I did. I offered dinner on Saturday. Maybe we split out of Essex and head over to Winslow. There are a couple of real good places over there."

"You want to risk running into your ex-wife?"

Venter thought momentarily and shrugged as he cut off a piece of pie. " Frankie? Doubtful that might happen, Jane."

She smiled at him as she refilled a coffee down the other end of the counter. Looking out to the sidewalk, she saw Rusk walking towards the diner from the other side of the road. "Marvin's on his way in." She said softly.

Venter hardly listened. The more he ruminated on the past several days, the more he could not escape the fact that weird incidents were increasing around the town. Wolves, unseen in years, attacked a defenseless bull, leaving it mutilated. McNab made it clear; wolves and dogs could not join together, yet the Romano sisters saw both together as they attacked their sheep. What the hell was the green, wavy light in the sky? He shook his head softly. It made no sense at all.

Marvin strolled in and slumped next to Venter. He pulled his hat off in a practiced motion and called out to Jane for coffee. "I just saw something real strange." He said in a soft voice as he looked directly at Venter.

Brought back from his thoughts, Venter looked at him blankly. "Good news for a change?"

Marvin pulled a pack of camel cigarettes from his pocket and lit one. He leaned towards Venter and whispered. "I went to the Jack Milbrook farm earlier. You won't believe me when I tell you, sheriff. One of the worst things I have ever seen."

Venter looked directly at him. "What? Not wolves?"

"Nope. Birds?"

Venter looked at him warily. "What the hell are ya talking about Marv?"

"Dead birds, sheriff. Hundreds of them on the ground."

"How could that happen, Marv?" Venter asked him hoping the answer would be simple.

"They flew into the goddam windows and the side wall of his house! You've never seen anything like it. Finches, they were, you know, the ones with the red beak. It was like an enormous swarm just smacked into the back of the house and killed themselves."

Venter pulled back from the bench. He looked at Rusk, trying to visualize what he was hearing. "Are you kidding, Marv?"

"No joke, sheriff. Looked like more than a hundred of the little things."

"Birds flew into his house? Does he know what caused it?"

"He says it just happened. He heard a thump on the wall and then another, so he walked out the back to investigate, and as he looked up, he saw a huge flock of finches, like starlings in evening murmuration, rising and falling."

"Murmur, what? What the hell is that?"

Marvin puffed his chest out slightly as he answered. "Well, sheriff, you know starlings at night when they go into those patterns at dusk. You know, rising and falling and following each other, well, that is called murmuration."

Venter looked at his deputy with increased admiration. "Well, there you go, Marv. Learn a new thing every day."

"Anyways, the birds danced up in the sky and then swooped down together to go full flight into the wall, which killed most of them. Jack ended the misery of the ones that crashed but didn't die."

"For no reason? Were they pursued by something?"

Marvin shook his head. "I think he was still in shock when I got there," Marv responded. "He is at a loss to understand why."

"I told you, Tom!" Jane said as she overheard the whispering. "Strange things are happening around here, and no one is anything about them."

Venter looked at her. "What would you have me do, Jane? Stop a hundred birds flying into the back wall of a house?" He shrugged as he looked at Marvin, who took a sip of his coffee. "Damndest thing, Marv."

Rusk lit a cigarette and took a long drag. He leaned back on the stool and shook his head. " It might just be a natural accident, sheriff."

"Accident?" Jane scoffed as she returned, placing an ashtray next to him. "You are blind, the two of you. Things are happening around here and you need to find out what!"

"It's not our business, Jane. We uphold the law, not protect citizens from goddam wolves or birds for that matter."

"What about the wave light in the sky?" She demanded.

Venter turned to his deputy. "You saw the light, Marv."

Rusk shrugged. "Nope. Probably campfires."

"And pigs will fly," Jane commented as she moved down to the other end of the counter.

"You want to bring Winslow into this?" Rusk looked at Venter with a shrug. "Do we need them for this?"

"Nope. All the mayor will do is complain that we aren't working on policing business. I'll go back and see McNab and tell him about the birds. Maybe he has an answer. I can't think of any other solution."

Rusk pushed his coffee cup towards Jane, who was heading down the bench, refilling as she went. "Yep, I agree."

Venter turned his attention to his deputy, who exhaled a lungful of smoke. "When you spoke to the Romano sisters about the attack, they agreed that dogs and wolves were after the sheep. Right?"

Rusk nodded. "Yep. Dogs and wolves together."

"McNab said that isn't possible."

"He did, but that doesn't make it impossible, does it?"

"What are their names again?"

"Meg is the older one, and Jamie is the one who manages most of the farm."

"Maybe you should go out and have another look in the morning. It might be wise to calm them down. We don't want complaints"

Rusk nodded. "I'll head out early and then to the eighty-five."

"They got a phone?"

Rusk shook his head. "Nope."

"How many did you end up informing about the wolves?"

"Six properties, including Jack Milbrook. I went to several others near the eighty-five turnoff, but no one was around. Those I spoke to haven't seen a wolf in many years. One of them had never seen a wolf, but they are a long way from the hills."

Venter nodded as he downed the last of his coffee. "Good work, I'm heading off to see McNab. You might as well come along, but I need to go to the office first."

Rusk nodded, picked up his hat from the counter and followed Venter.

CHAPTER 30

Venter sat at his desk in a less-than-conciliatory mood about the developing issues of predatory wolves. He had never seen any wolves or coyotes in the entire time he had worked in Essex. He picked up his hat and motioned to Marvin at his desk. The two walked briskly toward the major intersection. Within minutes, he stood outside McNabs" office.

The old glass-fronted shop with a dirty window adorned with the words 'Veterinarian Clinic' had held McNabs office for over forty years. Venter waited for Marvin to catch up as he stood on the sidewalk surveying the town road and the shops. Ford pickups and two delivery trucks took up some of the spaces on the road.

Together, they opened the door into a well-worn reception area. A light tinkle came from a bell above the door. The room appeared sparse. It held five wooden chairs on one side and an old desk on the other. The walls were adorned sparsely, with two aged university degrees in gold frames and a large poster of a Hereford bull with a blue ribbon around its massive neck noting "first prize" 1937 beneath the aging photo.

McNab came out from the back. "Just the man I wanted to see. I've been getting calls from people saying you and Marv have been out alerting people about the wolves. And dogs, for that matter! I thought we had an understanding, Tom." McNab's face was red, and his tone aggressive.

"Now, now, Harold." Venter said to calm him down. "Only the farms and one ranch closest to the warehouse. They need to be on the lookout."

McNab pointed to the chairs that lined the wall, and as they sat down together, Venter sat close to him. "Why are you here?' McNab asked quickly.

THE WOLVES OF ESSEX

"Marv, tell Harold about the birds."

Rusk told McNab about his visit to Milbrook and what he witnessed at the back of the house, the broken windows, the dead and dying birds inside and outside the farmhouse. "Out of nowhere." Marvin added at the end of the story.

McNab listened patiently until Marvin finished. He adjusted his spectacles as he looked at the two of them. "Jack Milbrook is okay?" He asked as Marvin nodded his head. "Well, it's nothing more than a natural occurrence. It can happen to any species. They lose bearing and go off course, which is usually quite unnerving. It's a pity about the finches, but they will breed and come back into force. That is mother nature's way."

"There were more than a hundred birds!" Marvin replied.

"Quite." McNab slowly nodded his head. "As I said, many species have the same issue. Whales beach themselves and birds go off compass."

"What about the wolves and dogs?" Venter asked quickly. "You know about the Romano farm. We need to force the issue and send out information to everyone in the county, Harold. We'll do it nice and slow, no rush and no excitement. Otherwise it will just take up more time, later." Venter folded his arms waiting for the response.

McNab removed his glasses, cleaned them, looked at them through the light, and replaced them. "Now listen, sheriff, if you start telling everyone about these wolves, you will panic the town. Their immediate reaction will be that their entire stock is under attack, leading to unrest and fear, and the response will overrun me. People always overreact to threats, whether that threat is a few wolves or Bangs disease."

Marvin looked at the McNab. "What the hell is Bang's disease?"

McNab shook his head. "Don't worry about it, Marv. It's just another thing we have to keep an eye on when it comes to herds. I am saying that the townsfolk, farmers, and ranchers will get panicky, and

I am sure we don't want that issue. The people you have told are now trying to pass on the information, which can only cause uncertainty."

Venter waited a moment before he responded. "Harry, you saw the bull; you know about the Romano farm, and we have been to Bob Carter's place to view the calf, where we saw wolves on the upper paddock."

McNab nodded. "Well, as I said, Tom. These isolated attacks may be the work of a pack of wild wolves who have run out of prey and are going for easier food. They will return to the hills, I am sure of it."

"I am not convinced. The townsfolk, the ranchers and farmers, are they safe?"

"Of course!" McNab replied defiantly and aggressively. You're the expert, are you? These wolves have foraged down here and will take off to the hills of their own accord. They are wild animals. Eventually, they will return to their habitat."

"If they don't?"

"They will."

Venter could feel his anger rising. "Just supposing they don't, Harold. What then?"

McNab looked at him blankly as he thought momentarily about the question. "They are wild animals, Tom, and while they aren't protected, like eagles, they are still wild. Therefore, we need to be careful about killing any species."

"They are killing stock. You don't care about that?" Venter said bluntly.

"All animals serve a purpose. Wolves, coyotes, and mountain lions, prey on weak and slow animals, keeping the *system* in place. The strong survive, and the weak die off. But they will return to their territory. It's in their DNA."

Venter removed his hat and dropped it on the chair beside him.

"What *system* are you talking about, Harold?"

"Nature, Tom. Every animal plays its part. The world is tied together; the trees, the insects and animals, the air we breathe. It all ties together. The real problem is us. We are the ones dominating the world. There is a cost to all wildlife."

Venter stared at McNab briefly. "There may be a 'system' as you call it, Harry, but the wolves are killing defenseless animals. The bull is dead, as are sheep and calves. That's enough evidence to take them out. Don't you agree?"

"They are on a foraging expedition. Maybe they are heading back right now."

"Harold, it's time to show some sense in all this. If they are on a killing spree, they must be stopped. This is your area, not mine, so why don't you take it over?"

McNab looked surprised at Venter's anger. "I am the town vet. My job is to advise." McNab looked at him placatingly. "Let it be, Tom. It will resolve itself!"

"For Chrissakes, Harold, the wolves are *not* eating their prey. They are simply killing them in vicious attacks!"

"There may be a reason for that, Tom."

"The bull is hardly easy prey." Venter said in response.

"The attacks are just isolated occurrences. I doubt they will be repeated."

"I don't think it is worth taking that risk!" Venter said gruffly. He shifted in his seat uneasily. "My concern is they will move towards the town."

McNab shrugged. "Why in hell would they do that, sheriff? There are many recorded instances throughout California of wolves coming down from their territory to forage. Give it a couple of days and see how it goes. But, returning to my earlier point, it may be better to leave off telling the town. If they get wind of it, they will think the worst and, except for Bob Carter's bull at the disused area of Essex, the attacks have been well out of Essex. I am sure you have better things to do with your time?"

Rusk shrugged as he lit a cigarette. "We run the risk that the community is not told, and the issues keep occurring." He blew a long stream of smoke into the air.

McNab motioned to the door. "No smoking in here, son. Outside with that."

Marvin got up as requested and disappeared out the door as Venter stood and put on his hat. "My concern is the townsfolk. That's my responsibility."

"I get that, sheriff," McNab spoke consolingly. "I am sure everything will calm down. Okay? Trust me on this."

Venter reluctantly nodded his head. "Okay, Harold. You win this time."

"Good, " came McNab's reply. He rose from his seat and put a consoling hand on Venter's shoulder. "There is no point in stirring things up. A loss of a bull and a few sheep? I am sure Essex can put up with those losses. This wolf issue will quieten, and they will return to their territory. Of that, I am quite sure."

Venter remained unconvinced. "If the killing continues, we start culling. If it involves safety for the townsfolk, we will come out blasting."

McNab gave him a stern look and walked towards the surgery door. "Patience, Tom. They will disappear."

As they walked out together, Venter turned to Rusk. "I don't believe what McNab is saying. As far as I'm concerned, a wolf is an animal that is born to kill. We need to be careful."

CHAPTER 31

Charlie Nesbitt guessed it was very early that morning, around three, when he heard the unmistakable sound of howling assaulting the night air. The sound awoke him suddenly as he lay on his back on his camp stretcher.

The high-pitched sound drowned the low tones of crickets and frogs in the calm night air. It sounded like several packs of wolves were joined in the spine-tingling serenade. Nesbitt slowed his breath and listened. Perhaps they were higher up, towards the forested hills. Wolves worried him. They were the natural enemies of dogs, and his deerhounds were his livelihood.

After a brief discussion with Jesse, early that morning, he decided to cancel the dog show and head home. He felt an increasing urgency to get up and start work. At first light, he began to set up the dog trailer with new straw and clean cages to take his dogs back on the road to Pomona. The last thing he needed was a confrontation between a roaming wolf pack and his deerhounds. His dogs would fight and in all likelihood come off second-best.

Pomona was a long drive. He had completed it many times over the years. Pulling a trailer with seven dogs meant heavy going in any weather. Drivers inexplicably become less courteous on dirt roads where passing pickups, and trucks rarely yield to anything, including dog trailers.

On the return trips from wherever he set up his show, he would pull over on the side of the road in a favorable spot. He always pitched a tent, fed the group of dogs, and set up a bed for him and Jesse between two wool blankets to ward off the cold or inevitable insects that seemed to forage only at night.

He often thought to himself it would be a nice change, for once, to pull up in front of a comfortable motel and stay the night on clean sheets. He knew it was not a reality he would ever experience. He never seemed to have enough cash or to find a motor inn allowing dog trailers to park outside with them inside. So, he traveled with his dogs.

That morning, a cold fall wind from the north bit as it cascaded over the hills. It chilled him as he scattered the old hay from the cages around the tent area. The old tents, army issue, left marks on the ground from the lack of sunlight on the grass, and holes where tent pegs were driven into the ground.

Earlier in the morning, the dogs became agitated at the howling. He walked around talking to them, but they continued to whine despite his attempts to calm them down. Several of them growled menacingly at things they sensed in the distance. Since his Deerhounds sense of smell was ten thousand times more sensitive than his, he was hardly surprised at their unrest. They could smell the movements of wolves.

Looking around the back of the old showground towards the hills, he could see brilliant shafts of light spearing through the clouds. In his experience, it meant the weather was changing towards sun and a little more warmth. Good news.

With the care of an experienced dog trainer, he walked to each dog with a soft word and a pat on their muzzle and neck. Satisfied they were calm enough, he let them off the run, one by one. He cautioned them not to move further, and they complied with wagging tails and attentive posture.

Except for his lead dog, Marco, the rest stood their ground, sitting obediently and waiting patiently. Marco seemed unusually nervous and eager to get to the trailer. Nesbitt patted him affectionately on his head. The dog whined and howled at being cooped up in the trailer cage and now, for the first time, seemed eager to be put into his cage.

With practiced ease, Nesbitt led two young female staghounds to the trailer door. He picked them up and placed each in the smaller cages at the front, closing the cage doors as he did so. As he loaded the smallest of the two dogs, he saw Marco standing at attention, his nose high as he snuffled the air.

"Come on, Marco. Here, boy, come." Nesbitt called out with a whistle. He watched as the fur on Marco rose up. A low, menacing growl increased from its throat as he stood firmly before the other dogs. His eyes were fixed on the opposite side of the field.

Several other dogs started to whimper, and others looked quizzically at Marco and growled in unison. Suddenly, Nesbitt saw with horror what the dogs sensed. He stared, disbelieving at the sight.

Immediately, subconsciously, he stepped back several paces, looking across the field and then at his staghounds, who started to panic. Agitated and growling, they moved around. Nesbitt noted the hair on their backs had risen and they looked nervous and unable to sit still.

Nesbitt started to retreat to his tent as he sighted a pack of wolves—maybe eight or nine, he thought—sprinting at high speed from the forest end of the field directly towards his campsite. Even from the distance, he could hear the wolves growling savagely as they neared the middle of the showground field.

He thought feverishly for a moment as he watched in horror at the wolves bounding towards them. He realized he had little time to protect the dogs and his wife. The tents would not offer protection. He decided to get his dogs to the trailer cages to protect them. As he looked, he realized the deerhounds were darting in different directions despite him shouting desperately at them to follow him to the trailer.

He grabbed at his lead dog, but it took off, loping towards the oncoming pack. Nesbitt knew enough to know the action was certain suicide. "Jesse, Jesse!" he shouted as she walked outside the tent at the urgency of his voice.

He pointed to the wolves, who were moving at high speed past the middle area of the showground as they bounded in long strides in his direction. As she looked over, she screamed, "Oh, my God. Charlie, come on. We've got to get to cover." She immediately turned to the tent beside her. "Here. Here!" She shouted

"Not the tents. Come this way." He urged. Breathlessly, he grabbed her arm and moved quickly towards the trailer some twenty yards away, calling the dogs to move with him.

Panicked and spooked, the dogs moved quickly away from the oncoming wolves. One of the males followed Marco as he sprinted headlong towards the wolf pack that had reached a point less than forty yards away.

Nesbitt repeatedly called out to bring them to safety. "Marco, here, boy, here." He screamed at the top of his lungs. None of the dogs heeded his call. Four of them headed off toward the small stadium adjoining the tents while Marco, followed by another male, sprinted toward the lead wolf. In desperation, Nesbitt moved towards the trailer.

Suddenly, six wolves split off, following the largest of the pack. They were led by a giant gray wolf, almost half larger than the rest. They were headed directly to where he and Jesse stood near the trailer. He was undecided about what to do. He had no rifle or anything he could use against a charging wolf pack. What the hell could he do to fend them off?

The truck was on the other side of the pitched tents, and the pack had almost reached it. He realized the trailer was their only refuge. He grabbed his wife by the hand, pulling her to the rear of the trailer cages.

In the distance, he heard the anguished cries of his lead dog. While the other deerhounds barked and snarled, keeping a distance as they moved away from the wolf pack. One wolf attacked his lead dog, bowling it over onto the ground.

Finally, Nesbitt reached the trailer door pushing Jesse into the cage used for the larger dogs. Looking behind him in terror, he jumped into the cage beside her. He held the door closed with his finger around the door wire.

Jesse screamed in panic. "What the hell is going on, Charlie?"

Nesbitt felt sweat pouring off his head and shoulders. "I don't know, Jess." He uttered as his breathing subsided. He didn't know. He had never experienced anything like it.

CHAPTER 32

After some deliberation, Milbrook disposed of the birds by digging a trench towards the fence built parallel to the back of the house. The trench lay beside he rose bushes his wife had planted some years before. She loved the garden with its view to the hills beyond, sitting below the light gray granite of the upper reaches of the mountains surrounding the farm and most of Essex.

He carefully placed the finches into the bottom of the shoveled-out furrow by softly upending the bags he used to collect the dead and broken flock. He felt an overwhelming sadness as he looked down at the trough of tiny birds with their beautiful red beaks and bright neck feathers.

The finches lay nestled with several owls and a bald, headed eagle, lying pristinely on its side. The broad wings and beautiful feathers of the fallen eagle sat in perfect order, lying lifeless above the finches. What was the point of the act? He shook his head as he surveyed the loss of such magnificent creatures.

He was not a meticulous man by nature, but he kept a reasonable count of the finches that had suicided against the boards and those that had flown recklessly through the glass windows. He counted more than one hundred and fifty small finches had followed each other into the rigid boards.

Some of the less injured birds had died slowly. He wondered if they could have survived such a horrible collision? He had no choice but to wring the necks of the broken birds that lay, barely alive on the ground. It was the humane thing to do for those birds that lay in pain.

As a rancher for so many years the event had saddened him. There was little he could do but walk around, pick them up, and gently place them into the bottom of a sack. The load had become so heavy he had to drag it around on the grass with both hands.

The grassy area offered the evidence of the slaughter. Fragile, tiny feathers lost by the reckless birds stuck fast in the grass. As he picked up the remainder of the birds he watched the feathers as they moved softly in the breeze. Some lifted into the wind to be taken to a place of rest away from the carnage that littered the ground.

He shoveled the excess dirt back into the trench with infinite care, finally using the shovel head to flatten the ground. He noted with satisfaction that the grass would grow over the area, finishing near the troughs his wife had dug around the rose garden. The bird's resting place would be hardly visible from the house. A proper resting place.

Despite his bewilderment as to what caused the mass suicide, he felt relieved that there had been no reoccurrence of bird flocks forming in large groups. He had not heard a single bird call over the last day. That absence alone seemed strange. He realized he had not seen a bird in the sky or the trees since the headlong suicide of the flock into the wall. Perhaps, they had died somewhere else.

CHAPTER 33

Nesbitt slumped on the hay as he and Jesse pulled their cages shut. At least they had protection. In the distance they watched the marauding pack of growling, slavering wolves head across the final twenty yards to where they sat cramped and uncomfortable in the trailer cages built for dog's half their size.

Within several moments, the wolves reached them. As a group, they milled around the trailer, sniffing and snarling as they stalked Nesbitt and his wife. "Get outta here, get away," Nesbitt shouted in desperation and anger.

As he shouted, the largest of the pack launched at the side of the cage where Jesse sat, trying to hold on to the door wire. Its snout, foamed and dribbled saliva, barking savagely at the cage side with long, yellowed teeth, trying vainly to bite her. Each time it bit into the cage wall, it retreated and launched another vicious attack.

Horrified by the sight of the pack, they watched eight gray and black wolves stalk around the trailer. "Jesse, look at that." He watched in astonishment as his disheveled, seemingly friendly dogs returned to the trailer to sit with the restless wolf pack. Then, his lead dog appeared from the side of the tents and loped towards the cages.

As Marco approached he stopped and subordinated himself to the wolf next to him by lowering his front legs, waiting until the wolf moved. Then, without any resistance, he followed. As his dog neared, Nesbitt stared at him, incredulous at the scene he was witnessing. His lead dog should be mauled or dead.

He knew that fighting a full-grown wolf was suicide. Yet, the wolf and the wolf pack had let him live. His one-hundred-forty-pound dominant lead dog deferred to the wolf that trotted around the cages. As they neared the trailer, Nesbitt could not believe what he witnessed. Marco licked the wolf and finally sat back on his haunches.

He shook his head slowly, trying to comprehend what was happening around him as he watched the same large wolf move forward. It stood growling and baring its teeth, then moved before him, intently watching the cage. The wolf bared its teeth each time he moved position in the uncomfortably small area. Several times, it attacked the side of his cage in frustrated rage.

"What are we going to do, Charlie." Jesse whispered anxiously. "We can't stay here forever."

"It will be fine, Jess." Nesbitt said in an unconvincing tone. He sat motionless trying to figure out what to do. He opened the cage door slowly to see if there was any reaction. As it opened, one of the female wolves launched itself at the door, snarling and aggressive. He quickly pulled it shut and sat back towards the end of the cage away from the door. He watched as white bubbles of saliva dripped down the wire.

"Look." Jesse said, pointing to the other end of the trailer. Male wolves clustered around the trailer end where he had put the female deerhounds. They whimpered at the females through the cage walls, encouraging them to join them, but the cages were firmly shut. The largest wolf who had been guarding Nesbitt moved over to the front cage and nuzzled the wire.

The two female deerhounds sniffed and then pulled away from the cage wall. With caution, Nesbitt began to open the cage door once more. A wolf swiftly rushed towards it, attempting to bite the wire before he closed it, which he did with a loud thud. "Goddamit," He shouted out loud.

"You have to do something!" Jesse called out. "I am feeling sick. We need to get out!"

Nesbitt looked at her through the wire. "Whatever you do, don't move! It will be okay, Jess. Take it easy. They will leave soon enough," After several minutes, he tried to find a more comfortable position. The cage was too small to stand in or stretch out entirely. He tried to ignore the pain of sitting in a bent-over position, as he looked around the old showgrounds. No one was around, and there was no way out of the cage. He sat there wondering how long the pack would remain.

Finally, the largest of the wolf packs moved over to Marco, who was lying on his side. He looked up and nuzzled the alpha, who immediately let out a low howl. Several minutes later, Nesbitt and his wife watched as the last three deerhounds returned. They walked slowly and cautiously toward the pack until they were at a close distance. Instantly, they entered a submissive, crouched position.

"Look at that!" Jesse screamed.

"I don't believe what I am seeing!" Nesbitt whispered to his wife. "Dogs and wolves? What the hell is happening?"

CHAPTER 34

Milbrook held a shovel in his callused hands and stood back to survey his work. He decided to return to the house when he heard the movement of something behind him. His first thought was that one of his herd had found its way to the house. Not the first time it had happened which meant he needed to check the gates.

He turned and stopped, frozen at the sight. Five giant black wolves stood several yards from him. They stood so close, so motionless, that he could easily see the color of their eyes. Four held his gaze with an intense yellow glow around their iris. The fifth, by far the largest of the group, held bright green eyes. The intense glare of each wolf firmly fixed on him.

The largest wolf stopped five yards away and waited for the others to pass. It stood quietly as the others went into a crouch and inched slowly towards Milbrook. Low growls came from their snouts as they moved slowly forward. "Get outta here! Get away!" he shouted without any effect. He waved the shovel end at them to no effect.

The sight was mesmerizing and frightening. He had never seen a wolf up close, and their size astonished him. He quickly realized they must each weigh well over a hundred pounds. They crouched in readiness, each taking an angle of approach with jaws open and poised to attack. He noticed the hair on their backs was raised.

Feverishly trying to evade them, he stepped to the left towards the house, but each time he took a stride, the wolves reacted by pacing slowly with him, moving closer. As he moved, the lead wolf lowered its head and started to growl.

Panicked by the confrontation and realizing he was trapped, he stepped forward and swung the shovel head down onto the nearest wolf. It ducked quickly as the blow glanced off its shoulder.

Instinctively, the other wolves moved to his right to attack him from the side.

He swung the shovel again, leveling another sharp blow to the nearest wolf, searing a wide gash in its side. It screamed with agony as the others launched towards his legs and bit into his side. The nearest wolf bit his ankle and held on as the rest came forward.

Using his broad hands, he tried to bludgeon them with the blade of the shovel, but their grip and weight pulled him slowly toward the ground. Milbrook screamed out in pain as the grip on his thighs and calves became tighter and more violent. One wolf bit into his thigh and shook it violently from side to side as Milbrook started to scream.

He looked down in shock to see blood pouring out from the bottom of his work trousers. One of the wolves had punctured his femoral leg artery. In a vain attempt to staunch the flow, he placed his hand on the wound. It was a mistake. As soon as he lowered his arm, another wolf bit onto his forearm.

Raucous sounds of low-pitched snarling and growling increased as the pack, including the injured male, intensified their attack. He kept beating them away with one arm, wielding the shovel, trying fruitlessly to ward off the attack while holding one of his hands to his bleeding leg. The more he fought against the assault, the more entangled he became.

Finally, in desperation, he attempted to roll away and then stand, but heavy jaws clamping his arms and legs stopped any movement. They clamped their teeth on his arms and legs and slowly pulled him down to the ground. All he could hear was a chorus of clawing, snarling wolves and his heavy shouting underneath a fog of brutal pain.

Finally, in desperation, he freed his hands and grabbed the neck of the nearest wolf. It made no difference. It broke free of his grip and clamped its teeth on his neck, shaking furiously until his body went limp. Moments later, Milbrook lost control, his muscles succumbed to weakness, and darkness enveloped him. His shouting slowed, and finally, surrendering to the loss of blood, he stopped moving.

The alpha wolf, calm and motionless to this point, moved across to the inert body, sniffed it, and assisted the pack in ripping his body limb from limb. The attack lasted until the limp and ragged body of Jack Milbrook lay on the ground next to the trench where he had laid the finches to rest half an hour before.

The lead alpha moved off with its snout in the air as the pack trotted obediently behind. Momentarily, it stopped and looked to the sky to the North and then directly towards the sun. It barked loudly towards the pack who moved beside him as he took off at a trot.

CHAPTER 35

With a menacing look and snarl at Nesbitt, the largest of the wolves joined the other pack members. After circling the trailer cages for a minute, it sat with them on the grass.

He was in the middle of a nightmare that he could not understand or change. Nesbitt almost pinched himself. He looked at them in disbelief. What he saw before him contradicted everything he knew about dog behavior. Everything.

The scene before him was verging on ridiculous. The dogs and wolves were cohabitating without aggression? It made no sense. The wolves had attacked him, but the dogs, trained by Jesse and himself, joined them.

He sat stiff and immobile in the small trailer cage while his dogs mingled with a large, feral wolf pack, displaying friendly but subservient behavior to them. He would never have believed it if someone else had told him the story.

Now and then, he heard a snarl and noticed a wolf staring at him, its fangs showing. He started to sweat as he tried to reposition himself against the back of the wire cage. He called out to his dogs, but they neither looked in his direction nor acknowledged his instructions. He was stuck in the cage. He doubted they would survive if he or his wife left and made a run for the truck.

"Do we make a run for it?" Jesse asked him with desperation in her voice."

"No chance," He replied abruptly. "We stay put until I figure something out."

There was no way out without encountering the pack that sat alert on the grass five yards away. His only hope was waiting for the wolves to disperse, getting his dogs back into the trailer cages, and getting out of there.

"Can you answer me!" Jesse shouted. "What are we going to do, Charlie? What the hell are we going to do? We can't get out of here. Who is going to come and find us?" Nesbitt stared blankly at her and then at the wolf pack that mingled freely with his dogs.

"I don't know, Jess. How in God's name could his happen?" He lowered his head and tried to change position to relieve his back pain. Every time he attempted to open the cage door, the closest wolf would raise itself to stare quizzically at the cage door with a low, deep growl coming from its throat.

"Look at the size of that wolf." He stared as it lay on the ground with its head raised. It was the largest canine he had ever seen, with a black-tipped, long, bushy tail. Its coat looked to be a mix of gray and brown fur. It looked like a distant cousin of a German shepherd he had seen at a dog show some months before.

He guessed the wolf to be five feet long and its tail two feet longer. All members of the wolf pack were large, but as he looked over at the alpha sitting outside the group, he realized it stood twice the size of the nearest male and must weigh at least one hundred fifty pounds or more.

"Why didn't our deerhounds protect us?" Jesse cried as she looked hopelessly at her dogs, who lay motionless next to the wolf pack that had finally congregated at the far end of the trailer.

"I have seen nothing like it, Jesse. Wolves and dogs don't bond! They can't bond! They are too different species. Any first-year veterinarian can tell you that! "He leaned towards the cage wall that separated the two of them. "Look at Marco! He is lying on his side next to the pack leader and licking him!"

"I don't believe it?" Jesse whispered, shaking her head in disbelief.

"Look at the size of that wolf. He is almost twice the size of the other males. It's like looking at a small horse."

"Thanks, Charlie. That makes me feel better."

"Just be quiet, Jess. They'll move on, I am sure of it." Nesbitt said, trying to comfort her.

"They'll kill us if we leave these cages, won't they?"

"It's not worth the risk. It will be okay, hon, sit tight."

"That's easy for you to say." She replied haughtily.

"Don't panic, Jesse. We will wait until they leave."

"What if they don't?" Came the curt reply. Nesbitt could not think of an answer as he sat on the straw of the small cage, hunched over and unable to sit up or stand. His legs ached.

"I am tired, hungry, and thirsty. Do we have any water?"

Nesbitt shrugged. "It was too early to put water into the cages. If they don't leave, I will run to the pickup."

Jesse looked at him as she tried to move up to her knees but found she didn't have the space. "They will kill you! Please have a look at them. Do we even have a gun?"

Nesbitt shook his head. "I didn't think there was any need to bring one."

CHAPTER 36

Susan stood outside the house late the night before, fascinated by the light that moved in green waves across the sky above the Essex hills. She watched for half an hour, fascinated by how the green light moved, and then, abruptly, it disappeared, replaced by blackness below the blaze of stars across the sky. With an early start the next morning she retired to bed.

She wished, as she had so many times, that her husband was with her to see the sight in the heavens above the Essex granite cliffs. The wavy lights were magnificent. He died just after the war, and with no recourse but to manage the farm, she toughed it out and assumed his duties. While some of the labor proved difficult, she learned to enjoy the running of a large citrus orchard. A new tractor would help, but that lay on the wish list. Money, as always, was tight.

The two-hundred-acre farm held an extensive orange tree plantation. Thankfully, due to the reliable rainfall and rich, dark soil around Essex, she had never experienced a poor crop. However, her trees produced the best oranges in the county, and she held blue show ribbons to prove it.

The war years offered higher returns for the fruit, but as the war requirement stopped, so did the price. The bills kept coming, and despite her sending letters to change the name, they lay in her letterbox, noting Susan and James Constant. So, she gave up and accepted them as they were; addressed incorrectly. She paid on time as well the money was available. And if she missed a payment? Well, she paid it when she could.

She missed her husband's companionship the most, and she was at the age when most people left her alone. It was probably her fault, she thought. She and her husband had kept mostly to themselves, and perhaps she was paying the price.

That morning, over fifty bales sat neatly arranged in the barn, away from the elements. The bales were pulled out when the small number of cattle she held required feed away from the parched fields in the middle of summer. Susan checked the stringing on the last bale and hefted it onto the line of bales across the back wall.

Stacking bales remained a chore she disliked. It required strength to place them above each other, and for that, she needed her husband. She dropped one last bale onto the lower level as she heard a strange noise coming from the outhouse at the back of the grove. It sounded like a thud, then stopped and started again. It sounded strange, almost surreal.

She listened for a moment. She thought one of the louvers of the windmill that brought bore water to the surface had broken. She shut the barn doors and went to the outhouse just thirty yards from the homestead.

Walking towards the sound, she breathed the scent of fruit budding and ripening under the California sky. The sun was starting to make its presence felt that morning as the heat rose, and citrus trees responded with extended leaves to soak up the light.

She walked quickly to the small building which housed mainly farm implements. It also held two old saddles she no longer used since her husband died and the horses had been sold. The sound was coming from the side of the small building built well away from the windmill, so she changed her mind about the louver.

As Susan turned the corner, she froze. A giant black-furred wolf stood beside the outside wall with its back facing her. It was throwing something heavy against the boards. As the small, bloodied body fell to the ground and started to move, the wolf picked it up and threw it again. It held a near dead fox in its jaws.

She stood transfixed at the sight, staring at the wolf and wondering quickly what to do. With rising panic, she became breathless and disorientated. She stood still for a moment, realizing that if she ran, the wolf would sense her movement, and if she stood still, it would eventually face her when it was tired of playing with the fox. Either way it would probably kill her.

She had not seen a wolf in years, and on the rare occasions, she and her husband saw one of them from the hills, it had disappeared as fast as it arrived. The markings on its long body were familiar. It resembled a timber wolf, she knew that much. It held lustrous black and brown hair with a long tail and a broad head. From its snout came a menacing snarl as it repeatedly threw the fox carcass against the timber wall, sniffed it and threw it again.

She stepped back softly, moving towards the house. Panic took over. She found herself sprinting across the open ground. Behind her she heard the sound of paws on the ground and a loud pitched growl. "Get away, get away." She shouted, not daring to look behind her. The farmhouse was barely twenty yards away.

Suddenly, the wolf was upon her. She turned to confront it. All she could see was the size of the wolf in midair launching itself at her with its massive jaws open and snarling from deep in its throat. "Stop!" She shouted. "Go away!"

She screamed again as the mass of muscle hit her, knocking her breath away. With the sound of its violent snarling filling her ears, she fell heavily to the ground, trying with all her strength to push it away. No amount of holding or pushing made any difference. The wolf used its weight to push her flat to the ground until she could no longer move. It stood above her, peering at her face.

"Please, " she said softly, realizing the wolf could snap her neck in two with one clamp of its heavy jaws. She could smell its reeking breath as it moved over her to pin her completely on the ground. Not knowing what to do, she let her head fall to the side.

In the distance, she could see the house as her ears filled with the deep guttural sound. It stood over her, staring hard, with almond-shaped eyes that appeared slanted. The ferociousness in its eyes lined up with the outer base of its held-back ears. She knew that look on a dog. It was the position before an attack. She wondered where her dog had gone. It had disappeared. She thought about screaming, but who would hear?

Terrified, she turned her head to look directly into its eyes. They were amber in color, brilliantly lit by the sun. She dropped her hands to her sides, realizing it would be impossible to fight it. She had no weapon, and there was nothing near her that she could use. She hoped the savaging would be quick.

Suddenly, there was a howl from near the barn, and the wolf immediately raised its head and sniffed the air. It glowered at her, but its growling lessened. The next moment, it pulled back from her as barking around the barn increased in volume. Finally, the wolf stepped back several yards, waiting to see if she moved. It growled menacingly, stopped, and looked towards the copse of trees at the top of the adjacent pasture.

Astonished, Susan watched as the wolf appeared undecided about what it would do. She remained motionless, she turned her body and her face to the ground. Slowly, it moved away. She started to cry and found it difficult to breathe. "Be strong, goddamit." She said to herself. She kept her eyes averted from the retreating wolf. She heard it move back further, its attention caught by something else.

She raised her eyes, and in the distance, she could see other wolves roaming together around the orchard. Her wolf trotted to the outhouse, picked up the fox, and threw it in the air. After a bark from the paddock nearest the orchard, it headed quickly towards the field at the back of the barn. It let out a howl as it picked up pace.

"Oh, my God!" The only words she could muster as she rose from the ground and staggered to the farmhouse. She was sweating. She looked down to find her pants stained with urine by the time she reached the door. "Oh, my God! She screamed out loud.

She felt pulsing fear and heavy anger at what had happened. She was angry that wolves would invade her property and fearful of what the wolf might have done to her if it had not heard the call of the other wolves. She had been moments from death, and she knew it.

Wishing her husband was still with her at the farm, she realized she had little choice but to kill the wolf. Wolves were vermin; predators to be destroyed. She held very few cattle on the farm, but they were at risk as well.

Spurred by pulsing adrenalin, she grabbed her .22 rifle from the rack next to the door and headed back out the door with the gun raised and the breech cocked. How many bullets would it take to kill a large wolf? Why, in hell, did it leave her alone? It could have killed her instantly?

She moved past the outhouse, ready to retreat if she needed to escape. Cautiously, she crept around the side of the large barn to the fence that separated the large field from the orchard. A light wind ruffled the grass tops. The wolf was nowhere to be seen.

The remains of a cow carcass lay bloodied and strewn at the other end of the fence. She had not heard it cry out. She did not understand why until she looked at its mouth. It had teeth marks and had been crushed. The wolves had clamped its snout and ripped it apart, limb from limb. She felt sick as she looked at it and vomited next to the fence.

Fearfully, she checked the other side of the barn and walked slowly through the orchard. Nothing! She stepped back inside the house, shaking and unable to control the fear. The wolf was so much larger than her. Why did a wolf come so close to the farmhouse? Why did it leave? She shook her head in disbelief. Where did the rest of them go?

Safely inside the homestead, she poured a glass of brandy and sat on her rocking chair near the fireplace to sip it and calm her nerves. Where did they come from? She needed to let people know. Then, she needed to find her dog—a black-and-white sheepdog. Where did it go? Perhaps it was dead, destroyed by the wolf pack.

CHAPTER 37

They dozed that night, and very early the following morning, Nesbitt and his wife whispered to each other as they warily watched the wolves. They had tried to sleep, but the cramped positions offered only one option: sitting on the straw with bent knees, making everything more difficult. The hours passed slowly, with Jesse groaning now and then as her position in the cage brought on cramps.

Nesbitt checked his watch. Several wolves, followed by one of his dogs, trotted off into the distance. They returned about an hour later and joined the group at the other end of the trailer.

"Maybe if we let the two girls go, they will take off," Nesbitt whispered as he attempted to move from his tight position. His back was spasming as he sat on the straw. "What do you think? Because I can't think of anything else to get the pack moving. They may be staying because of them."

Jesse shrugged as she looked at the cage next to her. Anything will be worth trying at this stage. I am so thirsty. I am still sweating. It is unbearable. We need to do something! You think that is the reason they won't leave?"

"I can't think of anything else. They seem to be grouped down at that end of the trailer, so maybe, just maybe, that is the reason."

Jesse sighed as she leaned back against the cage wall. "Well, there's no point in the girls staying in here. They won't help us, that's for sure. Do you think they'll attack the girls if we push them out of the cages onto the ground? Those wolves don't look like they are in any hurry to get going, and they look hungry."

"We have to try."

Jesse nodded. "I can't reach their cage handles."

"We just need to push the cage doors." Nesbitt looked around for something to use. He spotted the cage-locking pole on top of the trailer wire. "They might attack males, but two young females? Unlikely."

Jesse thought about it for a moment. "I guess it's worth a try."

"You see the long pole above you, up on the roof of the cage? If I can get my hands on it, I can push the cage doors open and give the girls a nudge, but I will have to open this cage door to grab it."

"There's no other way?" Jesse asked. "Can't you pull it through the cage top?"

Nesbitt just shook his head as he looked around. "Don't think so. It's too long. I don't have the leverage from inside here. I can only get a half hand through the wire."

"What about me?" Jesse replied quickly. "Let me try."

Deftly, she put her hand through the top of the cage, grabbed the long stick, and pushed it across the top of the wire until she grasped the end. With some effort, she up righted it and brought it down through the cage top and towards where Nesbitt was sitting. As it passed, he fed the length out the back of his cage and finally fed it to where Jesse sat.

"Okay, I'll pass it through to you. You need to push the cage door open at the front and jab her to get out. She should jump out of the cage."

Jesse took the stick and slowly fed it through the cage walls until it reached the gate of the first female. With a grunt, she pushed the unlocked cage door. " It won't budge."

'Push it harder.' Nesbitt urged.

Jesse pulled the stick back and shoved it hard at the wire door. Finally, it opened. She gave the female a nudge with the end of the stick. The female stood up but did not move.

"Harder." Nesbitt whispered.

After a harder push, the female deerhound moved slowly, pushed against the cage door, and jumped to the ground. As she did, Marco came over and gave her a lick. Finally, she slumped down as the wolf leader sauntered and sat beside her.

"Well, that proves they will not attack her. Pass me the stick." Nesbitt repeated the procedure from his cage, and without prodding her, the second female jumped lazily down from the cage. Within a minute, the wolf pack and the deerhounds got up and moved toward the nearest hill.

"You see? You see?" Nesbitt said excitedly. The girls were the only reason they were staying. Let's leave it for half an hour, and I will run for the truck. It should be light soon."

"What if they are still here?"

Nesbitt waited patiently and finally cracked open the cage door. He waited breathlessly for any sign of the wolf pack. There was nothing. They had disappeared.

Jesse whispered. "What time is it?"

Nesbitt checked the luminous dial on his watch. "Close to six. No wonder I am tired. I still haven't slept."

"Will they still be here?" She asked anxiously.

Nesbitt shook his head. "If they are still around, we would have seen them. The truck is at least thirty yards behind the last tent. I cannot see them if they are still skirting the area. Let's wait a little longer and see what happens."

"Then what?" Jesse said as she tried to change position in the cage.

"We head for town. These wolves must be killed, and we must try to regain our dogs. But. God knows where they went. Could be here or in the hills. Who knows?"

"The dogs, be damned." Jesse shouted without taking a breath. "I want to get packed up and out of this town, Charlie. Don't you go thinking about hunting wolves? Hear me?"

"What about our dogs?"

"For all we know, they could be dead by now," Jesse replied as she looked at his face in the rising sunlight. Nesbitt thought better about trying to persuade her, but he knew the pack needed to be killed and killed quickly.

"I know what you are thinking, Charlie Nesbitt. If we get out of this goddam cage, we will not help anyone around here. We are heading home. Dogs or no dogs. You hear me?"

CHAPTER 38

"I can't see how any of this is your business, sheriff," Mayor Perkins said loudly and authoritatively down the telephone line. "McNab may be right. Just leave it alone. I spoke with him, and he seemed unconcerned. Just stay out of it."

Venter sighed involuntarily. "I have no desire to hunt and shoot wolves, mayor, but we have a problem on our hands with the livestock kills. People are starting to complain."

There was a pause on the other end of the line. "A bull was killed, right? Yes? You told me all about that, sheriff." Perkins said in a condescending voice. "The bull was well away from the farm, and there have been a calf and few sheep. That doesn't seem much to worry about."

"People are worried and complaining. The… " Venter started to explain as Perkins interrupted.

"This hardly constitutes an emergency, sheriff," Perkins replied, his voice offering exasperation. "We have other problems, such as speeders on the eighty-five and increasing crime in Winslow. Wolves are pests, vermin. It is up to farmers and ranchers to deal with them alone—not ours!"

"There are other issues, mayor. We have strange lights up..."

"What?"

"Do you have anything different in the night sky over Winslow?" Venter asked quickly."

"What the hell are you talking about, sheriff?"

"Well…"

Perkins rudely cut him off. "To be honest, sheriff, I don't care. Keep your duties on whatever needs to be done in upholding the law. Let the community get rid of any pests. It is not our responsibility or duty. Tell the veterinarian to work something out."

Venter cursed under his breath, realizing he was wasting his time. "Will do, mayor."

"That's the spirit, sheriff. We will see you next week for our meeting."

Venter took a moment to replace the receiver. He looked over at Beth, who had a wry smile as she leaned back in her chair. "That went well?"

Venter shrugged. "Remind me next time not to call."

"Of course, " she replied sardonically. "We should get the new two-way by the end of next year, if at all. You might also bring that up at your meeting next week."

CHAPTER 39

Quietly and cautiously, Nesbitt opened his cage door, holding his breath as it squeaked. He pushed it wide enough so he could move gingerly to the ground. As he landed on the hard-packed earth, he let out a loud grunt from the pain spreading from his lower back to his legs. "Damn it." He said under breath as he rubbed his lower back.

He moved slowly around the trailer to see if wolves or dogs were nearby. Realizing that the pack must have left with his dogs, he walked over to a tent and pulled out a water bottle. Gleefully, he hurried back to the cage, where his wife sat uncomfortably in a cramped position. She grabbed the water bottle from his hands and drank. "Are they gone?"

Nesbitt looked towards the large field where the wolves had entered. "I sure hope so. Stay here, Jesse, and let me check around."

"Be careful! " she replied softly. Welcoming the relief, she slowly slid over the straw through the cage door to place her feet on the ground. Her stiffness and cramping increased painfully. Without a word, she walked around the trailer to regain circulation in her legs.

Nesbitt stopped momentarily and cautiously glanced at the tents. Some twenty yards away, he could see the back of the truck by the side of the largest tent. He needed to get to the truck and head to the town, where he would get a rifle, return, dismantle the tents, hopefully find his dogs, pack up, and leave.

As he neared the back of the truck, he heard the ominous sound . He stopped and listened, wondering if he was hearing things. The wolves and his dogs had left. He was sure the pack would have departed together.

As he inched closer, he saw his lead dog, Marco, move cautiously from the shade of the tent. Nesbitt softly called for the dog to come to him, but his smile vanished when he saw the dog's behavior. Hair had risen on its back, and its lower jaw dropped to release the dripping saliva that covered it. A low, menacing growl came from deep in its throat.

Behind him, Nesbitt could hear his wife's voice, watching from the safety of her cage. "I can hear him. Come back!"

He backed away as he murmured to the dog. "Marco, Marco, come on, boy. It's me, your friend." He put his hand out towards the dog, but it continued to snarl, suddenly moving into a low, stalking crouch as Nesbitt backed slowly toward the trailer.

He looked at the mass of the one hundred-and-fifty-pound male deerhound, realizing for the first time in his life what damage a dog of that size could do if it attacked him. "What the hell? Marco, it's me!" Marco started to circle him, and Nesbitt knew what that meant. Keeping his eyes on the dog, he backed quickly, turned, and ran for the cage. He scrambled inside as Marco came bounding up against the side.

His lead male was now pacing the perimeter, watching and growling. There were no other dogs in the vicinity, so where were the rest, and why was Marco the only dog guarding the trailer?

He looked over at Jesse, who had started to cry. "We raised him. Why is he doing this?" She shouted, trying not to look at Marco as he trotted around the perimeter of the trailer.

"He doesn't know what he is doing, Jess."

"What the hell does that mean?"

"It means something has completely changed his behavior. He is no longer the dog we raised."

"You're not making sense." Jesse said as she gulped more water.

I can't explain it, but he's become a predator like the wolves. Just look at him; look at the way he is acting. He's changed."

"That is ridiculous, Charlie! How could he change in a day?"

Nesbitt rubbed his lower back. "I wish I knew."

"What are the chances of someone coming here?"

Nesbitt looked blankly at her. He had no idea. They were both tired, hungry, and thirsty. There had to be a solution, but what? In frustration, he hit the side of the cage.

CHAPTER 40

Jamie Romano heard her sister shout. It turned into a high-pitched scream of panic. Leaving the iron pan frying on the wood stove, she pulled a rifle from its mount in the hallway, dashed out the front door and down the two steps to the front of the house.

Searching desperately for her sister, she ran around the house to determine where the screams were coming from. Finally, she doubled back, running breathlessly along the side of the farmhouse. She noticed that the gate to the lower paddock was ajar, which struck her as unusual. Being considerate in all things, Meg would not have left it unlocked. She constantly checked and shut gates to prevent stock from venturing out.

Looking over the pasture, she saw Meg running towards her through the long grass. Behind her in pursuit were several large dogs, chasing her across the broad expanse of the paddock, snarling viciously as they moved close enough to bite at her legs. "Get the gun!" she heard her sister scream. "*Get* the goddam gun!"

Meg reached the gate. In horror, she watched the hound launch itself into mid-air. It caught the back of her dress and pulled her slowly to the ground as she fell from the force of the attack. Jamie raised the rifle, trying to aim so that she did not hit her sister as the dog started to rip at her dress, snarling and growling.

Jamie dithered for a moment, thinking that they could shut the gate against the dogs once Meg got through. In the same instant, she realized they would quickly get through the fence horizontally or have the size to vault the gate if it blocked their path.

She hefted the rifle, pulled back the bolt, checked the breech and ran towards where she had fallen.

"Shoot, shoot." Came the scream.

"Stop moving! I can't aim properly." Jamie screamed. Every time she aimed, the dog changed its snarling attack. Jamie moved closer to her sister as she saw the other dogs launching themselves down the hill, towards the gate.

Meg turned over and away, trying to fight off the dog as it bit savagely into her leg, drawing blood that increased the violence of the attack. Clutching helplessly, she grabbed for anything she could find while she screamed in horror and pain.

Scrabbling around for anything to beat the dog off her leg, she found a rock near her hand. "Shoot, Jamie, shoot!" She screamed.

Jamie pulled the trigger, and all she heard was a click. The rifle had jammed. In desperation, Jamie pulled the breech back and ejected the round.

Screaming at the pain, Meg picked up the rock and smashed it into the dog's head, swearing as she realized it was not stopping the attack. One hand desperately held the dog's left ear. She continued to pound the other side of the its head with the rock, but it did not seem to faze it. "Jamie, what the hell is wrong with you, shoot!"

'I don't want to hit you!' Jamie shouted.

Meg hit the dog as hard as she could and instantly rolled away hearing the loud percussion of the rifle discharging. The dog dropped to the ground, panting heavily, with a wound to its neck. As it tried to rise, it whimpered pitifully and finally stopped moving.

Jamie cocked the gun and shot at the two dogs that stood snarling, suddenly uncertain about continuing the attack. She hit one on in its hind flanks, and it took off with a howl. The other started to advance, growling and slavering spit from its open jaw.

Jamie grabbed at her sister's arm. Meg got to her feet and retreated with her sister as she tried to staunch the flow of blood from her bitten leg. As they backed, Meg grabbed the rifle from her sister and put a shot into the nearest dog that was advancing several yards from where they moved. It fell quickly to the grass as another moved forward.

Meg counted five dogs, two on the ground and the rest stalking them. She half ran as she limped to the house door ten yards away. The closest dog bared its teeth, yellowed by age, and started to move towards them.

Meg started to cry as she realized her dress was wet, soaked in blood from her leg. Jamie held the gun at the ready as they backed up the two steps to the front door and finally slammed it shut.

Meg fell to the floor in disbelief. She started to sob as she pulled her skirt up to look at her leg. Bite marks had ripped the skin and blood flowed constantly from the wound. "Jamie, move! Get vinegar and a bandage. Hurry!"

Jamie looked at her, still immobile from the shock of the attack. She looked blankly at Meg and seemed unable to talk. At her sister's urging, she walked to the kitchen, grabbed a glass bottle of white vinegar, and hurried back. She passed the rags and vinegar and finally turned on her heels towards the kitchen

"Where in hell are you going?" Meg called out as she moved strands of gray hair off her face.

"To see if they are out the back."

"Don't worry about that. They can't get inside. Help me."

"But…"

"Stop dithering, Jamie'" Meg shouted as she poured vinegar over her wound and ripped her skirt. She fashioned a bandage and tied it around her leg to the wound, then applied vinegar to the rest of her leg. "Pull the bandage tight from the back." She turned over on her front so Jamie could tighten the bow behind her leg.

With effort, Meg finally rose and walked gingerly to the door. Slowly, she pulled the curtain aside and peered out. Outside, the wounded dog lay on the ground as the other stalked around it, snarling as they kept vigil on the front door.

To her astonishment, a wolf joined them. The wolf looked almost twice the size of the dogs that sat with it. It stood tall with matted gray hair, a long jaw, and white teeth that bared into a menacing growl as it saw her looking out the high window of the front door.

"Look out there, " she breathed softly. Jamie peered out at the pacing dogs. "What is going on? Why are they here!" she said as she moved away from the window. "Let's shoot them!"

Meg sat with a thump on the couch. "It may bring more, Jamie."

"You think there are more?"

Meg sat there disconsolately as she tried to understand what had happened. "I went to the top to pick some carrots. I looked over at the number two field and stopped in shock. There were at least five sheep on the ground. They were mutilated."

"The dogs did that?"

"Must have." She bent over, crying again. "Oh, my dear God, I was frightened. I saw them beyond the fence line, and a moment later, they started running towards me. They were barking and snarling as they came, so I just ran off towards the house."

Jamie put her hand on her sister's arm to comfort her. "But, you made it back. It's okay."

"It's anything but okay!" Meg put both hands on her head as if she could not believe what had happened. "It's like a dream, a bad nightmare."

"It's no dream, Meg. I just shot one of them. We need to get help." Jamie said sternly.

Meg looked at her as she lifted her leg onto the sofa. "How would we do that?"

"We need to get outta her."

"To where?" She asked excitedly. I'm not going outside, and neither are you, Jamie. You don't want to get attacked like what just happened to me. I am lucky to be alive. If you weren't here I would be dead, ripped to pieces like those sheep. Well, God knows what I would have done."

Jamie looked at her with a perplexed look on her face. "Well, we can't stay here."

"At least we are safe."

"I wish we had a telephone." Jamie said wistfully.

"Amen to that," Meg said as she looked up at her sister, who started to cry. Meg took her hand and made Jamie sit on the couch with her. "We are safe. That is all that matters."

"Why did it happen? Two of those dogs are ours! Why would they attack us?"

Meg re-inspected her wound, relieved that the bleeding had slowed. "I don't know, " came the flat reply. "But we are not leaving until those dogs and that wolf have gone elsewhere. If they see us, they will take us down before we get halfway to the barn or the pickup. Have we ever seen a wolf around here?"

Jamie stood up again and looked around, anxiety on her face. "Not for many years. It must have been before Papa died. Well, we can't just stay here, can we?"

"For a while," Meg replied as she tested her leg and gingerly stood up. "I might need a fresh bandage and, I sure as hell need something to drink. Then we need to bar the doors and pull the curtains across all the windows so those monsters can't see inside."

CHAPTER 41

That night, Tom made himself a cup of black coffee, pouring it from an old, red metal percolator his wife had used and left behind when she dissolved the marriage. He disliked alcohol and had never smoked. When he received the cigarette packets in his K rations he gave them way. It made him popular.

He could hear his wife talking about their first purchase after they married. "It's Italian made," she would say quite proudly, inferring that it produced better coffee, but he could barely tell the difference between her coffee and his when it came to making more.

He sat down with a light grunt at the pain from his shoulder. He opened the book he had started some weeks before, determined to finish the last chapters. The weather was changing towards cold and it reminded him that he needed to clean the fireplace and start stacking logs for the coming winter months.

The familiar sounds of frogs croaking and the incessant clicking of crickets joining in the night serenade outside the farmhouse gave him comfort. The cooing of owls was missing, and he only realized it as he turned from the passage he was reading and looked around the room.

He heard it again. A pulsing, like a low rumble. It pitched and descended. He put the book down on the chair arm and padded slowly around the house. The sound wasn't from inside house, and when he finally got up to look outside, it ended. He sighed, wondering if it was his imagination and returned to his armchair.

A half hour later, he finished the chapter, laid the book on the table next to his chair, and walked outside the back door to relieve himself. He looked up towards the hills to the East. He saw the light that so many had spoken about above the hills. It brightly illuminated the low point of the horizon. The sky held an eerie emerald glow, like a flashlight shining back and forth through green cellophane. The light pulsed, creating waves in constant rhythm. He immediately chided himself about making the excuse of campfires.

Mesmerized by the light, Venter kept his eyes on the horizon at the junction of the night sky and the granite cliffs lit up by the iridescent light. It illuminated the entire sky above the town. The effect was eerie and disconcerting. Where did it come from?

The effect alternated brilliantly green, disappeared, and then appeared again. He wondered if the trees dancing against the wind at the top of the hills made the light appear as if the glow was changing and thought for a moment that it made more sense. Perhaps the glow was constant, with an optical illusion created by the trees?

Venter held his arm up, watching the waving light reflect off the back of his hand. Abruptly, the light disappeared. He waited fifteen minutes, but the sky remained dark and foreboding with the brilliance of stars above. The light had come and gone. The strange, green waves of the light reminded him of the ocean on his honeymoon with Frankie. Sitting on the foreshore, he watched waves peak and fall away, diminished to the appearance of boiling water.

Finally, he gave up waiting and returned to his chair in the lounge room, noticing the pulsing sound had not returned. He picked up the book and continued reading. What the hell was it? There were no doubt queries coming into the office in the morning. The remaining question in his mind held no answer. If the waving light appeared and disappeared at night, where did it go?

CHAPTER 42

Venter made his way to the office early. He arrived just at seven under a crystal clear, blue sky. It lifted his spirits and made the drive relaxing and enjoyable.

After spending much of the past days on livestock kills by wolves and dogs that seemingly arrived out of nowhere, he decided to leave the issues to McNab and that meant he had time to process his neglected paperwork.

The mayor's words rebounded in his mind. It was not his problem, and any eradication of the wolves, wild dogs, or both was someone else's problem. However, to his mind, it made the issue more complex.

He entered the office and promptly filled the coffee jug, waiting a minute for the dripping water to fall onto the grounds. His second step was to pull all the paper out of his tray and dump it, with the appropriate sigh, in the middle of his desk. He read several reports regarding drunk drivers in Winslow and the increasing number of vagrants and shysters seen in or around the county.

An hour later, almost half of the paper had been redistributed into files or the trash. He took a last sip of cold coffee and sat back in his chair as the two-way clicked furiously for a minute. He ambled over to the old system and clicked on the receiver. There was no response except the sound of static that moved towards a high-pitched crescendo, then retreated to a dull monotone and increased again. "This is Sheriff Venter. Come on? Anyone on?" With no answer, Venter returned to his desk and pulled the last two files from his tray.

Several minutes later, the phone rang on his desk. There was silence on the other end of the line when he picked it up. He replaced it angrily, wondering if someone was playing a joke on him. Finally, it rang again. "Sheriff Venter speaking. There had better be someone on the end of the line."

"It's me, sher…, sheriff. Lena, Lena Peterson."

Venter groaned quietly as he listened to her voice. "Hi Lena." Venter waited for a reply. He asked quickly as he thought about the visit to Chance's farm.

"Her voice was strained and high-pitched. "You need to come to the farm. Quickly!"

"Are you okay, Lena?"

"I am alive, but you must get here, sheriff." She implored him.

Venter stopped talking for a moment as he digested the news. "I am on my way? Where is Chance?"

"Well, I woke up this morning and could not find Chance anywhere. Then I……." The line suddenly went dead. He called back with the same result. Nothing. Her voice seemed tinged with fear and that meant Chance had been at her again.

Venter picked up his hat and called again, but there was no answer. He thought briefly of his last visit. Maybe he hit Chance too hard? He got up, didn't he? Perhaps he injured him, and the injury disabled him sometime later. Venter felt a heavy feeling of unease flooding through his mind. The only other explanation is that Lena took a shovel or something to Chance, but that hardly comforted him.

Beth came walking in, grimly smiling as he opened the door. "Did you look for the light?"

Venter nodded. "I saw it on the horizon. It was quite weird. Just above the hills and a long way out. Did you see it? Weirdest thing."

"Everyone has seen it." She replied briskly. "Where are you going?"

"I am heading out to the Peterson ranch. There is a problem. "

"What? Beth asked, suddenly curious.

"She didn't say. There was a connection problem on the phone."

She smiled at him. "There's a connection problem everywhere if you ask me. The two-way hardly works. It's been like that for three days."

Venter nodded. "I'll head out to the farm. Chance has disappeared, but that is all I heard. The line went dead."

"Well, I hope she's okay." Beth said as she moved towards her desk.

Thoughts raced through his mind as he recalled his last visit to the farm and the fight near the entrance to the barn. He had hit him hard, but he was a big boy and seemed unfazed by the fight. Unnerved by the conversation he put his gun belt on before he entered the car.

He put the key in the ignition and started the cruiser. Aggravated about the need to return to the Peterson place, he took off in a cloud of dust, almost forgetting to slam the cruiser's door shut. With the siren on, he moved quickly up the road past the old church and towards the turnoff to the eighty-five.

The dust trail behind the cruiser billowed across the dirt shoulders of the old road as he hit the accelerator. As he reached the highway, he looked out to crop pastures and grassy fields bleached by the sun that appeared to stretch to eternity. Now and then, a single cow and a small flock of sheep raised their heads with little interest and continued grazing.

Fifteen minutes later, he pulled up in front of the house. Tom got out of the car and put on his hat as he watched Chance's wife come running down the steps from the house, holding a rifle in both her hands. "Careful with that rifle!" He shouted out as she approached.

Tears distorted her anxious face as she ran into his arms. "Thank the Lord you have come, sheriff. It's terrible, just terrible!" She cried as she motioned for him to walk back with her.

"Lena, calm down." Venter said as he looked into her eyes. "It can't be that bad. I'll take care of it. Where is Chance?"

"You are too late for that," She shouted hysterically, her eyes filled with tears.

"What do you mean?"

"Follow me and keep a sharp eye out as you walk." Regaining her composure, she strode out in front of him.

"What do you mean?"

"You'll see soon enough."

What has happened? Is Chance okay?"

She shook her head quickly and urged him to follow her. She wiped tears from her eyes with her hands, finally lifting the folds of her dress to dab at her eyes as she walked. "I woke up this morning and called out for him as we were sleeping in different bedrooms because of our problems. We weren't speaking. I went looking for him for breakfast because he was always around then, and he liked a cooked meal. I looked everywhere. At least I thought I did."

"What time was this, Lena?" Venter interrupted her.

"Donno." She said truthfully. "I think around six thirty."

Venter stopped her as they walked past the old barn with the rusted doors. "But you found him, right?"

"I think he's dead."

Venter stopped momentarily, astonished at what she said. "Did I hear you right?"

Lena Peterson, her arms cradling the rifle across her body, cried again and urged him to follow her. "I found him at the side of the barn. Follow me, but I don't want to look at him again. It's just too horrible."

They reached the barn as she pointed down the side hidden from the house. "You look, I can't go there again," she said.

Venter stepped around the old door and down the back of the barn lined with rusted remains of farm machinery lying unused against the wall. From where he stood, he could see the prone body of Chance Peterson on his side against the barbed wire fence.

Venter moved cautiously down the side of the barn wall. He gasped as he saw the body lying face down with one arm caught in the bottom of the barbed wire fence. He prodded him with his hand. "Chance!" He called out. There was no response. With some effort, he rolled Chance onto his back and stood up, stepping back in shock.

Chance's torso lay bloodied and torn with teeth and bite marks across his body. Half of his face ripped away. What was left was a pulpy morass of flesh and bone. All he could think of was the calf he saw on the top paddock of Carter's farm.

Venter put his hand on the man's neck to check for a pulse and realized there was little chance of finding one. Feeling nauseous, he stood up, thinking about what to do. This would mean the medical examiner and assistance from Winslow.

He finally walked back to where Lena stood, looking terrified. "How did this happen?"

"I don't know," She answered immediately as shock seemed to quiet her until she slumped against him. "Is he dead?"

Venter nodded unable to think of anything to say. He paused for a moment. "Lena, did you hear anything last night?"

"Not from Chance, but the sheep were crying out last night. Sometimes, if a storm is coming, they get restless and bleat, so I thought it was just a change in the weather on the way."

"There was no storm last night. Anything else?" Venter asked as he looked further around the farm. It looked as if Chance had been ravaged by wolves. "Where are the sheep?"

"In the North field. Chance put them up there two days ago, as its more sheltered from these winds that keep changing direction. Why do you want to know?"

"Listen, Lena. I want you to return to the house and stay there, okay? I'm going to have a look around."

"What about Chance? Are you just going to leave him there?"

Venter shook his head. "I will need to call Winslow, but first things first, Lena. I need to make sure you are safe. I won't be long. I need to check around the property."

"But, why?" She asked plaintively.

Venter took a breath as he looked at her in a distressed state. "I need to find out if there are any animals around here that might have done this to Chance," he said.

She cried again as she looked up at him." You be careful!" Venter nodded his head. "You have a gun?" She asked quickly.

Venter nodded and motioned towards his revolver hanging at his hip. "Now, you head back to the house, Lena. I won't be long." She glanced at him with tearful eyes and turned on her heels to return to the refuge of the old house as Venter took off in the opposite direction.

He walked up to the fence line of a vast field towards the top of the farm, which led to the foothills of the rise towards the vista of the granite cliffs. He looked up to the steeply rising hill and the forest stretching up towards the granite cliffs. He could feel the wind strengthening as he walked.

He moved slowly along the fence line, stopping every twenty steps to look around. There was nothing out of the ordinary. He listened for sounds, realizing there were no birds in the trees that he could see. He moved slowly up the hill towards the field where Lena had told him the sheep were enclosed.

Stopping momentarily to catch his breath, he hiked further up towards the following fence line, moving around several tall boulders jutting from the grass in the middle of the field. Unable to see the sheep, he traversed the paddock through a wide copse of elms next to the fence that separated the lower field from the long grass fields at the top of the rise.

From his position, he could look down towards the house and the barn near where he had stood with Lena. He could almost see where Chance lay at the side of the barn.

There was a strange scent on the wind, almost like the stench that carried on the wind outside an abattoir. The smell was faint until he reached the fence line on the other side of the trees. He stopped in disbelief at the sight that lay strewn across the upper field.

"Goddamit." Venter said softly to himself, leaning on the fence wire. He lifted his hat off his brow and surveyed the unmoving bodies of more than a dozen sheep and several lambs. Each lay on the field in pools of their blood. Each lay savaged and brutally dismembered.

Without thinking about the danger, Venter crouched down and crawled through the wire to inspect the one nearest to him. A lamb, probably not over five months old, lay before him. Something had beheaded it. The thought of the violent attack unnerved him as he looked further around the blood-soaked grass.

Across the field, the grass lay littered with animal legs, heads, and torsos scattered in piles. As the wind's direction changed slightly, the smell hit his nostrils: a mixture of the scent of recently spilled blood and decaying flesh.

The kills were recent, he thought, as he observed the color of the ripped meat. The invasion of ants and other insects on the carcasses was barely evident. The kills were maybe that day or the night before.

He looked up the hill to see the standing figure of a large, black-coated wolf staring in the opposite direction. His skin crawled as he looked further around. Two wolves and what looked like a large, light-colored dog sat serenely near it.

THE WOLVES OF ESSEX

He watched as the wolf played with the carcass of a sheep held firmly in its jaw. The wolf threw the carcass high into the air, picked it up again, and shook it violently. He realized the pattern was the same. It played with the remains of the sheep, without eating it. Venter watched it cautiously.

Besides the group of wolves and dogs near the top of the paddock hill, another dog, larger and darker in color, approached slowly. It nuzzled one of the wolves and stared down across the paddock. It then sat slowly on its hind legs and let out a long, high pitched howl. Within seconds, a response came from the timbered hillside—it came from an unseen wolf.

The breeze was moving away from the pack. He knew enough to know they could not pick up his scent. Venter stooped down to view the sheep's carcass further up the hill. The flesh appeared ragged, with cuts across its neck and torso, resembling the damage Venter observed on Chance's body nearby, only two hundred yards away. The sheep carcass below him was also not eaten. It did not surprise him. It was the same pattern as the bull, the calf, and the sheep scattered before him. The wolves and dogs were not killing for food.

A sudden movement at the top of the hill caught his attention. He looked up to see the large dog nearest him immediately stop its attack on a dead carcass and stare intently at him. An icy shiver went down his spine. He stood still and waited.

As he watched, he realized the dog had sensed his presence. It lowered its head, pivoted slowly from side to side, and raised its snout to scent. If McNab was right and dogs could smell up to five miles, he realized it was time to retreat slowly back to the farmhouse. He took several small steps back to the fence as slowly as he could towards the fence wire.

The dog sensed him. It was snuffling the light breeze. Venter felt his blood grow cold as he realized the air current was changing towards him. He watched the dog stand to attention with its head slightly lowered. Glowering and slavering, it took several steps with unwavering attention towards where he stood.

Venter watched, wondering momentarily what he should do. The hound was moving with its teeth bared. It moved down the hill in slow, deliberate steps. The hair on its back started to rise as deep growls came from its open snout. In seconds, it gained full flight from where it had stood over the sheep carcass. The pack of wolves and dogs at the top of the hill immediately became agitated.

Venter could feel a rising panic. He thought quickly about retreating, hoping the dog would not follow him through the barbed wire fence into the adjoining field. The copse of trees behind him? No, he thought, that would not stop a dog of the size coming down the hill, and he was too old to climb trees, even if he could find one in seconds to climb. He needed to head for the open ground of the field below. The large rocks might give him protection.

Concentrating on the dog moving towards him, he pulled his pistol from its holster. He swore as he realized the chambers were empty. Feverishly, he reached down to his belt and watched the dog springing towards him; he had no choice but to try to fill the revolver as he moved. He pulled four cartridges from his belt as quickly as he could and pushed them into the chambers of the police issue pistol, dropping several bullets on the ground as he ran the ten yards to the fence.

In his alarmed state, he wondered how many bullets would stop a charging one-hundred-pound dog the size of the one charging in bounds down the paddock towards him. If the other wolves and dogs followed, he was going to die. He had little choice but to retreat.

He wasted no more time. He re-holstered the pistol as he neared the fence. Just as he reached the wire, he slipped on blood surrounding a sheep carcass lying on the grass five yards away. The momentum pushed him into the barbed wire strung across the posts, entangling his shirt.

Swearing, he pulled himself up and moved through the top two wire strands as quickly as he could, tearing his shirt as he wrenched himself through. Behind him, he heard the dog snarling as it vaulted down the paddock slope. The dog was less than ten yards away when it also slid across a bloodied carcass and careered into the grass, finally coming to rest against the fence and trying to raise itself to continue the attack.

As the massive size of the dog came closer, Venter could see bloodied foam running from its jaw and down its neck. The dog's broad chest looked to be layered with what could only be congealed blood. Suddenly, he realized it was the same dog that Chance had set on him on his visit to the farm.

Why a farm dog would kill its owner and all the sheep that lay inert in that field was beyond his reckoning. There was little he could do but retreat to safety. But where? It was at that point that he saw another dog. It appeared to be slightly smaller. It was moving into attack position, emitting the same menacing howl as it appeared at the top of the field. It descended the hill towards the fence line he had just struggled through.

Venter sprinted towards the open ground. His thoughts were clear. He could kill the pursuing dog if it continued its attack by confronting and shooting it point blank, if he got the chance. He slithered through the copse of trees, tearing at his belt to remove three more cartridges. In a headlong dash he continued down the paddock toward the rock outcrop. Feverishly, he thumbed the rounds into the empty barrel positions one by one.

An enormous granite boulder sat high out of the ground ten yards away. He reached it and turned around. Behind him, the dog was snarling and barking. It stopped five yards away, eyes fixed on Venter. It crouched low and started to move side to side in an agitated state, ready to attack. Venter thumbed the safety off and aimed.

Out of practice with a pistol, Venter fired the first three shots, all of which missed as the dog moved frenetically around him, trying to gain an advantage. The dog reacted, enraged by the sound of the gun. Finally, it leaped into midair.

Venter fired the fourth shot, heard a loud yelp, and, without a second thought, he fired the last two rounds. One hit the dog in the side of its neck, and a second later, it smashed onto the side of the boulder with a resounding thud. Panting heavily and bleeding profusely, it lay twitching on the ground.

As he looked up, he saw the other dog, a black-and-white breed he had seen at the top of the hill, become airborne as it vaulted the top of the fence. It hit the ground in a savage sprawl, sliding several yards before it came to a stop. In an instant, it raised itself. The dog charged down the hill towards him. Would the wolves follow? If they did, he realized he had no way of escape.

Venter reached for ammunition. There were no rounds left in his belt. He had not used his pistol since he started as sheriff, and he had little need for ammunition. He hardly checked his belt, and at that moment, he wished he had.

He looked around for something to use against the dog. Finding an old tree branch, he picked it up, but it crumbled in his hands. He scrambled up the boulder and grabbed his pistol by the barrel to use it as a cudgel.

A moment later, the second dog reached the bottom of the boulder. With a giant leap from its back legs, it flew into the space before him landing with all four feet on the rock. It was all he could do to hold his hands up to try to fend the dog off. It bit at his legs and moved forward to bite his flailing arms. Venter tried to balance on the top of the rock.

Suddenly, he heard a shot; the galloping dog screamed and fell to the side of the boulder. He watched the dog slump, grunting and bleeding from its side. With a cry, it lay a yard from the other hound on the bloodied grass at the bottom of the rock.

Breathing heavily, Venter glanced to the fence at the top of the paddock. There were no wolves in sight. He changed his attention to the sound of the rifle, as he realized it was Lena, standing twenty yards away, still with a rifle held firmly into her shoulder, still aimed in his direction. As the dog bellowed a last grunt, she finally let the rifle fall to her side. "Are you okay?" she shouted out.

He could barely hear her as he stopped over to regain his breath after the run through the trees to the middle of the field. He stepped back warily to look at the dog. It was dying a painful death. Blood oozed from a wound to its head and neck, but even as he lay in a bloodied mess, it continued to try to rise towards him. Anger overtook him. He looked around for a rock, which he found several yards away. With one massive blow, he smashed the rock into the dog's head to finally kill it.

He looked over at Lena, who stood next to the inner fence, dazed by what had happened. She started to cry as Venter approached. "Seems I owe you one. That was a hell of a shot! Let's get back to the house pronto," he said.

Lena looked at him, her face white with shock. "What the hell is going on, Tom? What the hell is happening?" She shouted on the verge of hysteria.

"Come on, we have to move. There might be others on the way." He said as he looked towards the trees at the top of the field for movement. He could see glimpses of at least one dog towards the copse of trees at the top of the rise. He grabbed her arm and felt her go limp against him as he held onto her rifle in his other hand.

He moved as quickly as he could to the farmhouse, constantly looking behind him and wondering why the wolves had not attacked. What started this? What weird force was driving dogs to act so aggressively? There was no reason for it.

He had no ammunition left, and he wondered if her rifle held many rounds. As he reached the steps of the house, he looked over to see another dog sniffing at the fallen mongrel near the boulder. It raised its snout and stealthily approached the fence line near the house. It reached the wire, crouched, growling, and sniffing the air.

CHAPTER 43

Rusk got up from bed earlier that morning, a little later than his habitual six thirty. He downed half a cup of coffee, dressed, and left his small house on the North side of Essex, near the old town road.

Aggravated by the need to revisit the sisters farm he threw his bulky gun belt and hat on the passenger side of the front seat and made his way in the opposite direction of Winslow towards the Romano farm. The road condition, half laid with bitumen and half dirt road due to erosion and lack of repairs, made the journey more challenging. He hummed a tune with the thought that it would be a quick visit as he spent several minutes thinking of excuses to leave.

Rusk could see light mist settling across the top of the granite cliffs that held up the escarpment supporting a long ridgeline. From several years of watching the seasons around Essex, he knew that within several hours, the mist would disappear, dispersed by the heat of the sun. The result would be a clear day where one could see almost forever.

He followed the ridge in the distance to his right until he found the turnoff to the farm. The front held a sign that barely showed the original writing of *Romano farm*. It resembled old parchment laid down by an ancestor who no longer lived. He had never met the older man, Georgio Romano. He died just before Rusk took the position of deputy of Essex, leaving his daughters to run the place.

Rusk stopped the cruiser ten yards from the front door, watching several dogs move off to the side of the house at the car's horn. Exiting the cruiser, he closed the gate behind him and called out to the sisters, but there was no answer. He walked to the front door, noting that all the windows had heavy curtains across them, which was unusual for that morning. Pulling the curtains aside in the early mornings was almost a ritual to welcome the day in most farmhouses where the owners rose early to start chores.

THE WOLVES OF ESSEX

He knocked heavily on the door. "Meg, Jamie, you there?"

Finally, he heard a shout from inside. "Is that you, Marvin? Come in quickly!" The door opened, and Jamie grabbed him by the arm as he heard the movement of something behind him. In the next moment, he felt the vice-like grip of strong jaws clamping onto his leg, biting deeply into his flesh. He let out an involuntary grunt as the pain in his leg became overwhelming.

Instinctively, he fell back, looking at the head of an enormous dog that had bitten his leg and was pulling him down onto the boards of the small deck outside the front door.

In shock, he reached for his pistol. He cursed his tardiness as he realized he had left it on the cruiser seat. He tried to hit the dog's head with his hand in a feverish attempt to stop its growling.

The pain made him bellow. He had no way to stop it. Within moments, he fell to the ground, trying to grab the dog's snarling head with his right hand. He stared at the slavering dog in horror. Its strength was unnerving as it held onto his leg, biting fiercely and growling incessantly. He shouted in pain as he repeatedly hit the dog with his balled fist.

He looked away momentarily, sensing more movement, and saw a large, gray wolf approaching him. It crouched and lowered its broad head. He glanced at the brilliant yellow of its flashing eyes as it moved closer with open jaws.

Jamie stood immobile, not knowing what to do but shouting at the top of her voice. "Meg, Meg, get the rifle." She opened the door. Meg came limping through with the rifle raised. "Get away, goddamn you!" She hissed as she saw Rusk fall backwards. She instantly slammed the stock into the dog's head, which made it pull back. She hit it again, and it released its grip momentarily. "Jamie," She breathed heavily. "Help Marvin. Get him in inside, now!"

As Jamie stooped down, Meg raised the rifle. She shot the dog straight through the top of its head. As it slumped it released its grip. Immediately as she turned to face the snarling wolf. She shot it in the flank, but as she pulled the trigger again, the gun jammed. She hit the stock on the floorboard to release it, but the trigger would not budge. "Pull him, Jamie. Pull him now!" She screamed.

With little strength left and fighting the pain from the wound on her leg, she gathered her strength, brought the stock up, and smashed it down on the side of the wolf's head. It pulled back with a howl of pain, bleeding profusely from its ear. As she brought the stock up, she realized it had splintered in two.

The wolf retreated several yards, unable to keep its balance. With Meg's help, the three fell into the hallway. Jamie reached back to slam the door shut with her foot just as the snarling jaw of another dog reached inside. With a yelp, it pulled back as the door smashed into its snout. Using both her feet, Jamie held the door shut.

The next sound they heard was the impact of another hound as it launched against the timber door, scrabbling at the door, trying to gain entry. Jamie stood up to peer through the closed curtains. "Look at the size of that goddam devil!"

The growls continued, following a high-pitched wailing as Rusk felt the back of his thigh to hold the bleeding wound. "What the hell is going on here? How long have they been out there?" He shouted as adrenalin coursed through him. "Meg, are you hurt? Were you bitten?"

Meg raised herself and moved over to where she had left the vinegar and bandage made from a torn sheet. "Yes, to both those questions, deputy. I got attacked yesterday afternoon. If Jamie had not been around, I would surely be dead." She raised her hand and pointed outside in disgust.

"I wasn't much help. I panicked." Jamie fixed her fallen hair into a bun and sat on the closest chair. "The dogs and wolves? They are out of control. They will kill anything that moves!"

"What the hell is happening here? " Rusk shouted as agitation took over and the shock of the experience settled in. "There were only two dogs when I arrived, and they took off at the sound of the cruiser. Where did the wolves come from?" he said with a grunt at the pain.

Meg glanced at Jamie, who still held a stricken look, which Meg took to mean shock. She put her arm on Rusk, still sitting on the floor. "It's okay. We are inside. They can't get in," she said.

"There are more?" Rusk said quickly.

Meg nodded. "They are out the back as well, waiting. I was attacked by dogs yesterday afternoon. They came out of nowhere. I still can't believe what happened."

"They are your dogs?"

"Two of them." Jamie replied. "I don't recognize the others."

Rusk gazed at Meg with a look of astonishment. Her appearance was ragged, with her long hair falling in strands and her leg wrapped in a bandage. "When did you say you were attacked?"

"Yesterday afternoon. Late, late in the day," she replied almost matter-of-factly. "Undo your pants, Marv." She said abruptly. Rusk gave her a sideways glance and shyly undid his belt. She watched as he pulled the soiled slacks to his socks and inspected the wound. "Not as bad as mine, but it drew blood. I am going to bathe it in vinegar and bind it. We only have vinegar, but it works. Okay? We have to stop any infection."

Rusk nodded, relieved that the damage was not worse. He tested his leg, wondering if he could stand. "And the wolf?"

"Wolves." she corrected. "No, I have not seen them before. They are timber wolves. You can tell by their coloring. We have not seen a wolf in these parts for quite some years, so who knows where all these monsters have come from?" After she finished the binding, he pulled up his pants and tried to stand but thought better of it. "Dogs and wolves attacking? I am told it is impossible!"

She pointed to the door. "Oh yeah? It's possible, Marvin." She replied with a dour look. "The animal that attacked me came out of nowhere yesterday afternoon. When I went to the back of the pasture, I found several of our sheep. They had been ripped apart. Those things out there slaughtered them. This was not killing! It was destruction. There is no other word for it. Destruction!"

"Did you see wolves?"

Meg shook her head. "This dog, this massive hound, came out of nowhere, galloping down the hill towards me. I watched it for a moment and took off towards the house."

Rusk looked at her, perplexed. "But, dogs? Why would they attack?"

"We asked that question twenty times last night, and there was no answer. Why here, why now? Why attack at all? It borders on the bizarre. The entire world has gone strange."

"It's the work of the devil," Jamie said with a frightened look on her face. She looked at the frown on her sister's face and stopped talking.

"Can you move your leg?"

Bracing against the pain, Rusk moved his leg slowly. Heavy bruising surrounded the teeth wound. 'Yeah, I'll live.'

"Is it broken?" Jamie asked.

Rusk tested his leg. "Nope, good enough. I'll see the doc when I get back to town."

"It's not that easy," Jamie said sternly as she approached where he was sitting. "They are out there waiting." She said angrily.

Rusk looked at her strangely. "What do you mean waiting?"

"You'll see. They are waiting for us," Jamie looked at Meg and then at Rusk. "They will kill us if we leave this house."

"Where did your attack happen, Meg?" Rusk asked, suddenly officious as he started to calm things down.

"Out near the back gate. I consider us both lucky if you saw what they did to the sheep! And the lambs!... It was horrible." She started to cry.

Rusk looked up at Jamie. "We need to find a way out of here."

"It's not that simple. The one we shot yesterday afternoon is still alive. It limps but is holding guard on the other side of the house, with more wolves outside than yesterday. I know it sounds strange, Marv, but Jamie is right. They are waiting to kill us."

"I doubt that." Marvin added.

"Marv, you have no idea of the violence of those dogs and wolves. You encountered one. Try fending off a pack! Those wolves are bigger than the dogs. They are huge and brutally violent." She shouted at him.

She nodded at Jamie, and together, they helped him stand. "Come over here," Meg said authoritatively. Rusk moved stiffly to the where she stood.

Rusk winced and shook his head as he counted five dogs and six large wolves. Strangely, the dogs were different breeds. A cattle dog was sitting at the front, and there were two black-and-white sheepdogs and an Alsatian that looked similar to the wolf as it sat on the grass. Some moved agitatedly, while others, such as the cattle dog, sat on their haunches staring at the door.

As he watched, a deerhound, the same as he had seen at Nesbitt's tent, walked around the corner of the house and settled near the front door. He wondered how it had gotten away from Nesbitt and out to the farm from the showgrounds—a distance of at least twenty miles.

"Why would these dogs attack us? What the hell did we do?" He whispered as he moved away from the safety of the window glass.

"Nothing." Jamie sternly replied as she walked to the door window to peer out. "Look at them out there. Those brutes are waiting for us. Dogs and wolves."

Rusk limped over to the door. Outside, the dog that attacked him lay motionless on the porch with a swarm of flies on its head, feeding off the pool of blood beneath its body. A wolf sat at its side, licking the wound to its hind leg where Meg shot it. Blood from the blow to its head had congealed along its jaw and ear.

"That's the wolf you hit with the stock. Why is it still there?" Rusk asked slowly. "It doesn't make sense."

"It's unholy. Last night, the howling almost sent me mad, " she retorted. "Anyone got a machine gun?"

Rusk thought for a moment as he tested his arm again. He needed to contact the sheriff, and they needed to get reinforcements to kill the pack that sat vigil outside the farmhouse. "You don't have a phone, right?"

"Nope," Meg replied. "A bit late now."

"Any suggestions, deputy?" Jamie asked quietly.

Rusk looked out of the window. "How many rounds do you have in the rifle?"

"Very few and, anyway, the rifle stock is broken. All we have left is an unusable rifle with half a stock. How are you gonna use that?" Meg replied. "It will be difficult to fight our way out of here."

"You got any other rifles?"

"Nope." Meg replied as she put her hand on her sister's shoulder. She started to cry at the frustration of their situation. "It will be okay, Jamie. We will get out of this."

"Unless they tear us apart first. What happens if they come through the windows?"

Rusk put his hands on his hips as he looked around. "Would dogs do that?" He asked.

Jamie stared at him momentarily. "Given what they did to Meg. I wouldn't doubt it."

"Here is the truth, Marvin. They are not killing for food. These devils are killing for the fun. Our beautiful sheep are on the upper paddock, ripped apart." Meg said in an emotional voice. "These dogs and wolves are out to kill. Nothing will stop them other than a bullet. They kill and eat nothing."

"Amen." Jamie added.

Rusk found a chair to sit in and slumped backward. His leg was hurting as the shock of the attack receded. He thought briefly about the cruiser and how to get to it without being attacked.

Meg squatted down beside him. "We need to wait it out, Marv. Let's see if they move off."

Rusk looked at her with a calming smile. He knew Venter had been right. They should have killed them all. Damn, McNab.

CHAPTER 44

In his haste to return to the house, Venter realized he had left the fence gate open nearest the house. He cursed his carelessness without mentioning it to Lena, who looked at him with despair in her eyes. Her face still held the scars of Chance's beating. "The one that chased you was Chance's old hound." She said abruptly, as she wiped tears from her eyes. She got up to get water from the kitchen.

"I thought I recognized it. And the second dog?" Venter asked.

"He was our sheepdog. He was four years old and a better dog you could not find. And now? My God, why did it attack you?"

Venter shook his head as if to say there was no answer. "There are a lot of strange things happening around Essex." Venter added without telling her what they were.

Venter regained his feet and peered out the window towards the paddocks surrounding the farmhouse. "I interrupted that goddam dog as it was attacking what was left of a sheep. This is not the first time I have seen dead livestock." He shook his head at her. "I have no idea of what is happening."

Lena stared at him as she finally got up. "I need something to drink. You?"

Venter nodded as he approached the old telephone with its side cradle on the wall. He picked up the receiver and clicked it several times, but there was no response. He clicked it again and looked over as Lena entered the room.

"It was working this morning. Then it went dead." She said firmly as she walked to the kitchen for water. "What now, Sheriff?" She asked as she returned.

Venter looked at her as he greedily gulped the second glass down. "Someone needs to look at Chance, and that has to be Doctor Lowes, as he is the closest thing we have to a medical examiner. I know you are having a tough time, Lena, but we must arrange these things. Let me try to get to the two-way in the cruiser."

"You will be coming right back?" She cradled her left arm in her hand. "It still hurts. From Chance." She said softly.

Venter nodded as he made his way to the front door. As he opened it, another large dog, a white and black crossbred with a broad head and powerful shoulders, confronted him. It had been sitting on the step outside the door, poised, ready to attack.

Venter pulled back in shock as he glanced at its size. It would tear him to pieces. He immediately shut the door and pulled his pistol to reload it, realizing he had no ammunition. "Now we have another dog guarding the door."

"Don't go out." Lena asked, terrified by the tone of his voice.

"Is it your dog?"

Lena peered out the window at a mid-sized cattle dog with white markings on its fur. It stood immediately outside the door, snarling and dribbling. "That's not ours." She said immediately. "Why would it be acting like this? How in hell did it get here?"

"You don't know this dog?" Venter questioned her as he looked out at the dog through the safety of the window.

Lena nodded as she took a seat next to the window. "No. Can we get around it?" She dried her tears and ran her hand over her hair.

"How?" Venter asked. "I need to get to the cruiser and get us back to town."

"Let me try." She looked at Venter as she rose and moved to the front door. Venter gave her a questioning look and tried to stop her, but she was intent on meeting the dog outside the door. He stood beside her with the rifle as she turned the handle and stepped onto the verandah.

As she moved from the doorway, the dog backed away, snarling, froth falling from its jaws to the timber stoop. The fur on its back raised, and instantly, it launched itself off its hind legs at her, trying to bite at her legs.

The force of the attack pushed Lena back. She fell heavily against the door frame trying to maintain her balance. Venter immediately raised the rifle, firing two rounds at point-blank range into its body, then aimed at the twisting body, finally shooting it in the neck.

Slowly, it fell to the ground. He looked at the dog with the thought that if he had put the same rounds into a man, they would be dead before they hit the ground. The dog was still trying to rise. "Damn you!" He shouted in frustration, cocked the rifle, and shot it again in the head.

Venter assisted Lena inside and set her down on the nearest seat. "Listen, I am going to make a run for the cruiser in case more are out there, so I need you to stay put. I will be back as soon as I can. Don't open any doors or windows! Wait until I get back. Okay?"

Lena looked at him with a stern look across her face. "I'm coming with you, sheriff. I ain't staying here." She grabbed his arm as he stood there.

Venter looked around the room. "Okay. Before we go, have there been any changes in your dogs' behavior before today? Have they been acting differently?"

Lena looked up at him with bewilderment on her white face. She nodded. "They have been agitated over several days, but the wind has been up. Sometimes, the wind change makes them a little restless. But, you know, nothing out of the ordinary until late yesterday afternoon. Late afternoon, or thereabouts."

"What happened?"

"The night before Chance and I heard howling from the hills. We hadn't heard that before. When we went out, we saw this light at the top of the hills to the North. It was weird, but the moon was up, so I thought it might be a… What do you call it? An illusion is the best way I can describe it."

"Did the light come in waves?"

Lena nodded. "Yep, and then they disappeared." She sat down suddenly, slumped shoulders in the chair. "I have to tell ya," sheriff. None of this makes sense to me. Why would those dogs attack Chance? He raised those dogs, and both of them were his companions. He had them since they were puppies.

Venter nodded as he listened. "I met that large dog. Thank God it was tethered at the end of a chain."

She nodded her head knowingly. "Chance told me."

"You got back several days ago?"

She looked at him with a tear in her eyes. "I should have left him. But what then? What have I got?" She pointed out towards the barn to change the subject. "Chance always chained the dogs up at night, so I don't know how they got off or why they attacked him."

"All I know is that a dog was playing with what was left of a very dead, sheep carcass on the top of that hill before it sighted me." Venter looked at her and shrugged his shoulders. "I am at a loss to give you any idea why I was attacked. If it was not for your sharp shooting I would be dead. Just like Chance. I am worried about the town."

Lena walked around the room, arms crossed across her chest. "What? Do you think what happened here is happening other places?"

Venter rubbed his chin, thinking about her question. "Maybe. If it is, then people are in danger, and that changes everything. Everything!" He added.

"Why us? Why here?" She asked, perplexed.

Venter decided not to answer. He moved to the door to open it slightly. He looked out and then closed it again. "Do you have any other dogs?"

"No." she replied as he moved the curtains to look outside. "But, there are more of them out there. I can feel it. We need to be careful."

CHAPTER 45

Venter stepped warily over the bleeding, inert body of the dog near the door. They closed the door gently behind them, trying not to make a noise. With Venter holding onto Lena's arm, they walked quickly down the drive and got into the cruiser.

The engine started the first time, and he thanked God under his breath for that miracle. He settled her in and drove down the old dirt road towards the eighty-five and the Essex township.

Lena pointed to the side of the barn as they passed. The carcass of a black and white dog lay on the ground with its throat torn out. "Oh, my God." She gasped. "Will you look at that dog? Look what they did to it!"

Venter slowed the vehicle, looking over to where she was pointed. "Is that your dog?"

"No." Lena replied. "I haven't seen it before. Why would a dog come to this farm?"

Something clicked into place as Venter thought about it. "The dogs are following the wolves! It's the only thing that explains their behavior. I doubt the wolves would follow marauding dogs."

"You think that is what happened?"

"Lena, it's the only thing that makes any sense in this nightmare." Suddenly, Venter pointed to the distance to a lower field next to the barn. "Look! " he shouted. Across the paddock, moving towards the side of the barn where Chance lay, a large gray wolf moved with a smaller dog beside it. As if sensing the cruiser, they started to trot quickly towards it.

"We need to go." She shouted.

He hit the accelerator without urging as the cruiser lurched down the road. The engine spluttered and coughed. "Not now, dammit." He shouted, coaxing the accelerator while waiting for the cruiser engine to run correctly. Finally, the motor calmed, and the car moved down the dirt road.

"You okay?" He spoke as softly as his exhaustion would allow him.

She nodded. "Thanks to God you came when you did. I would have been next."

"Well, you saved my life." He said finitely. "That was some shot."

"It might have been luck." Lena nodded as she quietly gazed out of the car window. Venter looked at her, thinking she was moving into immobility caused by shock. Within several seconds, he heard the click on the two-way and pulled the microphone off its cradle.

"Beth, that you?"

Her voice was indistinct as the static increased and subsided. "I can't…raise..Mar..."

"Beth, if you can hear me, we got real problems out here." He replied sternly. "Chance is dead. Dogs attacked Lena and me."

The two-way sprang to life. "Oh…oh, my God. Chance Peterson is dead? Why? How did that happ…?"

"Dogs, we think. Lena shot one of them, heading for me. Is the town okay, Beth?" Venter asked with concern in his voice.

"As far as I know."

"Where is Marv?"

There was a sigh on the other end. "I've called and called, but no answer, so only hell knows where he is. This goddam two-way stops working most of the time. I keep getting a high-pitched whine."

"Like the other day?"

"Yup. Must be interference somewhere."

Venter changed the subject quickly. He needed Marvin. "Did he head out to the Romano farm this morning?"

"Yup." I spoke to him briefly on the way, but that was some time ago—four hours or more. No one seems to have any explanation as to what is happening. The light above the hills is spooking everyone."

Venter looked over at Lena, who had slumped semi-conscious on the seat beside him. "I've got Lena in the car. I'll drop her off at the office. When Doc Lowe returns from Winslow, he can look at her. I think she must be in deep shock." Venter leaned over to wind her window down several inches to give her air.

"What do you want me to do?" Beth asked with concern, masking her voice.

"Whatever is happening, it is escalating." Venter spoke slowly into the microphone, trying to keep the panic he felt away from Beth. "I want you to alert the town. Tell everyone to meet me at the church in three hours. Get onto it, Beth, and don't delay! Make sure McNab is there."

"Will do." Came the affirmative reply.

"I will head out to see Nesbitt before he departs. Maybe he can help. Beth, you there?" Venter asked, frustrated by the static on the line.

"It's hazy, sheriff. I can… hardly hear. Speak slo..."

Venter shook his head as he considered what to say. Frustration rose as he realized he had almost died on Lena's farm. Wolves and dogs were cohabitating. They were running and hunting together, meaning McNab had underestimated the situation.

"Are you there, Tom?" There was no answer. She clicked off and walked up the street to tell them about the meeting. She carefully checked the street and the side lanes as she passed each corner. There was nothing out of place.

CHAPTER 46

Venter reached over and patted Lena's shoulder. "You okay?" He asked consolingly.

Lena lay her head back on the seat, staring out the passenger window as they motored down the town road towards the town center. Suddenly, she raised her hand towards the scrub on the side of the road. Venter looked over to see a large black timber wolf standing near a large bush twenty yards from the road.

"It's heading to town."

"Maybe." Venter replied.

"They are coming." She said softly.

'What do you mean?' Venter asked quickly.

"Them! The wolves and dogs.

"Look over there, sheriff."

Venter looked over at her as she motioned for him to slow down. "What?"

"Look!" she exclaimed as she pointed out the window.

Venter slowed to a crawl. He leaned forward to look out the window. A pack of wolves and dogs trotted in the distance, walking around the old buildings in the disused warehouse area at the back of the town. Venter counted six wolves and four dogs.

"Mark my words, sheriff. They are coming for us," she whispered. Visions of what had happened on the farm stayed in her mind, as she looked despondently out of the window. " I knew they would. It's not just on our farm, Tom. They are everywhere."

"Nonsense." Venter said roughly.

"You are wrong, sheriff. "Look over there. They are coming for the town."

"What do you mean?"

"Can't you see! They are moving directly towards Essex. Why else would they be moving in that direction? It would be best if you alerted everyone. You saw what they did to Chance."

As Venter slowed further, one of the dogs picked up the scent of the cruiser and stopped in a stooped pose, head lowered, ready to attack. "Wolves on the street doesn't mean they are all heading for town. They might be in the area," Venter replied as he tried to calm his thoughts and assess whether there was an immediate threat. Essex was a rural town. How could Essex be a target for dogs and wolves?

That's not all!" Lena shouted, alarmed at the vision above her. "You need to listen, Tom Venter. Look!" She pointed skywards.

Venter followed the direction of her pointed finger, peering out of his side window. "Look up there. What in hell is that? Now, that is the strangest thing I have ever seen."

A large flock of birds circled above them, moving clockwise, positioned well above them in the sky. They were circling directly above the town. Venter slowed to a stop to look. Sunlight reflected from their wings. "Are they eagles?"

"Sure, looks like it." Lena replied. She twisted her head to look up through the top of the cruiser window. "How about that? They keep following each other. Any reason they would do that?"

"Beats me." Venter wound down his window to better view the circling birds.

"Ain't never seen that before." Lena looked up again at the birds and then across at the wolves and dogs that had immediately stopped to look at the cruiser.

Venter pulled to a stop next to the warehouse where they had inspected the bull remains barely three days before.

"Over there." Lena pointed at a group of wolves milling around the front of the old gates. Venter barely had time to react as a wolf leaped onto the car's hood, snarling and clawing at the windshield, while a large, dark-haired dog launched itself at the slightly open passenger window on Lena's side.

"Oh, my God!" Lena shouted. Venter hit the accelerator, and the cruiser took off down the road. The wolf lost its balance as the car moved, falling heavily onto the dirt at the side of the road. He watched in the rear mirror as the wolf, seemingly unharmed by the hard fall, quickly rose and sprinted off to catch up with the pack. He gunned the motor to outrun them.

"Don't you see what is happening? They are coming for us!"

"That's ridiculous, Lena."

"Look! Look for Christsakes. These monsters are heading for Essex. Can't you see that? I don't want to go to the town! Take me somewhere safe. They are heading into the town!"

"Lena, it will be okay. There is nowhere safer than the office, and that is where we are going!" he replied breathlessly, accelerating down the old town road.

Five minutes later, he turned the cruiser from the side road through the intersection that took him down the main street and towards his building. As he expected, Beth had done her job to alert the township. The street lay deserted except for two trucks.

Several minutes later, he stopped the cruiser as close to the front door as possible and sat to scrutinize the street and area near the office. It appeared to be clear as he leaned over to Lena. He shook her gently. "Are you okay to walk?"

"I don't think so." She looked at him imploringly. Blond hair with streaks of gray, dirty and disheveled, lay plastered across her face. Her face drained of color. "Why are the birds, the eagles, I mean.... Why are they up there in the sky like that? It's so strange." She peered through the windshield at the circling birds above the town. 'They are beckoning the wolves."

Venter smiled thinly at her. "Nonsense, Lena. McNab said they will move back to the hills soon. Let's get you inside. We can wait it out there."

"You believe him?" She asked incredulously.

Venter pulled his revolver and checked the chambers, finally placing one more round into the cassette and clicking the safety on. Slowly moving his head, he double-checked the surroundings, then got quickly out of the cruiser, swiftly skirting around the car's trunk to open the door.

He grabbed her arm, picked her up, and carried her from the car door up the two steps to the front door of the office. He finally pushed her inside. Beth grabbed her from the open doorway.

Venter quickly returned to the cruiser, took his rifle from its mount, grabbed the ammunition box from the trunk, and returned to the office. Once inside, he slumped onto his chair and pulled his hat from his sweating head.

Beth brought water and put a cold compress on Lena's head. She looked over to the sheriff's desk. You okay?" She asked with concern in her voice.

Venter shook his head, trying to determine what was happening to the town. "Very nearly got ripped apart by dogs this morning, Beth. Did you get the townsfolk together?"

Beth nodded. I asked everyone to be there on time. Several of them thought I was kidding."

Venter nodded his head. Well, we are going to need help. Have you heard from Marv?"

Beth shrugged. "Nope, and I have tried a few times."

"Try again." Venter said to her as he wiped his forehead.

She returned to her desk and hit the button several times. "Marvin, you read? Over. Marvin, you….." She finally got up from the desk. "Did you hear that?"

"The static, you mean? Venter asked.

"Nothing. The damn thing hardly works, and I'll tell ya another thing."

"Which is?" Venter said impatiently, realizing he would not get a response until he questioned it.

"The phones are hardly working. Madge told me after she tried several times. I could hardly understand what she was saying, and then the damn thing cut out."

"What the hell is going on?"

Beth shrugged. "Beats me. Maybe the genius will know."

"Who?'

"McNab!"

CHAPTER 47

Venter stood beside Sean Hallgren, the Parish of Essex priest. The priest held his hands together before him, slightly bowing his head to the audience. He was short in stature, with sand-colored hair and a broad face. His eyes were cornflower blue behind oval spectacles.

After waiting for the group to settle, he finally raised his head and looked at the people before him. "Thank you for coming. Sheriff Venter wants to speak with us all, " he said softly. "Sheriff? Over to you."

Venter stood on the pulpit step, just above the eye level of the fifteen others standing before him. He looked over the assembled people. Eddie Crooks stood at the front with Meg beside him. Beth had asked as many from the town as she could for the meeting.

"What the hell is all this about?" Eddie asked, standing with his arms folded. "Some of us have a business to run."

"Thank you, Father, and thank you all for coming," Venter said, raising his voice as he spoke. "The reason for this get-together will sound strange, at least I think it will. Things, strange things, are happening around Essex that don't make a lot of sense. All of you know that a bull was killed near the old Sturger warehouse. We had two expert opinions, and we have enough evidence to know that wolves took it down. There have been other instances of attacks and kills."

"There ain't no wolves around here." George snorted as he listened. "Ask Harold."

McNab moved to the front and turned to look at the townsfolk. "There are wolves, George. I can't tell you where they came from, but they are here and attacked the bull. We saw the prints."

"Wolves?" Forrester said from the back of the assembly. "Not in the past years. Never seen one. Has anyone here seen a wolf lately?" A murmur of discontent spread across the crowd. Some shook their heads.

Madge moved forwards. "What has this got to do with anything, sheriff? A dead bull, and what I hear is a dead calf. So?"

Venter used his hands to quieten them. "I was attacked at the Peterson farm this morning by two dogs. Both had to be shot! Now listen up," Venter looked around the crowd in front of him, there is a chance we may all be in danger."

"Those dogs might have attacked anyone. Everyone knows about how Chance's bred his dogs. You're unharmed, so what is the issue?" Eddie said with an irritated tone.

"I agree," Forrester said with a dismissive wave. "We all have things to do. The wolves will head off soon enough. Has anyone here seen a wolf?" He looked around the group.

Venter shook his head. "Nope, it was not like that. They attacked full-on, and there were wolves there as well. They wiped out the sheep on that hillside above his farm. Now listen, everyone. We need to take precautions."

"Why? Do you think they are coming around the town? Why would they do that, sheriff?" Forrester raised his voice from the back. Venter could see his face as he spoke. He stood taller than anyone in the group.

"What about those lights in the sky at night?" Meg asked in her brusque way.

"I've seen them." Meg shouted out. "And I am not alone."

Venter shook his head. "I don't want to alarm everyone, but I believe we may be in danger. Wolves and dogs are banding together, and if, and I emphasize, *if*, they enter the town, we need to be ready."

"Who said they are coming into the town."

"Nonsense." Crooks shouted loudly.

"Shoot em all." Eddie said with a snort.

Venter held his hands up to quiet them. "I drove Lena Peterson into the town, and there were quite a few wolves and dogs, on the outskirts."

"How many?"

"I counted more than ten wolves and as many dogs."

"Sounds like an overreaction to me," Billy Ray said from the side of the group. No one has seen anything; only you, sheriff."

Several people looked at McNab as he made his way to the front of the crowd. He moved up to where Venter was standing. "Listen, everyone; the sheriff is overreacting. Yes, the pack has killed some livestock, but the dog attack may have just been territorial. I have spoken to Sheriff Venter and told him there is no need to alarm everyone. They are foraging and will return to the hills to their marked territory in due course."

"When?" Forrester asked quickly. "I hear there have been stock losses in several places. Don't worry about the town. What about the ranchers and farmers?"

McNab nodded as he listened. "Calm down, everyone. They will disappear soon enough."

"And the dogs?" Venter looked directly at him. "Harold? What about the dogs?"

"As I suggested, sheriff, they are following the wolves, which is consistent behavior. That is the difference in the breeds. Wolves lead, dogs follow. The dogs will calm down once the wolves head off the hills. The dogs will return from where they came."

"Really?" Venter replied. "If dogs attacked me on the Peterson property, there is every reason to believe that if dogs or wolves encounter one of us, they will do the same."

"What do you mean, *if?*" Eddie asked, looking at Meg.

"I think what the sheriff is trying to point out is we need to be prepared if they move towards town," Beth said quietly from the side of the crowd.

"How do you know that? Have you seen.. ," Jane said, moving to the front of the crowd.

Venter didn't wait for Jane to finish. He raised his hands up to quiet the crowd. "You need to listen to what I am saying!" Venter started to shout. "When Lena Peterson and I drove in from the highway, we saw dogs and wolves outside town, near the old warehouses. That was several hours ago."

"How do you know they are heading here?" Forrester asked.

"I don't. What I am asking you all to do is be prepared." Venter replied as he looked around at the disbelieving stares.

"Wolves and dogs?" Eddie asked incredulously. "That just don't make sense, sheriff."

"I agree." Forrester nodded solemnly. "My Collie seems okay."

"Don't make sense to me." Eddie added. "Sounds like nonsense. Dogs and wolves. What the hell you talkin" about, Tom?"

"Listen, everyone! A dog and a wolf attacked the cruiser as we stopped near the Sturger warehouse, where the bull was taken down. That's anything but nonsense. As I said, I was confronted by two dogs this morning, and if it were not for Lena shooting one of them as it attacked me, I would not be standing here!"

Jane raised her arm. "Where are they all coming from?"

Venter looked perplexed by the questions as he stood there with Beth by his side. "I don't know. No one knows. But I do know one thing for certain. They are attacking anything that gets in their way."

"How many could there be? Some dogs and a few wolves? Harold is right. They'll head off in due course," Madge said, her voice low and fragile.

Venter stared at her for a moment and shrugged his shoulders. "Maybe. Is it worth taking the risk?."

"How many?" Forrester asked from the back of the assembly.

"Hard to say. If you combine wolves and dogs? From what I saw on the way in here? Quite a few." Venter replied.

"You ain't answering the question, sheriff. How many do you reckon?"

"If they all gathered? My guess is up to a hundred."

There was a distinct murmur across the crowd, which immediately silenced. "A hundred? You must be exaggerating, Tom." George chortled at the idea.

"I thought you said a lone wolf attacked the car on the outskirts?" Jane looked directly at him

"There was a dog as well." Venter responded quickly. "There was a pack of wolves on the side of the road after the attack. The one that attacked, a large, black timber wolf, fell off the hood when I accelerated. It picked itself up and joined the others."

McNab listened to the murmuring in the group and finally put his hand. "I don't want everyone overreacting to this issue. I am sure it will go away. Listen to what I am saying. In the unlikely event some enter the town, everyone must stay safe. Understand?"

"What about the wavy light last night? That's weird as well." Billy Ray looked around at everyone. "Everyone has seen it, right?"

"What now?" A voice came from the back of the crowd.

Venter looked around the group. "Do you have any other questions before we move on to what we need to do to protect ourselves?"

"Do you *really* believe these wolves and dogs will come here?" Meg asked quickly. She motioned to those around her, "Into the town, I mean."

Venter paused for a moment as he considered the answer. "My job is to keep you people safe, which is what I am doing right here and now."

"Why Essex?" Madge asked bluntly.

Beth put her hand up to quieten them. "Trust me when I say I wish I knew."

"If they arrive." Eddie said quickly. "Just shoot em" all."

Venter looked at them, noticing their concern. "From this point on, everyone should stay inside. I will get Marvin, and we will take them down if they enter the town. One by one, if necessary."

"I'll help." Eddie said with a grimace.

Venter smiled at him. "I'll let you know, Eddie. I've got experienced men with me, but I'll call you if I need your help."

McNab moved to stand next to Venter. Everyone quietened as he started to speak. "Now, now. Listen, everyone. I believe that they came down to Essex for the easier game to kill."

"For God's sake, Harold, look at what is going on around here. They are not eating the prey that they kill." Venter said angrily.

McNab put up his hand. "Let me finish, please. They are timber wolves on a foraging expedition. I can assure everyone they will eventually move back to the hills once they have had their fill. I don't agree with the sheriff and last time I looked I am the expert here. A small number might be around, but they will disappear soon enough. I have asked him not to start shooting but to give it a little time. At least two to three days."

Venter glowered at him and moved slightly in front of McNab. "Just stay inside until we find out if they will come into the town. The farmers and ranchers can take care of themselves."

"So, will this request to stay inside be short-lived?" Forrester added.

"A day or two at the most." McNab added.

"Then what about the dogs? Why are they with the wolves, Harold?" Meg asked abruptly.

McNab shrugged. "Well, as you are probably aware, dogs and wolves do not get along, so it just might be that dogs are following the wolves. The wolves kill the prey, and the kill attracts the dogs. They feast once the wolves have moved on."

"Why would ordinary house dogs do that? Assuming they are the dogs on the farms and used by the ranchers." Meg questioned with a look at those next to her.

McNab smiled knowingly. "Give it time. They will disappear, I am sure of it."

"Says, who? You?" Meg said with a sideways glance at the veterinarian. "What if the sheriff is right?"

"They will return to their territory. It's in their DNA."

"What?" Eddie asked quickly.

"Genes, Ed." McNab said firmly. "But, as a precaution, stay inside for the next day or so. Maybe catch up on your paperwork, " he said with a quick laugh.

"Who else has seen those wavy lights at night?" Billy Ray asked quickly. "That's weird, don't you think?"

"You mean the light in the sky at night that everyone has seen but hardly anyone is paying any attention to?" Jane glowered at McNab. "Has anyone seen the birds flying above the town? What about them? Is there any explanation for that?

McNab shook his head. "A natural phenomenon is the only explanation. Has anyone heard of the northern lights? Nothing more than that. An atmospheric disturbance which will dissolve soon enough, And the birds may be in the throes of migrating."

"What? Above Essex?" Billy Ray shouted out.

"What the hell are northern lights, Harold?" Eddie shook his head in disgust and turned towards the small crowd near the pulpit.

"They happen in the northern latitudes and look eerily similar to the light we have seen above the cliffs."

"So, it has never happened before, but you think it's a natural occurrence? Is that what you are saying?" Billy Ray asked as he moved closer to the front. "Guesswork is all you got, Harold?"

McNab looked at him and shook his head. "No guesswork, Billy Ray. There is a scientific explanation for everything happening."

Standing higher than the rest at the back of the crowd, Forrester cleared his throat. "Harold, let me get this right. You reckon the lights, which everyone has seen, are natural, but we have never seen them before. You are also saying that the wolves or dogs or both will head off towards the hills once they have had a feed. Is that what you are saying?"

McNab nodded. "Yes, Simon. I believe so. Yes, that would fit with wild dog behavior."

"We're talking about timber wolves."

"Wolves too." McNab added with a reassuring nod.

"Goddam wolves, huh?" George shrugged and sighed.

Venter raised his hand to quiet the increasing conversation. "Listen to me, everyone. My job is to make sure you are safe—first thing. Return to your business or home until this all calms down. Some of you live on your premises and others live away, so either way, you stay off the streets. If they come to town, we will handle it."

McNab motioned to Venter to move to the side of the group so he could whisper. "We won't be hunting them, sheriff. You don't have the right to do that!"

Venter glared at him. "Harold, the time of letting them do what they want is far past this hour. They attacked me! They will kill if anyone gets in their way. You can go back to your office if you like, but if they come near this town, they will be shot."

"Says who?" McNab countered.

"Me, Harold. I am the damn sheriff, and I will protect this community. Look, Harold, there are issues you know nothing about. I will tell you after the meeting."

McNab looked at him quizzically, nodded, and moved to the side of the group.

Venter returned to his position next to the priest, who raised his hand to the group. "Are there any other questions? Everyone is busy, so we must wrap it up."

"Have you spoken lately to Winslow?" Meg directed her question to Venter.

He shook his head. "Nope. Before you ask any other questions? What are they going to do to help us?"

"Not much." Beth's reply sounded tired.

Venter motioned to the door. "Okay. I will keep in touch as things change. Keep safe. That is an order." He barked with a tired smile.

"What about that dog breeder? Can he help?" Meg asked.

Venter looked directly at McNab as he answered. "I'm heading out to see him right now. I'll check around."

The group moved slowly to the church front doors in deep discussion. As they disappeared, Venter motioned McNab to join him near the side door. "Listen, Harold. I have not told anyone. Chance

Peterson was killed probably last night or very early this morning by dogs or wolves or both. That is why I went to their farm after a call from Lena. She found him on the side of the barn."

"You should have told me before."

"I just got back from the Peterson farm!" Venter responded aggressively.

How was he killed?"

"He was ripped from head to feet. It could only have been canines or wolves." He added.

"That does not make sense, Tom. Why would dogs kill the person that feeds them?"

Venter shrugged as he whispered. "Keep this to yourself, Harold. This is why I called this meeting. If they are coming into town, we need to protect everyone."

McNab thought for a moment before he spoke. "Yes, I quite understand. However, as I have said, I still believe they will return to the hills. Chance might have taken a wrong turn or somehow enraged one of his dogs."

"Or he might have been attacked and killed by wolves," Venter retorted.

"Did you look at the prints?"

"No. That was the last thing on my mind."

McNab nodded. "Okay."

"Keep this to yourself, Harold. Okay?"

McNab nodded and strolled out of the church with Forrester.

"What now, sheriff?" Hallgren asked as he rearranged books that sat on the front pew.

"Nothing, Sean. Just stay inside."

"Okay." Hallgren nodded as he attended the books.

"Let's get back, Beth," Venter said as they walked out the back door. Together, Venter and Beth walked back to the sheriff office.

"Let's hope no one gets hurt." Beth said with a worried look.

"Amen to that. I'm heading off to the showgrounds to see Nesbitt."

"Can he help?"

"I sure hope so. If Marvin contacts you get him to come back to the office and stay put!"

"Will do." Beth replied. She walked stiffly up the steps to the office.

CHAPTER 48

Venter drove towards the old town road, turned left, and headed to the showgrounds. As he left the town precincts, he watched the front of disused buildings, inspecting the weed-infested areas and deserted blocks of land. To his relief, there were no wolves or dogs. Perhaps McNab was right.

He reached the edge of the town and pulled to a stop. In a curious mood, he stopped briefly to look back. Far above the town center, birds were still flying in formation, following each other clockwise. He thought briefly of Lena when she pointed them out. 'Weird,' she had muttered under her breath. Perhaps it had something to do with the finches Marvin had told him about at the Milbrook ranch.

He shifted into high gear and watched the countryside pass. He couldn't find any explanation for the connection between eagles above the town and finches. McNab's explanation seemed obvious: migration for the eagles and loss of bearing for the finches. It made sense when he thought about it.

Finally, the showground appeared at the top of the old blacktop road two hundred yards from the highway. Slowing down the cruiser, he approached the tents slowly, relieved that Nesbitt had not departed.

Spotting the truck, he parked next to it. He searched around the enclosure lines for Nesbitt and his wife, wondering where the deerhounds were. Perhaps they were walking them? He walked freely around the tent lines and the truck until he heard a shout from the other side of the large tent.

"Sheriff! sheriff! Watch out! There are wolves around the tents! Be careful!"

Venter immediately became cautious as he walked guardedly towards the trailer, astounded to find Nesbitt and his wife inside two of the cages. He made his way to the rear of the trailer to where Nesbitt sat. "Thank God you are here," He said in relief as Venter approached. "I hope that pistol is loaded!"

"What in the hell are you both doing in the trailer?" Venter asked quickly.

"Keep a lookout!" Nesbitt replied as he left his cage and helped Jesse from the trailer to place her feet on the ground. She almost collapsed from the pain of standing after sitting in the small cage for so many hours. He faced Venter. "You got your rifle here?"

Venter nodded. "In the cruiser."

"We need it. Keep your revolver handy. This place was crawling with wolves. They attacked us, and we made it to the trailer just in time."

"Wolves attacked you?"

Nesbitt nodded as he checked Jesse. "We have been sitting in the trailer cages since late afternoon yesterday. It was the only safe place we could find as they barred the way to the pickup."

Where are your dogs?" Venter interrupted.

"Gone with the wolves!"

Venter looked at him in disbelief. "What? I don't understand."

"Trust me, neither do we! Our dogs joined the wolf pack, and they accepted them! They barred us in until late last night when they started to move off; my deerhounds and the wolves. Finally, I decided to make a run for it. I got out to make it to the truck over there early this morning, and one lone wolf was waiting near the tent. It attacked, and I had no choice but to retreat to the trailer. Did you see any?"

Venter pulled his revolver loose from his side pouch and checked the barrel as he looked cautiously around. "Nope. I couldn't see any wolves when I drove in. There were none that I could see when I walked around before. Maybe they have moved off."

Nesbitt nodded warily. "Maybe."

"We saw some of them heading towards town." Venter said softly as they moved away from where Jesse stood.

"How many?" Nesbitt gasped.

"Not sure. A lot, I guess, but there could be more."

"Did you see our dogs?" Jesse asked.

"Why?"

"They've disappeared!" Jesse blurted out as she leaned against the trailer for support. "You have never seen anything like it. Our dogs! Dogs we have bred from pups. They left us and joined the wolves. They stood around the trailer for hours. Charlie kept saying they couldn't mix. Didn't you!" She shouted at her husband."

"It's not that easy, Jesse." He replied.

"Well, it sure as hell was easier than what you said! We saw dogs and wolves sitting with each other next to the trailer. Well, there is your proof!" She said sternly, looking at Nesbitt with an angry look on her face. She moved over to where they were standing. "We need to get to town for supplies and leave this godforsaken place."

"The town is closed." Venter said abruptly. "There is no point in heading there. Nothing is open. You can come back to the office."

Nesbitt looked startled as he tried to stretch his legs. "Who ordered the closure of the town?"

"Me." Venter replied. "Like I said, wolves are moving outside the town. They are taking down anything they can get their teeth into. They attacked the cruiser while I was heading to the office with a passenger." Venter omitted to tell them about Chance Peterson, a man they had never met.

"Dogs, as well? They are with the wolf pack?"

Venter nodded. "Charlie, this is not just a single wolf pack. It is far more!"

Nesbitt looked at Venter, his face gaunt and stressed. "What do you mean, *more*?"

"My guess is there are many more than a pack. There are a lot of them, Charlie. Not just a few. Dogs attacked me on the Peterson farm this morning while wolves stayed at the top of the paddock, where both dogs and wolves had killed the sheep in the paddock. They were playing with the dead sheep carcasses as I approached the area. One huge dog attacked me, and I had to shoot it. A second attacked, and shot before it could kill me."

Jesse looked at Venter with shock on her face. "Dogs? And the wolves did not attack?" She looked at her husband, who stood immobile. He kept looking around the camp for any movement.

Venter shrugged as he thought briefly about it. "I am at a loss as to why this would happen anywhere. Why in Essex, of all places?"

"Why did you come out here?" Jesse asked quickly. "I am happy you did, though." She smiled wanly as she said it.

"I need help, so I came out to see Charlie to ask his advice," Venter replied.

Nesbitt shook his head and pointed to the forest area at the back of the showground. His voice was low and thoughtful. "Dogs and wolves together? It is a pattern of behavior outside anything I have ever witnessed," He stroked the light beard on his chin as he thought momentarily. "It can't be true. It simply does not make sense."

"Then why are they killing anything that gets in their path?"

"Again, I don't know. Wolves kill for food. However, most domesticated dogs would not know how to kill anything."

"Charlie? You mean including our dogs?" Jesse asked as she walked closely with them towards the large tent.

Nesbitt shrugged. "You saw them, Jess. They would have killed us if we left the trailer. You want my advice, sheriff? Kill them all and kill them quickly."

"Can you help? McNab will do nothing."

"What do you want?" He asked quickly.

"To help kill them if they enter the town."

Venter followed them towards Nesbitt's truck. Immediately, he heard the low growl of a presence on the other side of the fence. "It's that wolf!" Nesbitt looked agitated as he looked at Jesse. "It disappeared for a while, and now it's back. It must be defending."

"What do you mean?" Venter asked as he crouched beside Nesbitt, pointing to the other side of the tent. "Why would it defend this area? There are no other wolves that I can see."

"My best guess is that they have marked this area. Maybe Essex has become part of their territory. First things first, we need your rifle." He whispered.

In the next moment, a large, snarling, gray wolf came bounding in full flight around the tent line towards them. "Oh, my God, look at the size of that monster," Jesse screamed as she hid behind her husband, scared enough to pull his arm to run back to the trailer.

"Move! Move!" Nesbitt shouted as he ran with her. "Sheriff, follow me," he cried. Venter held his ground, raised his pistol to eye level, and fired. The second round hit the wolf in the chest as it rose, and the third caught it in the middle shoulder as it slumped.

Within four yards of where they stood, the scowling, black, and brown wolf hit the earth with a thud and a dying growl. It lay on its side, panting with quick breaths, its long tongue on the grass. Venter rose from his crouched position, walked over, raised his pistol, and shot it through its head.

Nesbitt came running up to him. "Good shot, sheriff!"

Venter re-holstered the gun and looked around and towards the hills. "They must be from up there," he said, pointing to the ridgeline. "But, where are they heading?"

Nesbitt and his wife ran towards him. "You okay?" Venter asked.

Anger contorted her face. She looked over at her husband with her hands firmly on her hips. "This is not our problem, sheriff."

Venter looked at her imploringly. "I understand. I don't have many to help me, but I understand if you want to get the hell out of here."

"How many did you see when you were attacked?" Nesbitt asked, giving a sideways glance to his wife.

Venter thought for a moment. "There were at least ten wolves on the hill at that farm and, maybe, half as many dogs. They had mutilated the sheep, but they were not eating them.

"That many?"

He nodded. "So, they can't be from this area; it is too far away."

"Not possible!" Nesbitt said with a concerned look. "It's simply not possible to have so many wolves. When we first met at the bull site, you told me there were no wolf sightings in the area for years. No one had sighted a wolf. Isn't that what you said?"

"Can you ask me an easier question, Charlie? All I know is that wolves and dogs have joined to create packs. It is not ten or twenty of them. There are more."

"More? What do you mean?" Jesse asked.

"I don't know. Maybe fifty, maybe a hundred." Venter said slowly. He felt tired and drained of energy. He replaced his pistol in its holster.

"A hundred wolves?" Jesse looked at him. Her face blanched with fear.

"If you combine the wolves *and* dogs." Venter replied as he turned to Jesse. "I'll get that rifle for you. If you decide to stay, we will need it."

Nesbitt stared up towards the hills and across the ridge line to the back of the showgrounds. "Maybe you are overestimating?"

Jesse nodded her head as she listened. "I think the sheriff is right, Charlie. If you combine the size of our dogs and wolves, no one can fend off the savagery of that strength. Maybe the dogs are learning from the wolves and the town is in their path?"

"What do you mean path?" Venter asked quickly.

"Maybe the town has some attraction for them. What else could it be?"

Nesbitt looked over at his wife, who stood before Venter. "There is only one possible reason. The wolves have decided Essex is their territory and they are defending it. The townsfolk are in the way."

"Is that possible?" Venter asked as he looked around.

"I can't think of any other reason." Nesbitt nodded.

Venter stared at both of them. "I saw the wolves on Peterson's farm earlier this morning, so the same pack at the farm could not have been here. Peterson's wife, Lena, identified two dogs from their farm, one she had not seen before. The farm is probably thirty miles away, so there is no possibility they could be the same pack. There are more than we think."

Jesse grabbed her husband's arm. "Charlie, I am tired, hungry and cold. I don't feel like fighting packs of wolves and dogs to defend a town. It's not our town!"

"Come on, Jesse." Nesbitt said soothingly. "No one is saying that wolves and dogs are taking over a town."

"Really? It would not surprise me." She replied abruptly.

"You want to call Winslow?"

Venter shrugged. "It's Saturday afternoon. No one in the council works on a weekend. They are all at church tomorrow. I don't know what else to say, Charlie. Also, what the hell could they do?"

Jesse looked at the expression on her husband's face. She placed her hand on her husband's shoulder. "No!"

Nesbitt looked at her with an imploring look. "The sheriff has come out here to help us. We have to help, Jesse. We have no choice. Our dogs are involved. If they are with the wolves they are attacking as well."

"Then we need to move back to town to my office now! We have limited time." Venter started to move towards the cruiser.

"Is the office safe for Jesse?"

Venter looked relieved as he stopped and turned back to face him. "It is the safest place in the town." He sauntered off towards the cruiser, watching the areas around the tents. "Follow me."

"Where is deputy Rusk?"

"That is the next problem. We can't locate him, and the two-way is hardly working. I sure hope he is okay."

CHAPTER 49

Rusk peered out the farmhouse window curtains, hoping the wolves had disappeared. As he watched, several wolves and a sizeable cream-colored dog resembling a Labrador cross with some other hound focused on the house and the front door. They seemed to hear everything, even the slight turning of a latch.

"Meg, I have to get back to town." Rusk said softly as he peered out the window. "I will bring back reinforcements!"

"Do you have any suggestions on how you might do that, Marv? We have maybe five rounds left in the rifle, and you don't have a gun."

Rusk smiled grimly at her. "Well, I do, but it's in the cruiser. The only way is to distract them. I will make a run for it."

Jamie padded over to where they were standing. "What sort of diversion did you have in mind?"

Rusk walked over to the stand and grabbed the rifle. He cocked the breech, opened the door slightly, and pulled the trigger. The deafening sound filled the hallway of the house. The dogs and wolves scattered.

He timed their return with his wristwatch. It took them some minutes to arrive and several more minutes to settle, intently watching the house. "That's the only thing I can think of unless y'all have a better suggestion," he said.

"What if they attack you as you head to the car?" Meg said, looking out the window and silently counting the wolves and the dogs. There were four wolves and as many dogs.

"Then you stand at the door and shoot as best you can."

"What? With a broken stock?"

Rusk went to the kitchen, grabbed two large tea towels, wound them around the stock, and tested it against his shoulder. "That might work," he said. "Ready?"

Jamie nodded. She walked to the door with him. "Move fast, Marvin," she roared. She opened the door, aimed at one of the wolves, and pulled the trigger. The wolf screamed, and the dogs retreated from the sound away from the house.

Rusk limped as fast as he could towards the cruiser some twenty yards away, situated just beyond the fence. He ignored the pain as the raucous snarling of dogs following him filled his ears. Breathless, he kept running towards the fence. As he reached the gate, he started to open it and finding the lever stuck he started to climb over the top. As he scaled the fence upright, one of the dogs caught his trailing foot.

He kicked at the dog's head as hard as he could and fell to the other side of the fence in a heap, shouting in pain. The rifle discharged behind him, and he watched as the dog whimpered and fell to the grass.

"Go! Get in the car!" He heard Meg's voice scream out from the partially opened door. He raised himself from the dirt, feverishly searching for the door handle and trying to shake the sweat pouring into his eyes. "Get in, get in, Marv!" Meg's voice was loud and clear. Finally, he found the handle. He pulled the door and threw himself in as a wolf approached the cruiser. He could hear it behind him.

As he tried to close the door, the black head of the snarling wolf attempted to enter the car, holding the space between the doorjamb and the seat. It growled heavily, biting at his leg as he held the door while moving his leg away from its jaws.

He pulled desperately on the door handle, trying to force the jaws from biting into his flesh. The wolf's head inched toward his leg each time he softened his grip on the handle. Snarling from deep in its throat could be heard above its labored breathing as it fought to move further into the door.

Shaking and breathless from the exertion of running for the car, Rusk reached over desperately, grabbing at his pistol lying on the seat. He held the door with his sweating hand, grabbed the gun with his right hand, cocked the hammer, and pointed it between the wild, brilliant, yellow eyes of the scowling wolf. He pulled the trigger twice in succession. The face of the wolf exploded, splattering him and the inside of the cruiser dashboard and seat with blood. "Goddam," He muttered as he tried to regain his breath.

He watched the decapitated body of the wolf fall slowly from the side of the seat to the ground, its gray and black fur drenched in blood. Stunned, he slammed the door shut just as another wolf attacked the opposite side of the car. Wide paws scratched and pawed the side window of the cruiser as saliva ran down the glass.

"Get away!" He shouted feverishly as he tried to clear his eyes.

With his free hand, he wiped the spattered blood and brains from his face and turned the ignition key, praying it would start. He looked over at the window where Meg was waving. He waved back feebly, put the cruiser in gear, and took off down the dirt drive with several dogs chasing him. As he looked back, he saw several wolves milling around the fence.

Once he had traveled several miles down the road, he stopped. He looked for a rag and finally found one in the side of the door. He wiped his face thoroughly and dried off the inside of the front windscreen and dash. There was blood and matter everywhere, but at least he could see.

He saw movement in the distance towards the tree line of the hills to his left. Several large, black-coated wolves came into view from the bottom of the tree line, loping towards the South. He wondered where in hell they were coming from and where they were heading.

As he drove off, the radio crackled to life. "Marv, this is… Beth. You.. there?"

"I'm here, Beth." Marvin replied trying to hear her voice above the crackling on the two-way.

"Thank God!" Beth said in a concerned voice. "I have been trying… to contact you since early this morning."

"Got holed up at the sister's ranch. Dogs and wolves surrounded the… pla. I got bitten by one of them. I don't know what's going on, it's the strangest thing I've ever seen. I ain't seen a wolf around here ever, and now they are surrounding the house. What the hell is go..?"

Beth hit the side of the unit with her hand in frustration. "Damn thing hardly works. If you can hear me, Marv? Listen, Marv. This morning, dogs attacked the sheriff at the Peterson farm.

Marvin pulled the cruiser up on the side of the road as the reception improved. "How can that be if the wolves are at the sister's ranch?"

"They are everywhere!. Last night, the sheriff said dogs attacked and killed Chance Peterson!"

Rusk's breathing stopped for a moment. "Killed? Are you sure it was dogs, not wolves?"

"Nope. By Chance's dogs, apparently. His dogs have gone crazy. Nobody knows why." There was silence and a loud crackle as the two-way refused to work and returned on air several minutes later. "Marv, are you there? Come in, Marv. Are you okay?" she repeated. "You hurt?"

Marvin moved the cruiser twenty yards down the road until he could hear her voice. "I got bitten, but I'll live. Where is the sheriff?"

"He went out to see the dog breeder."

"What for?"

"We are going to need help."

"Is he on the radio?"

"Can't raise him, I've tried. You might be closer. If you speak to him, tell him Frankie called. His daughter has disappeared."

"Allie?"

"Tell him to get to a phone and call Frankie."

"Will do. I'm heading in."

"Then be careful, Marv. The sheriff saw wolves and dogs on the outskirts near the old warehouses. They are on the move."

"To where?"

"To the town, we think."

"Are you serious? Beth! Heading to town? How many?" The two-way stopped. Marvin clicked the receiver several times and waited, but Beth's voice had disappeared. Swearing under his breath, he threw the microphone onto the passenger seat beside him, watching the curly cord go limp.

CHAPTER 50

Venter pulled up outside the office. He cautiously looked around and waited for Nesbitt and his wife. Charlie parked his truck near where Venter left his cruiser. He motioned to the office. "Let's get inside," he shouted to Nesbitt and Jesse, who followed him quickly into the office area.

He walked in, feeling relieved as he smiled thinly at Beth. "Where's Lena?"

Beth motioned to the back of the office and the jail cell. "She's sleeping, and not much will wake her," she replied quietly.

Venter nodded and mouthed the word *thanks* to Beth as he saw Marvin pull up in his cruiser. The deputy limped up the steps to the door. The door closed, and finally having the space to check his pistol, he opened the barrel, replaced two cartridges, and stood there looking blankly at Beth and the others. "It's been a hell of a morning. I can tell you that."

"How did that happen?" Beth asked with a sympathetic voice as she inspected the bandage.

"One of the dogs surrounding the house attacked me as I went in. We had to shoot a wolf outside the house and another dog to get into the cruiser." Marvin nodded. "The sisters are stuck in that farmhouse and can't get out. The place has dogs and wolves around it, attacking anything that looks like it is moving. Even themselves."

"Are they safe in that farmhouse?" Beth asked, looking concerned. "Pretty scary, if you ask me."

"Meg is injured. They are safe inside the house for now." Marvin replied with a heavy sigh.

Venter moved to his desk and sat down heavily. He felt tired and drained from the past two days. The issue of the dead bull seemed so long ago he could scarcely remember it. *What the hell is happening?* He thought to himself.

The infiltration of dogs and wolves was officially out of control, and he had no more idea of why they had appeared than when he first looked at the bull. Nesbitt must be right, he thought as he sat back in the comfort of the chair. *Territorial*. It was the only answer that made sense.

Nesbitt moved over to the desk, sitting on the edge to whisper to Venter. "Something has affected these wolves and dogs. We have no choice but to take them out and quickly."

"Amen to that." Rusk replied tiredly.

Beth looked at Venter and then at Marvin. "Did you tell the sheriff about Frankie's call?"

Rusk shrugged. "My two-way ain't working."

"What call?" Venter asked.

"From Frankie, about two hours ago. I could hardly hear what she said, as the line had heavy static. Allie has disappeared."

"What, from Winslow?"

"Don't know. She just said call her."

Venter picked up the phone and started to dial his ex-wife's house. There was no sound on the line. "The phone is dead," he said in disgust as he replaced the receiver. "Did she say anything?" He directed at Beth

"Nope," came the reply. "Just ring her back."

Venter picked up the phone again and called McNab's surgery. He depressed the cradle several times and finally replaced the receiver.

"Nothing?" Nesbitt looked over at Rusk with a worried look.

Venter tested it again. "Two-way isn't working, telephone is no longer working, and we have dogs and wolves hunting us. This is a goddam nightmare. And now my daughter has disappeared? Did Frankie say there were wolves in Winslow?"

Beth looked at him. "Nope, she didn't mention it, but I could hardly hear."

"We need to take these monsters out. Nothing else is gonna work."

Rusk nodded. He retrieved one of the rifles from the wall mount. "We don't have much ammunition, maybe fifty rounds, including the rifles and pistol. Charlie has nothing in his truck, leaving us with a problem. Do you have any suggestions?"

"Kill as many as we can." Nesbitt replied slowly. "Do we have any other choice?"

"We could try to run them over in the cruisers!" Rusk said with anger in his voice.

"What about Winslow?"

Venter nodded at Nesbitt as he sat on the side of his desk. "It's Sunday, and as I said to Charlie, what the hell could they do? Either way, we need to move on this. Beth, did you hear from McNab?"

"Nope," I rang him earlier, but there was no answer. I did speak to him briefly when I spoke to those in town I could get a hold of, but that was before the meeting."

"Well, to my mind, that has to be the first port of call."

"Why? McNab told us not to kill the wolves and to let them go."

Venter just stared at his deputy. "He may have ammunition."

"McNab was sure the wolves would leave." Rusk said as he looked outside one of the windows.

Venter looked at him hard. "Have you been outside? You got attacked this morning, just like me, and you think these animals are going to retire to the hills? You think the dogs are going home!?"

"No, boss." Rusk replied deferentially. "Just trying to find a way out of this, that's all. I ain't an expert. Old McNab is supposed to know what he's talking about."

"There is no way out of this!" Venter growled. "We have to take out as many as we can. Charlie, are you okay with a rifle? I mean, accurate?"

"Accurate enough, I guess."

"We have little in the way of choices here. If we take them down, everyone must understand that we work together, not apart. We cover the angles and shoot to kill."

"If they arrive, " Beth said, looking out of the side window that looked up the main street to the shops.

Venter shook his head slowly. "They are coming. I don't know when, but they will come. Charlie is right. They have staked this town as their territory."

"What about us?" Beth asked as she looked at Jesse.

"This is the safest place. Here's more ammo," Venter pulled his pistol out and laid it on the desk alongside two boxes of ammunition he found in his desk drawer. "Marv, check the rifles and ammo."

As Rusk sauntered off to get the rifles from the cupboard, the phone on Venter's desk jingled lightly. He moved over and picked up the receiver. "Yes, yes, who is it."

He could barely hear the voice at the other end of the line. "Daddy, help me…"

"Allie?" He shouted out. "Where are you?"

"At th …..dogs" The line went dead as Venter continued to shout. "I can't hear you, Allie. Speak up. Speak up!" Finally, he threw the received down on the desk. "Where the hell is she? Why don't these things work?"

Beth moved over to the telephone, clicked the cradle, replaced the receiver, and pulled it up again. She listened and then repeated the procedure. Venter stood with his arms folded and a stricken look. "Anything?" He whispered.

She replaced the receiver and tried again. Finally, she heard his daughters distraught voice. "Sheriff, I could hardly hear her, but I think Allie is at your house."

Venter glared at Beth with disbelief. What the hell was Allie doing at his house? How many times had he told her not to arrive without telling him? What happened in Winslow?

Marvin moved over to where Venter was standing. "What's next? Y'all going to the house?"

Venter nodded and grabbed his keys. "If there are no wolves, bring everyone you can find back here. If they are around the town, I want you and Charlie to pull everyone together to the diner and then back here if you can. Everyone else stays here. Understood?"

"Will do." Beth replied.

"You boys need to get to McNabs first and get him to help. If these hounds from hell enter the town, you must take them out. Make every shot count!" He moved over to Rusk and spoke quietly to him.

As Venter reached the cruiser, he waved briefly and took off. Beth called out to Marvin, who limped to where she stood. "Look!" Marvin rubbed his eyes and looked again. Three wolves and a dog were moving slowly towards the intersection near McNabs office.

CHAPTER 51

Venter sped down the town road, leaving a trail of dust behind him as he gunned the cruiser up another hill towards his house. A double-barreled shotgun sat beside him, and twelve cartridges sat next to it in a neat box describing their gauge and length.

He touched his sidearm for surety, feeling safer that it was still in its holster. It was fully loaded. He would not make the same mistake again as he thought briefly about the trip to the Peterson farm.

He reluctantly reduced speed towards the turnoff to the road that led up to the old house. The big cruiser slewed around the gravel corner. He compensated by turning the wheels in the opposite direction and took off, speeding along the worn tracks on the road.

As he drove, he saw several dogs but no wolves. The dogs looked at his speeding car with interest. They seemed to be heading east, moving in the opposite direction along the fence of the farm he passed. They did not move against the cruiser, but if his guess was correct, they were heading toward Essex town. What the hell? He pushed the thought out of his mind and concentrated on his daughter.

He headed up the last hill, fruitlessly trying the two-way. There was no console light. It was completely dead. The pulsing sound it emitted that morning and the day before disappeared. Was it the two-way, or was it some other issue? He shook his head, almost too tired to think about it.

Before leaving the office, he had instructed Rusk to take Nesbitt with him and head towards McNabs' shop, forcing him, if necessary, to help and kill any wolves or dogs entering the town. "Make sure he helps," Venter had whispered to him. He advised him to ensure they were near shelter if they were overrun.

Marvin had looked at him askance as he pulled him aside to give him the orders. "There are no wolves or dogs in the town," Marvin said as he pointed to the main street.

"They are coming?" Venter had replied gruffly.

"How do you know?"

"Lena said it as we drove in, and I think she is right. They are entering the town for a reason that none of us understands. If we get the way of what they want, they will kill us. They might just kill us, anyway. Somehow, Essex has become their lair."

"Don't take this the wrong way, sheriff, but you are starting to sound crazy."

"Have a look around, Marv. Think of the last three days."

Rusk nodded his head. "I still think we are overreacting."

"Maybe, Marv. Don't take anything for granted, okay?"

He had left them two rifles and ammunition, and Marvin had his pistol. Miraculously, Marvin had found another half-empty box of bullets in the rifle cupboard, which would help if they had to continue shooting. How many wolves and dogs could there be?

As Venter pressed the accelerator he realized little of the past three days made sense. Had he followed his instincts and not McNab, the town might be better positioned. What worried him most was the memory of Chance's dead and ripped body near the barn. It had been a confronting vision with his arms and legs torn away from his torso. If it could happen to him, it could happen to anyone. His daughter included. He hoped to God she was okay.

Another thought infiltrated his mind as he drove faster towards his house in the low foothills. What about Winslow? If Essex was under attack, did that mean the attack was across the county?

CHAPTER 52

Rusk and Nesbitt cautiously left the office, armed with rifles. Rusk held the rifle in one hand and firmly onto his handgun with the other. They exited through the office back door, which allowed access to a small laneway leading to the main street. Slowly and guardedly, they walked down the laneway to the street corner. Nesbitt tapped him on the shoulder.

"Marv, a word of warning. Wolves have excellent night vision but not so good during the day. They use their noses to scent prey and track by vision. We need to stay upwind if possible."

"Where the hell is upwind?"

"I'll let you know." Nesbitt said as he stepped from the line of a building and walked up towards the shops on the main street. "Look!" Rusk whispered as softly as he could. They watched as two wolves trotting ahead on the opposite side of the street, moving agitatedly with lowered heads and fur upright on the back of their necks.

"What about dogs? Do they see any better?"

"Some of those dogs are my staghounds. They see better than any breed."

'Is that meant to be good news?" Rusk nodded as he peered around the corner of the building that turned to the shops. The street appeared deserted. The street curb held several trucks near the diner, but the rest of the area was clear. "There's something wrong." Rusk whispered as he looked back down the laneway. "Those two wolves have disappeared. Where have they gone?"

"They may be up towards the stores, but that's not far away, so it beats me where the hell they are."

Rusk nodded. "Let's get to McNabs. It's on the next corner, and we can work forward from there."

Rusk and Nesbitt moved side by side, holding their loaded rifles at the ready. They crossed the small intersection of the main street and a side street that led up to the town road. They reached McNab's front door and bustled inside.

McNab was nowhere to be seen despite Rusk calling out his name. He nodded at Nesbitt. They made their way to the back of the surgery through the adjoining door. The smell of alcoholic spirits filled the air.

On the left side of the room, the wall held cages with several injured cats, one of which had a plaster cast on its back leg. What appeared to Rusk to be a ferret sat agitatedly in another cage. He called out several more times as Nesbitt investigated two smaller back rooms. He found shelves of chemicals in one and what looked to be an operating table in the other. Rusk called out, but there was no answer.

Rusk cracked the back door and peered out. He gasped at what he found. "Good lord, have a look at this." Nesbitt moved to where Rusk was standing. Astonished, he looked out at a body lying bloodied on the ground. "Who the hell is that?" Nesbitt said, shocked by what he saw. He glanced over to see Rusk shaking his head. "A town vagrant," Rusk replied briskly, "by the name of Bing. Bing Weathers, a town drunk and the man who found the bull."

"Bing! Can you hear me?" Rusk looked carefully around before opening the door.

"He's been mauled." Nesbitt felt ill as he held his rifle high and slowly ventured out to the concreted area at the back of the office. Several pieces of rusted machinery lay near the back door, and old wire cages were stacked near the back wall.

Bing's body lay at the rear of the concreted area, suggesting that he had been running when he was taken down. He lay with his head towards the door. His legs were severed. His eyes stared vacantly into space.

Rusk shook his head as he inspected the area. "He must have been trying to get away and ran to the back of the surgery to get away from the wolves."

Nesbitt adjusted his glasses as he walked solemnly around the body. "They dragged him over there." He pointed to an area where there was a spill of blood. "Did you know him?"

"I booked him for drunk and disorderly more times than I can remember. He was harmless. He must have been out there at the wrong time." Rusk sighed and motioned for them to return inside. Together, they checked their weapons and reached the front door. Rusk got to the store window and stopped Nesbitt with his hand. "Mother of God. Look out there!"

On the sidewalk, surrounding the storefront, a large group of wolves milled around, snarling, and moving impatiently as they stalked the front of the surgery. Upon sighting them inside the store, several wolves attacked the window, smashing into the glass to try and break it.

"I'll check the back," Nesbitt asked anxiously. He hurried to the back door and returned as quickly as possible. "They are guarding the back entrance as well," he said. "What the hell do we do now?"

Rusk looked out of the window, uncertainty etched on his face. "Where has Harold gone? We need to head to the diner. Hopefully, he will be over there."

"How do we do that?" Nesbitt asked nervously. "There must be twenty or more wolves and dogs out there."

"We open the door and start firing. Once it's clear enough, we run over. Okay?"

Nesbitt looked at Rusk with a shake of his head. "Deputy, I've counted twelve wolves and maybe eight dogs out there, which doesn't count the ones out the back. Do you want to shoot your way out of this? Are you serious? We won't get past the sidewalk."

Rusk looked at him. "Where in hell do we go if we don't try to get to the diner, Charlie? Stay here! Those people over there at the diner don't have protection. They are going to end up like ol' Bing out there. I am under strict orders from the sheriff. Protect at all costs."

Nesbitt put his hand roughly on Marvin's shoulder. "Listen! I've seen these wolves up close at the showground. They will kill us if we take two steps outside."

Marvin stepped back to think. He could feel the intimidation by watching so many wolves and dogs milling around the sidewalk and road. "You must have some idea, Charlie?" Rusk asked as he sat down briefly on one of the surgery chairs.

"Alpha's. He said almost to himself.

"What?" Marvin asked.

Another wolf threw itself against the old door of the surgery, picked itself up, and attempted to break the window by catapulting itself against the front glass. As it fell another took its place.

"They will break in eventually, Charlie. When that happens, they will tear us apart." Marvin waved his hand around the small waiting room. Marvin stared at Nesbitt with fear across his face. "I would rather face them than be killed inside here."

"Okay, Marv, have it your way. You see those larger wolves out there amongst the others?"

Rusk peered out, his sore leg ached, reminding him of the bite at the Romano farm. "Yup, " he replied.

"Well, they are the leaders—the Alphas of the group. The smaller ones are the Betas. They follow the Alphas. When we start firing, the wolves and dogs will scatter, but the first ones we shoot must be the Alphas. If we take them out, the rest will get confused without leadership. But, for how long is anyone's guess," Nesbitt pointed to several of them. "You see them?"

Rusk counted as best he could. "Three of em." Right?"

"The ones we can see. There might be more." Nesbitt nodded as he checked the breech of his rifle once again. "Truth is, deputy. If there are three Alphas, there are likely more than twenty Betas, and I'll tell ya something strange."

Rusk looked at him blankly. "What?"

"The dogs are mimicking their behavior."

"Is that meant to be good news?"

"Maybe not." Nesbitt shouted as he looked through the glass.

"Look!" Rusk checked his rifle as he looked at several dogs moving across the road to join the wolves crowding outside the door. "Christ almighty, are they waiting for us as well?"

Nesbitt tapped on the window with the butt of his rifle, watching the restlessness of the wolves increase. "See the Alpha's? We shoot them first and make a run for the diner."

"You sure about this?"

"Shoot quickly and then we move together. If we take the alpha group down, the rest will be disoriented. But listen, Marv. It won't last long. They will regroup!"

They rechecked the rifles. Suddenly, they heard gunfire from the other end of the street. Marvin leaned close to the window to look down, and he could see Eddie shooting in the distance. A group of dogs moved fearlessly down towards his gas station. He counted ten dogs and then saw a wolf join them.

CHAPTER 53

There was a violent shuddering of the wheels as Venter applied the brakes. The cruiser skidded across the gravel several yards to a halt. He looked over to see another car, one he had not seen before, next to the side of the house. He realized someone must have brought his daughter to the house that morning after he left early.

He opened the cruiser door and went through the swirling dust to the front steps. "Allie, Allie, where are you?" He shouted as he looked around, finally charging up to the front door.

As he reached for the handle, he looked down the veranda towards the end of the house. Suddenly, his old dog came charging around, dripping saliva from its jaw as it finally sighted him. Venter could see clumped fur on the dog's back and neck, rigidly upright and growling as it approached.

The door handle did not turn. Venter instantly assumed his daughter had locked the latch. "Stop, Butch, stop." He shouted out, instantly realizing the dog had lost control of its senses. He raised the rifle he held in his right hand, quickly took aim, and shot the old dog between the eyes as it took a snarling jump toward him. He fired a second shot, and the dog hit the ground and slumped. It stopped breathing before it hit the boards.

Venter slumped against the door momentarily, allowing the coursing adrenalin to diminish and his breathing to return to a nearly normal state. He felt tired, more tired than he could remember.

His thoughts returned to his daughter, so he put his shoulder to the door and entered. He found his daughter slumped on the floor in the hallway behind the door. He dropped his rifle gently on the floor as he kneeled next to her. "Why didn't you open the door? What's happened, Allie?"

Allie pointed towards the door and started crying.

"Are you okay, Allie? Are you okay? " Her hair was messy. Tears streaked down her face as she reached out to him, finally encircling his neck with her arms. She pointed towards the front door. "Jarrad."

"Who?"

"Jarrad. He's out there."

"Who's Jarrad?" He asked gently.

"He's the boy who brought me here."

"Is he okay?"

She started crying again and pointed back towards the door. "He pushed me inside, slammed the door, and told me to lock it, which I did. He had a rifle in the truck, but then I heard him shout not to come out when those monsters attacked him," She started to cry hysterically, holding her hands up to her face. "They got him!"

"They?" Venter asked as he sat beside her.

"Dogs. There was a group of dogs. Butch was with them. I didn't see them until we got out of the car! They started stalking us. They were so quiet we didn't notice them until we were near the house. They came out of nowhere. They just appeared! How could that happen?"

"Is Jarrad out there?" Venter asked softly, trying to calm her down.

She nodded as he started to rise. "I am too frightened to go out." She grabbed him to pull him back, but he resisted with a reassuring nod. "I will just check on him. He will have found cover."

"Don't leave, daddy. I'll come with you if you are going out."

Don't worry, Allie, I'm armed, I'll be okay. Stay here and keep the door closed."

Allie looked up at him imploringly. "What was that shot before? Are they still out there?"

Venter looked at her with a pained look. "That was Butch. He attacked me, and I had to shoot him. I didn't see any other dogs around."

"Oh my God." She started to cry again. "Poor Butch. What is going on, Daddy? Why would Butch attack you? I mean, why did those dogs attack us?"

"No one knows, Allie. Everything has gone strange." He rose and went to the door, taking a minute to check the outside. Butch lay on the boards in a pool of blood. Flies covered the bleeding wounds.

He opened the door quietly, moved into a crouched position, and pulled his pistol out as he walked. He checked the barrel and held it steady in his right hand, alert to any movement as he moved forward.

He moved slowly down the steps, looking to his left and right as he walked towards the pickup. Two minutes later, he saw the boy sprawled out on the ground, unmoving and obviously dead. His body had been ripped, just like the sheep, the bull, and Chance.

Venter moved to the side of the old pickup. Bloodied handprints were on the door. Why? He wondered. Maybe the boy tried to reach the pickup for shelter as the dogs assaulted him and reached out for the door trying to get away. Whatever happened, the boy did not make it.

Venter looked inside the truck, noting that the rifle was still in its rack. He closed the door to check the back tray. There was an old tire on the boards and a tire lever—nothing else.

Holding his pistol high, Venter checked the perimeter of the house. Except for a light breeze nudging the trees there was no movement. Perhaps his old dog, Butch, was too tired to move off with the other dogs and had stayed behind. Whatever was affecting the wolves and dogs in Essex had a similar effect on Butch. That was the only explanation. His old dog, irascible but friendly, attacked when he moved towards the door. The dog was clearly under the influence of something that Venter did not understand.

Where had the dogs gone? Why were there no wolves in the attack? A shiver went up his spine as he thought they might have taken off towards the town. He checked around the pickup, the cruiser, and the perimeter of the house. He headed back to the front door.

Allie remained slumped on the floor, so he sat down with his daughter and put his arm around her shoulders.

"What happened? Is he okay?"

"No, he is not okay, Allie. The dogs got him. Now, answer me a question. Why are you here?"

"Mom and I argued, and Jarrad said he would take me away. We came here."

"Were there any problems in Winslow? Dogs? Wolves?"

Allie shook her head. "No, Daddy, nothing. Why did that pack of dogs attack Jarrad?"

"I don't know, Allie. Many things are going on, and there seems to be no reason for any of it."

"I want to see, Jarrad."

Venter shook his head firmly. "No, Allie. It's not a pretty sight. I don't want you out there. I just thank God you are okay. You need to return with me to Essex. It's unsafe for you to stay here."

"Poor Jarrad! It's my fault. I shouldn't have let him go back to the pickup."

Venter shook his head as he held her. "No, it's not your fault, Allie. Have you called your mother?"

"The phone doesn't work, daddy."

Venter got to his feet, tested the telephone, and nodded slightly. "Dead line. Okay, grab your stuff and come with me."

"I don't like it around here. Can't we go back to Winslow?"

"Not at this stage, Allie. I need to put you in the office with Beth to know you will be safe. If you stay there, I know you are protected."

"Then what?"

Then I have to help Marvin and another man with our issues in town."

"You mean the dogs?"

Venter nodded, wondering if he should tell her the entire story, and decided against it. She had enough for one day. He now had two dead people. He wondered if there were more casualties.

He stood by the door, waiting for his daughter and concentrating on his issues. "Come on, Allie! " he shouted as he kept watch outside the house. What attracted the wolves and dogs to the farms around the county and the town? What the hell could it be? If the predatory actions of wolves and dogs changed, why not coyotes, bears, and other animals? His mind offered no hint, no answer. Whatever force worked on the wolves and dogs created the same effect on the birds. They did not attack, but they acted weirdly. The finches and the eagles above the town stuck in his mind. Why? The frustration boiled in him as he hit the door with his hand. 'Allie, what is taking you so long!?"

Instinctively, he knew McNab was wrong. These were not natural occurrences. A green wavy aurora in the sky that lit up the back of his hand as he held it up? Birds flying to death into the side of a house and birds that flew in clockwise precision above the town? He searched his mind for an answer. There was none. His anger mounted, and he shouted again at his daughter to hurry the hell up.

CHAPTER 54

On the count of three, Nesbitt opened the door of McNab's office against the snarling mass of agitated wolves pacing outside the door. They stepped outside the door and started firing.

Marvin dropped two of the Alpha wolves before he became surrounded by Betas, who attacked him, biting at his legs, ripping his pants, and lunging for his arms as he tried to push them off to get away from the pack. "Charlie, move with me," he shouted as he tried to stay beside the dog breeder.

Nesbitt was not as good a shot. Shooting one at point-blank range caused him to swivel his rifle just as an Alpha bounded into the air, finding his shoulder with its powerful jaws. The weight of the one hundred forty-pound wolf took him down onto the sidewalk. He tried to pull his rifle around to aim, but the size and weight of the animal made a shot impossible as it snarled and tore at his flesh.

He desperately attempted to pull the jaws off his shoulder as the Alpha wolf clamped its teeth and shook its head violently. Searing pain intensified as he lay back, shouting at the pain, unable to move under the attack.

He shouted out to Rusk, who fought his way over to where Nesbitt had fallen, using the butt of his rifle to bludgeon the wolf away. He put one accurate shot from his pistol through the head of the returning Alpha. As he turned around, he shot another, realizing it was a smaller wolf; a Beta.

"The diner is across the street. Can you make it?" He asked breathlessly.

"Take my arm," Nesbitt said in a hoarse whisper. Marvin grabbed him with the strength the adrenalin surging through his body offered. He pulled him up to a standing position as quickly as he could. Together, they walked, shoulder to shoulder, backing up across the road, keeping their body forward to the encroaching wolves.

Losing the alpha males had made the pack hesitant to attack, but several Betas growled brutally towards them as they approached from the front and sides. "Don't take your eyes off them, Marv. If they see a sign of weakness, they will be on us in a second."

"They are circling to my left." Marvin hissed as he clouted one with the butt of his rifle. It was like hitting hard rock, hardly fazing it as it kept approaching.

"Don't shoot. Just keep backing up. We are almost there. If you shoot, you will set them off, and they will attack. Since the Alpha isn't leading, they are unsure what to do. It's our only chance!

"How far have we got?" Marvin followed Nesbitt's instructions and kept his eyes on the front wolves, lashing out with his rifle each time they approached. He hit one wolf in the side of its head and it instantly backed off.

"Almost there," Rusk looked behind him as they stepped up onto the sidewalk. He could see two people at the window looking out as they approached. Their faces filled with horror, they shouted soundlessly through the glass front of the diner. Rusk could only guess at what they were saying.

Nesbitt watched a large Alpha wolf bounding up the street towards them. "Marv a male Alpha is coming! Get to the door!"

"Open the door." Marvin shouted desperately at Jane, who nodded as they neared the diner entrance. Rusk bashed the two nearest wolves with his rifle stock, hitting as hard as he could muster. As the Alpha neared, he raised his arm, holding onto Nesbitt's arm, and fired. The sound of the pin could be heard just above the snarling. Instantly, he realized the breech was empty.

"I am out of ammo. We go in together. Don't let them get to your side, and I'll do the same. If they follow us in, we are all dead!"

Nesbitt grimaced at the searing pain that pulsed through his shoulder as they neared the entrance. He pushed hard against the door of the diner with the heel of his boot. He passed his rifle through the slightly open door and pulled Rusk with him until someone grabbed Nesbitt's arm and roughly rustled him inside.

As Rusk followed, one of the wolf pack desperately lunged to bite into his leg, ripping a large hole in his trousers. As he fell through the door he kicked desperately trying to pull his leg away. He raised his pistol and put a round through the head of the wolf. With a dying growl, the Beta sank slowly to the sidewalk surface with blood oozing from her mouth.

In the resulting commotion, Rusk fell heavily against the opening door, falling against George who manhandled him through. A moment later the door slammed shut and a chair was positioned against it to stop it from moving. As he heard the door shut he let his body slump to a seating position on the cool of the tiled floor. The relief was overwhelming. He felt breathless and unable to move. "You okay Charlie?" He called out between breaths. All he heard was a grunt in return.

CHAPTER 55

Rusk finally laid his sore body on the floor in utter exhaustion. Nesbitt, grunting at the pain in his shoulder, leaned against the side of the long diner counter. "How many goddam wolves and dogs are out there?" He said out loud. "I have never seen anything like it. Where in hell did they all come from?"

George stood by the window as Jane moved to help Nesbitt to a seat in one of the booths. As she passed the inside of the long window she pulled back in shock as a lone wolf smashed its body against the glass. A moment later, it stood with its tongue hanging out of its mouth, snarling through the window.

Jane pulled Nesbitt's shirt back and probed around the wound. "George, get hot water and some iodine and rip up some clean towels for bandages, okay?"

"Will do." He said and hurried off towards the kitchen.

Sit here and let me have a look at that bite." She said softly. "And bring scissors, George!"

Rusk raised himself to a sitting position looking in dismay at his ripped trousers and the milling wolves outside the glass. "They are gonna try anything to get in. If they do, they will kill us."

"Then we need to stop them! Are you sure you are okay, Marv?" Jane asked as she inspected his disheveled appearance. He was covered with dirt, and his trousers and shirt were heavily ripped from the attack.

Marvin nodded wearily as he stood and sat on one of the stools, peering out at the street. He looked at Jane. "Y'all don't need to ask," he snapped. "No one knows what's going on, least of all me. The only question is how this is going to end. We will have to kill em' all."

Nesbitt groaned, waiting for the bandage. "It sure as hell won't be easy, Marv. Have a look at how many are out there."

"Is there any chance of a coffee?" Rusk muttered to himself, as he felt his sore leg.

"Anyone seen Harold?" Nesbitt asked.

"Oh, my God. Harold? He's out there." Jane replied with a sad expression. She pointed to the back of the diner. "He saw some wolves at the other end of the street, so he came over earlier to warn us not to go out. A sound came from the back of the garbage cans, and he told us to stay put. He walked out the back to investigate. Said he'd be careful."

"And?" Rusk asked quickly.

George shook his head. "I heard him shout so I went out the back, took one look and came running back here. It was horrible. Worst thing I have ever seen. It must have been dogs. There were no wolves that I saw. Maybe it was both, but the wolves were gone."

"Large with dark fur?" Nesbitt held his shoulder as he sat uncomfortably. Several times he changed position.

"Yeah, but I didn't wait around to check. As soon as I saw Harry ripped and lying on the ground, I took off. It was one hell of a sight. I can tell ya that."

Nesbitt silently shook his head as he looked at Rusk. "They are our dogs. I am sure of it."

"You certain?"

"Deerhounds." Nesbitt said solemnly. "They could easily take him down."

"He wasn't moving?" Rusk asked George.

George looked at Rusk blankly. "Moving? Deputy, he just lay there, torn apart. It was a gruesome sight and not one I would ever want to see again. Jes' thinking about it gives me the shivers."

Jane put her hand out as he approached. "Give them to me, George." He handed her a small bottle of iodine, rags, and a bowl of steaming water with a floating cloth. Jane soaked the rags and applied them to his wounded shoulder. Nesbitt let out a howl. "Goddamit, that stings."

"Good." she replied, "then it's working." She took the cloth, wrung it out, and wiped the area around the wound, cleaning his arm and hand as she finished.

George passed her a ripped tea towel, which she wrapped around the wound after applying the iodine, and finally stood him up. "It would be best if you took it easy; otherwise, that bleeding will start again. You got some serious teeth punctures, but the wound is smaller than I thought."

Nesbitt nodded, and with considerable effort, he stood up, found a different booth away from the front, and sat down with a long sigh. "What now, deputy?"

Rusk shrugged. They could not leave, and fighting the wolves outside seemed impossible given the battle as they approached the diner. Their numbers were considerable. Each time they shot one, two seemed to take its place. "Is the phone working?"

George shook his head." Nope, deputy, ain't worked for two days."

Rusk moved over to the window, gazing at the street before him. He noticed something peculiar as he surveyed the area. A pack had surrounded several of the wounded wolves. Some stood motionless beside their fallen brothers, others licking the wounds.

He counted what looked like three dead alpha males and four other wolves lying prone on the ground. Five dogs lay dead or dying on the road. As he watched the scene, one of the wolves sensed his presence inside the glass and took off toward him and the diner window. With full force, it jumped into the glass. Almost as if it did not see the window.

Rusk stood dumbfounded at the attack. He immediately moved back as the glass window wavered but held in place. The animal fell heavily to the ground. Several seconds later, it stood up, barely conscious, and slunk off towards the others.

On the sidewalk outside, wolves and dogs began to move agitatedly in front of the window after the wolf had jumped against the glass and retreated. Some wolves were sitting on the other side of the street where he had shot the two alphas. He counted quickly. Eight wolves and seven dogs were moving with eyes fixed on the occupants inside.

"Look at that." He said to Nesbitt, who rose gingerly from the booth and plodded to the window. "Protecting the wounded."

"Are all the alphas dead?" Rusk asked Nesbitt.

Nesbitt stood up slowly and made his way to the window. "I think we got them all but eventually, the Betas and the others will work it out. Don't be fooled by their behavior. They are watching us. If we try to move out, they will attack. Wolves don't take prisoners," Nesbitt said dryly. "At this point in time, we are in a cell, and they are the jailers."

Jane gave the bloodied rags to George and moved towards where Rusk was standing. "The question remains. How do we get out of this jail?"

CHAPTER 56

Venter pulled his daughter out of the cruiser by her arm, up the two steps, towards the office entrance. He had urged her not to dawdle, but she seemed unresponsive. In desperation, he bundled her through the door and into the office.

Her eyes were downcast, and she seemed unable to speak until Beth approached and led her to a chair at the radio desk. "It'll be okay," she said soothingly. She pulled up a chair next to her, sat down, looked over at Venter, and shrugged. "What's next, Tom?" she said.

Venter walked to his desk at the back of the office, and slumped in his swivel chair. He felt exhausted and unable to think of what to do next. He felt hungry and thirsty. "Did you see wolves or dogs around when Marv and Charlie left?"

"Before he left, Marv reckoned he saw some up towards the diner."

"Phone still not working, I guess?"

Beth nodded. "Correct." She handed Allie a cup of water and stood next to her while she drank it.

"Is Lena okay?"

Beth walked over to the cell at the back of the office and returned. "She's okay. She's still sleeping. In shock, I guess," She motioned to Venter to speak to her at the back of the office. "What happened at your house?" she whispered.

Venter told her the story.

"Another? Dead?" She questioned

He nodded. "This time it was dogs. No wolves."

"Can't say I have ever seen a dog attack someone? Makes no sense to me."

"I saw it happen once, but nothing like what I saw outside the house. According to Allie, she did not see a wolf, only dogs. When I checked around the house, the dogs had disappeared. They must have killed Jarrad and then taken off. The question is, where did they go?"

"Who is this Jarrad?"

Venter shrugged. "I can't ask her in the state she's in, but I suspect he is her boyfriend."

"Oh." Beth nodded her head.

Venter whispered to her. "Let's leave that alone. She's too young for a boyfriend, so I will assume, and hope, they had a friendship."

"What are we going to do about these bodies? Chance is dead, and so is this Jarrad boy. We need to get the authorities from Winslow out here asap."

"Granted." Venter replied. "The phones don't work, and I need to see where Marvin and Charlie have ended up. That rules out a trip to the council chambers at Winslow. Goddamit, I hope they are okay."

"I could drive over to Winslow," Beth added impatiently.

"We need you here," Venter said, shaking his head. "We have Lena and Allie here, and I'm worried about what might happen to you on the way to Winslow."

"We have to do something!"

Venter looked at her as he thought briefly about it. "There is not much you can do, Beth. Either way, I need you here."

"Somehow, we need to get word to Winslow."

Venter stared at her. "What are they going to do? You heard Perkins when I told him about these strange events. We are heading into the late afternoon, and there is no chance of going home, so we will need to set the office up so people can sleep here. We have coffee and little food, but that's about it."

Beth looked at Allie and smiled reassuringly. "Okay." She said flatly and sat down.

When he weighed the events of the previous three days, it became obvious that the violent behavior of the wolves and dogs first coincided with the mutilated bull. Wrong place at the wrong time. No doubt about it. His best guess was that the wolves, aided by the dogs of the district, ripped the big bull and the rage, if he could it that, continued as they attacked livestock indiscriminately, including a calf and many sheep on two farms as they moved around. He wondered how many other farms had been invaded.

The evidence showed that dogs, maybe wolves as well, murdered Chance and Jarrad and nearly killed him. How many others had been killed? How would anyone eliminate such a significant threat if it was widespread across the county, or the country? Was that possible?

He clearly understood the behavior. In each case, the attack was unpremeditated against an animal that could not defend itself. Also, all of the attacks and resulting violence were brutal and unrelenting with dogs and wolves combining in the assaults. So, something was driving their behavior, and it had not happened, to his knowledge, anywhere else. Allie had told him that Winslow was unaffected. But, was it, or only at the time his daughter had left with Jarrad? The thought unnerved him.

The evidence was overwhelming. The attacks were not killing for food but for the hell of it. He believed that the wolf packs had taken control, and dogs, including Nesbitt's deerhounds, had followed behind the packs. The dogs were copying the behavior of the packs, and maybe working independently from the wolves.

It stood to reason that most farms and houses kept dogs throughout the Essex district. That meant a large number of dogs had joined the wolf packs. Why and how they would cohabitate and hunt with a natural enemy eluded him? An icy shiver went up his spine as he considered the possibility of more wolves and dogs arriving in the town. The only question that remained front of his mind related to Essex. Why were they converging on his town?

Beth's voice brought him out of his thoughts as she stood beside his desk with her arms folded. "There is not much else I can do, sheriff. Allie has settled, thank God. I don't want to wake up our other guests. The question is, what are you going to do?"

"Find Marv and do what we can to take em' out."

"What if there are more coming?"

Venter gave her a grim smile. "Then we have a larger problem. Either way, they will not back down. They are moving into this town to kill. Of that, I am sure. Why this town? God knows, because I can't think of a plausible reason. We are now the hunted."

"I don't think you understand, Sheriff." Beth said in her most serious voice.

"What do you mean?" He said, rising quickly from his seat.

Beth had walked down to the window in front of the radio desk. "Have a look outside," Came the reply. "There are more!"

He scurried down to the front window as he heard his daughter scream. "They are waiting for us!"

CHAPTER 57

Venter did not see the snarling dog as he hustled out the door towards the cruiser. He instantly heard the growl and as he looked behind him a massive German shepherd was barely three yards behind him in a slavering crouch. He shouted at it, pulled his revolver and shot it at point blank range. Blood from the spurting wound sprayed the front of his pants as he angrily shot it again. Bleeding profusely, it slumped backward on the ground near the cruiser rear wheel.

He opened the door and slammed it behind him, immediately checking the two-way. Red light blinking, the lack of signal stared back at him. Nothing worked! How was that possible?

He threw his rifle on the seat, looking over the hood, directly into the growling face of a small black-and-white dog. He stared at it realizing it was a sheepdog, a kelpie of all things. It bounded onto the hood, pawed, and snarled at the glass that separated it from the interior. He started the cruiser and hit the accelerator as the dog fell heavily onto the blacktop, rising instantly and moving to the outside of the office to join another dog and two wolves standing outside the door.

He drove quickly down the main street, took a right at the intersection, and onto the access road to the town road. He looked back in his rear-view mirror, astonished at the number of wolves and dogs milling around the middle of the intersection. Many were sitting around the iron World War Memorial in the middle of the street.

He stopped the cruiser and looked around. Some of the dogs and wolves began to follow the cruiser, as others appeared to be guarding the sidewalks towards the main group of shops. Venter could not make sense of it so he slowly motored down until he saw the diner. Jane and Marvin were waving at him as he stopped outside.

Marvin motioned urgently for him to come in. He looked up and down the street, watching the wolves who had sensed his presence start running towards him. He fired his pistol to disorientate them and slammed the cruiser door behind him. He was inside within five long steps.

"Is everyone okay?"

"Thank God you are here." Jane moved quickly to him and put her arms around him. "We're okay. Just okay!"

Marvin approached him and pointed to Nesbitt, sitting in pain at the booth, his right hand gingerly around a coffee cup.

"Anyone else here?" Venter asked.

"It's just us, sheriff. They got Harold. They got him out back, and there is not much left."

Venter grimaced at the news. He put his arm around Jane. "You okay?"

"Sort of, " she replied quickly. I was worried about you. It has been a hell of a day."

"Charlie, you badly injured?"

"He'll live." Jane replied. "They make them tough, these dog breeders."

"Not tough enough." Nesbitt replied. "We got attacked over at McNab's surgery, fought our way out and across to here."

"How long ago?"

"Maybe two hours or more." Rusk replied. "Did you find Allie?"

Venter nodded. "I think her boyfriend dropped her off. He was attacked outside."

"How bad? Jane asked.

"He didn't stand a chance," Venter replied sadly. "Allie is a mess, so I left her at the office. Did you fight your way here?" he asked Nesbitt.

"We shot three Alphas, but one of them survived, or so we think. The other two fell, and that was enough to disorientate the other Beta's and Omega's in the pack. We forced our way into the diner."

"Omega's?" Rusk asked.

Nesbitt shrugged. "Part of the pack hierarchy."

"How many wolves and dogs are there?"

"Hard to say. We shot some, but they kept coming. There might be up to thirty or more betas, plus several alphas. As I explained to Marv, the betas will be reluctant to attack if the alpha isn't leading. I know that much about wolf pack behavior."

"And the dogs?"

"Not so many," Rusk offered. "Maybe fifteen, but we shot four of them."

"I shot one at the office." Venter noted. "I counted two wolves down there. Did anyone here see them clustering around the middle of the intersection? They are sitting, and some are standing around the old memorial."

"Why the hell would they do that?"

"I have no idea." Venter shrugged as he moved to the window to look at the street before him.

"It's made of iron, isn't it?" George added. He walked over to the booth and poured another cup for Nesbitt. "I can't say that might mean anything. Maybe the iron attracts them?"

"Why would iron attract dogs and wolves? That makes less sense than what is happening out there," Jane looked over at Venter. She removed her cap and adjusted her hair. 'I don't see bears or coyotes. Why only dogs and wolves. None of it makes sense."

Venter nodded with a wry smile. "I agree."

Nesbitt moved his shoulder with a wince. "I am sad about Harold. He was good man and a great veterinarian. I don't understand why he went out knowing the savagery of the wolves. Why would he do that?"

Jane shrugged. "He didn't believe they would continue to attack, and he told Marv and me, and everyone at the church, to leave them alone. He said they would head back to the hills by themselves. Perhaps he thought they would leave him alone. I think he was trying to prove something."

"Those monsters are the disciples of the devil." George added. "Nothing more or less."

"Hey, look at that!" Marvin pointed out the window.

When Venter saw the mass of wolves, he stepped back from the diner window, moving Jane with him. He looked at Marvin, who had pulled back from where he was standing. Instinctively, he reached for his pistol to check the breech. "They're back." He shouted.

Outside, half of the sidewalk had suddenly filled with wolves and dogs. Some were fighting amongst themselves, jaws flashing and muscles bulging as snarls took over and fights broke out.

One dog trotted back to the opposite side of the street and turned. With its head down and jaw tightly closed, it sprinted towards the diner window, launching against the glass. It hit with a resounding thud as the window wavered but held. "What the hell is it doing?" Rusk looked perplexed. "Is it trying to break through the glass?"

Venter watched as it fell, badly dazed with blood dripping from its black nose. Within a moment, another took its place, snarling and bounding towards the window to throw itself against the glass, which yet again shuddered and finally calmed.

"Up there," Jane said, pointing to the top left-hand side of the glass nearest the door. A small but noticeable crack had appeared.

"What the hell will we do if they break in?" Jane looked at Venter and Rusk. "How many dogs and wolves are out there? What if they get through?"

"They will certainly kill us. I know that much," Nesbitt said in a measured tone. "That dog that hit the window? That was Marco, my lead dog. Those wolves are heavier, so that window won't last long. They are trying to get at us, and unless we do something, they will rip us apart." He looked at Jane and Venter, standing several yards from the window.

"We have nothing we can use to bar the glass, for Chrissakes." George wiped his brow with a handkerchief. "How much ammo do you guys have?"

"Maybe twenty rounds? Marv?"

"Less!" He replied solemnly. "Several in my pistol as well."

Nesbitt looked at his rifle. "Not many. We don't have enough ammo to kill them if they get through. Anyone got a suggestion?"

Venter looked out of the diner window. "Just one. Somehow, we must get out of here and back to the office. We can defend there more easily and have the jail cells at the back for protection. They may be able to get through glass, but no chance against a metal jail cell. Somehow, we have to divert their attention and get to the cruiser."

"How?" Jane asked.

Venter walked to the back door, and everyone else moved back as a wolf smashed against the lower part of the window. It fell hard to the ground, seemingly winded, but unhurt.

Others followed the pattern as the wolf picked itself up, throwing themselves with a thump against the glass. As each fell, another took its place. Saliva and the blood from injured jaws dripped down the bottom of the wide glass front.

Nesbitt stood unsteadily from his booth, gingerly approaching the front door to inspect the glass. It had begun to crack from the top and the side. "The only thing I can think of is to make a ruckus at the back of the diner, which should attract them away from the front to give us time to get out."

Rusk nodded. "That might work. We get the cruiser as close to this door as possible and pile in. This front door opens inwards, so we should be able to crawl through the cruiser window if it is next to the door and into the back seat. Sheriff, do you agree?"

Venter shrugged. "Anything is worth a try. The glass will not hold much longer."

Involuntarily, he stepped back as what appeared to be the most prominent wolf in the group hit the middle of the window with a resounding smack. A crack started to travel from the side across the panel, almost reaching the middle.

"Several more of those and the wolves will pour through the broken glass. Let's get to it."

Venter moved to the back of the diner, pulled the door slightly, and peered outside. As he stepped out, he could make out McNab's motionless, bloodied body. He picked up the nearest trash can and threw it into the air. As soon as it landed, he sent another one after it.

"It's working." Marvin shouted from the front.

Venter raised his rifle and felt the recoil before releasing the stock from his shoulder. He watched as wolves and dogs bounded around the corner of the building directly toward the sound.

As a large group of wolves and dogs approached, he shut the door tight and jammed the top of a chair under the handle. He ran to the other end of the diner as Marvin opened the door. Within five steps, he was inside the cruiser. He jammed the key in the ignition, wondering why he had taken it out in the first place.

"Go. Go!" Marvin shouted as he looked down the street.

Wolves were loping around the corner after hearing the cruiser engine start. Venter rammed the cruiser in reverse, hitting one of the returning dogs. Moving backward, the car hit another wolf on its side, propelling it with force as it screamed in pain. With a loud yelp, it got up and limped towards the others.

Venter put the gear in first, moving the cruiser so close it scraped against the building wall until the back door was next to the diner door and the side of the vehicle rigid against the window and the wall either side of the front.

"Let's go," Venter shouted. Marvin pulled the diner door open. Venter immediately leaned back to unwind the rear window, allowing access to the inside.

He looked around feverishly. The snarling group could only access the car's interior by climbing over the roof and attacking the open window opposite the diner door. "Get in, get in, before they work out how to come over the roof." He shouted desperately.

George pushed Jane through the window and tried to follow her, but his size made it difficult. Wolves pawed at the other side of the cruiser, snarling and barking. One finally scrabbled onto the hood, and as it moved, it lost its footing.

Venter handled his pistol, edged it into the space between the door frame and the window, and fired three shots in succession. The point-blank bullets hit one wolf and a dog that had gained a footing on the hood. One went down with a smashed back leg, and the other took the bullet through the chest as it fell sideways with blood spraying over the black hood, leaving a shimmering spill that dripped down to the front fender.

Marvin pushed George through the open window and rushed over to assist Nesbitt as he faltered, trying to get up from his seat. With the strength that comes from fear and adrenaline, he moved him over to the cruiser window.

"George, get in the front seat." Venter shouted over the screams of pain coming from Nesbitt as he crawled through the window, snagging his ripped shoulder on the side of the window frame.

Marvin pushed him through as hard as he could and, within a moment, propelled himself through, landing on the seat, head down, but inside. He quickly righted himself, wound up the window, and looked out the back at the crowd of wolves clawing at the cruiser sides.

"Close the window," Venter shouted as he put the cruiser into gear. A dog jumped on the hood. He gunned the engine. There was a tearing sound as the cruiser doors moved away from the wall. Marvin looked back to see four wolves chasing after them. Another dog threw itself against the diner window. As it picked itself up, glass shards began to fall to the pavement. A second later Rusk could see the window collapse. He watched as wolves and dogs vaulted into the diner.

"What do we do now?" Jane asked, brushing the hair from her face. "What about everyone else?"

The wolves gave up the chase, falling away one by one. One hundred yards up the street, he slowed the vehicle. "Everyone okay?"

"Charlies in a lot of pain." Marvin replied, "But he'll live."

Nesbitt grunted. "Anyone got an aspirin?"

Venter slowed the cruiser as he pointed to the gas station. Eddie Crook's bloodied body lay outside the front door of his shop, almost against the bowser. "He must have been taken while we were inside. When I drove up, there was no sign of him."

Jane grabbed Venter by the arm. "We should check. He could be alive."

"Marv?"

Marvin checked around the car, cautiously opening the back door. He could see the group of dogs and wolves moving quickly down the road towards him, so he promptly moved to where Eddie lay, shook his head, and returned. "He's dead," His words hung over the interior of the car. "Goddamit, why was he out there?"

Jane turned to Rusk and put her hand on his arm. "It's all so sudden, Marv. No one knew it would turn out like *this*."

Marvin shook his head. "Who knows? He may have just come out to look around and got taken from behind. These bastards move so fast. Look what they have done to the diner window."

"At least we are out of there."

"Do you think this is happening in other places?"

"My guess? Yep, it must be. That light above the hills can't be just here, over Essex of all places."

"You mean Winslow and the rest are under attack by wolves and dogs?"

Nesbitt nodded. "Why would Essex be the only area affected? I think the wolves and dogs share one common thing."

"Which is?" George shifted his bulk around on the seat.

"The attacks are compulsive. They do not differentiate between animals and us. They are not foraging to kill humans. The wolves are killing, and the dogs are joining them in response. It is almost as if the wolves have control of the dog's behavior."

"But why dogs and wolves?" Venter asked. "Why not coyotes or bears or goddam foxes, for that matter? It's unbelievable."

Rusk nodded as he considered it. "You're right, sheriff. There has not been a coyote in sight."

Nesbitt held his shoulder as he looked at Jane. "There must be a solution."

It could not be much worse." Venter said softly. "We don't have a telephone that works, and the two-way hasn't operated for two days. Winslow is forty minutes away. If Winslow are overrun, what will we do? We need to wait it out."

Marvin nodded. "I agree with the sheriff. We need to stay put until tomorrow morning."

Venter drove slowly around several of the back streets in the safety of the cruiser. He sighted two wolves in the vicinity. Two dog carcasses lay on the side of the road. Each dog had been brutally torn apart. The head was ripped, and the legs pulled from the torso. There was no visible consumption of the carcasses. Venter guessed there was a fight with wolves, and the dogs came off second-best.

"They're gone from the monument." Marvin added with a long look as the cruiser motored the distance to the office.

"Is that good or bad news." Jane looked over at Rusk.

"What time is it?" Venter said as he pulled up at the office. He looked around. The wolves and dogs he had earlier left behind had disappeared.

Marvin checked his watch. "Heading to five. Why?"

"Do wolves get restless in the afternoons?" Venter directed his question to Nesbitt, who rubbed his shoulder with a wince of pain. "Wolves are nocturnal, Tom."

"How good is their hearing?"

"About five miles. Better than domestic dogs, anyway."

Venter turned the next corner, asking Marvin to check out the back of the cruiser. He could see the wolves moving down the street but not near the car.

"We've got time before they mount an attack." Nesbitt said as he looked out the window.

"How long?" Venter asked.

"Not long enough."

CHAPTER 58

Venter grabbed a cup of coffee from Beth when she offered it to him. He wolfed down several cookies as he checked the back cells where everyone would sleeping that night, and returned to his desk.

The office had never held as many occupants as it did that evening. There were eight of them scattered around the floor. Lena stayed in the rear cell on the old bunk. She lay there without complaint but had no interest in eating or drinking.

"She is still in shock, Tom." Beth whispered when he entered the door with the others. Venter nodded. There was little to say.

He spent a short time with his daughter to understand if she could talk and function after the horror of the attack at the house. She seemed okay, but he felt suspicious that she was hiding the loss of Jarrad and was unable to speak of it. She said little staring vacantly at him when he asked her how she was feeling. It unnerved him.

"We have little in the way of food, " Beth said softly, holding a half-pack of cookies. We have cookies and bread, but plenty of coffee. We even have cream left."

Venter stood up and nodded to Rusk as he leaned back against his desk. "It's getting dark, so we need to bunk down tonight, and tomorrow morning, I will make a run for it with Charlie to the hospital in Winslow. After he is secure, I will get to the council chambers and get the county coroner. We have three dead out there. God knows how many more. The women can take the four bunks. If they get in, we can defend from here."

"If?" Jane asked with a flutter of nervousness.

Venter shrugged and smiled. "Harder glass to break. We should be okay."

"Good." Beth snapped. "There are four bunks and plenty of blankets to find some comfort. What are you boys going to sleep on?"

"Y'all take the bunks; we'll share the floor." Rusk said with a wry smile. "I'm so tired I could sleep on barbed wire."

"Sounds great." Nesbitt commented quickly as he slunk into a chair.

Beth returned to her desk to pick up her cup. She suddenly stopped and stooped forward, dropping the cup to the floor. It broke into pieces, scattering on the old floorboards. "Oh. look, look! Sheriff! Come here!"

Venter moved quickly to the front of the office and peered out the window, looking up towards the intersection. In the fading light of the main street, he could make out the mass of gray and black shapes spread across the road and sidewalk. Wolves and dogs were moving towards the office.

"Oh, dear God." Beth's face looked white from fear. "How do they know we are here?" Her face was white as she turned to the rest of them. "What are we going to do?"

Venter sprinted back to his desk, grabbed his rifle, and headed for the door. "Marv, get your rifle and follow me. For the rest of you, get back to the cells, lock the doors, and stay there! If they get in, you stay in the cell and fight from there!"

Nesbitt rose, trying to use his good arm to lift himself from his chair. Venter shook his head at him. "Nope, Charlie. You stay here and take care of everyone else. Do what you must, but everyone will be safe behind those bars, so no one leaves." He handed Nesbitt his pistol and with his rifle in hand he followed Rusk, slamming the front door behind him with a thud.

Venter pulled his deputy by the arm to position him beside the Ford opposite the main street. Rusk set himself behind the cruiser hood, keeping his feet firmly on the ground. Venter moved to the back of the car, looking up the street. "Use the hood to keep your hands steady, okay?" He said breathlessly.

"Is this gonna work?" Rusk asked nervously.

"We don't have a lot of choice. It is now or later. Either way we need to make a stand. Like it or not, this is it!"

Rusk nodded as he checked the breech of his rifle and jingled the rounds that lay at the bottom of his right pocket. He pulled them out and laid them next to the gun. He looked up the road with a scared look on his face. A bustling pack of salivating wolves and dogs kept moving towards them. "How many are there?"

Venter sighted his rifle after loading it. "There must be fifty or more! I bet that they will slow as they approach us. They will scent, which might make them wary of coming closer, and that is when we open fire. We won't kill fifty but we can take quite a few out."

"For Chrissakes, sheriff, I hope you are right. That didn't work on the way to the diner."

"You shot several of the Alpha wolves, right?"

"I think so, sheriff. That's what Charlie said to aim for, so I did. I understand that the pack responds to the Alpha leader, and they are usually the biggest. So, we shoot em first."

"Will do." Venter replied nervously.

Rusk pointed to several of the larger wolves. "See, over there, the largest ones at the front? They are the Alphas!" He was sweating. The more he wiped his face, the less it helped. He wondered if he could hold the rifle properly.

"Kill what you can."

"What happens if they overrun us?"

"We need to fight until we have no ammo left and then we need to get back inside somehow. We guard each other against side attacks."

"Have a look at the size of that pack!" Venter could hear the panic in his deputy's voice. He felt the same way. The sight of so many vicious animals was confronting and frightening. He shook his head wondering if it was just a bad dream until he heard Rusk load another round into his rifle. Venter squinted at the moving mass of fur. At least fifty, he guessed at a quick count. There were more wolves than dogs. He could hear the fevered panting as they approached.

"If they overrun us, Marv, they will tear us apart. Make every shot count. We fire until we have nothing left, then we fight our way back inside."

Two of the lead Alphas stopped some twenty yards from where he and Marv stood behind the cruiser. They snuffled the air, looking hesitant to move forward, almost as if they sensed the rifles aimed at their heads. "Not long now," Venter whispered.

Suddenly, the Alphas parted and spread out until the wolves following them stood two deep and stretched across the sidewalk and across the road with an Alpha at each end.

"What now?" Rusk said quietly. "Why are they stopping?"

Venter shrugged, trying desperately to understand why they had halted their advance. He watched as they fanned out further, flanking the cruiser. He watched as packs of wolves and dogs moved in different directions. The combined growling became the only sound he could hear.

"Be careful. I reckon they are trying to outsmart us, Marv. They are going to attack from all sides. That means you will have to watch your side. Going over the cruiser's top will be difficult, but if one of us falls, the rest is easy to work out."

"Let's head back inside! We can shoot from inside!" Rusk spoke hoarsely, watching the restlessness starting in the pack.

Venter shook his head. "Too late, Marv. You saw what happened at the diner. They will come through the windows, and we have people to protect."

Goddamit." Venter heard the hissed reply.

"This is what we're paid for, Marv." Came the soft reply.

"I never saw anything in the rule book about fighting wolves and dogs, sheriff," Rusk snorted as he waited.

Slowly, the mass of black-coated wolves shifted towards them. Venter also counted eight dogs moving up behind the lead pack, but were less aggressive in their stance and behavior. The largest Alpha to the left of the cruiser growled deeply, bared its teeth, and moved stealthily with eight more wolves in its group. Several dogs started to move shift direction towards the cruiser. "Now, Marv. Let it rip."

The sound of gunfire echoed off the building and down the long street. Venter aimed for the head of the first enormous wolf, assuming it was an Alpha. He took it down in one shot. It fell hard to the ground.

Marvin shot twice at an approaching wolf, missed, cursed, and shot again, finally wounding it in the neck. They loaded as quickly as possible and kept up the firing until they were shooting at the mass of wolves and dogs milling in front of them. The sound of their heavy breathing and screams of agony from the pack filled the air.

Loud gunfire lasted for less than five minutes, but it felt like an eternity. The quicker they shot the front wolves, the more amassed in front of them. The quicker the betas followed the charge, the more rapid the gunfire. Venter reached into his pocket. He was out of ammunition. As he checked a wolf, a female Beta, jumped up onto the hood, slipped and fell back. Another took its place as Rusk fired at its head. It slumped and fell back.

"You empty?" He shouted.

Rusk placed a small handful of shells on the cruiser hood. Venter grabbed them quickly as he clouted one smaller alpha with the stock of his rifle and shot it as he retreated.

Among the smell of gunpowder and the percussion of the rifle rounds ringing in their ears, the agonizing growls of wolves and dogs filled the area. Around them, dogs and wolves lay dying on the road and sidewalk. One alpha, shot by Marvin, raised itself on all four legs, snarled, reeled, and finally fell over, presumably dead.

Wolves moved around the end of the cruiser, avoiding the gunfire at the front. Rusk grunted in fear as he looked desperately to his right at a smaller wolf that had sneaked around the back tire and moved into a crouch. "Sheriff, they are coming around the sides. Look, look!"

Venter did not have time to check to his side. He had counted fifteen or more had been taken down, but still some moved forward. Finally, two bounded towards the cruiser hood, directly towards where he stood. While one slipped, Venter took the advantage and fired a shot through the gray-furred chest of the other at point-blank range. It grunted at the pain and fell back to the blood-soaked ground.

Venter searched vainly for more bullets in his pocket, but there were none. "Marv, I'm out. Let's move." As he turned, a small wolf launched at Venter's leg. It missed and finally clamped it jaws into the top of his boot.

Venter grunted in agony. "Shoot, it's got my ankle. Get, it off!" He screamed out. He could feel sharp teeth crunching through his boot and into his heel. He tried to raise the stock of his rifle as the wolf violently pulled his ankle back towards the pack.

Within a second, Rusk moved over to where Venter was falling to the ground. He grabbed the rifle from Venters hand, prayed there was a round left, and shot the beta through the eyes. "Pull it off me, Marv. I can't get away," Rusk bent down, grabbed the wolf by its jaw, prized them open, and manhandled Venter to pull him up with his last ounce of strength.

Together, they hobbled up the steps as another lone wolf galloped around the back of the cruiser toward them. "Go!" Rusk shouted as he pushed Venter through the door. He shot at the wolf as it launched itself towards him, missed and clubbed it as it came close. In a moment he opened the door and slammed it shut behind him with the sound of the wolf hitting the outside of the door.

Venter grabbed at his heel. "Is it bleeding?" He shouted. He felt no pain, just the coursing blood that pounded at his temples from the exertion of the battle.

"Move back to the cell." Venter shouted over the unbearable sounds of dying wolves and savage dogs that kept howling, snarling, and growling outside the door.

Within a minute, another, more ominous sound began. The frantic sound of wolves and dogs throwing themselves at the door and windows. Each crash against the door made the building tremble.

"They are going to get in," Venter said as he tried to breathe. Rusk nodded, shouting at the pain from his leg as he dragged himself along. They reached the first cell, pulled the door shut, and fell on the floor, panting to regain breath.

"I think we just saw hell." He stuttered before trying to sit up.

Slumped on the cell floor, they drank slowly from cups of water passed to them by Beth through the bars of the adjoining cell. Nesbitt and George were in the cell with them. Beth, Jane, Jesse, Lena, and his daughter, Allie, sat in the next cell, further away from the door. The women seemed calm but alert to the sounds from outside.

Outside, the night had turned pitch black. Venter checked his watch. It had been over an hour, and the wolves had not broken through the window. The sound of smashing bodies against the front of the building lessened. A piece of good news, he thought to himself as he sat exhausted on the floor with his back resting on the cell wall.

Finally, with effort, Venter raised himself and strolled around the cell to test his foot. After taking off his boot, he examined the wound and felt relieved to see that the skin was bruised with some minor bleeding. The force of the wolf's jaws had clamped on his boot and broken skin, but had not punctured his flesh. "You got any ammo left, sheriff?" Rusk asked slowly as he winced at the pain from his leg where it was bitten at the Romano farm. He felt the wound area. It was tender and painful, but the bleeding had stopped.

Venter checked his handgun. "None. You?"

Rusk shrugged. "Four in the pistol. The rifle is empty."

Venter felt steady but tired. Nesbitt rose to stand with him. They gazed out the cell window towards the hills to the East of the town. The night air felt cold and unwelcoming. "Four rounds will not be of much help the way things are going," Nesbitt said with a slight shrug of his shoulders.

Venter nodded. "In the army, they used to say that when in trouble, use what you have, not what you want. Not that it helped much when we ran out of ammunition."

"What now?" Nesbitt said. "The wolves have us cornered. If they break in, we have nowhere to go."

"I understand that!" Venter replied, suddenly angry. "I have four people dead out there, and those are only the ones I know about! I'm not going to lose anymore. We must bunk down tonight because everyone is exhausted and safe behind these bars. No arguments!"

"Okay, okay, just settle down, Tom. Just saying it as it is. What about the morning?" Nesbitt asked quickly.

"I fight my way out and get to Winslow for help."

"Can't you go now?" Jane asked quickly. "Maybe we could start a diversion."

"Are you serious?" Marvin looked at her with a frown. "It is knee-deep in wolves and dogs out there, and you can't see your hand in front of your face, it's so dark. We need to rest, don't you think? We have four rounds left."

"I agree." Venter replied. "We will fight on in the morning." He returned to his sitting position and his water cup.

Nesbitt stayed at the window, looking up at the blaze of stars blanketing the sky above Essex. "Clear night, " he said to no one in particular.

Calm descended on the office as each made themselves comfortable. The raucous sounds made by the wolves lessened. Now and then, they heard the sound of another attack on the door. Venter offered silent thanks that the building was old but soundly built.

" Maybe they need sleep as well." Beth said from her bunk.

Venter pulled an old pillow under his head and fell asleep quickly and easily. He had never felt the fatigue that washed over him that night. His daughter was safe and close to him in the next cell, and they were protected. He considered it the only good news of the day.

Some hours later, Venter awoke from a gentle hand nudging his shoulder. He tried to ignore it and push it away with his hand. He finally woke reluctantly at Nesbitt's voice above him. Venter looked up wearily. "What?" he asked.

"Come with me." Nesbitt said softly.

"Where the hell are we going?" Venter asked groggily.

"You need to see this." Nesbitt helped him up, and together, they walked softly to the window at the back of the cell.

'What?" Venter asked sleepily.

"Look!" Nesbitt pointed to the window. "You need to look up there."

"What?" Venter asked again. He felt physically and mentally tired, and even the thought of rising made him feel worse. Stiffness had invaded his body.

"So?" Venter said as his aggravation increased.

"The light above the hills."

Venter peered out for a moment. "So, what?"

"It's disappeared."

CHAPTER 59

Early the following day, Venter turned his tired and sore body over on the floorboards that had been his bed for the night. His arms and legs hurt. He looked at Marvin, who had removed his boots as he lay on the hard floorboards. His face looked drawn and thin. He doubted either his deputy or himself could fight another battle. They had been lucky to get away from the invading wolves and dogs the previous night.

Jane looked at him from the other cell. Everyone else appeared to be resting. "Marvin snores like a horse." She whispered with a broad smile. She gazed at him through her drowsy eyes, her hair tousled and her clothes ragged from sleeping on the hard cot.

Venter nodded and slowly sat up. He looked through the bars at the office, and it remained intact. "Are you okay?" he whispered back. She smiled again. "The sounds have stopped. Listen?" She said softly.

Venter stood with a grunt and moved over to the cell door. A cup of coffee and a plate of eggs would go down a treat, he thought to himself as he leaned against the bars to listen. Jane was right. There was no sound coming from the front or side of the office. He expected to hear shuffling, growling, and the occasional fight, but it remained strangely silent.

He nudged Marvin awake, and he quickly sat up. "What's up? What happened?"

Venter bent down to speak to him. "It's okay, Marv. Thank God, they didn't get in. It seems quiet outside."

Rusk nodded. "That's good news, right?"

Venter checked his ankle and sat next to Rusk to whisper. "I don't think we can fight them again, Marv. I need to get to Winslow for reinforcements. I will take Charlie with me to get treatment for his shoulder."

Rusk rubbed his forearm as he gingerly stood up for a moment and then slumped down again as pain took over. "What y'all want me to do?"

"Sit tight and do what you can if the wolves come in. They can't enter the cells, so we'll make sure you all have water and food left. I'll drive straight to Winslow. Explain to them what has happened and get help."

"What if they have the same problem, sheriff?" Beth asked with a sleep-laden voice.

"Then, we will have to deal with that issue. We need help, Beth, and that's the only place I might get it. Also, we need more ammo. Whatever they have, I'll bring it back with me. I'll try to get supplies, like food and bandages. Marv, you said we have four rounds left?"

Rusk nodded as he shuffled to the cell door, looking warily around the outside of the iron bars.

As they spoke, the others slowly woke up. "What time is it?" Jesse asked as she rubbed her eyes."

"Six thirty," Venter replied, looking at Rusk. "You let us out the door and then get back here, okay?"

Rusk nodded as Venter prodded Nesbitt. "Charlie, you have the worst injury. You need to come with me and go straight to the hospital at Winslow."

Nesbitt looked over at his wife. "Jesse?"

She nodded. "We'll go later, Charlie. I feel safer here." She met him at the bars, separating the two cells. "You need to get help. I think that the wound is infected. Don't worry, Charlie. We will be okay in the cells."

Nesbitt nodded and turned to Venter. "I'll follow you, sheriff."

"When we get to the cruiser, we both pile in, one after another, through the same door. If they attack, I will shoot, but you go in fast."

Rusk checked his pistol and passed it to Venter. The three moved out of the cell toward the office door. Rusk peered cautiously out the window toward the town center, remembering the sisters farm and how the wolves stood guard outside the front door and side windows.

"How many?" Venter questioned as he checked the pistol and waited next to the door. He felt uneasy, wondering if a sprint to the cruiser would give them the time to get inside. He had seen enough of wolves to know what they were capable of in attack.

Rusk moved his position to view as far as he could up the main street and then checked the front porch. He looked quizzically at Venter and then rechecked the window view towards the town.

Nothing moved. The street was vacant.

CHAPTER 60

Marvin opened the office door softly, keeping his eyes on the steps that descended to the sidewalk and the cruiser, eight yards away. The car looked like it had been involved in a severe collision, with the passenger side buckled in from the diner when Venter broadsided the wall to get close to the door.

He looked at Venter and shrugged. He mouthed the words. "The wolves are gone".

Venter stared at Rusk in disbelief. With his hand on the latch, he moved cautiously through the doorway with his hand held at waist height, the hammer of the pistol cocked back, ready to fire. He could feel his pulse rise as he stepped out onto the porch, fully expecting an attack.

Slowly, he made his way down the steps, swiveling his pistol to his right and left as he moved forward. Behind him, Nesbitt grunted in pain as he took the first step, looking for approaching wolves, ready to move his broken body to the car as fast as he could.

A tall gray dog strolled around the corner as Venter reached the cruiser door. Eyeing them, it walked casually towards them with its tail wagging. With its head held high, it emitted a light whine as it approached. Venter aimed the pistol at it as it came forward.

"Don't! Don't shoot," Nesbitt said with a gasp. "I know that dog."

"That's a goddam huge dog, Charlie. It looks like it is ready to attack!"

"It's recognized me. I know it's behavior like the back of my hand. It will not attack."

"Says who? You?"

"It's my dog, sheriff. I should know."

Venter looked at him, stunned. "One of yours? The group that took off with the wolves?"

Nesbitt crouched slowly to avoid pain from his shoulder and held out his hand. The hound padded softly to him and licked his fingers, finally sitting calmly beside him. "Yep, one of mine."

With nerves jangling, Venter walked cautiously around. He checked beside the cruiser and the front of the office with a slow shake of his head. Holding the pistol high, he inspected the bodies of wolves and dogs lying in broken, bloodied, lifeless shapes around the perimeter of the car and on the sidewalk. One dog, lying wounded on its side, whined slowly as he moved past. He stood next to it and surveyed the scene.

One wolf lay hanging over the front of the cruiser hood with its tongue slumped from its mouth below dead eyes. Venter pushed it off as he kept alert. Wolves and dogs lay in various stages of rigor mortis. The area looked like a battlefield, which Venter realized it had become early the night before as they fought to save their lives.

He nudged several with his boot as they lay on the road, noting with satisfaction that they were dead. He grunted as he returned to where Nesbitt stood leaning against the cruiser passenger side.

"The wolves have disappeared," Venter whispered to Nesbitt as they looked at the surreal sight before them. The carcasses of dogs and wolves lay across twenty yards in front of the cruiser and towards the front of the sheriff's office.

"Look over there." Nesbitt pointed to several dogs lying in the sun on the sidewalk ten yards away. Venter watched the dogs with heightened suspicion. He held his pistol trained on them as he hurriedly looked around. One of the dogs lay on the ground, and the other stood, tail wagging and head high as it sighted them.

There was no aggression, slavering, or growling. The frenetic movement he had witnessed in the last several days had disappeared.

As he watched the dog's behavior, he thought it must be some sort of diversion. Were wolves intelligent enough to do such a thing?

One of them, a sheepdog, paddled over to Nesbitt with a wagging tail and licked his hand. It sat beside the deerhound and finally lay down at Nesbitt's feet.

"What is this?" Venter asked, disbelieving what he was witnessing. "Is this a ploy? Are they hidden somewhere?"

Nesbitt shook his head. "The wolves have disappeared, probably to the hills. It seems the dogs have lost their aggressive behavior. Something has changed. It's back to normal, maybe?"

"There is no goddam *normal* around here, Charlie. Get in." He roared as he slammed his door. "This can't be right. Can you cope with the pain while we have a quick look around the streets? I want to get you to Winslow, but I need to have a look."

Nesbitt nodded as he tried to find some comfort on the hard seat. He leant back as comfortably as possible and held his arm.

Venter reversed the cruiser onto the blacktop, driving guardedly up the road toward the town center. Nesbitt started to unwind his window, but Venter stopped him. "Listen, Charlie, don't tempt fate. We have no idea what is going on. You reckon they are intelligent? Maybe they are up to something?"

"Doubtful. The one thing I know about wolves is that they are reclusive if they are not hunting. They have taken off to the hills."

"Who says they are not hunting? They were hunting last night; you witnessed it. Maybe they have left the town for somewhere else?"

"What? Dogs and wolves? We saw the dogs. The wolves have taken off."

"Why, Charlie? Why take off? They are here somewhere."

"They have left, sheriff. If you don't believe me, where are they?"

"Why now, Charlie?" Venter queried, unable to accept the carnage had stopped. They reached the intersection, passing the war memorial where the wolves had assembled the previous day.

Venter stopped the cruiser, examined the area, got out, and stood beside the door. There was an eerie silence in the town. The shops were closed, no one was in sight, and the roads lay empty as far as he could see.

"Goddam it, it doesn't make sense," Venter said, shaking his head. None of it makes any sense, including the last several days. Why, in damnation, would they attack everything and disappear overnight? It's like a goddam nightmare, and then we wake up to find everything is okay."

Nesbitt turned to him as they drove down a back street towards the main road. "It's over, sheriff. They have returned to the hills, just as McNab said they would. Whatever happened, has changed."

Venter shook his head. "That is ridiculous. Last night, all of them, dogs and wolves, were trying to kill us, and now, this morning, it has all stopped. Not possible. Something is happening, and we don't have any idea what it is."

"Have a look around!. They are gone. It's over! Whatever happened, for whatever reason, has stopped."

"But why?" Venter growled. "Why would they just move away? And the dogs? Why are they friendly all of a sudden?"

"There is only one explanation."

"Which is?"

"Remember last night at the back of the cell? The waving light everyone in the district saw in the sky? It stopped."

"So?" Venter asked through the open door of the cruiser.

"The light disappeared last night, sheriff. That has to be the reason," Nesbitt said slowly as he continued to look around the deserted street. "It's the only connection."

"How in hell would an aurora in the sky at night make dogs and wolves attack anything they came across? Including us?"

"Maybe the light affected them?" Nesbitt added as he got gingerly out of the car.

"That's ridiculous! Why didn't it affect everything else?" Venter replied with a haughty look.

"Well, we looked last night. The light in the sky had disappeared, and if you put the two events together, it makes sense. The behavior started when the light appeared above the hills and has now disappeared. The wolves have gone, and the dogs are quiet."

"Why?"

"Beats me." Nesbitt said with a thin smile. 'I don't have much interest in trying to understand why. We are safe. That is all that matters."

Shaking his head, Venter returned to the cruiser and waited for Nesbitt to settle himself. "Let's check a few backstreets, then I will take you to Winslow. I hope Winslow is safe and did not get taken down the same as Essex."

Venter drove slowly down the familiar old town road, a road he had travelled hundreds of times, towards the Sturger warehouse and the site of the bull killing. As he neared the derelict area, he slowed to a stop. "There's a wolf! See it? Up towards the hill."

Nesbitt followed the direction of Venter's finger. Sure enough, at the end of the old road, a large, grey wolf stood glancing momentarily in their direction. It held no interest in the car. A second later, it turned and trotted off towards the forested hill in the background. Venter stopped the cruiser to see what it would do. It stopped a second time, lowered its head, looked back, and continued towards the forest, finally disappearing into the undergrowth.

"You see, Tom? It's over. They are returning to the hills."

"I'm not convinced, Charlie. If you are right what happens if the light returns?"

Nesbitt shrugged. "Why would it return? It might have been a strange event. Stranger things have happened."

"You serious? Have they? I can't think of one, Charlie!" Venter replied, looking unconvinced.

"The light has stopped, and the predators have gone. We should count our blessings."

"Then, the light could return, maybe for the same reason it occurred in the first place. We don't even know *why* it happened, and we don't know if the light was seen in other areas."

"Does it matter, Tom? It's over."

"It matters, Charlie. We need to know why."

"Maybe it's just one of those things." Nesbitt raised his hand and pointed out the front windscreen as he spoke. "You know. What do they call it? An anomaly?" Maybe just a mysterious anomaly."

"Four dead and more that I don't know about? That is more than just an anomaly, Charlie! It's a goddam massacre."

EPILOGUE

AUGUST 1948

George Richards drove slowly up the long dirt road leading to the top of Mount Wilson heading to the observatory perched above Pasadena. He could not forget the date—precisely his birthday, Wednesday, the twenty-fifth of August 1948.

Above him, perched on the mountain top, the Hooker telescope, the largest aperture telescope in the world in that year of 1948, offered a view of the heavens unmatched by any viewing platform in the United States, or anywhere else for that matter. It held a comforting thought in his mind. No one else could view the heavens better than him on that afternoon and night.

The drive took fifteen minutes. He drove carefully, spending the time to avoid potholes and the myriad of sharp tree roots that grew at the side of the gravel road. He had lost count of the tires he had punctured on the road over the years and was careful not to have another.

His journey from the blacktop highway at the bottom took him up the 5,710-foot peak to the tall structure and the massive dome that held the telescope. When George reached the top of the mountain, it was past one thirty in the afternoon. He parked near the observatory and looked out towards the vista that never ceased to amaze him. Bathed in sunlight, snow-clad mountains stretched across the horizon.

As an astronomer, he spent his time under the eyepiece of the giant apparatus, viewing the planets floating majestically and elegantly in the black of space so far away from Earth. The colors of the planets varied so differently, from the red of giant Mars, the Greek god of war, to the multicolored rings of Saturn.

As he slowly exited his pickup, he looked at the sky with a wide smile. The air above the mountain remained clear of clouds for the first time in a week.

For the following two weeks, George decided to concentrate on the great planet of the heavens. Mars, the colossal red planet, fascinated him as it had over time for so many astronomers who had spent the time to view it with awe. It remained a magnificent sight.

Discussions with astronomers constantly raised the question: Did Mars support life? If so, what sort of life? The broad culverts and stained surface areas that appeared through the scope might be rivers or large seas. It was as enticing as it was frustrating. The thought of a spaceship that could take him there filled him with momentary excitement.

He entered the bottom of the domed structure and started the climb up a long set of stairs that winded him each time he climbed them, so he took his time. Some minutes later, he arrived at the landing.

The floor was usually busy in the late afternoon as administration officials finalized their reports for the meteorology for the various government departments.

He walked through the cluttered desks and chairs, he spotted the man who had just spent the previous four hours under the telescope's viewing glass.

"Hey, Steve." George said to him as he walked closer to the man's desk. "I thought you'd be long gone by now."

Steve, a large man in disheveled clothing and dragging on a pipe, shrugged as he concentrated on picking up a large bundle of papers and a dog-eared notebook. "I'm trying to finish a report, George. A clear night is coming up, though. Happy days, if you get my drift."

"I get it."

Steve raised his head and looked directly at him. "I was watching the sun corona this morning. There is strange activity on the corona. Very strange."

"Strange? What do you mean?"

"Weird. Never seen anything like it. What are you spending your time on?"

"The god of war. Mighty Mars."

Steve thought momentarily, "Well if you get bored, put the filters on this afternoon and look at the corona in the right upper quadrant. "

George smiled thinly. "Will do."

"Concentrate on the right hemisphere. About ten degrees East."

George nodded and took the small folder from Steve as he passed it over. "Until at least seven tomorrow morning."

"Long night?"

"You betcha."

"I tell you, George. I could set my watch on your punctuality."

"On time is half an hour late," George replied with a light smile. He pushed his glasses onto his nose. "But I'll take that as a compliment, Steve. Is the coffee fresh?"

The man laughed. "Fresh from early this morning. I'd be putting on another pot if I was setting up."

George shrugged as he took a cup of over brewed coffee and gathered his charts. He made his way up the flight of stairs to the viewing platform, which consisted of an oversized, comfortable chair under a long cylinder that tapered to a small point just above the chair. There was room to stand rather than sit, but George enjoyed the comfort of sitting. Standing for extended periods hurt his knees.

The viewing glass was large enough for one eye to view the heavens. Above him, the mighty apparatus balanced on giant gears capable of adjusting its attitude and focal length in minute degrees.

George settled himself. After changing some of the adjustments, he peered through the eyepiece after judiciously applying the special filters that allowed the sun's corona to be studied for activity.

Over an hour later, after making several short notations regarding the small amount of activity he could see, he wondered what his colleague had been talking about?

He spent fifteen minutes fitting a different filter onto the eyeglass to protect his eyes and illuminate the area. The sun appeared as a bright, white disc with eruptions, like electrical sparks from its surface.

He checked the notes regarding the hemisphere where the activity had taken place and could see nothing unusual except for some restlessness of the surface on the right quadrant. He rested back in the chair and sipped his cold coffee, which he had left, as an unbroken habit, on a small table next to the chair.

After several minutes, he returned to the eyepiece. Just at that moment, his eye widened as he pulled back in rapt astonishment. He immediately changed to a white light coronagraph to watch the massive MCE.

It pulsed out from the sun's surface, displaying a massive white core, a dark surrounding cavity, and a bright leading edge. It was a massive coronal mass ejection from the sun's corona. In twenty years, he had never seen anything like it.

He thrust his head forward to look again. *Wowwee*. Was the only word he uttered as he reached for his pad and pencil. He had witnessed the most magnificent sight of his astronomical life.

A massive, solar-arcing plasma ejection erupting millions of miles into space! What a sight! Such a massive explosion would make it easily to Earth. He decided to leave a note for Steve when he finished that night. It might be worth alerting the agencies. Astronomers looked forward to it every day, but it rarely, if ever, occurred. Something magnificent, something new! This was both, and he was the first to see it.

It made the dust storms on Mars pale compared to the glorious sight through the filter. Now, this was something different. This would be something to crow about to the others. He had never seen activity on the corona with such intensity. It erupted, spewing out maybe more than a million miles.

The End